# THE FABER BOOK OF
# BEST NEW IRISH SHORT STORIES
## 2006–7

### EDITED BY DAVID MARCUS

*faber and faber*

First published in 2007
by Faber and Faber Limited
3 Queen Square London WC1N 3AU

Typeset by RefineCatch Limited, Bungay, Suffolk
Printed in England by Mackays of Chatham Ltd

A CIP record for this book
is available from the British Library

ISBN 978-0-571-23045-7
ISBN 0-571-23045-8

2 4 6 8 10 9 7 5 3 1

# Contents

# Introduction

In early Victorian times the short story was virtually ignored by Britain's great novelists. Was this the case in Ireland too? At the time many of the Irish were speaking Irish, and so they didn't need to worry about stories, because where they lived in their counties, they had their *seanchaí*. A *seanchaí* was a traditional storyteller, versed in folklore. He would gather as many people as possible, indoors or out of doors, to listen to his stories.

In more recent times it has been a pattern with some new British writers to start with one or a few short stories and soon move on to novels. In Ireland, on the other hand, most writers were employing both forms. Take some of Ireland's outstanding male writers of the past, each of whom produced novels and short stories. George Moore, 1853–1933; James Stephens, 1880–1950; James Joyce, 1882–1941; Liam O'Flaherty, 1896–1984; Sean O'Faolain, 1900–1991; Frank O'Connor, 1903–1966; Michael MacLaverty, 1904–1992.

And consider some of the great Irish women writers of the past who also wrote novels and stories.

Maria Edgeworth: Born in Britain in 1767, her family went back to Ireland in 1782. In 1795 her first publication was *Letters to Literary Ladies*, and her first novel, *Castle Rackrent*, 1800, won her a place in the literary history of the English-speaking world. Then in 1804 she wrote a collection of short stories, *Popular Tales*.

Somerville and Ross: Edith Somerville, born in 1858, met her cousin Violet Martin in 1886. The most famous of their novels is *The Real Charlotte*, 1894 – the most memorable of all in Irish fiction – and they also wrote short stories.

## Introduction

Norah Hoult: Born in Ireland in 1898, her first published book was a collection of short stories, *Poor Women*, in 1928. One of her best-known novels was *Holy Ireland*, 1935. She published over twenty novels, and her second short-story collection, *Cocktail Bar*, was published in 1950.

Elizabeth Bowen: Born in Dublin in 1899, her first book, published in 1923, was a collection of short stories, and her first novel came in 1927. She published a dozen novels and ninety short stories. She died in 1973. Harold Pinter wrote the screenplay for a television adaptation of her novel *The Heat of the Day*, published in 1949.

Mary Lavin: She was born in the USA in 1912 to Irish parents who returned to Ireland when she was nine. As a short-story writer she had an international reputation. Her first collection – indeed her very first book – was the world-famous *Tales from Bective Bridge*, published in 1942. She wrote twelve story collections and two novels.

Irish women writers of today also write stories and novels, but, as Ireland has always had more male than female writers in print, since my first editorial years it has been my desire to see Irish women writers produce novels as well as stories. In these pages virtually all of them have already beaten the drum.

David Marcus

# First Light

## JOHN BANVILLE

Of the things we fashioned for them that they might be comforted, dawn is the one that works. When darkness sifts from the air like fine soft soot and light spreads slowly out of the east then all but the most wretched of humankind rally. It is a spectacle we immortals enjoy, this minor daily resurrection; often we will gather at the ramparts of the clouds and gaze down upon them, our little ones, as they bestir themselves to welcome the new day. What a silence falls upon us then, the sad silence of our envy. Most of them sleep on, of course, careless of our cousin Aurora's charming matutinal trick, but there are always the insomniacs, the restless ill, the lovelorn tossing on their solitary beds, or just the early-risers, the busy ones, with their knee-bends and their cold showers and their fussy little cups of black ambrosia. Yes, all who witness it greet the dawn with joy, more or less, except of course the condemned man, for whom first light will be the last, on earth.

Here is one, standing at a window in his father's house, watching the day's early glow suffuse the sky above the massed trees beyond the railway line. He is condemned not to death, not yet, but to a life into which he feels he does not fit. He is barefoot, and wearing pyjamas that his mother found for him somewhere in the house, threadbare cotton, pale blue with a bluer stripe – whose are they, were they? Could they be his own, from long ago? If so, it was from very long ago, for they are far too small for him, and pinch at the armpits and the fork. But that is the way with everything in this house, everything pinches and scratches and makes him feel he is a child again. He is reminded how when he was a little boy here his grandmother would dress him up for Christmas, or his birthday, or some Church festival, tugging him this way and that and spitting on a finger to plaster down a stubborn curl,

1

and how he would feel exposed, worse than naked, in those already outmoded scratchy grey tweed suits with short trousers that she made him wear, and the white shirts with starched collars and, worst of all, the tartan dicky bows which afforded him a wan, vindictive pleasure to pull out to the limit of their elastic and let snap back when someone was making a speech or singing a song or the priest was holding up the communion wafer. That is how it is: life, tight-buttoned life, fits him ill, making him too much aware of himself and what he believes is his unalterable littleness of spirit.

He is called Adam. He is about to be thirty, the young son of an ancient father, 'product', as he once overheard that rascally father say with a phlegmy chuckle, 'of my second coming'. Idly he admires the dense mud-indigo shadows under the trees. A kind of smoke hovers ankle-deep on the grey-seeming grass. Everything is different at this hour. An early blackbird flies across at a slant swiftly from somewhere to somewhere else, its lacquered wing catching an angled glint of sunlight, and he cannot but think with a pang of the early worm.

Now, gradually, he is becoming aware of something, hard to identify, a tremor that is all around, as if the air itself were quaking. It grows more intense. Alarmed, he takes a soft step backwards into the protective dimness of the room. Clearly he can hear the sluggish thudding of his heart. A part of his mind knows what is happening but it is not the part that thinks. Everything is atremble now. Some small mechanism behind him in the room, a clock, surely, sets up in its innards an urgent, silvery tinkling. The floorboards creak in trepidation. Then from the trees at the left the thing appears, huge, blunt-headed, nudging its way blindly forward, and rolls to a shuddering halt and stands there gasping diesel smoke. The lights are still palely on in the carriages, they make the dawn draw back a little. There are bent heads in the long windows, like the heads of seals – are they all asleep? – and the conductor with his ticket thing is going up an aisle, clambering along hand over hand from seat-back to seat-back as if he were scaling a steep incline. The silence round about is large and somehow aggrieved. The engine gives a steamy snort, seeming to paw the earth. Why it should stop at this spot every morning no one knows, or will not say. There is not another house for miles, the line is clear in both directions, yet it halts just here. His mother has complained repeatedly to the railway people, and once even was moved to write to someone in the government, but got no reply.

'I wouldn't mind', she says in a tone of mild sorrow, 'what noise it made going past – after all, your father in his wisdom insisted on us setting up home practically on the railway line – it's the stopping that wakes me.'

Thinking of his mother he instinctively listens for her step above him, for he knows she is awake. Though large and rambling the house is mainly made of wood and sounds travel easily and far. He does not want to deal with her, just now. Indeed, he finds it always difficult to deal with her. It is not that he dislikes or resents her, only he does not think she is like a mother at all. She is absurdly young, hardly twenty years older than he is, and seems all the time to be getting younger, or at least not older, so that he has the worrying sensation of steadily catching up on her. She too appears to be aware of this phenomenon, and to find it not at all strange. In fact, since he was old enough to notice how young she is he has detected now and then, or imagined he has detected a certain tight-lipped briskness in her manner towards him, as if she were impatient for him to attain some impossible majority so that, coevals at last, they might turn arm in arm and set out together into a future that would be . . . what? Fatherless, now, for him, and for her, husbandless. For his father is dying. That is why he is here, foolish in these too-small pyjamas, watching the dawn break on this midsummer day.

Shaken by such thoughts of death and dying – for he believes that despite everything he loves his father – he fixes his attention on the train again. One of the seal-heads has turned and he finds himself regarded across the smoky expanse of lawn by a small boy with a pale pinched face and enormous eyes. How intensely the child is staring at the house, how hungry his scrutiny – what is it he is seeking, what secret knowledge, what revelation? The man is convinced the boy can see him, skulking here in the shadowy depths of the room, yet how could that be, for surely the window from outside is a black blank, or the other extreme, blindingly aflame with the white-gold glare of the sun that already is swarming strongly up the eastern sky. Apart from those avidly questing eyes the boy's features are unremarkable, or at least are so from what of them can be made out at this distance. But what does he want to stare so? Now the engine bethinks itself and gives a sort of shake, and a repeated loud metallic clank runs along the carriages from coupling to coupling, and with a groan the brutish thing begins to move off, and as it moves the risen sun strikes through each set of carriage windows in turn, having its revenge on the still-burning bulbs, putting them to shame with its irresistible, harsh fire. The boy, craning, stares to the last.

Adam is cold, and the soles of his bare feet are sticking unpleasantly to the chill, tacky floorboards. He is not fully awake but in a state between sleep and waking in which everything appears unreally real. When he turns from the window he sees the early light falling in unaccustomed corners, at odd angles, and a bookshelf edge is sharp as the blade of a guillotine. From the depths of the room the convex glass front of the clock on the mantelpiece, reflecting the window's light, regards him with a monocle's blank glare. He thinks again of the child on the train and is struck as so often by the mystery of otherness. How can he be a self and others others, since the others too are selves, to themselves? He knows, of course, it is no mystery but a matter merely of perspective. *The eye,* he tells himself, *the eye makes the horizon.* It is a thing he has often heard his father say, cribbed no doubt from someone else. The child on the train was a sort of horizon to him, and he a sort of horizon to the child, only because each considered himself to be at the centre of something, to be, indeed, that centre itself, and that is the simple solution to the so-called mystery. And yet.

How lucky they are, these blithe self-regarders. For us, the deathless ones, to whom everything is present everywhere at every instant, the world is uniform in all directions. Think of that.

Adam pads across the floor – at his passing the clock on the mantel gives a single, soft, admonitory tinkle – and opens a white door into the hall and stops short with a muffled grunt of fright, his heart setting up again its slurred clamour, like an excited dog pawing to be let out.

He quickly sees that the figure in the hall is only his sister.

'For God's sake!' he says. She is squatting monkey-like on her haunches at one of the little low doors in the white-painted panelling that closes off the space under the stairs. 'What are you doing?'

She turns up to him her little white face and yet again he sees in his mind the child's face at the train window.

'Mice,' she says.

He sighs. She is in one of her states.

'For God's sake,' he repeats, wearily this time.

She goes back to rummaging in the cupboard and he folds his arms and leans back against the wall and watches her with a show of supercilious impatience. She is nineteen, nearly twenty, and still so much child. He asks how she knows there are mice in the cupboard and she snorts.

'Not here, you fool,' she says, the sleek black back of her head – another seal! – aquiver with contempt. 'In my room.'

She rises, wiping her hands on her skinny flanks. She does not meet his eyes, but bites her lip and frowns off to the side; she does not meet anyone's eye, if she can help it.

'What in God's name are you wearing?' he asks.

Something in faded blue silk that hangs limp on her meagre frame, the sleeves and legs comically too long.

'They're Pa's,' she says sulkily.

He sighs again.

'Oh, Pete.'

Her name is Petra, called by him Pete. She is tiny and thin with a heart-shaped face and haunted eyes. Until recently her head was shaved and what hair she has is a bulrush-brown nap that covers her skull evenly all over. Her hands are the scrabbly pink claws of a rodent – he thinks: *The mice must have recognised one of their own*, and chides himself, half-heartedly.

'How do you know?' he asks.

'How do I know what?' – a petulant whine.

'About the mice.'

'I see them. They run around the floor in the dark.'

'In the dark. And you see them.'

She blinks slowly and swallows, as if she might be about to cry, but it is only a tic, one among the many that afflict her.

'Leave me alone,' she mutters.

When she was little she used to sleepwalk, appearing at the top of the stairs with her eyes rolled up into her head and her mouse-claws lifted in front of her chest. At the memory the small hairs stir at the back of his neck. His loony sister, hearing voices, seeing things.

With a cocked big toe he pushes shut the cupboard door. She makes a gesture towards it, her left arm jerking out stiffly from her side and a finger childishly pointing and then the arm falling weakly back.

'I thought there were traps,' she says sulkily, 'there used to be traps, in there.'

When she did that with her arm he caught a whiff of her: a faint, musty, greyish smell, like the smell in the room of an invalid. She does not bathe enough. 'I despair of her,' their mother says, 'really, I do.' As if they had not all done that, long ago, except for Pa, of course, who likes to insist she is his muse made flesh. Or liked, that is: Pa is in the past tense, now.

The light here in the hall is murky still but the sun is burning gaudily in the front door's stained-glass panes as if, Adam glumly reflects, he and his sister were locked indoors while a party was going on outside. In their comically ill-fitting pairs of pyjamas they stand before each other in silence, at a loss, each thinking and yet not thinking of what it is that constrains them so: their dying father, whose sleeplessly sleeping presence fills the house like a fog. No one in the family these days dares to speak above a murmur, though the doctors blandly insist that nothing any longer passes beyond the portals of Pa's hearing – but how can they be so certain, Adam would like to know, where do they get such assurance? His father is in another kingdom now, far off to be sure, but may it not be that news from the old realm reaches him still?

'Why are you up so early?' Pete asks, accusingly. 'You're never up this early.'

'These short nights,' Adam says, 'I can't sleep.'

This answer she receives in silence, resentfully. It is she who is supposed to be the wakeful one. Her unsleepingness, like their father's dying, is a pervasive pressure that makes the air in the house feel as dense as the air inside a balloon.

'Is the Dead Horse coming down today?' he asks her.

She gives a shrug that is more a twitch.

'He said he would. I suppose he will.'

They can get no more from that subject, and fall silent again. He has that feeling of irritated, vague desperation that his sister so often inspires in him. She stands as she always does, half turned away, at once expectant and cowering, as if hoping for an embrace and at the same time in dread of it. As a little girl she had no tickles and would squirm away from him with a scowl but then would lean back again, droopingly, unable to help herself, her sharp, narrow shoulders indrawn and her head held to one side, seeming miserably to invite him to try again to make her laugh. How thin she had been, how thin and bony, like a sack half filled with sticks, and still is. Now she lifts a hand and scratches her scalp vigorously, making a sandpapery sound.

'There's nothing wrong with her,' their mother will say, 'nothing clinical', and will pause, drawing her lips into a wrinkled rosebud shape, and then burst out again – 'It's just nerves, that's all!'

Adam feels light-headed, weightless, seeming to float a millimetre above the floor. Something to do with oxygen in the brain, or a lack of it. His sister is right, he is not used to being up at this hour – *everything is different* – when the world looks like an imitation of itself, cunningly fashioned yet discrepant in small but essential details.

He has not seen his father yet. Arriving late last night he had pleaded tiredness and gone straight to bed. To have visited the old man then would have been gruesome, like a nocturnal viewing of the remains, or breaking into the vampire's crypt. Although he has not told her so, he thinks his mother should not have brought Pa home from the hospital. Keeping him in the house is a throwback, something Granny Godley would approve. Yet this morning he is sorry he did not go at once and at least look at him, his fallen father, for with each hour that passes it will be so much the harder to force himself up those stairs and into that room, the same room into which for so many years his parents would retire to spend together their mysterious, married nights. He does not know how he will behave at the side of what everyone has acknowledged is a deathbed. He has never seen a dying person before.

His sister is still scratching, but with decreasing momentum, absently, like a cat losing interest in its itch. He wishes he could help her, could assuage even one of her inflamed sore spots. Yet he resents her, too, has always resented her, since before she was born, even, his usurper. *Oh, she'll see to you, that one,* Granny Godley would say gleefully – *you'll think your arse is haunted!*

'Come on,' he says to his sister now in his brusque yet not untender tone, 'come on, and we'll have our breakfast.'

And sister and brother, these waifs, shuffle off into the shadows.

It is shadowed too in the sickroom, where Adam Godley at the centre of a vast stillness is silently going about his dying. Yes, he is Adam too, like his son; this frequently causes confusion and some difficulty. Apropos of which, I should before going any further give some account of myself, this voice speaking out of the void. Men have made me variously keeper of the dawn, of twilight and the wind, have called me *Argeiphantes*, he who makes clear the sky, and *Logios*, the sweet-tongued one, have appointed me the guardian of crossroads, protector of travellers, have conferred on me the grave title *Psychopompus*, usher of the freed souls of men to Pluto's netherworld. For I am Hermes, son of old Zeus and Maia the cavewoman.

You don't say, you say.

I understand your scepticism. Why in times such as these would the gods come back to be among men? But the fact is we never left – you only stopped entertaining us. For how should we leave, we who cannot but be everywhere? We merely made it seem that we had withdrawn, for a decent interval, as if to say we know when we are not wanted. Now and then we cannot resist showing ourselves to you, out of boredom, or mischievousness, or that lingering fondness we feel for this rough world of our making. When on a summer's day a sudden wild wind rushes through the treetops, or when out of the blue a soft rain falls like the fall of grace upon a painted saint, there one of us is passing; when the earth buckles and opens its maw to eat cities whole, when the sea rises up and swallows an archipelago with its palms and straw huts and a myriad ululating natives, be sure that one amongst us is annoyed.

But what care we lavished on the making of this poor place! The lengths we went to, the pains we took, to make it plausible – planting in the rocks the fossils of outlandish creatures that never existed, distributing fake dark matter throughout the universe, even setting up in the cosmos the faintest of faint hums to mimic an echo of the initiating shot that is supposed to have set the whole shooting match going. And to what end was all this labour, this dissembling? So that the mud men that Prometheus and Athene between them made might think themselves the lords of creation. We have been good to you, giving you what you thought you wanted, and look what you have done with it.

All this, of course, is cast in the language of men, necessarily. Were I to speak in my own, divine voice you would be baffled – in fact, you would not be able to hear me at all, so refined is our heavenly speech, compared to your barely articulate gruntings. Why, the music of the spheres has nothing on us. And these names, Zeus, Prometheus, grey-eyed Athene, even Hermes, these are your inventions. We address each other only as air, as light, as something like the quality of that deep, transparent blue you see when you peer into the highest vault of heaven. And heaven – what is that? For us there is no heaven, or hell, no up, no down, only the here, which is a kind of not-here . . .

This moment past, in the blinking of your eye, I girdled the earth's full compass thrice. Why? For diversion, and to cool my heels. And because I could, and you cannot. Oh, yes, we too are petty and vindictive, just like you.

Old Adam Godley has suffered a stroke. By the way, is that not a curiously innocuous, even pretty, way of putting it – as if one of us had laid a hand too heavily on his brow. Which is entirely possible, for we are notorious for not knowing our own strength. Anyway, for some time prior to this stroke old Adam had been subject, all unbeknownst, to a steady softening of the brain due to a slow extravasation of blood in the area of the parietal lobe. In other words he was already a goner before that catastrophic moment when, enthroned at morning within the necessary place – to put it as delicately as I may – he crouched too low and strained too mightily, extruding a stool as hard as mahogany, and felt, actually felt, a blood vessel bursting in his brain, and pitched forward on to the floor, his face to the tiles and his scrawny bare bum in the air, and passed at once, with an almost delicious smoothness, into death's vast and vaulted ante-chamber, where still he bides, poised upon the point of oblivion.

He is not alone. He senses the multitude of his fellows all about. And he has me, as I have him. When the time comes we shall go together, he and I, into whatever is next.

His wife has entered the room, making hardly a sound, as is increasingly her way in these days. She feels she is becoming more and more a wraith, as if Adam in his last illness were siphoning something vital from her, drop by glistening drop. She closes the bedroom door softly behind her and stands motionless a moment, letting her eyes adjust to the dimness. A teeming sword of early sunlight is falling through a parting in the heavy curtains, breaking its blade across the foot of the bed. With a qualm she acknowledges to herself how restful she finds it here. There is a dense, intent quality to the silence in the room, it is like the silence inside her, and soothes her heart. Ironic, this hush, considering the constant clamour with which her notoriously noisy husband used to fill their lives. But this morning, as every morning this past week, he is still and lifeless-seeming. She can make out his form now, supine in the bed, but though she listens intently she cannot hear him breathing. Perhaps . . .? At the unthought thought something stirs in her, a yearning something, and then she is ashamed, or tries to be. Yet why should she reprove herself? – everyone says the end will be a blessed release. Those are the words they use: *a blessed release*. Yes, she reflects bitterly, a release, that is, for all except perhaps the one being released. For who can know but that Adam in some part of his mind might not be in a way awake and experiencing wonders? People who are deeply asleep seem unconscious but still may be dreaming the most fantastic things. Anyway, even if she cannot hear him she knows he has not gone. The elastic link between them has not been broken yet, she can feel faintly still the old, twanging tug.

She advances to the bed soundlessly on slippered feet. In their early days together he used to call her his geisha girl for her pattering, rapidly stepping gait. She recalls the antique kimono he brought back to her from Japan – *a kimono from Kyoto!* – cut from heavy, jade-green silk, a garment so exquisite she could not bring herself to wear it. He shouted at her, of course, and threatened to take the thing and give it to one of his girls, the girls he said she imagined he had in every city that he visited. Then he looked at her, with his head back, savagely smiling, showing his teeth, daring her to call his bluff. For it was a bluff, about the girls, about there not being girls: they were legion, she knew it, and he knew she knew it. That was the way of lying that amused him most, saying the truth in tones of high, mocking irony so that to challenge him would make the challenger seem a hapless dolt.

She stands at the side of the bed feeling at once there and not there, though not anywhere else, either. Uncanny to enter here each morning and find him just as she left him the night before, the blanket moulded smoothly to his form, the sheet uncreased, the cockscomb of silky hair – still black! – rising unruffled above the high white dome of his forehead. She has always loved his skin, the moist, cool, translucent paleness of it that the years have not succeeded in sullying. She hates, knowing how he would hate them, the two narrow tubes that are threaded into his nostrils and held in place with strips of clear stickingplaster. There are other tubes, farther down, hidden from sight by the bedclothes. What a trouble there was settling him here, Dr Faulkner fidgeting and the nurses cross. But she had insisted, surprising everyone, herself included, with her vehemence. *He must be at home*, she kept saying, ignoring all their advice, *if he is to die he must die here*. Old Faulkner, who looked like Albert Schweitzer and had been the family's physician since Granny Godley's time, had squeezed her hand and mumbled something through his moustache, but the two young nurses had narrowed their eyes at her and stalked off, their backsides wagging professional disapproval.

By now she can hear her husband breathing, the faint rustle of air in throat and chest. At the end of each indrawn breath comes a tiny flutter, like an impatient twiddling of fingers. She realises what it is that is familiar about this sound: it is how he used to sigh when she had done something that particularly exasperated him, with just that little fluttering flourish to show how annoying she was and at the same time how inconsequential.

She feels something brush past her in the air, it seems more than a draught. She has felt it before, in recent days. Whatever it is it is not benign; she has the impression of haughtiness and a bridling resentment; it is as if something were bent on jostling her out of position. Try as she will to prevent it the notion has insinuated itself into her mind that this angry visitant is Adam's long-dead mother, Granny Godley the old witch, come back at the end to assert her claim to him over that of his mere wife. There are other strange things, too, other haunting effects. She has glimpses of figures that cease to be there when looked at directly. She wakes in the night with a start, her heart pounding, as if there had been a tremendous noise, an explosion or a clap of thunder, which had shaken her out of sleep but of which there is not even an echo remaining. When she speaks to people on the telephone she is convinced there is a third party on the line, listening intently. She tells herself it is all in her imagination, but I know better. It is my presence that she senses, the whirring of wings at my heels that she half hears.

Her name is Ursula. She dislikes the name. Why would anyone call a child after a she-bear? Adam had looked it up, of course, and was able to tell her gleefully of St Ursula martyred along with her eleven thousand companions – 'What a day that must have been, eh, *im alten Köln*?' The children had named her La, and still call her that. Adam is Pa and she is La. She wonders if there is ill-intent behind these pet names. She has not been a good mother. She did her best with Adam but poor Petra was too much for her. Having Petra was the start of all her troubles.

She touches her husband's hand where it lies on the blanket. It has an unsettling feel, the skin brittle as greaseproof paper and the flesh pulpy underneath; it is like a package of scrap meat from the butcher's, chill and sinewy. That malignant force pushes past her again, or through her, rather, as if it is she that is without substance, as if indeed she and not this other were the ghost.

Her head is very bad, today, very bad. She needs a cure for it. But it is too early. Even for her kind of medicine it is too early.

In the well of the kitchen the morning light has a sharp, metallic sheen, and the square of sunlit garden in the window behind the sink is garish and implausible, like a primitive painting of a jungle scene. Adam and his sister are seated at one end of the long deal table, hunched over cereal bowls. When their mother appears at the top of the three wooden steps that lead up to or down from the rest of the house they sense rather than hear her – Rex the ancient Labrador lying on his bed in the corner gives a few listless thumps of his tail but makes no effort to get himself up – and they stop eating and lift their faces and look at her. She sees again with a faint start how alike they are, with the same broad brows and little sharp chins and ash-blue eyes so pale they are almost colourless. Family resemblance she always finds uncanny, even in her own offspring. Both of them take after her – hers is the wide forehead and sharp chin and azury eyes – which is another source of her husband's many-sourced resentment.

'How is he, today?' her son asks. For some reason she finds just now his palely candid gaze well-nigh intolerable. He was always remote, even as a child; perfectly loving and good, but far away, in his own world.

'Much the same,' she says, and Petra laughs, who knows why, making a nasty sound. She thinks sometimes that both her children hate her. She feels as if she were not their mother but a person put in intimate charge of them, a guardian, say, or a bitterly resented stepmother. Yet these are the creatures she carried inside her and gave birth to and fed from her own breast. 'He seems peaceful,' she says. It is the same answer she gives when anyone asks.

Her son regards her as she hovers on the stair at the far end of the long, low room. He cannot focus on her properly. She has a quality of being not entirely present, of seeming to hesitate on an invisible threshold that is there under her feet wherever she steps. She is wearing a cotton dress like a smock and a baggy, greyish-brown cardigan the hem of which sags almost to her knees. Her hair, which is the colour of a polished knife-blade, is pulled back in two flattened wings and pinned at the nape of her neck. She descends the steps and comes forward and stands by the table, absently kneading the wood with the fingertips of one hand, like a blindman reading braille.

'You're up early,' she says to both of them. 'Did the train wake you?'

Neither will answer. Petra, looking aside frowningly, says: 'Roddy will be here at ten.'

Her tone is truculent, as if to baulk disparaging comment. Roddy Wagstaff, also known as the Dead Horse, is her young man, or so convention has it, though it is apparent to everybody that her famous father is the one he comes to see.

'Oh,' her mother says, and a shadow passes over her already shadowed face, 'then there'll have to be lunch.'

Since Adam fell ill the household has been content to shift for itself, but a visitor will have to be fed, Adam would insist upon it.

'We could take him into town,' her son says. 'Isn't there a new place, what's it called?'

'Oh, yes,' Petra says with a sneer, 'let's all go into town and have a lovely lunch – we can bring Pa and sit him at the head of the table and feed him soup through his tubes.'

She glares at her cereal bowl. Under the table her left leg is going like a sewing machine. Adam and his mother exchange an expressionless look. Her father's collapse has been for Petra a great excitement, being at last a calamity commensurate with the calamitous state of her mind. The question of lunch is let hang. In the corner Rex the dog gives a contented, shivery sigh. He can see me plainly, lolling in mid-air at my ease in the midst of these troubled mortals, but it is nothing to him, his world being already rife with spirits.

Petra has her subject now and will not let it go. In a thick, tense voice, goitrous with sarcasm, she embroiders upon the notion of a family lunch in town to which her father would be brought – 'in a hammock maybe or a sling slung between us or one of those things with two poles that red indians drag the wounded along behind them in' – and at which they would all celebrate his achievements and make speeches and raise toasts to his greatness as artist, man and father. When she gets going like this she has a way of speaking not directly to the others in the room but to the air beside her, as if there were present another version of herself off whom she is bouncing her taunts and who will give to them, thus relayed, an added ironical cast. Adam and her mother say nothing, for they know there will be no stopping her until she has exhausted herself. The dog, lying with its muzzle between its paws, eyes her with wary speculation. The tabletop vibrates rapidly along with the girl's bobbing knee. Adam tries to eat his cereal, which has gone soggy; he recalls himself again as a child, sitting at this table, listening to his father talking and feeling his throat thicken and his eyes scald with inexplicable tears he dare not shed, shaming tears, hot and heavy like melted metal. He looks sidelong at his sister and sees the silvery light shaking in the spoon-shaped hollow above her clavicle as she tries not to choke on the torrent of words that keeps welling up in her unstaunchably.

Their mother, standing by the table, cannot stop herself noticing the cereal bowls her son and daughter have been eating from: why does it so irritate her that they are unmatched? Petra's is decorated around the rim with Beatrix Potter animals. Anthropomorphism – how Adam would gnash and seethe. She has tried not to be resentful of her son for so far refusing even to enter the room where his father lies dying. Yet she does resent it. She supposes he is afraid. She drifts to the window at the sink and looks out at the sunlit day, a hand lifted to her face.

'And and and,' Petra is saying, her voice ashake on the sliding crest of its arc, 'and and and *and* . . .'

. . . And I it is who have contrived these things: this house, the train, the boy at the train window, that slanting blackbird, the dawn itself, and this mother musing on love and her losses, and her troubled daughter at the table gabbling out her woe, and the son, young Adam, who in a moment will make up his mind and rise from the table and ascend those three short steps and be wafted upwards on my invisible wings into the presence, the absence, rather, of his earthly father.

# The Written Word

## Michael J. Farrell

'There are no heart transplants in the Tarantula Nebula.'

Up to that point he was just an old man blathering, but what he said seemed a mouthful. So I looked at him.

'No liver transplants, either. And, if you ask me, no livers.' He was talking either to himself or to me, there was no one else available. He peered into the distance, somehow seeing the Tarantula galaxy, of which, up to that moment, I had never heard.

I'm retired myself. In the late morning, if weather allows, I walk by the rambling River Inny until it reaches the town. I stop to pay my respects at little bridges that only local farmers know, the stones blotched piebald with lichen. I exchange a few thoughts with the water below, a leisurely trickle in summer but impatient in winter and often taking shortcuts across the road. Since I have nothing else to do, I think a lot.

By about noon I get as far as Curly's, an eatery. There are sixteen tables, seating two to as many as eight, all covered in red oilcloth. I sit by the window, the near chair so I can still see the river. I don't need to order any more. The girls know I'll be having a grilled ham-and-cheese sandwich and coffee. In about an hour I am on my way across the square. I walk on the grass, the grass doesn't mind. On my left is the church, a squat structure in dark stone, and atop the spire an iron cross slightly tilting, though nobody agrees with me about this. On my right is a red plastic filling station. People call out greetings as I go and I wave back at them. Waving saves me having to remember their names.

Ours is, in short, an orderly little world and no loony bin. I make a beeline for the green wooden bench facing the fountain. I am a lover of water in its various manifestations and worry that global warming will reduce it all to steam. For years I had the bench to myself though I always sat on the south end to leave room for others.

Until that day, some years ago, when the stranger was there ahead of me – and on my end of the bench. We exchanged a few words. I intended to leave it at that but he talked on regardless until he made his odd remark about heart transplants.

'You have a point,' I remember saying to him. I had no idea what point he had, but my modest encouragement added fuel to his fire.

'Thank you,' he threw me a glance. 'Diversity must be desirable or there wouldn't be so much of it. But now, tragically, diversity is reaching a dead end.'

'How do you mean?'

'Take fingers and toes,' he said. 'We've had five on each extremity for as long as we can remember.' I nodded solemnly, egging him on. 'Toes in particular have suffered from stagnation since we invented footwear.'

'But fingers have developed, how shall I say, a certain dexterity.'

Now he looked at me foursquare. With a smile, I was convinced, of approval. He must be nearly eighty, I figured. He had a rugged, outdoor face that sported what I would call a debonair moustache, it was easy to be debonair in our neck of the woods. He wore a shapeless cloth hat of a kind popular in Austria. It covered, I would later learn, a cranium reminiscent of certain Tibetan monks. His eyes were tight together, but that wasn't it; they seemed all alert and circumspect. If any eyes could see the Tarantula Nebula, his could.

'If I had it to do again, I'd assign eight fingers to a hand. Ten if you want, it's up to you.'

There it was again. Some mighty intimation. Sounding off in his understated way as if – yes, and the eyes twinkling as if he were, to say the least, an eccentric. Or, to say it bluntly, a headcase.

'We humans should long ago have developed wings, anyone can see that.' He was wearing a green corduroy suit and already in September an orange scarf. He didn't look crazy. Average, that's what he looked. 'If birds could make the leap to flight there's no excuse for us with our bigger brains and know-how.'

'But it's not your – problem.' Later I could think of various ways I should have nailed him, bons mots to tie him in knots. 'I mean, you're not –' Some of the best questions don't need to be asked.

'Yes, I am.' He was so quietly sure. Of whatever it was. I glanced around, suddenly suspicious lest some television programme might be

pulling my leg. Everything seemed normal, including this odd customer. I felt an urge to be angry with him. But I'm woefully liberal by
disposition. He couldn't help himself, I concluded, he just needed to
take his medicine.

'And ears,' he said. 'Skin and cartilage higgledy-piggledy and not
even efficient after billions of experiments. Do you not care?' It was like
the question about beating your wife, only different. I was suddenly
tired of his self-possessed hauteur, like a bloody sultan, though I have
nothing against sultans.

'I need to be going.' It wasn't a lie. 'My name is Owen,' I added,
wanting him to divulge his own.

'Luke,' he said. He held out his hand and I shook it. Five fingers. Of
a soft old average hand.

'Luke?' people repeated with blank faces when I made enquiries. In
the days that followed I took care to arrive early and reclaim my end of
the green bench. Yet I would scan the square, and there was a twinge of
loss when he failed to appear. We may have done poorly in the fingers
department but we people are miles ahead when it comes to curiosity.
Had I seen that nutcase, people would ask, and I would shake my head,
until I wondered had I imagined him on a day I myself had forgotten
my vitamins.

But after a week or two, when my guard was down, he was there
ahead of me, and on the south side of the bench. For a moment I wanted
to push the old rascal off. I hoped that, after we exchanged a civilised
word or two, he would mind his own business.

'Here's what I'd do if I had it to do again. I'd scrunch all the land
together into one big continent.'

'And all the water, I suppose, into one big ocean?' I countered to slow
his gallop.

'No islands. Everyplace contiguous to everyplace else.'

'No need for boats.' The devil made me do it. 'None of your
oil tankers polluting the earth. No need for aircraft carriers and
armadas, and forget about your yachts and skiffs and ocean cruises. No
Caribbean, for heaven's sake, nor Mediterranean, nor Cape of Good
Hope.'

'It's not a game.'

'I'm sorry,' I said. He seemed so hurt.

'No Christopher Columbus,' he then relented and joined my game.
'No Vasco da Gama.'

'So what about the seashore?'

'We keep it. We didn't create all that sand for nothing.'

'We? Who's we?'

'A few molecules one way or the other, a few electrons and other subatomic whatnots here or there in the initial conflagration, and we could have an earth made of iron. Or wool or sawdust.'

'Or gold?' I opted to humour him.

'Not gold,' he said sourly, not opting to humour me. 'There's truth, for starters. And goodness goes without saying. But beauty is ambiguous. A gold earth would be tawdry and unsuitable. On a golden earth what do you do for flowers, or weeds, or people for that matter? What do you do for acoustics?'

Out of his mind. But then he smiled slyly as if to say, it's only a game. I went home confused. I alerted people – he's back. Provided a few extra details until someone remembered him. Harmless, everyone then agreed. His name is Pepper, or Davis, something like that.

His appearances became more frequent – a week, four days, then two in a row. Even when I got there first I gave up my end of the bench to him.

'We should abolish the automobile,' he said one noisy day in town.

'How?' Leading questions, I discovered, made his day.

'Petroleum is the culprit.'

'We're back to molecules and electrons, am I right?' I was getting the hang of it. Even in our own town donkeys and carts had succumbed in one generation to a constant stream of cars. However slow the donkeys in the old days, we never had a traffic jam. This must surely be food for thought.

'And chance,' he said. We were becoming friends. 'Never forget Murphy's Law.'

'It would mean a return to beasts of burden: the donkey, the camel, not to mention pigeons. Think of all the hay and potatoes.'

'No need. We'd be strong as horses ourselves if we had exercised the appropriate muscles and mental neurons for the past million years.'

'And speedy as a speeding bullet,' I was enthusiastic.

'As a jet plane,' he amended. 'Creatures of infinite possibility.'

And that was just the physical side. When he thought I was ready he steered me – I don't know – upward or inward to where the molecules were more refined and the considerations more intangible.

'I'd abolish hate.' The pale October sun was too weak to make shadows. The cross on the church steeple cocked its head and paid attention. 'This would call for a radical realignment of all the other emotions.'

'Is there any future for love?'

'We need a new vocabulary. Did you notice there's no word for disinterested love? That's because it so seldom comes up in conversation.'

'Or vice versa.' I wasn't sure what I meant by this. In discussions like ours one threw words in the air and hoped some at least would come down with significance attached to them. 'What about justice?' I forged ahead. 'What about revenge?' Once one started asking such inflated questions there was no obvious place to stop.

I forget what he answered. At a certain stage words lose their point: either inadequate or superfluous. He had touched my arm. And turned the smouldering eyes on me. For a while that October day I could see through him. No metaphor, this, nor mystical experience. Behind where his head should be obstructing my view, I could see leafless trees. I saw crows on the branches. And behind them Rooney's pub.

Was this a holy fool? In the gritty heroic ages holy fools kept all manner of tribulation at bay. I wondered then whether God, commonly believed to be dead, could rise again. God had a history of surprises.

'I don't even know your name.'

'Pepper.'

At Curly's, next day, the waitress wore a knowing grin, and I could soon see why. Luke Pepper had come in from the cold. Had ensconced himself at what I considered my table. A shiver ran through me. Where I sat now might be decisive. I opted to be gracious and asked if I could join him. He looked different indoors, more fragile. He had removed the hat and his skull shone radiant in the light of a fake Tiffany lamp.

He, in turn, was getting a first good look at me. What he saw was a shorter man, chunky. My demeanour, I suspect, is more solemn than average, the reward for a lifetime of burying the dead. My hair is unusually dark for my age because, when a few grey ones popped up not long ago, I bought a bottle of black stuff at the pharmacy. I have a ruddy complexion and shave once a day, including the area where a moustache would otherwise grow.

'The heavenly bodies,' he got down to business. 'We're only one or two discoveries away from a breakthrough.'

'Hubble,' I enthused. 'Fantastic pictures.' In the narrow confines of Curly's our conversation grew more discreet. It was insane to think we were alone in the universe, we both agreed. Astronomical numbers were trotted out, and no matter how vast my numbers Luke always topped them.

'Will they be like us, then? Little green persons or more of the same?'

'It's more a matter of what we see than what's there.' He was whispering now. 'It makes sense to seek out civilisations at the same stage of development as ourselves. That means they would still be in their bodies. So they would need place-to-place transportation. Food, too.'

'What about reproduction?' Did I mention that I live alone and, frankly, am often lonely?

'I'd search for a planet where there are advanced forms of gratification,' he said, reading my mind. He made it sound easy. And it would be easy if one knew how to go about it – like following directions. I glanced around, but the locals seemed unaware that space-time was knocking at their door.

Luke, for the record, had vegetable soup and brown bread. Outside, I couldn't resist looking up at the infinite sky, and acknowledged it with a surreptitious nod.

He was at my table ahead of me every day, on the chair from which, for years, I enjoyed an exceptional view of the Inny. Our conversations became more ambitious, took aim at more distant stretches of the imagination. There were, among the stars, he would say, happy places. In one lofty digression he expressed interest in a more user-friendly heaven.

'And a more forgiving hell.' Being a liberal, I have always believed in giving the devil his due.

When he missed a day I felt bereft. Afterwards, I crossed the square to our bench. A bird had dirtied the south end. Instead of cleaning it, I settled for the clean side. The water had been turned off, exposing the stained stone base and rusty pipes of the fountain. Wild geese flew over, flying high, going away for the winter.

On the third day I grew concerned. Odd couple that we were, I had neither his phone number nor other particulars, but the consensus pointed to a little road I had always thought led nowhere. Too far to walk, I was told, so I set out early. Crows flew uselessly about, tilting in an enviable motion. Luke had the right idea about wings. I regretted never having become part of some radical movement that might have created enough commotion among life's molecules to cause buds to sprout from chosen shoulders until they were airworthy to soar. Failing that, I should have contrived some other wild plan to goose the universe, the crazier the better, failure would be more acceptable that way. I would die happy if only I could become one of the world's heroic failures.

By late morning I could see a white house ahead. Since it was the only one it must be the right one. The crows had abandoned me, probably for personal reasons. It is my custom, when out walking, to speak to birds that come within earshot, and likewise to farm animals. Not that I'm a mystic, but most animals are lonely, even in crowds, anyone can see it. Luke's place was a sprawling structure, a weather vane above the chimney, a once-elegant house turned shabby. A pair of stone eagles looked at me ruefully from crumbling pillars. There was an electric doorbell but I opted for the big brass knocker.

Luke was first a moving shadow behind frosted glass and then the door opened. He wore a loose faded shirt unbuttoned to mid-chest. His face was flushed, as if he might have come from a hot kitchen. A series of emotions, including panic, spread across his face.

'You shouldn't be here.'

'I was concerned.' Behind him in the dark interior of the house I could see nothing but books. There was time for only a glance before he led me outside, pulling the door behind us.

'I hoped you might come,' he contradicted himself. He walked ahead of me back toward the little silver gate between yew trees. Sat on the low wall and I sat beside him. 'If I had it to do again, I'd have met you when we were young.' He said it into space, the way he talked about the Tarantula Nebula. This made me nervous – what could he possibly be seeing? The sun came out, doubtless an accident of clouds and wind currents, but I sensed life was making some statement. Old apple trees survived in an orchard. One tree had fallen years ago, the trunk stretched flat on the ground, yet the branches refused to give up, growing faded yellow apples already raided by blackbirds.

I did not notice the door opening. Now a wraith stood there, white robe to her toes, face spectral, yellow-white hair cascading to her waist.

'Could you come back tomorrow?' He did not wait for an answer, ushered the woman into the house. What the fox said to the little prince kept whispering in my mind all the way home. About how we are to tame one another: just gently come a little closer each day.

Next noon I followed the trail of a high-flying jet out the road. If I had it to do again, I decided, falling for Luke's old gimmick, my knees would not ache nor my heart palpitate. Neither would I be sad. Luke's house would assume a new coat of white paint and then grow grander until it became a fabled city full of energy and interesting people and especially children rushing shouting into the future. I opened the silver gate noisily to alert the population against further surprises.

Luke was wearing the familiar corduroy suit, even the hat. Called me by my name as he ushered me into the claustrophobic interior. Apologised for yesterday's apparition. Led the way down a dim corridor. On the right, pots and pans hung from the ceiling of a small kitchen. Elsewhere scripts and cardboard boxes and folders were piled on sideboards, precarious and dusty, and stacked solid floor to ceiling. If a storm should blow down the thick stone walls, these other walls of paper would hold up the house. In some metaphysical way they had become the house.

Through open doors I could see other rooms similarly crowded: windows and alcoves stuffed with typescripts and printouts, bound in plastic or cardboard covers – as I would have imagined a publisher's emporium. Could he be? Or a magazine editor? But closed down, surely. Too much dust. More likely an archive. Or a heap of junk.

We came to a bedroom without books or papers. Items of antique furniture were strategically placed. A television set beamed silent pictures from a shelf high on the wall. The ghost lay on a wide brass bed amid gold wallpaper of an earlier era.

'My wife, Pamela,' Luke introduced her.

I took her hand, damp and limp, pressed it. She gave me a wan smile. She was nearly eighty, I guessed, but still a beauty. Around her ascetic face her long hair was draped over the pillow, hair that must have been her glory once, must have turned heads. Our audience was over in a minute. I squeezed her hand again and Luke kissed her cheek, but she was asleep. I was the last one on earth to shake her hand. She died the next day.

We were half a dozen at her funeral. As Luke scattered a token shovel of clay on her coffin, lusty singers wearing wings sang in chorus somewhere in the firmament. Or so I sensed – when death visits life it often opens cracks in reality through which mysteries slip in.

For a week Luke failed to appear in Curly's. One day, after lunch, I walked out the bleak road. Instead of the brass knocker I boldly rang the electric bell to drive grief away.

'I knew you'd come.' He shuffled ahead of me through the maze of paper. 'No one knew she existed.' He threw a glance over his shoulder. 'Oh, nothing sinister. Those who knew her had died. She has been eager to do the same for years. But, being married to me, she was always giving me another few months to get a grip on life. That's why she needed to see you; she always said I could never survive on my own.'

A room with bay window contained two rocking chairs and a desk on which sat a vintage computer pale brown with dust. From one chair he removed several typescripts bound by rubber bands.

'You'd better explain.' I spread my arms to embrace everything. But he left me and I could hear him in the kitchen before he returned with tea and six lumpy biscuits on a willow-pattern plate.

'The world has grown wobbly, Owen. The Big Bang got us off to a flying start, but look at all that went wrong since then.'

'Like this tea.' I was forever having to bring him down to earth. 'It's abominable tea.'

'Precisely,' he said without a smile. For hours he regaled me about prime matter and hylomorphism, about ambiguous shadows on the wall of Plato's cave. Mediocre tea, it seems, is only a symptom. More powerful forces need to be addressed. The universe is putting huge energy into expansion but not enough into cultivating a better brain.

'When you consider the primitive mess we came from,' I interrupted him, 'and how long it took to invent the wheel, for example, I'd say the contemporary brain is doing well. Including your own,' I added to humour him. I was out of my depth, having long ago rushed uneducated into the undertaking business. Luke waved my remarks aside.

'All we can do is hold entropy at bay.' Tons of molecules and other notoriously small particles were used up every day. Gone with the wind, he said. Suns, moons and stars were swallowed by black holes. A woman dies and all her knowledge so gradually collected and avidly hoarded is gone. 'When someone made the wheel, it didn't need to do anything, any more than a flower needs to be seen or a linnet heard.' He waxed for hours, as he said, adding words to the world. He made me promise to come back. Since I had no other friends I occasionally wondered whether our relationship was abnormal or typical.

Thereafter I always brought my own tea bag in my hip pocket. Luke adjusted stacks of paper to reveal a fireplace in the room with bay window. In it he inserted an electric fire boasting two feeble orange elements. Another blow against entropy, I suggested. He smiled good-natured agreement, but I wished he would let himself go and laugh and guffaw until the dust from all those books rose up and filled the room with dancing.

'The first wheel, the first submarine,' he was useless at small talk and always had a speech ready for me. 'Such things become obsolete. They're lucky if they make it to a museum. If you ask me, only ideas count.'

'Could we stop for tea?' He was, it turned out, a reasonably good baker, and would conjure up a different gastronomical surprise for each visit: bribes, I suppose.

A phantasmagoria of indifferent ideas roams the world, he announced after the rhubarb pie. Rocking gently in his battered chair he would look off into space and make room in the world for all kinds of poppycock: trivial ideas elbowing out profound ones by force of numbers; embarrassing ideas in search of a hearing; risky ideas ditto. He would trot out foreign names such as Bucky Fuller, Albert Camus and a Dane called Kierkegaard.

The universe, he said, was kept in circulation by a small coterie who took the initiative to explore this vast zoo of ideas, rejecting some and polishing others for the world to salute.

'The only humans who fully accept this challenge are writers.' A lifetime of dealing with bereaved people had made me a good listener, a rare species nowadays. I had only to nod encouragement to keep Luke's momentum up.

'The first word – I like to think it was spoken by a woman, though it could as well have been a parrot or a jackdaw. Who may have said *mountain*. Or *toothache*. Or more likely grunted, but with a certain nuance over and above the average grunt.' And he was off to the races. Our discussions, I am convinced, kept him alive that winter. We talked in ever smaller circles until his house full of paper could be ignored no longer.

'I was a doctor. I practised medicine for a year and a day. I dealt with aches and pains, nothing big like brain surgery. I fell for the usual dilemma: too much pain and too little time. I gave up. I thought, writing. Writing will alert people and then we'll all heal everyone else in a hurry.

'So I became a professional and wrote words morning to night. Raw words and sophisticated ones. See-sawed between past and future – the present always evaporated before I could write it down.' He became eloquent and expansive as if a different lingo were required to talk about writing, until I deflated him.

'Excuse me, now,' I said, 'but are we talking about articles for the paper or big bestselling books that nobody reads?'

'An occasional little magazine would publish an article.' Humility descended upon him. 'But no one ever seemed to read it. Eventually I had articles waiting at all the magazines, and novels at all the publishing houses. The rejection slips piled higher, a mountain of rejection. Finally I realised people were not ready. Too busy watching television. Attention spans of shrimps.' Bitterness gripped him for a moment.

'I was ready to go back to doctoring when Pamela walked through the door. She was, in fact, wanting to see a doctor. Until I told her I was a writer. She was a dancer, a ballerina from Vienna, Austria. You can imagine how unlikely it was that a ballerina from Austria would darken my door in the midlands.'

'People are overwhelmed and can't cope with you,' she confirmed his own pessimistic view. 'Yet there exists an audience worthy of you.'

'Anyone who makes such a lavish promise is bound to pay a price.' Silence followed. A grandfather clock ticked time away in the next room. I willed him to be human and fiercely bawl his grief to the heedless countryside. Week by week I could discern him approaching that decisive moment beyond which stretched eternity.

'I wrote to all the agents and editors and told them I was withdrawing my submissions because I had found a new audience. I never heard from one of them. You would think they'd be curious.

'The next day, going over the heads of publishers and other middlemen, I started writing directly for the universe. What are a few pages in a magazine compared to that? What good is a bestseller compared to that? I was surprised other writers had not thought of this before.' He paused to savour the memory of giving the status quo its comeuppance, sipped the lukewarm tea from his blue mug. In return for rhubarb tart I had agreed to supply him with tea bags.

'It was liberating. No more catering to passing trends. The world was interested – how could it not be? The world had time. The cosmos needed feedback. The cosmos, designed for give and take, is constantly running down unless we give something back. This is especially true of meaning. Everyone knows there is a dearth of meaning in the world.'

'In English, is it?'

'Yes, in English,' he said when he saw my stupid question was well meant. 'Reading has nothing to do with it. And publication, needless to say, is just a gimmick to make money. Only the writing matters.'

'So what did you write?' For months I had walked over and around his neglected heaps of paper without once being tempted to steal a look. 'Articles or what?'

'Articles, yes, if some small point needed to be made. At other times I wrote longer works, some running to several volumes. Forty or fifty novels, it's a while since I counted.' He waved to indicate the whole topsy-turvy house. 'Plays – for a while I thought plays. It depended on the mood of the world. I had only to read the morning paper to see what was needed. Whenever life was going well I'd respond with lyrical poetry. But I must warn you: in a world where people kill each other with such regularity, and galaxies crash into each other on a daily basis, it would be dishonest to write as if life were smooth sailing.'

He married Pamela. 'Not only was she a great beauty' – he said matter-of-factly – 'she also had loads of money, a necessary evil in contemporary life.'

'She must have been proud of you.'

'She never read a word I wrote. That time she came looking for a doctor, it was about her eyes. Some rare disease. I would read to her on winter nights, until she informed me the reading was superfluous.' Another silence and a sip of cold tea.

Spring came. I tried to coax him out of the dank house back to Curly's for vegetable soup. He would say he needed to write, but he never wrote.

'When I saw you on that bench, I resisted at first,' he confided one day. 'I was looking for someone young to keep the thing alive longer. That was nonsense, of course. Once the words are written they have made their point.'

I held his hand when demons played with the knocker on the decaying front door. I made him cups of tea, then fed him sips on a spoon. Finally closed his eyes.

An April shower was nudged aside by the sun on the day of Luke's funeral. The priest turned a blind eye on his heresies and sprinkled the pine box with holy water. The church steeple stood at attention, the cross proud. Since I was the only mourner, the priest suggested I say a few words.

'He never gave up,' was all I could think of saying. And added, 'Goodbye, Luke.' And winked at his soul flying off on swift wings. Lucky old bastard. Everyone knowing him already and greeting him all over the universe, Luke waving back at them and no need to learn their names. Luke's spirit shining in the sun or ducking out of curiosity into black holes to verify his theories. Editors and agents and glossy magazine magnates left out of the loop while the universe thundered that it got his message, agreed with his gist.

The clay was still fresh over Pamela. Soon they would be snug side by side. If molecules were half as smart as Luke always said, this would be a lively graveyard hereafter. Subatomic whatnots would learn their way around, would visit each other in the dead of night, would mingle and multiply and start something new.

If I had it to do again, that's what I'd say.

In his will Luke left me the house, and all the words therein. I walk out once a week and switch on the electric fire to keep decay away. I will live as long as I can, in case anything unexpected should happen.

# A Literary Lunch

## ÉILÍS NÍ DHUIBHNE

The board was gathering in a bistro on the banks of the Liffey. 'We deserve a decent lunch!' Alan, the chairman, declared cheerfully. He was a cheerful man. His eyes were kind, and encouraged those around him to feel secure. People who liked him said he was charismatic.

The board was happy. Their tedious meeting was over and the bistro was much more expensive than the hotel to which Alan usually brought them, with its alarming starched tablecloths and fantails of melon. He was giving them a treat because it was a Saturday. They had sacrificed a whole three hours of the weekend for the good of the organisation they served. The reputation of the bistro, which was called Gabriel's, was excellent and anyone could tell from its understated style that the food would be good, and the wine too, even before they looked at the menu – John Dory, oysters, fried herrings, sausage and mash. Truffles. A menu listing truffles just under sausage and mash promises much. We can cook and we are ironic as well, it proclaims. Put your elbows on the table, have a good time.

Emphasising the unpretentiously luxurious tone of Gabriel's was a mural on the wall, depicting a modern version of *The Last Supper*, a photograph of typical Dubliners eating at a long refectory table.

Alan loved this photograph, a clever, postmodern, but delightfully accessible work of art. It raised the cultural tone of the bistro, if it needed raising, which it didn't really, since it was also located next door to the house on Usher's Island where James Joyce's aunts had lived, and which he used as the setting for his most celebrated story 'The Dead'. In short, of all the innumerable restaurants boasting literary associations in town, Gabriel's had the most irrefutable credentials. You simply could not eat in a more artistic place.

The funny thing about *The Last Supper* was that everyone was sitting at one side of the table, very conveniently for painters and photographers. It was as if they had anticipated all the attention which would soon be coming their way. And Gabriel's had, in its clever ironic way, set up one table in exactly the same manner, so that everyone seated at it faced in the same direction, getting a good view of the mural and also of the rest of the restaurant. It was great. Nobody was stuck facing the wall. You could see if anyone of any importance was among the clientele – and usually there were one or two stars, at least. You could see what they were wearing and what they were eating and drinking, although you had to guess what they were talking about, which made it even more interesting, in a funny sort of way. More interactive. It was like watching a silent movie without subtitles.

A problem with the arrangement was that people at one end of the last supper table had no chance at all of talking to those at the other end. But this too could be a distinct advantage, if the seating arrangements were intelligently handled. Alan always made sure that they were.

At the right end of the table he had placed his good old friends Simon and Paul (Joe had not come, as per usual. He was the real literary expert on the board, having won the Booker Prize, but he never attended meetings. Too full of himself. Still they could use his name on the stationery). Alan himself sat in the middle where he could keep an eye on everyone. On his left hand side were Mary, Jane and Pam. The women liked to stick together.

Alan, Simon and Paul ordered oysters and truffles and pâté de foie gras for starters. Mary, Jane and Pam ordered one soup of the day and two nothings. No starter please for me. This was not owing to the gender division. Mary and Jane were long past caring about their figures, at least when out on a free lunch, and Pam was new and eager to try everything being a member of a board offered, even John Dory, which she had ordered for her main course. Their abstemiousness was due to the breakdown in communications caused by the seating arrangements. The ladies had believed that nobody was getting starters, because Alan had muttered I don't think I'll have a starter and then changed his mind and ordered the pâté de foie gras when they were chatting among themselves about a new production of *A Doll's House*, which was just showing at the Abbey. Mary had been to the opening, as she was careful to emphasise; she was giving it the thumbs down. Nora had been manic and the sound effects were appalling. The slam of the door which was supposed to reverberate down through a hundred years of drama couldn't even be heard in the second row of the stalls. That was the Abbey for you, of course. Such dreadful acoustics, the place has to be shut down. Pam and Mary nodded eagerly; Pam thought the Abbey was quite nice but she knew if she admitted that in public everyone would think she was a total loser who had probably failed her Leaving. Neither Pam nor Mary had seen *A Doll's House* but they had read a review by Fintan O'Toole so they knew everything they needed to know. He hadn't liked the production and had decided that the original play was not much good anyway. *Farvel*, Ibsen!

In the middle of this conversation Pam's mobile phone began to play 'Waltzing Matilda' at volume level five. Alan gave her a reproving glance. If she had to leave on her mobile phone she could at least have picked a tune by Shostakovich or Stravinksy. He himself had a few bars by a young Irish composer on his phone, ever mindful of his duty to the promotion of the national culture. 'Terribly sorry!' Pam said, slipping the phone into her bag, but not before she had glanced at the screen to find out who was calling. 'I forgot to switch it off.' Which was rather odd, Mary thought, since Pam had placed the phone on the table, in front of her nose, the minute she had come into the restaurant. It had sat there by the water jug looking like a tiny pistol in its little leather holster.

In the heel of the hunt all this distraction meant that they neglected to eavesdrop on the men while they were placing their orders so that they would get a rough idea of how extravagant they could be. How annoying it was now, to see Simon slurping down his oysters, with lemon and black pepper, and Paul digging into his truffles, while they had nothing but *A Doll's House* and soup of the day to amuse themselves with.

And a glass of white wine. Paul, who was a great expert, had ordered that. A Sauvignon Blanc, the vineyard of Du Bois Père et Fils, 2002. 'As nice a Sauvignon as I have tried in years,' he said, as he munched a truffle and sipped thoughtfully. '2002 was a good year for everything in France but this is exceptional.' The ladies strained to hear what he was saying, much more interested in wine than drama. Mary, who had been so exercised a moment ago about Ibsen at the Abbey, seemed to have forgotten all about both. She was now taking notes, jotting down Paul's views. He was better, much better, than the people who do the columns in the paper, she commented excitedly as she scribbled. No commercial agenda – well, that they knew of. You never quite knew what anyone's agenda was, that was the trouble. Paul was apparently on the board, because of his knowledge of books, and Simon, because of his knowledge of the legal world, and Joe, because he was famous. Mary, Jane and Pam were there because they were women. Mary was already on twenty boards and had had to call a halt, since her entire life was absorbed by meetings and lunches, receptions and launches. Luckily she had married sensibly and did not have to work. Jane sat on ten boards and Pam had been nominated two months ago. This was her first lunch with any board, ever. She was a writer. Everyone wondered what somebody like her was doing here. It was generally agreed that she must know someone.

One person she knew was Francie Briody. He was also having lunch, in a coffee shop called the Breadbasket, a cold little kip of a place across the river on Aston Quay. They served filled baguettes and sandwiches as well as coffee and he was lunching on a tuna submarine with corn and coleslaw. Francie was a writer, like Pam, although she wrote so-called literary women's fiction, chick lit for PhDs and was successful. Francie wrote literary fiction for anybody who cared to read it, which was nobody. For as long as he could remember he had been a writer whom nobody read. And he was already fifty years of age. He had written three novels and about a hundred short stories, and other bits and bobs. Success of a kind had been his lot in life, but not of a kind to enable him to earn a decent living, or to eat anything other than tuna baguettes, or to get him a seat on an arts organisation board. He had had one novel published, to mixed reviews; he had won a prize at Listowel Writers' Week for a short story fifteen years ago. Six of his short stories had been nominated for prizes – the Devon Cream Story Competition, the Blackstaff Young Authors, the William Carleton Omagh May Festival, among others. But he still had to work part time in a public house, and he had failed to publish his last three books.

Nobody was interested in a writer past the age of thirty.

It was all the young ones they wanted these days, and women, preferably young women with lots of shining hair and sweet photogenic faces. Pam. She wasn't that young any more, and not all that photogenic, but she'd got her foot in the door in time, when women and the Irish were all the rage, no matter what they looked like. Or wrote like.

He'd never been a woman – he had considered a pseudonym but he'd let that moment pass. And now he'd missed the boat. The love affair of the London houses and the German houses and the Italian and the Japanese with Irish literature was over. So everyone said. Once Seamus Heaney got the Nobel the interest abated. Enough's enough. On to the next country. Bosnia or Latvia or God knows what. Slovenia.

Francie's latest novel, a heteroglossial polyphonic postmodern examination of postmodern Ireland, with special insights into political corruption and globalisation, beautifully written in darkly masculinist ironic prose with shadows of *l'écriture féminine*, which was precisely and exactly what Fintan O'Toole swore that the Irish public and Irish literature were crying out for, had been rejected by every London house, big and small, that his agent could think of, and by the five Irish publishers who would dream of touching a literary novel as well, and also, Francie did not like to think of this, by the other thirty Irish publishers who believed chick lit was the modern Irish answer to James Joyce. Yes yes yes yes. The delicate chiffon scarf was flung over her auburn curls. Yes.

Yeah well.

I'll show the philistine fatso bastards.

He pushed a bit of slippery yellow corn back into his baguette. Extremely messy form of nourishment, it was astonishing that it had caught on, especially as the baguettes were slimy and slippery themselves.

Not like the home-made loaves served in Gabriel's on the south bank of the Liffey. Alan was nibbling a round of freshly baked, soft as silk, crispy as Paris on a fine winter's day roll, to mop up the oyster juice, which was sitting slightly uneasily on his stomach.

'We did a good job,' he was saying to Pam, who liked to talk shop, being new.

'I'd always be so worried that we picked the wrong people,' she said in her charming girlish voice. She had nice blonde hair but this did not make up for her idealism and her general lack of experience. Alan wished his main course would come quickly. Venison with lingonberry *jus* and basil mash.

'You'd be surprised but that very seldom happens,' he said.

'Judgements are so subjective vis-à-vis literature,' she said, with a frown, remembering a bad review she'd received fifteen years ago.

Alan suppressed a sigh. She was a real pain.

'There is almost always complete consensus on decisions,' he said. 'It's surprising, but the cream always rises. I . . . we . . . are never wrong.' His magical eyes twinkled.

Consensus? Pam frowned into her Sauvignon Blanc. A short discussion of the applicants for the bursaries in which people nudged ambiguities around the table like footballers dribbling a ball when all they want is the blessed trumpeting of the final whistle. They waited for Alan's pronouncement. If that was consensus she was Emily Dickinson. As soon as Alan said, 'I think this is brilliant writing' or, 'Rubbish, absolute rubbish' there was a scuffle of voices vying with each other to be the first to agree with the great man.

Rubbish, absolute rubbish. That was what he had said about Francie. He's persistent, I'll give him that. Alan had allowed himself a smile, which he very occasionally permitted himself at the expense of minor writers. The board guffawed loudly. She hadn't told Francie that. He would kill himself. He was at the end of his tether. But she had broken the sad news over the phone in the loo, as she had promised. No bursary. Again.

'I don't know,' she persisted, ignoring Alan's brush-off. 'I feel so responsible somehow. All that effort and talent, and so little money to go around . . .'

Her voice tailed off. She could not find the words to finish the sentence, because she was drunk as an egg after two glasses. No breakfast, the meeting had started at nine.

Stupid bitch, thought Alan, although he smiled cheerily. Defiant. Questioning. Well, we know how to deal with them. Woman or no woman, she would never sit on another board. This was her first and her last supper. I feel so responsible somehow. Who did she think she was?

'This is a 2001 Bordeaux from a vineyard run by an Australian ex-pat just outside Bruges, that's the Bruges near Bordeaux of course, not Bruges La Mort in little Catholic Belgium.' Paul's voice had raised several decibels and Simon was getting a bit rambunctious. They were well into the second bottle of the Sauvignon and had ordered two bottles of the Bordeaux, priced, he noticed, at 85 euro a pop. The lunch was going to cost about a thousand euro.

'Your venison, sir?'

At last.

He turned away from Pam and speared the juicy game. The grub of kings.

Francie made his king-size tuna submarine last a long time. It would have anyway, since the filling kept spilling out onto the table and it took ages to gather it up and replace it in the roll. He glanced at the plain round clock over the fridge. They'd been in there for two hours. How long would it be?

Fifteen years.

Since his first application.

Fifty.

His twelfth.

His twelfth time trying to get a bursary to write full time.

It would be the makings of him. It would mean he could give up serving alcohol to fools for a whole year. He would write a new novel, the novel which would win the prizes and show the begrudgers. Impress Fintan O'Toole. Impress Emer O'Reilly. Impress, maybe, Eileen fucking Battersby. And the boost to his morale would be so fantastic . . . but once again that Alan Byrne, who had been running literary Ireland since he made his confirmation probably, had shafted him. He knew. Pamela had phoned him from the loo on her mobile. She had tried her best but there was no way. They had really loved his work, she said. There was just not enough money to go round. She was so sorry, so sorry . . .

Yeah right.

Alan was the one who made the decisions. Pamela had told him so herself. They do exactly what he says, she said. It's amazing. I never knew how power worked. Nobody ever disagrees with him. Nobody who gets to sit on the same committees and eat the same lunches anyway. As long as he was chair Francie would not get a bursary. He would not get a travel grant. He would not get a production grant. He would not get a trip to China or Paris or even the University of Eastern Connecticut. He would not get a free trip to Drumshambo in the County Leitrim for the Arsehole of Ireland Literature and Donkey Racing Weekend.

Alan Byrne ruled the world.

The pen is stronger than the sword, Francie had learned, in school. Was it Patrick Pearse who said that or some classical guy? Cicero or somebody. That's how old Francie was, they were still doing Patrick Pearse when he was in primary. He was pre-revisionism and he still hadn't got a bursary in literature let alone got onto Aosdana, which gave some lousy writers like Pam a meal ticket for life. The pen is stronger. Good old Paddy O'Piarsiagh. But he changed his mind apparently. Francie looked at the Four Courts through the corner window of the Breadbasket. Who had been in that in 1916?

He couldn't remember. Had anyone? Ceannt or X or somebody nobody could remember. Burnt down the place in the end, all the history of Ireland in it. IRA of their day. That was later, the Civil War. He had written about that too. He had written about everything. Even about Alan. He had written a whole novel about him, and six short stories, but they were hardly going to find their mark if they never got published and they were not going to get published if he did not get a bursary and some recognition from the establishment and he was not going to get any recognition while Alan was running every literary and cultural organisation on the island . . .

At last. The evening was falling in when the board members tripped and staggered out of the Usher, into the light and shade, the sparkle and darkness, that was Usher's Quay. Jane and Mary had of course left much earlier, anxious to get to the supermarkets before they closed.

But Pam, to the extreme annoyance of everyone, had lingered on, drinking the Bordeaux with the best of them. They had been irritated at first but had then passed into another stage. The sexual one. Inevitable as Australian Chardonnay at a book launch. They had stopped blathering on about wine and had begun to reminisce about encounters with ladies of the night in exotic locations; Paul claimed, in a high voice which had Alan looking around the restaurant in alarm, to have been seduced by a whore in a hotel in Moscow who had bought him a vodka and insisted on accompanying him to his room, clad only in a coat of real wolfskin. Fantasy land. That eejit Pam was so shot herself she didn't seem to care what they said. Her mascara was slipping down her face and her blonde hair was manky, as if she had sweated too much. It was high time she got a taxi. He'd shove her into one as soon as he got them out. He couldn't leave them here, they'd drink the board dry and if they were unlucky some journalist would happen upon them. He stopped for a second. Publicity was something they were always seeking and hardly ever got. But no, this would do them no good at all. There is such a thing as bad press in spite of what he said at meetings.

He paid the bill. There were long faces of course. You'd think he was crucifying them instead of having treated them to a lunch which had cost, including the large gratuity he was expected to fork out, 1200 euro of Lottery money. Oh well, better than racehorses, he always said, looking at *The Last Supper*. Was it Leonardo or Michelangelo had painted the original, he was so exhausted he couldn't remember. He took no nonsense for the boyos, though, and asked the waiter to put them into their coats no matter how they protested.

Pam excused herself at the last minute, taking him aback.

'Don't wait for me,' she said. She could still speak coherently. 'I'll be grand, I'll get a taxi. I'll put it on the account.'

She gave him a peck on the cheek – that's how drunk she was – and ran out the door, pulling her mobile out of her bag as she did so.

Not such a twit as all that. I'll put it on the account. He almost admired her, for a second.

With the help of the waiter he got the other pair of beauties bundled out to the pavement.

The taxi had not yet arrived.

He deposited Simon and Paul on a bench placed outside for the benefit of smokers and moved to the kerb, the better to see.

Traffic moved freely along the quay. It was not as busy as usual. A quiet evening. The river was a blending delight of black and silver and mermaid green. Alan was not entirely without aesthetic sensibility. The sweet smell of hops floated along the water from the brewery. He'd always loved that, the heavy cloying smell of it, like something you'd give a two-year-old to drink. Like hot jam tarts. In the distance he could just see the black trees of the Phoenix Park. Sunset. Peaches and molten gold, Dublin stretched against it. The north side could be lovely at times like this. When it was getting dark. The Wellington monument rose, a black silhouette, into the heavens, a lasting tribute to the power and glory of great men.

It was the last thing Alan saw.

He did not even hear the shot explode like a backfiring lorry in the hum of the evening city.

Francie's aim was perfect. It was amazing that a writer who could not change a plug or bore a hole in a wall with a Black and Decker drill at point-blank range could shoot so straight across the expanse of the river. Well, he had trained. Practice makes perfect, they said at the creative-writing workshops. Be persistent, never lose your focus. He had not written a hundred short stories for nothing and a short story is an arrow in flight towards its target. They were always saying that. Aim write fire. And if there's a gun on the table in act one it has to go off in act three, that's another thing they said.

But, laughed Francie, as he wrapped his pistol in a Tesco bag for life, in real life what eejit would put a gun on the table in act one? In real life a gun is kept well out of sight and it goes off in any act it likes. In real life there is no foreshadowing.

That's the difference, he thought, as he let the bag slide over the river wall. That's the difference between life and art. He watched the bag sink into the black lovely depths of Anna Livia Pluribella. Patrick Pearse gave up on the *peann* in the end. When push came to shove he took to the *lámh láidir*.

He walked down towards O'Connell Bridge, taking out his mobile. Good old Pam. He owed her. For each man kills the thing he loves, he texted her, pleased to have remembered the line. By each let this be heard. Some do it with a bitter look, some with a flattering word. The coward does it with a kiss, the brave man with a gun. That wasn't right. Word didn't rhyme with gun. Some do it with a bitter look, some with a flattering pun. Didn't really make sense. What rhymes with gun? Lots of words. Fun, nun. Bun. Some do it with a bitter pint, some with a sticky bun, he texted in. Cheers! I'll buy you a bagel sometime. He sent the message and tucked his phone into his pocket. Anger sharpened the wit, he had noticed that before. His best stories had always been inspired by the lust for revenge. He could feel a good one coming on . . . maybe he shouldn't have bothered killing Alan.

He was getting into a bad mood again. He stared disconsolately at the dancing river. The water was far from transparent, but presumably the Murder Investigation Squad could find things in it. They knew it had layers and layers of meaning just like the prose he wrote. Readers were too lazy to deconstruct properly but policemen were probably pretty assiduous when it came to interpreting and analysing the murky layers of the Liffey. Would that bag for life protect his fingerprints, DNA evidence? He didn't know. The modern writer has to do plenty of research. God is in the details. He did his best but he had a tendency to leave some books unread, some websites unvisited. Writing a story, or murdering a man, was such a complex task. You were bound to slip up somewhere. Perfectionism is fatal, they said. Give yourself permission to err. Don't listen to the inner censor.

He had reached O'Connell Street and hey, there was the 46A waiting for him. A good sign. They'd probably let him have a laptop in prison, he thought optimistically, as he hopped on the bus. They'd probably make him writer in residence. That's if they ever found the gun.

# The Death of Billy Joel

## JOSEPH O'NEILL

For his fortieth birthday, Tom Rourke organizes a golf trip to Florida. He emails a total of ten men, but only three say yes; a few, including some of his oldest and, historically and theoretically, best friends, do not even summon the energy to reply. Two of the three who agree to join him, Aaron and Mick, are his regular golfing partners in New York and friends of only a few years' vintage. Only the final member of the quartet, David, was at college with Tom back in the eighties; David, who now lives in Chicago, is able to make it chiefly because the January weekend coincides with a business trip to Nashville. It would have surprised the Tom of twenty years ago, when he and his contemporaries clambered aboard the world with a piratical energy he now finds marvelous, to have learned that only one of his undergraduate soulmates would answer such an important summons. But the Tom of today is not surprised, or even disappointed. A foursome is perfect for a golf trip. And if he is to walk the plank into his forties – and it seems, a little incredibly, that he must – then Aaron and Mick and David, who are more or less his own age, will make fine witnesses. In fact, Tom is not too concerned about the milestone, at least not yet, because he actually has almost a month of his thirties left. The only moment of alarm comes when his mother, on the phone from Connecticut, says, "Let me tell you, the years between forty and fifty go by in a flash." The remark both scares and disappoints him: she has failed in her never-ending duty, thinks Tom, who has not without guilt created two children of his own, to make the business of life and death seem less frightening to him.

Tom makes all the arrangements. He books the hotel and the tee-times and three round-trip tickets to Tampa/St Petersburg. David will make his own way in from the west coast. The New York–Tampa tickets are only $230, all taxes included, but that does not stop his companions from wondering out loud, in the taxi to La Guardia, if he might not have got a cheaper deal.

"I got them on Travelocity," Tom explains. "They were the cheapest available." He is handing out the sheets of paper, printed out from the web, which these days pass for airplane tickets.

Aaron says, "You didn't try JetBlue? JetBlue doesn't turn up on Travelocity."

"Yeah, well, these are the tickets I got," Tom says, a little irritated. Aaron knows more than he does about food, bars, music, anime, cocktails, clothes, and, Tom has now been reminded, the internet. Of course, Aaron has the time to investigate such things now that he is separated from his wife and son and spends much of his time with his brand-new twenty-six-year-old Venezuelan girlfriend.

The three New Yorkers fly off, scattered to separate window seats. Each, it seems to Tom, is glad to be alone, to moon undisturbed out of a thick plastic porthole. Exactly what is being mulled over by his companions Tom does not know, for the men's encounters are almost wholly confined to golf games, and the possibilities of self-revelation are few in the introspective cosmos of each round, in which the players, roving as couples in buzzing carts, mainly deal in tactful silences, terse or cheerful words of forgiveness and encouragement, and cackling monetary calculation. Tom presumes – not overly gloomily, he thinks – that his friends are grappling with the shaming inward puzzle that, in the last year or so, has come to preoccupy him: how the principal motions of his life – those involving his tolerant and industrious wife, his daughters, his decently affirmative work – have largely, and for reasons he cannot put his finger on, been reduced to a mere likeness of vitality. Which perhaps explains his and his friends' increasingly inordinate gratefulness for golf. Certainly, being out on the course is one of the few times Tom is convinced of his so-called place in the universe – convinced even though he understands that this adventure with golf, a cliché, expands the funnel of triteness through which he senses his existence inevitably and ever more rapidly pours.

Queens, when they fly over it, is all snow and inky roads, a newspaper made panoramic. The Hudson, Tom next sees, is mottled with large, semitransparent plaques of ice. It has been a freezing, miserable January, the second coldest in half a century, and he feels an enormous relief to be migrating south. At Tampa, the plane swoops down and around a bay made exotic by spectacular swirls of turquoise. The men all crane to look down, for it's their first time in Tampa. The land below looks watery, and flat, and generously quadrangular: the roofs, the lots, the blocks, the lagoons, all have a squarish spaciousness to them. It is a gray and rainy morning but not, according to the pilot, a cold one. Tom remembers how earlier in month, when the temperature fell to 1°, the monstrous cold was uncannily invisible in the sunny city; it agitates him, this recollection of the vicious unseen. Then he spots the ribbony fairways of a golf course, innocuous and pointless-looking from the plane, and is calmed.

At the airport, things go well. Their clubs and bags are practically the first to emerge on the luggage carousel – Tom feels a lurch of emotion at the sight of his small brown leather overnight bag bravely holding its own amongst thuggish black cases – and they have no trouble finding the Hertz office. Although Tom has booked a mid-size saloon, Aaron secures an upgrade to an SUV. They mildly argue on the drive to Clearwater about SUVs and their propensity to kill other road users and flip over, but underneath it all they are excited: to everybody's disbelief, none of them has ridden an SUV before. The most pleasing feature of the vehicle is its satellite radio. Neither Tom nor Mick knows how to work it but Aaron, of course, does. He finds a rap channel – fucking this and motherfucker that, which satellite radio is apparently free to broadcast – and then Mick, who has taken the front passenger seat on the grounds that he is bigger than Tom, searches for something more amenable. He opts for an eighties station. They endure a minute or two of Hall & Oates and a song featuring one of those watery saxophone solos which, the three men agree, they never want to hear again so long as they live. So Mick presses the button on the satellite radio gadget and they start listening to hits from the seventies. The first song up is 'Last Dance,' by Donna Summer; and Tom recalls the pre-teen parties from which his parents picked him up (he would push aside a curtain and there, uncompromisingly parked across the street, would be his father in the Chevrolet, sitting like a hitman in the dashboard's glow) and where 'Last Dance' signaled the last dance. To hear the song even now gives him an unpleasant feeling of time running out. Then comes Rod Stewart, whose appearance and marital career Tom has always found ludicrous; nevertheless he is overwhelmed by Rod singing 'You Wear It Well.' The song must be connecting him to something in the years past; and Tom thinks of his sister, who loved that song, his sister who is now in a marriage in Arizona and is lost to him in all kinds of ways. As the SUV comes to the end of the causeway that leads into Clearwater, the young Billy Joel begins to sing. Tom has never really warmed to Billy Joel and voices no protest when Aaron says, "I can't listen to this," and goes back to the rap station, or channel, or program, or whatever you call it on satellite radio.

The three golfers arrive at the Belleview Biltmore Hotel and Spa, at which Tom has booked rooms at a discount rate offered by Hotels.com that is, it turns out, slightly more expensive than the rate the Belleview Biltmore itself would have offered. There is a moment of slight tension as they thriftily debate whether to use the valet parking ($3): on the one hand it's raining, on the other hand there are free parking spaces not far from the entrance. What the hell, they decide, and they drive the SUV up to the door and let Aaron pay the valet $3 plus tip: they do not yet know that the valet charge really means a parking charge, and that it makes no difference whether the valet parks the car for them or not, and that when they check out they will be charged $3 on top of the $6 they paid the valet.

The men dump their bags in their rooms and head straight out to the golf club affiliated to the hotel, which has a course designed by Robert Trent Jones. There is a squabble about golfing handicaps in which Aaron shamelessly pleads for shots. The dominating conversational genre of the weekend is already fixed: amiable bickering with episodes of rather formal sunniness. It is raining softly as they arrive at the first hole, which gives them all the more reason to cut themselves a break and play off the white tees.

Aaron tosses a long white tee in the air to determine the honor. When it lands, it points at Tom. Hiding his sudden nervousness, he pulls out the huge driver his wife bought him for Christmas and, after a couple of practice swings, he hits. The ball slices beyond a small hill to the right of the fairway and disappears. "I'm not sure Robert Trent Jones is going to reward that," Mick says.

After nine holes, they stop at the clubhouse to buy lunch. Mick takes the opportunity to tally their strokes out loud, chortling as the totals spurt forward in horrible leaps of six and seven. None of the three men has played well. Aaron, who is especially disconsolate about his performance, buys a packet of cigarettes and offers his friends a smoke. "Jesus, why not, it's my fucking fortieth birthday," Tom says, and takes one. So does Mick, although like Tom he is officially, and certainly for all matrimonial purposes, a non-smoker. The cigarette makes Tom, who during his twenties smoked heavily, unpleasantly dizzy, and he resolves not to have any more, a resolution he will break after a triple bogey at the eleventh. They play on in rain. On the fifteenth green, as he watches the shadowy hole suck up the grubby moons clustered around it, Tom allows himself the thought that this uneventful golf course is, at green fees of $69, insufficiently superior to the New York public courses they play on at $35 a pop. Still, it was a fun round, the players agree to agree in the locker room afterwards.

At the pro-shop, Aaron asks the two clean-cut young men behind the counter, "What is there to do around here at night?"

"Drink heavily," one of them replies unexpectedly.

Aaron says, "I mean, is there anywhere in Clearwater that's kind of interesting? A bar, or someplace to eat?"

The two young guys look at each other with strange animation, and one says to the other, "What do you think?" and the other one, reading his mind, says to the visitors, "Ybor City. It's about an hour from here, across the causeway back towards the airport. There's a lot of good places round there."

Somebody told Tom, after he'd opted for Tampa on the advice of a golfing friend, that he'd picked the strip club capital of America for his weekend away. There has been no sign of any strip joints on the roads they've taken, and Tom is pretty sure, from the significant tone of the pro-shop guys, that Ybor City must be where these famous establishments are located. This knowledge fills him with both dread and anticipation: anticipation because, after all, there is the prospect of women removing their clothing; dread, because he really does not want to find himself, turning forty, watching strippers. Just shoot me and bury me now, he thinks.

"An hour away?" Mick says, looking at Tom.

Tom hears himself say, "That's too far."

"Way too far," Aaron says.

The three friends, who have all been thinking the same thing, decide with relief to eat out where they are, in innocent Clearwater.

They return to the hotel. Tom is rooming with Aaron, and Mick is paired with David, whose flight arrives later in the evening. They make arrangements for a car to pick up David at the airport. This is done with the help of the concierge. When they ask her to suggest somewhere to eat, she declares, "Frenchy's, on the beach. You guys will love it." She gets out a photocopied sketch plan of Clearwater and highlights the route to Frenchy's. She says it's a Friday night, and it'll be busy and – this is nice of her to say, because she's no more than thirty – full of "people our age." Tom takes the plan and inspects the bright yellow trail they must carefully follow, as if to treasure.

Before they go to Frenchy's, however, they relax for an hour. Aaron wants to go to the Jacuzzi – this is a spa, after all – and he asks Tom to join him. Tom, who has neglected to bring swimwear, is unsure; but in the end he follows Aaron down wearing two pairs of boxer shorts. They find a spot in a corner of the hot tub where they can stretch out and talk.

Tom volunteers, "Suzanne's grandmother" – Suzanne is Tom's wife – "once worked for Mr Jacuzzi."

"She knew Jacuzzi? Wow."

"She was his secretary," Tom says. "In California. Or maybe Minnesota. California or Minnesota. One of the two."

Aaron says, "And how is Suzanne?"

Tom says, "Great, just great." He shifts to let the current massage his upper back. He is glad he has made the effort to come to Florida. "How's it going with you and, ah, Consuela?" Tom is not yet accustomed to uttering this astounding name.

"Oh, fine," Aaron says.

Tom is tempted to put a more penetrating inquiry to Aaron about the latter's new situation and indeed about marriage and womankind in general. Tom feels his own unhappiness pressing at him and he judges Aaron to be a man of the world, with a superior sense of its realities, a man who might be able to clue him in to something. For Tom believes there must be some common knowledge that has been withheld from him, some widely yet carefully disseminated confidence, some trick of living that he, in his slowness and innocence, has not yet grasped. Tom believes that he has already identified one such trick, ambition: it has only recently dawned on him, as the uncertainly merited and somewhat preposterous success of various acquaintances comes to his notice – Tom is an advertising manager at a magazine aimed at the legal services industry – that those who achieve great positions are those who have the imagination to desire them. Why is it that nobody brought this fact to his attention years ago? Why has he been forced to make this discovery on his own? Bothered, he slides forward and lowers his head into the hot water. He stays underwater for a long time, holding his breath. In the aftermath of immersion – funny how a dip can make you feel better – his need to talk to Aaron has abated. It would be a delicate conversation, anyway, since Aaron's break-up with Annette is only six months old. Talk about clichés: one Sunday, Annette returns from a weekend away at a high school reunion in Wisconsin and declares herself to be a new woman and young again and demands that Aaron leave the house that very night; which, partly out of sheer amazement, he does.

Tom says to his friend, "You know what, I'm getting a little dizzy here. You want to head up?"

"Sure," Aaron says. "I'm all set here."

They go back upstairs and decide to shower. "You got to shower," Aaron says firmly, as if the matter were in issue. "You don't know what's in that Jacuzzi water." Waiting on his bed for Aaron to finish up in the bathroom, Tom turns on the TV and channel hops. He comes to CNN, and there, on the ticker, are the fleeing words ". . . Billy Joel, 55 years old." Tom immediately thinks, Billy Joel, dead? Only a month or so before he'd seen photographs of Billy – a white blubbery fellow with a graying goatee – in the *Post*. Billy was on some Caribbean island with his new girlfriend, and she was rubbing sun cream onto his back. Where was it, Tobago? Tom can no longer recall. But he is not surprised by the news, because the singer evidently had drinking problems. He recalls some fiasco of a concert with Elton John not long ago, when Billy was too drunk to perform.

"Billy Joel died," he says when Aaron comes out of the shower.

"No way," Aaron says, rubbing a towel against his head.

"I just saw it on the ticker. Aged 55."

"Jesus," Aaron says mildly. "Billy Joel. We were just listening to him in the car. 'The Piano Man'."

In the shower, Tom takes an interest in his feelings about the dead Joel. He notes, first off, that there is suddenly something slightly victorious about the business of lathering shampoo into his scalp: he is here, applying the anti-flake lotion and submitting to this hot adjustable waterfall, and Billy is not. Second, he detects relief, the relief you feel when you reach the end of a roll of toilet tissue, or – he is unwrapping a square of complimentary soap – when you finally get to throw out a withered nugget of soap. Yes, Billy was like an old bar of soap. Now that he's gone, the world seems minutely renewed. By the time he steps out of the shower cubicle, Tom is practically whistling.

It's raining more heavily than ever as they drive off in search of Frenchy's. Clearwater, supposedly a civilized place, looms as a bunch of newly built, empty malls. Aaron and Tom agree with a proposition, muttered by Mick, that there's nothing to do here but shop in the same stores as everyone else and look like everyone else and behave like everybody else. Meanwhile, in spite of their map, they are having trouble finding Frenchy's, and they stop off at a Starbucks to consider their options. Mick and Tom have espressos, Aaron orders a venti® – i.e., gargantuan – decaf soy latte. Tom says, "Venti. They've registered it as a trademark, or whatever."

Aaron says, "So if we use it we'll get arrested?"

"Yeah," Mick says. "Use it and you'll get into venti shit."

They head back out again. At last, venturing down an alley that leads to a car park, they find Frenchy's. It's a brightly lit place and there are TVs blaring out high school basketball, and loud green plants, and pastels randomly smeared on tabletops and walls and light fixtures. The patrons seem content, however. Old people and young people mix happily and without aesthetic difficulty. The men are fat or red-faced or both, and the single women tend to dress in a style Mick calls hooker manquée. There are no black people. Aside from one guy with a terrible duck hook on the driving range at the golf club, they haven't seen a black person since they arrived in Florida, not one. A waitress hands them cheery laminated menus. The three men wince at what's on offer, then order beers and steaks and calamari and green salads. While the food is being prepared, they go out with their drinks to the porch, which overlooks a soundless black void they take to be the sea, or the gulf, or the bay. Mick tosses a glittering butt into the darkness. "Venti fucking night," he says.

A little further down the porch, a young kid and his girlfriend are kissing violently. The girl seems to Tom wasted on this boy, with his fuzzy little mustache; and Tom is embarrassed by the realization that this species of tenderness, which he fears might mark the onset of middle-aged emotions, has recently been his invariable reaction to the sight of a pretty young woman with a boyfriend – that she is wasted on him. As if he, Tom, could somehow rescue her from her fate, as if he inhabited a universe in which he might multiply himself in order to rescue all of the women of the world. As if being with Tom would be so terrific. He wonders, not for the first time, how Suzanne puts up with him. Her responsibilities, even more mechanical and overwhelming than his, cause her anxiety and tiredness but not, for some reason, crashing, numbing doubt. Perhaps it is different for women, Tom thinks. Perhaps they are programmed to function more efficiently, more certainly. But then what about Aaron and Annette? Infuriated by the banality and uselessness of this line of thought, Tom goes back inside without a word.

They finish their meal quickly and Aaron says, "Let's get the hell out of here." Once back at the hotel, they thank the concierge for putting them on to Frenchy's, and go to the bar and have a drink. They review their golf scores and contentedly wade around in the small financial morass into which their various activities have placed them: they set off the cab fare to La Guardia against the hotel costs against the airfares against the valet money against the cost of dinner against the golf bets.

A member of the hotel staff approaches. "Mr. Rourke? Telephone message."

The message is from David. He has been caught up in Chicago and will have to fly directly to Nashville. He sends his apologies.

"Well, that's a shame," Aaron says.

"The fewer the merrier," Mick says.

They go to their rooms. Aaron and Tom undress into T-shirts and boxer shorts and get into bed. Then the hotel phone rings. Aaron picks up. "It's Suzanne," he says. He raises his eyebrows and whispers, "Booty call."

Tom takes the phone. "Hey, darling."

"How's it going?"

"Great. Just great. Although it hasn't stopped raining."

"Good, good. Listen, did you post that Verizon bill yet?"

"Which one? The one for the phone line or the internet line?"

"I don't know. The phone line, I guess."

"I don't think so. Though I certainly put a stamp on it. Why?"

"I can't seem to find it anywhere."

"It was on the desk, wasn't it?"

"That's what I thought. But I don't see it anymore."

Tom glances at Aaron, who is leafing through a magazine. Tom says, "Well, I don't know what to say, honey."

"I just don't want to be late with it, that's all."

Tom takes a breath. Then he says, "OK sweetie, let's not worry about it. It'll turn up. And if it doesn't, big deal, right? What's the worst that could happen? We'll pay it next month."

Suzanne, anxious, is silent. Tom says, "Listen, just assume I mislaid it, OK? You're in the clear, and I've mislaid it, OK? How are the kids?"

"Asleep," Suzanne says. Then she says, "I think I'll call it a day, too."

"Good idea," Tom says. "Call it a day, darling."

He hangs up with a sigh. Aaron says politely, "Lights out?"

The two men lie in their beds in the dark, backs turned on one another. Then Aaron's voice sounds in the room. "You know, Tom, about this thing with Consuela."

Tom is listening.

"It may seem great, and it is great, of course it is," Aaron says. "But there's no escape, is there? You know what I'm talking about? Whether it's relationship A or relationship B. Whether, I don't know, you're on a beach in Thailand with a bunch of underage hookers or whether you're watching 'The Battle of Algiers' with a hot little law professor. Either way it's one damn thing after another. You know what I mean?"

Tom senses that Aaron is warning him about something – putting him on notice of something important. This could be it: one of those inklings he needs. Tom says cautiously, "I guess so."

The two men lie there in their beds. "Well, I'm bushed," Aaron finally says. "Goodnight."

"Goodnight," Tom says.

The next morning they drive off to another golf course with the intention of playing thirty-six holes, although Mick is nervous about whether he will have the stamina to do it. At the first tee, the course starter has a New York accent. He tells them, as they wait for the group ahead of them to reach the green, that he worked for many years in Manhattan as a homicide detective. The ex-cop says that he'd thought about retiring to the east coast of Florida but preferred it here on the west coast on account of there being much less "bustle".

"You know what he means by 'bustle,' " Aaron says once they are safely out on the first fairway.

Mick says, "Nothing worse than coming all the way down to Florida to find yourself surrounded by more bustle. Not after twenty years of busting uppity bustle."

"Hustling bustle," Aaron says.

"Muscling bustle," Mick says.

They complete thirty-six holes, finishing just as the gray sky empties of light and their putts are impossible to read and straying balls, which in daylight stand out in the woods, can no longer be found. They drive back to Clearwater. Every few minutes, it seems, they hit a toll, and so there is a pleasant squabble over toll money and who has or has not contributed his share. During the hour-long journey, they listen once again to seventies music; and once again Billy Joel sings for them. "Hey," Tom is pleased to announce to Mick, "he died yesterday." Billy is singing, *I don't care what you say any more, this is my life*, and Mick immediately says, "This *was* my life," and Tom tries to think of something funny to say about uptown girls and downtown boys, but can't. When the Bee Gees come on, Mick asks, "What's the name of the dead Bee Gee?" and by a process of elimination, and discounting the death of the youngest Gibb brother who wasn't a Bee Gee, they come up with the name Maurice. "I knew a guy called Maurice," Aaron says, "Maurice Morris," and Tom, eagerly leaning forward from the back seat, tells the story of his childhood friend John Elder, who along with his father was an elder in the church, with the result that the father was known as Elder Elder the elder, which Mick trumps by suggesting that if they moved to Mexico the father would be called Elder Elder el Elder. Meanwhile they are listening to "Band on the Run" by Paul McCartney and Wings, and Mick makes a joke about Linda McCartney hooking up in heaven with the Piano Man, and Aaron says, with a hurt seriousness, "Come on, she was a nice woman," and the travelers fall quiet. Tom thinks back to 1980, when he was sixteen. Two girls he knew went to see Billy Joel live and met the singer afterwards backstage. They reported that Billy – Jesus, he must have been about 32 at the time, though he seemed so ancient – had been very kind and very respectful. Tom thinks about mentioning this incident, about saying something good about Billy Joel.

They take dinner at the hotel. There is no talk of Frenchy's or Ybor City.

The next morning, Sunday, they play one last round on the hotel course, this time off the back tees, and afterwards go directly to Tampa airport. There, Tom is again confronted by the irksome unworldliness that for some reason seems to be overtaking him. He is at the curbside check-in counter when Aaron says to him, "Don't check in here, it costs extra."

"It does?" Tom was not aware of this. The check-in man – a black face, at last – already has his luggage labeled, and silently stands by. When Aaron goes off to join the long line inside, the man says, in a booming theatrical voice, "Sir, just so you know, there is no charge for this service. If you wish to pay a gratuity, that is up to you. But there is no charge."

"It's not an issue," Tom says with a smile. "Let's do this."

49

"I just want to be clear on that," the attendant continues. "You don't owe me a nickel. You don't have to do anything you don't want to do."

"No, I completely understand. But you'll have no objection to accepting this" – Tom hands him a $5 note – "as a token of my appreciation."

"Tokens of appreciation are always welcome," the attendant says. "But I don't expect or ask for anything. No sir."

"No, no, no," Tom says quickly.

The three friends eat chicken fajitas in an airport restaurant. A final reckoning of all monies is made, with paper and pencil. Aaron asks for a special dispensation regarding the double payment of the valet, and gets it. They fly to Miami, change planes, and fly up home to New York. On this final leg they are seated together for the first time. As happened on the outward flight, they are starved and dehydrated by American Airlines, which offers them no more than a tiny bag of pretzels and one soft drink for the three-hour journey. To relieve the hunger and boredom, they buy $5 mini-bottles of Chilean Cabernet Sauvignon, messily split the *New York Times*, and make anagrams of a hard-on product – Levitra – that's advertised in huge spreads in the newspaper. Mick, an ad copywriter, doesn't even have to scan the word in order immediately to come up with *evil rat* and *vile art* and *I travel*. "Fucking venti," Aaron says in admiration. A single cab zigzags through Brooklyn to their respective homes. Tom is back with his family by nine o'clock.

The next morning, a Monday morning, Tom is walking to work down Fifth Avenue when he hears, piping out of the loudspeakers of a department store, none other than Billy Joel – which, given his death, makes perfect sense. He extracts his phone from his breast pocket and calls Suzanne.

"I forgot to tell you," he says. "Did you hear about Billy Joel dying?"

"No. He died?"

"Yeah. On Friday."

"Well, I haven't seen anything about it. Wait a minute." Suzanne, who works in a bank, consults people in the office. "No," she says, "nobody's heard anything about it. Are you sure?"

"I saw something on the CNN ticker about Billy Joel, aged 55. I'm assuming there's no other reason for him to be on the news."

Suzanne passes on what Tom has said. He hears indistinct talk followed by his wife's clear peal of laughter. "He didn't die, honey," she says. "He got engaged. To a twenty-two-year-old or a twenty-six-year-old, we're not sure which."

"Oh, right," Tom says. "Jesus, I went through the whole weekend thinking he was dead."

"Well, he isn't," Suzanne says. "Quite the contrary."

Tom continues walking down Fifth Avenue. It's cold. Ice is piled up everywhere. He has twelve more days left before he's forty. Tom perceives – as, suddenly apprehending the anniversary as a deadline, he quickens his steps – that he must in the meantime understand, somehow or other, to soap himself with the shriveling world.

# The Lover
Dublin, 1965

## DERMOT BOLGER

I met him first over fifty years ago, not long after he returned from the Amazon jungle. The mark of that humid swamp was indelibly upon him, in his eyes, in his stride, in his slightly haunted aura. What he had borne witness to in the Amazon changed him. Not just the tortures and exploitation, the casual flogging of natives to death – more as a warning to others than for any minor misdeed – and the indifference of other Europeans who rarely raised their heads from the profit columns of company ledgers on rubber plantations to take in what was occurring in their fiefdom of evil. He recognised and knew the depths of such evil because he was already haunted by similar images from his days in the Belgian Congo. For him no living creature was more vile than the cursed King of the Belgians who would force mothers to watch their children's hands being amputated if families on his plantations did not reach their weekly rubber quota.

His detailed Foreign Office report that revealed the atrocities of Leopold the Second was his first act of class betrayal, the day he cut himself adrift from the other white men who had gone to work for rubber companies in Africa. Such men trained themselves to see nothing or were gradually corrupted by the intoxication of absolute power, the insidious addiction of the opened box of cruelty on plantations in such remote locations that even God had ceased to watch over them. I don't know how I would have coped with the lure of such power because I have known little of that commodity in a life in which I have tried to go unnoticed. Once or twice in a dark bed when a kneeling man has cried out beneath me I have run my fingers along his naked back to circle his unprotected neck damp with sweat. Sometimes I have sensed their unspoken desire for my hands to choke the life from them during that moment when they are truly themselves, when they can feel my cock but not see my face. I have recognised their wish to die during the moment of climax and never again have to face the deceptions and evasions awaiting them once they put their clothes back on and retreated to the cold arctic wastes of their married lives.

But I am not a rough man. Occasionally I might tighten my grip on their necks slightly, just to heighten their passion and my own. Yet I never surrendered to the romance of the death wish. Unlike the zealots Casement hung around with at the end, my wish has been to survive. If they gave my kind medals then my chest could hardly hold the decorations from all the wars I have endured. I would be even more adorned than some of the other old men here in this crowd waiting for his body to pass outside Glasnevin cemetery. My primary wish was always to live and this is a wish that I shared with Roger Casement. Never once in the darkness did I feel a sense that he could not go on. On the contrary, his life force was always like a glow, the memory of which sustained me for days after I fucked him. I could feel his strength even as he yielded, I could close my eyes and still decipher the code of his body long after we hurriedly parted.

His strength came from the fact that he never lost his innocence, despite having forced himself to watch every act of cruelty and genocide in the Congo and then the Amazon. He had not flinched from keeping meticulous records, even when other white men realised that he was their enemy who had come to expose and shame them to the world. He had a royal commission to be there or otherwise they would have killed him as surely as they killed natives – quickly through flogging or slowly with impossibly hard work. They shunned Casement instead and sat on their verandas to drink whiskey and dream of white women before slaking their lust with compliant or non-compliant black girls. The rubber traders did not have him followed. That was their first mistake. They were too stupid to recognise the signs that I immediately noticed when I first saw him prowl along a country lane on the edge of Belfast. I say prowl because everything about him that evening reeked of desire and sex. Here was a man who wished to be fucked to the hilt. I had known rich toffs before, but generally they were primed to run away before I was barely finished tossing them off. Casement was a man who held your eye with his slightly fanatical stare. I knew within seconds of seeing him that he was bent and he knew the same was true of me and that the only reason we were both walking along that godforsaken country lane was because we knew how men who sometimes took the air there disappeared together into the ditches at dusk.

Other men from other secret societies were also meeting in remote country lanes that night in 1913, drilling and plotting and taking oaths. The Unionist tribe he hailed from were marching to prevent home rule from Dublin and the tribe he had joined who demanded nothing short of full Irish independence. Like my tribe in the ditches they were fired by passion, but it was not one I could ever share because their version of freedom would never include the likes of me. Still by then Casement had embraced yet another cause with a true convert's zeal. The Republicans were his other secret life. None of them knew – or perhaps they simply never wished to know – about his other life where he came quickly in my hands. Even today outside Glasnevin I see from the eyes of the crowds gathered here that they still don't want to know. From the moment the British authorities hung him for treason – subjecting his corpse to an anal examination so a doctor could confirm what they had gleefully leaked to the press – his Irish comrades have wished to claim only the man they knew. Now they have their wish at last. Last night the British exhumed whatever remained of him under cover of darkness in Pentonville Prison: a few ribs, several vertebrae, his lower jaw and the skull almost preserved whole. Quicklime had eroded the rest. Today a coffin containing those few bones is slowly making its way across the city, past vast silent crowds in a state funeral.

I don't know Dublin. I have never liked this city nor wished to live here. Still I had to come and be part of today, like I have discreetly attended the funerals of so many other men like him. The Irish newspapers have been remembering the courage that made him highlight the plight of Peruvian Indians, the bravery that saw him resign from the British Foreign Office to renounce his class and join the Irish rebels, the schoolboy zeal that saw him land in Ireland with his futile dream of bringing German guns to aid the short-lived Easter Rising. But I saw a more commonplace courage within him on that night we met. Gangs of youths often appeared for Belfast, eager to have sport by hunting us down. One evening I had to hide among briers that cut my skin to shreds as I watched rival gangs of Taigs and Prods unite to kick a couple of queers whom they unearthed. Both gangs were so consumed with hatred for our sort that they had momentarily put aside their religious differences. Whenever Casement began obsessing about how to unite Catholics and Protestants, I always said, 'Just give them queers like us to hunt down and hate, it could be their national unifying sport.'

Poor Casement didn't understand hatred. After the English hung him, he became a traitor and deviant to his former tribe and a martyr and icon to his new one. But for me he still remains the man I first fucked in an Antrim field with sheep unperturbed by our silent exertions. In that twilight the white candles of chestnuts were still visible in the dark mass of leaves above us. Nobody passed along the nearby lane during our passion and neither of us spoke as I ran my hands underneath his jacket and shirt so that my nails gripped his bare shoulders as I timed it so that we came together. On that first coupling I sensed that he had been touched by some foreign place, though it was much later before he talked about the Amazon. But I knew that he had always been a hunter for love and love had brought him to the strangest places. If those plantation owners had only followed him along the jungle paths at dusk they would have found enough ammunition to destroy him before he destroyed them. They would have seen him come in his extraordinary fashion as though you were his first love. They could have blackmailed him and possibly buried his report. But despite all their jibes and mock indignation, they would have laid awake long into the night, haunted not by the act that they had witnessed but by his sheer capacity for pleasure. Because, for all their whores on all fours and missionary wives, they would have known how to achieve such naked bliss as they would have witnessed in the eyes of Roger Casement when he finally came.

The crowd is twenty deep now as a man with a radio beside me reports that the state funeral is approaching Cross Guns Bridge. An old IRA veteran stands proud in the crowd, explaining to people why he received each of his medals. He is my age, in his youth he must have been handsome like I was handsome once. I want to say, 'You gave him a sense of fellowship but I gave him a sense of pleasure. For long minutes he was mine in a way that he could never be yours. I was his nation because we were equals and he was free to be himself in my arms.' If he had lived I wondered what he might have become. If the English government had not hung him probably in time the Irish would have, because he could never have settled for what they settled for. He had no wife or children to take the edge off his zeal. The comforts of office would never have soothed him because he had given such trappings away. Casement desired freedom, yet how can any man be free who fears a knock on his door or a mob in a country lane, who fears exposure and ruin. For long moments I gave him freedom and I was not alone in this. In the Amazon he was free to kneel in clearings for young men with the marks of whips still on their backs to fuck him tenderly or savagely, relieving one white man of his burden. I remember lying with him on those few occasions when we risked a Belfast hotel. I remember how when we first met I had to pretend not to recognise him and played along with the identity he invented. But slowly I gained his trust when he realised that the only two things I didn't do were tonguing and blackmail. Occasionally he made half-hearted attempts to convert me to his mania for nationalism, but generally he was happy to keep his two worlds separate. Now the older I get the more I remember the feel of his hands and tongue. And sometimes I curse him because I know how I shall never be remembered like he is being remembered now; no comrades will ever stand by my grave. I have enough money put aside for a headstone but no one will seek it out. My bones will lie undisturbed in Belfast soil. No pathologist will examine the ribs cracked when I was beaten up in a public toilet in 1936 or the fingers broken by a young man who came back to my flat in 1957 and demanded more money than I had. I gave the boy everything, yet he ransacked for more. But he never found the hidden ten shilling note that Casement gave me after our first encounter in that field. I accepted it because I was no fool but I never spent it and I never gave it back.

A young Irish soldier has just fainted in the colour party on the road in front of me, having stood to attention for two hours waiting for the hearse to pass. He lies exposed, with his colleagues unable to break from their rigid posses and assist him. Officers finally remove him from sight and order the soldiers to close ranks like he had never been there. I look around at other pensioners in the crowd and suddenly wonder how many others like me might also be here, unable to step forward and proclaim, 'I knew him, we shared love together.' I hear the sound of the cortège now, with the tricolour-draped coffin displayed on a gun carriage. This is the first coffin Roger has ever known, containing so much space and so few bones. I don't notice that I am crying as the gun carriage passes until a woman touches my arm.

'You knew him?' she asks.

'Yes.'

'You look like a veteran. Did you fight side by side?'

I don't reply. Side by side was not our style. She takes in the absence of medals on my dark suit. Maybe she is going to ask me something else, but I push past, joining the throng who had lined the road and are now trying to squeeze in through the cemetery gate. The open grave has pride of place in front of the O'Connell monument. Their nation's shaman, de Valera, is there, half blind, peering at his speech, but I have no interest in what he has to say. Finally the tricolour is removed from the coffin. Men kneel bareheaded while women cover their hair. One of their priests speaks nonsense in Latin. These words that I cannot understand move me strangely because I can concoct my own meaning for them. I can pretend that this burial is in honour of all the boys he once lay with, those with names he knew and those who were unknown. I can pretend that this empty coffin is meant for us all, that Casement has left space in the bed amid his few bones and the gathered fragments of shroud. All of us who must remain unknown and unremembered are represented in the box with him. Soldiers lift the ropes and the casket is lowered. Shots ring out and I stand up among the kneeling throng and lift my face to the sky. I can see white clouds over chestnut trees beside the Antrim field where I first waited for him. If only the comfort of a God actually existed, or there was a land where our queer nation could be free, then Roger Casement would be there now with his piercing gaze, waiting to welcome me.

# Snowblind

## Emma Donoghue

They were both heading for the Yukon goldfields when they ran into each other in St Michael, the old Russian port on the Alaskan coast. Goat (named for his yellow goatee) was a Swede and Injun Joe was from Iowa; folk said Injun looked more than half Indian but he didn't know. They'd both turned twenty-two that July and it was this coincidence that convinced them to hitch up. It has to mean luck, said Goat, doesn't it? It had to mean something.

Both of them had turned their hands to just about anything since hard times got harder round '93. Injun had been an apple picker, a ranch hand, a slaughterman; he'd even done a few prize fights till an Irish boy blinded his left eye. Goat had played three-card monte and thrown drunks out of a whorehouse. They were both as tough as hardtack, could tote seventy pounds, and scorned a quitter. Neither knew much about prospecting except that it was all they wanted to do. Goat said he was gold crazy, was that the word? It'd only been a few years since he'd come from Sweden with eighty-five cents in his pocket, his English was good but he didn't trust it. He claimed he'd take a fifteen-dollar poke of gold dust over a twenty-dollar banknote, he was sentimental that way, he just loved the sparkle of it.

After paying for the boat ride up the Yukon, the two fellows were down to their sleeping bags, tent and seven odd dollars between them. But at least they'd found each other. You'd got to have a partner or you wouldn't make it, that's what the old-timers said. It wasn't just that so much of gold-mining took four hands, it was the risk of going off your head in the dark of winter. In Fortymile – the shack-town just over the border into Canadian territory, where the two got off because Goat was sick of the tug of the boat against the current – they met a grizzled sourdough with six missing toes. He'd had a split-up back in '86, the two had divided their outfit fair and square and the toeless man had left his former mate to work the claim. It was a whipsaw that did it, he said. Whipsawing green logs put paid to many a friendship, because you got in a rage and couldn't trust the other fellow was pulling his weight.

The old sourdough asked Injun Joe if he was one of those lazy Stick Indians from the interior. Injun shook his head and said I'm from Iowa. Truth was he would have liked knowing what he was or where he was from on his father's side; his mother was pure Pole, she'd never said and he'd stopped asking long ago.

Fortymile was more of a camp than any kind of town – it looked like a heap of garbage washed up on the riverbank – but Injun reckoned it had all they needed, for now. Since every man in sight was a prospector, whether a veteran of Dakota, Idaho or Colorado or a tenderfoot like Goat and Injun, it was like being in a gang. A gang of loners, if such a thing could be. *Outside*, that was what they called everything outside Fortymile. McQuesten the storeowner boasted that no one ever starved to death, or not unless he was too stupid to roll out of his bunk and crawl into town.

McQuesten never refused credit, so Injun and Goat were able to outfit themselves on a promise of payback come spring. They kitted themselves out in gumboots, mackinaws, mukluks and the broadbrimmed hats that kept off rock splinters. (After all, Injun had to take care, he was down to one useful eye already.) They filled a wheelbarrow with kerosene lamps, a panning tank, a stew kettle, a saw and a couple of short-stemmed shovels, tin plates and forks, rope and coal oil, beans, cornmeal, baking powder, lard, salt, chocolate and tea, and on top, a fragile-looking copper scales and a phial of mercury wrapped in a handkerchief. This mountain of gear was too precarious to wheel around the wilderness, so they left most of it in the back of the store while they went off prospecting along the creeks of the Fortymile.

They'd pick a likely spot, spit in the can for luck, let the water wash away the mud, and peer into the bottom for the glitter. The first time they found some, it had a startling greenish tinge to it. Injun let out a yelp like an injured dog, and Goat got him in a half nelson and kissed his ear.

This was why the Yukon was the place to be, even if there hadn't been any real big strikes yet. In some goldfields, the stuff was veined into the hardrock, and only expensive machinery could blast it out, but the

Yukon gave up her treasure casually to any man who took the trouble to look for it. Placer gold – free gold, some called it – lying around in the white gravel in the form of good coarse dust or nuggets even. This first spot gave five cents worth of gold dust from the pan, when Injun weighed it with slightly shaking hands. The toeless fellow reckoned eight cents a pan's a pretty good prospect, he said, but Goat laughed and said this here looked pretty good to him. He wanted to stake their claim right away; Injun had to talk him into waiting to see if they could find a richer spot. (In Fortymile, Injun had got the impression Swedes were pitied for their willingness to stake a prospect other men would dig a shitpit on.)

At night the two fellows lay back to back in their sailcloth tent, and in the mornings they counted their bruises; the man with the fewest had to boil the coffee. That was their first game but soon they had plenty. After another week they found a bend in a muddy creek that gave ten cents a pan, and Injun felt the glow of being right, as well as the giddy anticipation of riches. Goat marked out the five hundred feet he liked best; Injun blazed a small spruce tree and pencilled on the upstream side, *One*, and their names.

That night they lay awake so long laughing and planning how to spend their fortune, they were baggy-eyed when they hiked into Fortymile to the Recorder's Office. The two of them were so ignorant, they hadn't realised that they were allowed a claim each, and that the discoverer of the strike was granted double, which meant three between them. They rushed back to their muddy creek the next morning and staked out another thousand feet, marking it *One Below* and *Two Below*. Injun put Goat down as the discoverer and himself as the second man, but that was just a formality.

In Fortymile they borrowed a mule to haul their outfit and a stack of raw lumber to their claim for building a tiny cabin. They left two stumps in the middle of the floor to sit on, and built bunks against the walls. The windows were deerhide (that was a tip another old-timer had given them); Injun was surprised how well they let in the autumn light. With a sheet-iron stove they were all set, and Injun soon had some flapjacks on.

At first he couldn't get the knack of sleeping on his skinny bunk instead of back-to-back in the tent, but at least it was warmer. The walls smelled of sawdust and pressed close, it was like living in a two-man coffin. Lucky we've got no third mate, he said in the dark.

Reckon so, Goat replied.

After a couple of days the cabin was fetid with smoke and feet. Injun pasted woodcuts from yellowed newspapers over the cracks: *Jumbo the Elephant*, and *A Lady Going Over Niagara Falls in a Barrel*, and *A View of Kew*. He found one called *The Forests of Scandinavia* to make his partner feel at home, not that Goat gave any sign of noticing.

In September, the leaves burnt red and fell, and all the Yukon's little veins froze up. Goat and Injun were so green, they'd never thought to wonder how to mine in the sub-Arctic winter. Sure you have to burn your way down, said the Irish fellows on the next creek over. So every night the two partners lit a wood fire in their dig, and every morning they scraped past the ashes into the hot thawed earth. The greasy black shaft they hollowed out this way was barely wide enough to let one man crouch. The other would winch the bucket of muck up with a windlass, and pile it in a dump. It was a fortnight before they hit the pay-streak – a dried-up creek channel – and started tunnelling sideways along it. Already their pay-dirt dump was as high as Injun's head. But the killing thing about northern mining, of course, was you never knew what you'd got till the spring melt.

Sometimes they got so tired of the crawling and scrabbling in the smoky dark, they splashed their faces with water and trudged into Fortymile. There was a snowed-in vaudeville troupe that gave the same turns every night till the crowd howled like malemutes. There were ten saloons, and the code was that any man who came in with a poke of gold dust to throw down on the bar bought hot hootchinoo for every-one in hearing, or real whiskey if a boat had come in. Fortymile men all seemed to have got strange nicknames like Squaw Cameron or Cannibal Ike. (Goat and Injun were too used to their own monikers to remember they'd ever been called anything else.) The stories told in the saloons were of goldmen; lucky ones, unlucky ones. A drunken sucker who got tricked into buying what seemed like a worthless stake, but it turned out a bonanza in the end. A Forty-Niner who washed out thirty thousand dollars but got so fixed on the prospect of being robbed that he slit his own throat before anyone else could.

The weather tightened like a fist. By October the mates had stopped shaving, since a beard was some protection even if it did form icicles around the mouth. Injun's droopy Indian-style moustache flowed right into his side-whiskers, he was like some old walrus, and Goat's goatee had spread into a yellow thornbush. When it got to fifty below, the mates gave up digging, lay in their bunks half the day in the smoky cabin. One of them might lurch out with scarves wrapped round his face to hack a deep hole in the river for water, or hobble into Fortymile – they were both plagued with blisters and boils on their feet – to get another handful of beans on credit. Long nights they curled like grubs in their foul sleeping bags, listing fresh things they'd a fancy for: apricots, cherries, tomatoes. They sang 'My Darling Clementine' and 'Break the News to Mother' and other old tunes they could only half remember. Injun hummed hymns from his childhood and Goat dredged up some sad Swedish songs. What's sad about them? Injun wanted to know, but Goat couldn't translate the words, he said they're just sad.

The code was, you helped other goldmen out, because otherwise who'd last a winter? A fellow was entitled to walk into your cabin while you were out, eat his fill, have a kip and go on his way, as long as he left a supply of fresh kindling in case you came in frozen. Once Injun arrived home to find Goat talking Swedish with some block-faced stranger over the last of yesterday's bread. He didn't like the fellow's manner and was glad he was gone in the morning.

That winter they made all the mistakes young men make from being in too much of a hurry to ask. They got stomach-ache when they didn't bother cooking their beans long enough, and toe-rot from sleeping in wet boots. The one thing they knew never to do was let the fire die out, because of that popular story about the two mates discovered in an isolated cabin, stiff as rocks beside an icy stew kettle with nothing but a pair of partly cooked moccasins in it.

In the night Goat and Injun kept talking, speech slurred from numb lips, just so they'd know they hadn't died. Your Yukon is a perverse kind of river, remarked Injun, did you know it rises fifteen miles from the Pacific and then meanders around for two thousand more before it falls back down into the Pacific?

Goat grunted as if to say he neither knew nor cared. After a minute he said this cussed place, why did Uncle Sam ever buy it off the Ruskies?

He didn't, Injun corrected him, that's Alaska, we're in the Queen's territory now.

Goat muttered something about what he'd like to do to the Queen.

Soap out that filthy mouth, said Injun, coughing with laughter, don't you know she's about a hundred years old?

Came a long blizzard when water froze on the walls two feet from the fire. Let me in, said Goat, stumbling two steps from his bunk to Injun's.

Lying like spoons they shuddered up some warmth. Injun woke from a doze to find his hand on Goat's britches and he couldn't rightly have said whether it was him who'd put it there. His left hand was so numb it hardly knew what his right was doing and he kept on doing. Then Goat thrashed round to face him and their breath was a hot Chinook wind.

What time is it? Injun wondered, what seemed like days later, and Goat said what does it matter? They stirred and slept, touched and rolled and slept, couldn't get out of the bunk except once in a while to throw a log on the fire. You do it. No, you! Numbskull Swede, lazy half-breed, they cursed each other with a curious fondness, tried to shove each other onto the floor, grabbed each other again. The wind made a fearful whining.

There was something wrong with their legs, they were bruised blue and red. Injun's joints ached and his mouth tasted metallic, like blood. Is my breath bad? he asked Goat, and his mate said sure, but I don't care. Goat's face was strangely puffy. We're a couple of beauties, he wheezed, laying his yellow beard against Injun's bared chest.

Injun woke up later, unnerved by the silence. The blizzard had to be over. He was starving and sore. Slowly he heaved Goat against the wall, tucking the sleeping bag round him, and got to his feet. He took a sip of water from the cup on the stove. His face in the tin plate was weirdly mottled. What had they done to themselves? It occurred to him that they were dying and his heart lifted oddly.

It took Injun the best part of the day to get to Fortymile. My partner and I, I reckon we're dying of gangrene, he told McQuesten, taking down his trousers in the back of the store. The owner snorted and said don't you fool boys know about scurvy? He sent Injun off with a bottle of lime juice, so sour it made him retch.

On the journey back the sun came up over the ice, and Injun had forgotten his wooden mask with the slit in it. By the time he made it home he was so snowblind he was surprised he hadn't stumbled into some abandoned shaft and snapped his legs. His eyes were full of scalding sand, the good one as bad as the bad; the whole world was scarlet with fire, and the more he rubbed the worse it hurt. Goat laughed but spooned stew into Injun's mouth like a mother.

Any way you looked at it these were awful days. They'd come all this way to work like half-starved galley slaves. Even after the lime juice fixed their scurvy, they had a damaged look about them. Some mornings Injun stumbled through the dusk, past the smog rising from their shaft, to peer at the brooding outline of their dump. How much was black dirt, how much gold? A tree made a sound like a pistol shot and Injun jumped, before remembering it was only the sap freezing. He could make out the purgatorial glow of other shafts on the next creek over, but the snow muffled all sounds. The world was empty but for small creeping things in their holes. He felt entirely temporary, and it occurred to him that the mine he and Goat were so painstakingly thawing and grubbing out this winter would, in years to come, close over again like a scar. Fortymile would fall to dust and wolves bed down in these shacks, the ice would seal over the trail.

But Injun always finished what he set his hand to and Goat was the same way. Also there was no way to Outside till spring unless they were insane enough to trek a thousand miles over the mountains. Also things had been different between them since the blizzard, they kept their kit on one bunk and slept on the other, or lay shoving and laughing and groaning in the dark. It was like a pact they didn't need to discuss.

Come May, at last, the cabin was green with mildew and the two partners coughed so wetly in the mornings it sounded like branches ripping off a tree. The creeks began to shrug off their ice; Injun and Goat's shaft seeped up to head-height and they had to abandon it. It was time to build a long sluice-box and divert some of the creek through it; time to see what they'd earned for their winter's punishment. They soon got a rhythm going: dump in a shovel of pay-dirt, let the water sweep the dross away, leaving the gold caught in the cross-riffles and matting at the bottom. Every three days they did a clean-up, lifting out the sluice-box and panning the residue.

After the first week it was becoming clear to Injun that they were losers.

Goat would hear nothing of it. The good stuff's lower down the heap, he insisted.

Injun rolled his eyes. The black dirt was speckled with gold, all right, but so was every sandbank in this part of the world. Their poke was mounting up slowly, miserably, but other men burst into Fortymile screaming like ravens, their pockets bursting with Midas dust. Goldmen went on sprees from saloon to saloon, the crowd bearing them along like champions, smashing furniture. The Irishmen on the next creek over boasted of washing out twenty, twenty-five cents a pan. Fortunes were made and drunk all that summer, while Goat and Injun bent and sweated their strength away.

One day Goat said he'd had it.

What do you mean, you've had it?

I've had it up to here with gold-mining.

Injun told him he just needed a whiskey. They walked into Fortymile, barely exchanging ten words along the way. Frost was tinting the mountains yellow already, the summer was on the turn. Injun picked up a page of newspaper in the street, it said the tenth of August. He blinked at it. Lookit, Goat, he said, I forgot my birthday. Yours too. Reckon we're twenty-three now.

Goat cleared his throat and spat, before turning into the nearest saloon.

Injun went on to the store, and handed over his meagre poke, but McQuesten snorted as he weighed it in his hand, and tossed it back to him. He agreed to extend their credit a month or two longer, in case the boys' luck was around the corner. Injun's mouth felt gummed up with shame. If you fancy a change, McQuesten remarked, I could use someone in the back of the store.

Injun stared at him.

I had a boy, but he's gone rushing off down-river at the first word of some discovery.

Thank you, said Injun, remembering his manners like some old relic of life before the Yukon. Thank you kindly, but my partner –

McQuesten nodded like he understood.

On the way back down the street, Injun thought of how it might be. If Goat had had enough of mining, if Injun took a job in town – then they wouldn't be mates like they'd been. There'd be no reason for their cabin, their games, their joint life. He made up his mind: he'd talk Goat into heading back out to their claim and laying into that dirt-heap again. Maybe there really was more gold at the bottom. Maybe they should give it another year.

The saloon was buzzing. Goat shoved a glass of whiskey to his mate's lips. There's been a prime strike on Rabbit Creek!

Where's Rabbit Creek? Asked Injun.

Off the Klondike.

The Klondike was the next big tributary of the Yukon east of Fortymile. That must be where McQuesten's last boy had gone. Injun felt oddly tired.

A fellow came in here with a shotgun cartridge full, Goat gabbled, poured it on the scale, old-timers never seen anything like it for colour and grain. I tell you, boy, it's going to be a stampede! Let's go before every inch is staked. Half this crowd's slipped away already, he said, draining his glass.

Injun snorted, but already he was imagining their hands yellow-green with gold dust, their raw new shack on the bank of the Klondike.

Goat was looking past him, waving at someone in the crowd. Oh, hey, I met up with Gundsson again, he's on for going thirds.

Injun turned, narrowed his eyes at the big-jawed man walking over. He recognised the Swede who'd turned up at the cabin that time. His throat tightened up. What do we need another mate for?

Goat laughed. Split the work and help tote the treasure-sacks, that's what.

Could Goat really be that dumb and blind? Had he no notion of what they'd be losing? I don't like him, said Injun.

You ain't even talked to him yet. Come on, don't frown, sounds like there's gold enough for everyone up on the Klondike!

The Swede was beside them, grinning with yellow teeth. Injun thought of him sleeping in their cabin, like some huge stinking bear, and wanted to punch him. Instead he folded his arms. Goldmen are so fickle, he remarked, soon as they hear of any half-discovery they'll desert their old dig.

Goat tugged his mate's shoulder hard enough to pop it out. Look, you cussed halfbreed, he said, can't your one eye spot the chance of your life?

Injun shrugged.

I tell you I've talked to a man who saw the nuggets on the scale. He says he heard the first shovelful from Rabbit Creek yielded eight hundred dollars!

This place has more liars than hell, said Injun.

What's the matter with you? Goat was red in the face. The river's choked already. Fortymile will be a dead camp by the morning. Come on, Gundsson can get us on a boat poling upstream tonight.

Injun refused to look at the Swede. I'm taking a job, he said, his voice thick with gravel. In McQuesten's store.

Goat's eyes were huge and pale.

Folk'll always need supplies, he added. Even if some of these fools find a few ounces on the Klondike, they'll be back here to record their stakes, won't they?

Mate, said Goat – putting his face close enough to Injun's to heat him with his spiritous breath, close enough to kiss him – our fortune's up there. He was pointing west.

I doubt that, said Injun, hoarse.

But I'm telling you –

Finders ain't keepers anyhow. Men who strike lucky, they never manage to keep it, do they? Just drink or gamble or lose it all one way or another.

Goat straightened up, still half-smiling. Well, damn your lily liver.

Best of luck to you and your countryman, said Injun, going to drain his glass, but it was dry already. He told Goat to take what he liked from the cabin before he went. He nodded to both Swedes and managed to get outside in the warm street before his face fell in on itself.

And with the certainty of a man who was still young, Injun said never, he said never, never again.

# Close

## Philip MacCann

He's just sneaked a woman into this house.

I'm trembling all over.

How absolutely dare he, what!

What would Mama have made of this?

Best not move from the old flowery sofa. Peer up at his window in the east wing.

Who? Did he? Aren't they?

Steady.

Top-up of vodka.

This drawing room is my austere little world. Winter sun through the slats striking the floorboards with an effect like bars. Gives on to generous, elm-lined De Crespigny Close, which has character. The rough charm of the past in decline. Above, so many twigs lacerate the heavens and virtually obscure them.

But what was that flicker!

I snatch my plastic leg from across the sofa. Slot it quickly into the old stump. Get the straps fastened round my waist.

I have enjoyed more dances than that young brother could ever know. Is that what they're up to? Is that what he's insinuating?

Reach for the check trousers, fling them on, I'm in business. Up on the legs. Make it across the bay of the window, swing the limb forward at the hip. Crane the head round the Sellotaped crack, peek up through the slats. The closest I can manage. Breathe in. Breathe out. Wipe the window. Strain the old eyes. Is that some kind of sweeping or swooping? So they want to rip my heart to pieces. Good views not on the agenda. I rest my fingertips on the glass.

Sundays are always a vexation to the spirit. Especially when God is
one's neighbour. I refer to the Church of St Gregory Thaumaturgus for
the deaf on 66 De Crespigny Close. The pavement positively blackens
with tortured flesh, unwilling to awaken from some dream or other of
light. (I will have none of this weak-willed apostasy.) Around one-forty
the righteous will emerge to a whole holy show up in our east wing,
dancing, flickering. There are none more nosy than the deaf. And the
way this neighbourhood has gone who can afford to attract attention?
Keep to oneself rather, reserve and tight lips. Rather than rake up the
past and what-not, trawling over ancient history. That young brother is
another Monsieur Eddy Grey. He knows no fear. Will not keep the lid
on. Well I prophesy this very day he shall be no more to me – nor I to
him – than a boarder in a first-landing room. If that.

Still can't see a bloody thing. Only my reflection close to me in the
glass. White, straggly hair on the old head, what.

Would be curious to forecast if the rain intends to spend its desire, by
the look of that sky. Look, a bag lady hobbling to the Minimart in the
spare ground across the Close. Scallywags made off with its security
camera and this a Neighbourhood Watch Area of twenty years standing. It's my duty to keep a close eye on Lawrence. Not that I myself
would have missed out on any fling when I was his age, but does one
need to fine-comb the past? Had hoped for no more than to pass the day
in peaceful repose on that big baggy sofa, re-reading *The True Bill Haley*
and smoking some more of the day's cigar. I shall resist delving into
Mama's old Tarot cards to help me guess who is up there with
Lawrence. One more top-up of vodka and I start on my short voyage
back to the sofa.

Yes I too got a lady up to my bedroom when Mama was alive. How
Mama went berserk, the bastard. But she was just right too, when
I think of it in retrospect. She had no wish to have kissing and laughter
up in the east wing in front of all and sundry. What else could she do if
I would not play the game? Didn't always see it her way though.
Velvetina a lovely girl. Mama was known to be a trifle hysterical. That
is to say, a cut above. Highly strung, voluptuous lady, given to psychic
attacks and pressing glasses of sherry on local schoolboys. Bloody
awful cook but she played the violin. Her own mother taught her
Marxism–Leninism at the university. Her father was an invalid of the
second category. Before the war they knew people in the Wielkopolskie

Orchestra. But in this country? One's pedigree was over the heads of the masses. Mama forever reminding us that others may be cotton, but we were silk. Told me she would just have to close the window up if I persisted. Led me into the kitchen to view a packet of six-inch nails. Pledged she would find the necessary boards. Was this what I wanted? People to start whispering? Next time I sneaked Velvetina in she dragged a board from the garden shed, right up the hall, tore the hall carpet, chipped the wood on the drawing-room door. I was rooted to the spot in terror. After that I called Mama 'Bastard' – though I won't dispute now she knew better in the long run, but why slam the board right down on one's toe?

A certain discomfort, that.

Toe turned purple.

Inconvenient the way gangrene crept up the old foot. Had it off one afternoon at the ankle. Was furnished with a metal one. Looked forward to being able to fit my own shoe. Gave up on Velvetina then. Took to painting model soldiers.

Became rather adept if I say so myself.

Could it be the plan of that young buck to get one into a whole condition?

Good views are bad news. No two ways.

Absolutely bloody.

Cheers.

An hour flies by as one weeps alone. One's moist eyes roam over the faded wallpaper. Withered sunflowers in the cracked vase. Mama's Tarot cards all this while untouched. The drawing-room door lies ajar and I can see ahead into the dark hall. Have been thinking a little about clairvoyance, a kind of . . . madness, which I find fascinating. Israel Regardie is brilliantly scathing of the practice, relating it, controversially, to the reversed Hierophant, and to idolatry. Waite called divination *the history of a prolonged impertinence*. Wonderful. The minister of the little church next door is a strange one and something of a specialist in metaphysics. Privately he recommends something called alt.tarot for the most pungent epigrams about Waite, the man, and his . . .

What was his phrasing in our recent genial altercation?

Epigrams about Waite's 'mischievous compounding of lies with truths, not all of which bear my Internet pseudonyms,' he said, whatever all that should mean.

Was that a creak from the ceiling?

I quickly get up. Make it over to the base of the first staircase, both my footsounds equally resonant.

Listen.

Can definitely make out . . . reverberated murmurs.

And no doubt whatsoever about creaks and cracks.

I ought to show that brother I'm serious. I should close him out for ever. I don't wish to hear noises of that ilk drifting downstairs into my life. He 'invades my space' (his youthful terminology). I daren't contemplate what's actually going on. Could he already have made a move? No. He'll be slower than I was when I was his age. When I had my own fling and make no mistake about it. And what of it? Flesh, mere flesh.

Clock chimes half-past ten. Time to turn in half an hour ago and more. Time for me to rap on the boards. So he must know I'm at my position. He must know I know too, but I oughtn't to let on and give him that pleasure. I can wait. Why should I rap when he ought to be down by now? Haven't to be careful where my stick lands. One should always be mindful of diabetics' toes. The metal foot proved too optimistic when amputation had to go to knee stage. Was disappointed to get a rod with an ugly large black boot attached. Managed it well though. Was complimented on my walk. Still . . . gangrene flourished up the thigh, you know . . .

I wallop that bloody stick on the boards because that intruding woman is raking it all up!

What sounds like 'Sh.' And silence now.

Another minute later and Lawrence descends the staircase buttoning his shirt. I grit my teeth. He comes up close. Through the gaps in my teeth I hiss, 'I wouldn't want to drag you away from any *pleasure.*'

He sighs long and noisily. Then: 'Eh yeah,' he mutters.

I lay my stick across my forearms. It's a bit of an old strain but he fetches me up. Jiggles me up the staircase in his arms. On the first landing we swing round towards my room. And in there he plonks me down on the legs. At this point I can pull the little string at my knee, so I can bend the leg. So I can drop down on the edge of my bed by the window and recover. In some sense it's a marvellous contraption. Take a breath, loosen my strap. Now it's quiet. I listen hard. Not a bloody peep from her ladyship across the landing. Whoever she is. Just the odd car passing on De Crespigny Close. I ease the leg off the old stump. Over me looms Lawrence. Could this be my moment?

'Thank you,' I say.

'Em, it's OK.'

I try to provoke with 'No . . . obviously' but this meets with silence. (Who was it said, 'No answer came the stern reply'? Such wit!)

'Obviously you're very happy,' I elaborate, smile, let my smile drop.

'Gloriously.'

'Yes, yes, I can imagine.'

And I snatch my petroleum jelly off my shelf, massage it into the fatty stump. The limb rubs, tends to inflame it. Am told Pampers do a soothing talc. I continue.

'Well, you know, I just have to watch it. Dancing. Whatever. This and that. Living it up. You know what I'm inferring. Lucky for some.'

His eyes watch me closely as I rub.

'Don't mind me. Barge ahead. Ruin your life. I don't want to see the consequences. I can close the window up . . .'

Brief glance into his eyes, then I resume.

'No, really, if that's what you're asking for. For everyone to wonder why I should board the window up? The whispering will start, you know. The whispering campaign. But it won't concern me if I'm not looking. If I can't see it, it's nothing to do with me, now is it . . .?'

'Enough,' he says sharply and turns to my door.

I call after him, 'Larry!'

For a moment his face is stricken with affection. Then he stamps across the landing.

I hurl my bloody leg across the bedroom. Strip down to balbriggans.

But what's that now? Chink of glasses? Can't be sure. He's devious enough to keep it all under wraps. Pop of champagne cork? I feel I'm tumbling, down a dark shaft. The thought of what human beings can descend to could warp the highest mind. If I must I'll press my thumbs in my ears because I haven't exactly wasted my life. There is what you can call the inner life of the spirit, for one thinks of these things as the end draws close. I've nothing more with Larry now. Time to bring down the hatches, old friend. He is in some terrible reality the reversed Fool, crossed by the chimeras of the . . . Seven of Cups? The dissembler! The shadow! From the darkness of my room I stare through my window out at the wet paving stones on the street behind. Stray dogs. A gang of roaming children.

Kept myself awake most of the night chattering. But in the morning I throw on the leg and shoes, mushroom-coloured trousers, any jacket. In my full-length mirror I regard the whole ensemble. The light is dull, sky like dark steel wool. Mossy jacket clashes with the old grey face. To kill off the morning I try different shirts, change the trousers, try the shirts once more. Each show up dandruff. None truly suit the knobbly hip. You're no beauty are you, mister, I tell the leg. We're getting nowhere. It's taking so long to find the right match and the light is worse than worthless. I change back into my jimjams. Still have to brace myself for the spiritual destitution to come.

Limp as quietly as I can along the landing to the top of the first staircase. My spot. I shall hang about here. Just keep still. Certain I smell perfume, which clinches it, does it? A bitch, eh, a bloody troublemaker? He's fine as he is. She's the last thing my Larry needs. You see, I am seeing the whole bloody mess twenty or so years down the road from now. Someone as irresponsible as he. With his history – to put it delicately. To put it mildly. To put it diplomatically. He was eight years under that doctor's close eye. Why oh why, frankly, was he ever born? No one can point the finger at me, I don't want to drag the whole thing up.

When he got out he bought an old Mercedes, a rusted affair. Drove it for a taxi firm, but could my brother be a regular driver? For a year and a half he was living in that taxi, his precious Mercedes. Well that says it all. That just proves what we knew all along. Then he had to go and buy a specific gadget. Very clever it was too, that gadget. Very specific. It intercepted the other taxi drivers' calls. Appears the police found him in a dustbin in Peckham Rye. I virtually collapsed when he approached me that day from an alley. One of those mellow, fresh afternoons I would venture out on the black boot before the full contraption. It was spring. Or was it autumn? Mama had recently passed away and my life was beginning. I was on my way back from the university. The Department of Fine Art. Terrific views. There was usually a bench free on the street where I could sit and watch the students, or else write a report. On my reactions to the rooftops and sky. What did I hear but 'Spare some change, mate?' 'Larry!' I exclaimed in panic. It is pointless to deny I was quite mixed up. Had to bundle him into the 49 and take him back in again. Then began such darkness that the former darkness should be called 'light'. Was better the way it was in the bad old days under Mama's ruthless thumb. Every day now I bleed inside, for frankly he is up to God-knows-what. Talking to people, will not be controlled. Thinking, digging, inviting probing women in. A milestone round my neck, strangling me, an albatross, literally.

Sh! – because by the sound of matters they're rising from Larry's bed. There! He emerges from his bedroom. But what was that adumbration in the room to his rear? He draws his door closed behind him, is slowly approaching me on my spot up the landing. Well, no more shrinking. It's time now. Time to face the music. Make your mind up time. Opportunity knocks.

He looks at me askance, sneers, 'You're something', bends his knees and scoops me up.

On our descent I catch his eye and manage a little twinkle. Launching in just yet would be premature. Only when we reach the bottom I say, 'Kitchen', so he carries me down the hall and right in. Once on my legs in the kitchen I ease myself into a chair at the big deal table. He sits across from me. According to ritual, opens my pouch. But he actually flicks it open the way I categorically request him not to. He takes out a syringe. His eyes are flitting from my right one to my left one. My old heart is fluttering away.

'I trust you don't think you're the first to live it up,' I commence.

'Christ get me out of this house. You're creeping around everywhere.' He shakes my insulin bottle so indelicately.

I clear my throat and say, 'I'm sure you remember the lady I once knew?'

I'm being ignored.

Then he speaks. 'Do you know what my friend says? My friend, Juliette. She says how incredibly alike we look.' The ceiling creaks, we glance up, and back. 'That old story, eh?' he says. 'Does make you think a bit. Mm?'

'Alike,' I say, 'but not *so* alike.'

He says, 'Really alike', and draws my insulin up with the syringe. I glance at both his eyes. He points the needle right at me now. Squirts it into my face. And he says softly, mockingly, 'Papa.'

'I want to show you a photograph of this woman,' I stammer as I wipe my face dry. 'There was another woman, son.'

But he is standing now and gripping my arm. He glares down at me, his whole face gaunt, and quivering all over – like a literal leaf. He screams, 'Son! Brother!'

Got to hobble to the conservatory at the back, quick. Lock myself in.

That went well. Could have been disastrous.

Sit on the piano stool at the woodwormy bureau in the corner now. Just have a bevy. One way or another, I shall get through this day.

Plunge oneself into something. Unlock the drawers. Poke through a few old model soldiers. Reds versus greens. From this window at the back I won't see a dicky bird. No danger here of peeping up without intent. He's off my mind. Because I don't want to get wound up watching him. Seeing him in those intimidating attitudes with God-knows-whom. Starting it all off. Dragging it all up. Then finding myself all a-flutter, emotionally a-flutter. Touch of the old tics. Palpitations sort of business, looking over the old shoulder, the twitches. He drags me categorically over the coals. Why can't he let things stay the way they were? Am I my son's keeper? That's the spirit, let it out into the open: *son!* Find I'm fidgeting with a folded passport photograph that was in with the soldiers, what?

Is it Velvetina? My old flame? Open it up.

Well, now. That is to say. Darling Mama? Eh what?

Top-up of vodka.

I intend to board up the drawing-room window.

There's nothing for it.

Because he oversteps the mark. Goes too far. Knows no limits.

That will get him thinking. That'll get him going.

Would have to get my hands on a section of board. Ten and a half by, say, seven and a half, what? Wouldn't have to be too precise. Three old cupboard doors would suffice. Say three and a something by seven and a half each. I'd willingly purchase them out of my Giros. Packet of six-inch nails and Bob's your uncle, I would be in business. Hammer them into the window frame and there I'd have it. Just the ticket. Any kind of board would do. Just to close the window up. What would his lady friend make of that? If that's what I have to do – I would do it. If people aren't going to respect one's space. I don't want to get wound up watching. People getting up to this, and that. No one is wishing to flirt with the devil. But in this set of circumstances, well, I say. A pair of curtains would merely be cosmetic. The thing to do is drag the kitchen table over. Unscrew the legs. Tilt the tabletop up on its end. Heave it up on to the windowsill. I'd manage a ladder, one way or another. Hold the table in place. And the nails. Gently Bentley, very precisely, hammer the nails right through the tabletop. Into the window frame. Block up the window. Once and for all. Close out that bastard.

Bang bang! I hear.

Steady.

Tap.

Stand up, scattering my soldiers. Drop my glass.

Tap, tap.

Make it to the conservatory door, clutching the photograph to my chest. Swing the leg up the hall – where it's chaos fundamentally. Front door lying open. Nails on our hall boards, a sheet on the drawing-room floor, tools everywhere. And Lawrence up on a chair, six-inch nails in his mouth. Actually hammering the shelves of his bookcase right into the window frames. No regard for woodwork. He keeps it up even as I gape. In between the whacks he shouts out words: 'Is . . . this what . . . you wanted? This should . . . keep you happy!'

I feel my whole life tumbling away in pieces.

I hold the photograph in my fist. Know of nothing else to do but continue limping up the hall and out to the garden in my jimjams. Pretend to notice nothing. Breath of fresh. Almost trip into the nettles and I can feel it starting to drizzle now. Have to blink to see through the darkening precipitation and my tears. It is a stark lithograph of an afternoon. High chimney pots defy the malevolent sky in a farce of trumpet keys: some up, some down. But look – a whole mob of rapscallions, piccaninnies too, down at our railings, hanging on them, looking in, jeering, as if we're bloody animals.

I tell you there is no more to be said.

This utter disgrace has finished me now.

Between him and me there will be the minimum human contract.

A stone actually lands at my toe.

Oh look, before the summer house, some woman is bawling at the rabble.

'Clear off, will you, you've had your fun!'

She's in our property. Oriental skin, dressed in trousers. It's her, isn't it, it's true. It's her. It is. Is she? Bloody newcomer. Stepping in where there's already a bond. Now she's turning round. She's approaching . . . me!

Grip the old walking stick.

'Are you all right?' she asks. 'I'm really sorry.'

I watch her strange features dance about in the flesh of her face. She tosses her dark hair with such charming lack of thought. The simple are at home in the world of objects. Slight rhythmic swaying there of the hips.

'Do you want to sit down?' she asks me.

What sort of innuendo is that? Getting me all mixed up, I say. Have to put a face on, keep up appearances and charm the beast. I clench my teeth hard in preparation to say something polite.

She watches. She waits.

Bang. Tap.

'Seen any good views?' I ask.

The little eyebrows knit together. Puzzled, I wager. Not good on our language.

'Excuse me?' she asks.

Right, enough of that. I swing back round and make off toward our ruined residence to the redoubled baying of those bloody young pups. Two more projectiles land close by and I halt and wave my arms wildly to protect my head. Never be seen to give in to a rabble. I turn round to face them out and I shout across our garden, 'I'm going back into the house now to make a pot of tea!' Cast a dirty glance over my shoulder, in the direction of Larry's little bit of crumpet. Then add, nastily, '*English* tea.' And off I totter. Postively trembling.

Too close for comfort.

Absolutely bloody. What?

Relaxing in the semi-darkness of the drawing room now. With a bottle of Pouilly Fumé and a few charming Nat King Cole standards, I'm doing battle with a certain kind of Saturday night ennui. And letting Capstan take the strain. Photograph of Mama tucked away, the sweetheart. The whole bloody window boarded up now. But who's complaining. Beautiful workmanship. Can't see a thing. Have nothing to complain of. Just me and the brother all alone once more. The woman has deserted. One's spirits do sink about that. Best not think of the human being there, but try to see beyond, to the sublime. I might drop the trousers. Hinge a little stiffish. Petroleum jelly out of the pocket. I work the jelly right into my hinge, rub it profusely.

Was that a door banging?

Get up on the legs. Hurl the hip forward. Quick, get to the window. A narrow crack between the boards gives a tolerable view. Can't see much so far.

Just be patient. All shall be well. Will probably make out something in a moment.

Rain dripping off the drainpipe there, forming a puddle.

Dare say Larry will come soon and sit on the windowsill. His favourite position since he was a boy. I do enjoy looking out for my son and brother, what.

I love to.

Steady.

# The Fall of Nineveh

## Patrick McCabe

It is axiomatic and so blindingly obvious as to barely merit stating at all that it ought not be permissible for a Catholic priest, particularly in the current climate, to pay visits to prostitutes on a regular basis. A fact I was more than aware of, and am in no way, here or anywhere else, seeking to justify my actions. Or, indeed, hold to account the person responsible for apprising my superiors of certain rather distasteful facts, for in so doing she was only discharging what she, as a daily communicant, and highly valued parishioner of my own for the greater part of my ministry in North London, considered to be her duty. Suffice to say that the whole regrettable episode proved infinitely harrowing, and I came bitterly to regret my shortcomings in this regard. An equal source of distress proved to be my subsequent encounters with the lady in question, whose disappointment she made no attempt to conceal, her eyes habitually lowered whenever she happened to brush past me in the churchyard.

No less traumatic proved to be the response, unsurprisingly, of my superior, a man whom I have always held in the highest esteem. That the duty which had fallen to him provided no sense of either triumph or vindication was painfully evident – he never once faced me that day we stood together in his study. Wounded and baffled, gazing out across the courtyard of the archbishop's palace, bearing the heavy protracted silences as best he could. Over the short number of years I had known him, we had come to develop a relationship I found immeasurably valuable – he was a scholarly man and one whose ideas and conversation had never been less than stimulating. He had a particular interest in the Jesuitical theologies of James Joyce. A notion upon which I was to reflect with bitter irony as I bade goodbye to him at his residence later that evening, making my way down the gravelled avenue with tears of anguish 'starting to my eyes', as the master might have had it.

The remainder of my journey on that occasion remains to this day something of a blur: but I do recall being deeply disquieted by obdurate recollections of that damp basement located amidst the urban sprawl of Brixton in South London, with its hideous implements and yet curiously drab, even nondescript surroundings – an unwashed candlewick bedspread, a discarded high-heel, and the lurking, hovering shadow of Mrs Beggs, an otherwise plain Home Counties, refined English lady, whose soft leather basque competently if not spectacularly effected the required metamorphosis, completed by the gauntlet in whose wet-look black fingers she turned the pink damask rose.

'You like it like this, don't you, dearie? You like a flower.'

Her bosom would heave and then I would hear her whisper, 'Smell it, certain! *Smell the rose!*'

And I would comply, trembling in my nakedness, hideously shamed in the grimy reproachful light.

When I arrived home to the presbytery that evening, my housekeeper handed me a telegram, informing me of my mother's illness. I didn't hesitate and caught the next available flight to Dublin, having arranged for a car to drive me to the midlands, to the undistinguished hamlet where I'd been born some fifty-five years before.

Illogically, in common with so many self-deluding, somewhat sentimental emigrants, I had been expecting the place of my birth to have changed very little, if at all. Almost to the point of being affronted when I realised the extent of its quite extraordinary transformation. As I came across the square, the second level school happened to be evacuating its boisterous charges. One of their number – a hobbledehoy in a navy-blue sweater, tossed a spent match into the wind and barked lasciviously, 'So then, Quinlan, will you get your sister to suck my cock?'

The response was heedless and indifferent, as transient as the match borne away by the breeze. They made their way towards the café on the hill, where their female counterparts idled coquettishly, displaying little interest in the preceding exchange. I spied a figure behind a twitching curtain, an elderly lady I remembered as an acquaintance of my mother's, gingerly withdrawing into the shadows. Her stonily impassive countenance suggested that the foregoing bawdy salutation had impressed itself with similar insignificance on her consciousness. I found myself wondering would it ever have shocked her, or had the much-vaunted sensitivities of that time been anything more than constructs either – routinely expected and soporifically delivered, in an exchange that meant little or nothing, certainly possessing no spiritual core? Such considerations bore me back to the town I used to know. I could hear it rising up – the babble of old men in the public houses, all of which were empty now, many of them in fact up for sale. The barber-shop was gone now too, the market yard shuttered, the open ground being cleared for the construction of apartments. No one dallied in the town centre any more; the shopping malls had seen to that.

When I got to the hospital I was directed towards a semi-private ward where my mother lay groaning beneath an oxygen mask. As I stood there beside her, she gave no indication of recognition; but she held my hand and that was something. The nurse had said: half an hour at most, so I left her then and booked into the Balla Arms. I lay there on the bed, the television on with the volume up in the hope it might distract me. The CNN footage of the Iraqi invasion was being rerun, the brash young soldiers in their desert camouflage, the jubilant imprecations of the liberated natives, the image of the dictator toppling in slow motion. An American professor denounced the looting of the Museum of Antiquities. It is no overstatement, he continued lugubriously, to describe Mesopotamia, the lands between the Euphrates and Tigris rivers, as the cradle of civilisation. It was here that agriculture, urban living, pottery-making, metallurgy and writing were all developed, he said. The camera homed in on a number of scattered stone tablets, the blowing sand covering their inscribed cuneiform.

I tried to sustain my interest but found it beyond me. I was in the grip of a melancholy which would permit me no release. The professor was debating the region and its history, systematically outlining events sur-rounding the capitulation of Nineveh to the Medes and Babylonians in 612 BC, paraphrasing Kipling as he concluded drily: 'All the pomp of yesterday becoming one with Nineveh and Tyre!'

His impassioned words, almost hypnotically, returned me to a time in the past that I had long since treasured; when I'd experienced a sense of pride and self-worth the like of which I'd never before known. It was the occasion upon which I'd been informed of my spectacular, and quite unexpected, success in the school essay-writing competition of 1965. It was an annual contest, traditionally set by the catechetical inspector to mark his Corpus Christi visit to our classrooms. It was to him I owed the honour of having my reward pinned to my breast in front of the class – an oval silver medal depicting the mother of God. I'd laboured many hours over the style of the prose and the tightly woven structure of the work itself, to the extent that, even yet, I could recall with accuracy many of its key phrases – disparate references which included, amongst others, *outer ramparts, severe depredations, winged bull colossus*. And my *coup de grâce*, over which I had exulted, the closing sentence I'd gleaned directly from the good book itself: *Nineveh is devastated, who will mourn her?*

As I'd watched the light fail across the town outside my bedroom window, I remembered, so consumed by my creation had I become, that the screams of animals burning in the fire and the pitiful pleas of flee-ing sinners seemed as real to me as the living souls who bestrode those dimming, starlit streets. To the extent that cold perspiration stood out upon my forehead and I found myself consumed by the strangest of sensations: of deepest foreboding and imminent catastrophe.

But all of that, now that I had been victorious, I considered, had been triumphantly averted, as I made my way in the direction of the chapel, there to spend hours in communion with the saints, among whose number I felt at home, as if through my success I now was counted among their number.

My feelings of achievement were more than justified, for the Corpus Christi prize was highly regarded in the diocese. It was even rumoured that the bishop had the final say in the adjudication procedure. And many of the previous recipients, I had been reliably informed, had actually gone on to receive – to the immense pride and honour of their parents – holy orders at Maynooth, Kiltegan and various other seminaries. I spent many hours ruminating upon the rituals of such establishments, envisioning my mother in the front pew, raising her eyes as I clasped my hands in the attitude of a penitent, the youthful deacon applying the oils to my anointed hands.

The intensity of these musings would completely overwhelm me, to the extent that I presently harboured a desire to assume the much-coveted position of the central figure in an important forthcoming drama – the Corpus Christi procession which took place every year. It was a major event in the liturgical calendar, a time when the town was purged and renewed in an act of homage to the Body and Blood of Our Lord Jesus Christ. Weeks were spent on the construction of private altars, which were prominently displayed outside front doors painted in bright gleaming colours and polished windows which shone as never before. Such was the fervour that burned within my breast that rarely an hour passed but I entered upon those hallowed cloisters, where indulgences fell upon my head in showers, as I fingered my glittering escutcheon of silver: the evidence that I had been singularly chosen.

The procession as a rule took place on a Saturday afternoon, and this year was to be no different. It was as if the automatic wail of the fire siren (which was tested each Saturday at 2 p.m. sharp) was acting as a warning to all prospective sinners as it wailed across the rooftops of the giddy, excited town. Our next-door neighbour – a lady not long returned from England, by the name of Doaty Finn, who was rumoured to be divorced, although no one had actually established this with any certainty – was snipping some flowers as I emerged in our doorway. Doaty was in her forties and bore a strong resemblance to Ruby Murray the singer, who crooned 'Softly Softly' and 'Miss O'Leary's Irish Fruit Cake'. I had seen a photo of Ruby, with her glossy curled perm and pastel lambswool sweaters. Doaty wore slacks: black Capri pants, in actual fact, a garment which most women in the town would have been very wary of indeed. It was commonly accepted that the Blessed Virgin Mary blushed every time a woman adorned herself in such a brazen manner. Once Doaty had said, quite out of the blue, 'Do you like lipstick? Methinks you think you do.'

I had made some hopelessly dry-mouthed reply.

Which had amused her, clearly, as she went *tut tut* and swept her fingers through my hair.

'Pink,' she said, 'that would be nice. Soft enough to be innocent, sweet enough to inspire. What do you think, my little soldier?'

I didn't know what to say.

'Pink,' she repeated, 'soft and sweet as the petals of a rose.'

When she called me that – her 'little soldier' – I found myself becoming suffused with an indomitable courage, an almost unquenchable yearning to defend her. I would stand for hours upon imaginary battlements, with my shield reflecting the burning crimson of the sun – awaiting plundering hordes, massing broodingly just beyond the horizon.

Topsy Burns was the oldest dog in the town, his age estimated at seventeen. He had come from Tipperary originally. Now he was crawling out of his hole beneath the hedge and looking about him with wild, defensive eyes. He glared at the sky until the sound at last abated, the moan of the siren as it skirled in and out of the arched alleyways and streets. Then he retreated, bristling yet. He had just disappeared into the darkened recess when Erskine Phibbs rose up, leaning over his back wall. Erskine owned a private patch of gravel situated directly in front of his house – between it and the gardens – which he guarded with a fearsome, almost psychotic vengeance. This he now surveyed for some time before making determined forays across its surface. Levelling it fastidiously with the sole of his shoe, small shudders of resentment rippling through his body. Presently he went back inside and Mr Coogan came cycling up the lane. He swung his leg across the bar, and came freewheeling towards us. Doaty was on her knees tending her flower bed with a trowel. You could see the outline of her body beneath her clothes. My cheeks burned. I averted my gaze and addressed Mr Coogan. He was gaunt, with high-waisted trousers and a military moustache.

'Doaty's flowers are coming on good, aren't they?' he said.

Doaty laughed, cupping the ejaculation as though she'd trapped a little bird.

'How's your father's hydrangeas?' he asked me then.

'Da says the best yet, Mr Coogan,' I replied.

He produced his pipe and set to the ritual of lighting it and puffing contemplatively, evaluating colourful rockeries and neatly trimmed borders. He tapped his soft palm with the bowl, lifting his nose to sniff the warm air.

'Bacon,' he said. 'Hard to beat the bacon. Isn't that right, Doaty?'

'Streaky,' replied Doaty, 'I always like a bit of streaky.'

'Streaky,' mused Mr Coogan, rubbing the bowl of his pipe as he spoke, 'you prefer the streaky do you then, Doaty?'

'O I do. I do, Mr Coogan. When I was living in Hendon, like, you know – why, I always used to get me a bit of streaky, like. I'd go down the 'igh street and get it, do you know what I'm saying?'

Doaty's voice was an unusual mixture of refined English and indigenous country Irish.

'My wife used to fry lovely bacon, Doaty. Whether it was streaky or not I couldn't tell you. But God it was lovely. It was the nicest bacon.'

A snatch of music drifted through an open window and Doaty sang along with it as she chafed at the clay with her trowel.

'Does the little soldier like his bacon?' she asked then.

I stiffened.

'I don't know,' replied Mr Coogan, as a cloud of blue smoke enveloped me. 'Why don't you ask him, Doaty?'

'Well, I don't know about him and bacon, but I do know he likes flowers,' she said.

She was standing before me now with a pink rose in her hand. Her fingernails stroked its long thin stem.

'You like them, don't you, soldier?' she said.

'Yes,' I replied, and lowered my head.

She raised the rose to her nostrils.

'Boys don't usually like flowers, do they?'

'It's going to be a nice day for the procession,' declared Mr Coogan.

'I love processions,' said Doaty, 'they didn't have them in England, you know. Over there you talk about processions, they think there is something wrong with you, they do. Unless it's for the Queen.'

'That's right. I daresay there's ones over there never so much as said a prayer in their lives.'

A small commotion commenced close by. In the doorway Mrs Paddy James was struggling awkwardly with a statue of the Sacred Heart. He held the first two fingers of his right hand, drawing attention to his thorn-crowned heart with his left. Mrs James sat it up on the windowsill and began assembling a display of bright flowers about its base. She stood back and admired it, then frowned disapprovingly and moved it ever so slightly. Her husband enquired as to whether she needed the white altar cloth yet or not. He proudly produced it and together they set to work arranging it to their satisfaction upon the small mahogany table, before lining up wax candles on the apron of stiff linen.

'Mrs James has nice candles on her altar,' observed Mr Coogan.

'Yes,' replied Doaty, 'Mrs James has the nicest house in the terrace.'

'And Paddy always gives her a hand,' continued Mr Coogan, picking his teeth insouciantly with a match.

'Yes,' said Doaty, 'it's good to see that.'

'Isn't it just,' said Mr Coogan, 'isn't it just, now, Doaty, isn't it just.'

Mrs James wandered over to us, applying her handkerchief to her moist forehead.

'It's hard work so it is. I say it's hard work, Mr Coogan.'

'It is,' said Mr Coogan, 'it is that, Mrs James. Isn't it a lovely day?'

'Do you know what, I'd say that's the hottest yet,' agreed Mrs James, 'our Bernie – you should see her back with the sunburn. She was up half the night, Mr Coogan.'

Mr Coogan gasped.

'Bernie? Half the night? No, Mrs James!'

Mrs James nodded gravely. I started momentarily as a rook swung abruptly out of the ash tree and looped in the air before settling back in the tree, where it remained gazing intensely at us.

'What you want for that is the Nivea cream,' suggested Doaty.

'Do you think so, Doaty? Is that good?'

Doaty smiled and insisted that would do the trick all right. The rook's glassy eyes switched back and forth in his head, then off he went careering into the heavens.

'We'll have to have the terrace looking well today,' said Mrs James with the tiniest hint of agitation, 'you should see Canal View. They have an Our Lady they got from the chapel.'

'The chapel above?' choked Mr Coogan.

'Yes. Father Vincent got it for them special. It's that height, all painted new.'

Mr Coogan's teeth ground in resentment.

'That's not fair. There ought to be no special treatment.'

'It isn't fair on the rest,' agreed Doaty, 'it gives them an actual unfair advantage. Isn't it?'

'No matter,' Mrs James went on, 'we did well other years. We always look well.'

'And sure that's the main thing,' said Mr Coogan.

'Our Lord doesn't be bothered too much about style anyway, Mr Coogan. A few flowers. A clean cloth and maybe a little cross or a rosary.'

'That's all's needed.'

Mrs James nodded and touched her husband on the elbow. 'We'd better be going in, Paddy,' she said, 'we'd want to get the dinner if it's our intention to receive.'

'Right so,' said Mr Coogan. 'We'll be seeing youse.'

Mrs James pushed the door and disappeared inside, dutifully followed by her husband.

We stood there staring after them for what seemed an age. Throughout which Mr Coogan tapped the bowl of his palm with the bowl of the pipe and Doaty began snipping carefully at the flowers, humming a song I didn't know. Mr Coogan exhaled a protracted sigh, his gaze fixed on the louche blue calligraphy of the slowly unwinding smoke. Doaty lifted her head before pausing for a moment and lapsing deep into thought. Then she rested her small hand on the nape of her neck.

'I think I have a touch of sunburn, Mr Coogan. It's so sore.'

Through an open window came jaunting the gay sound of orchestral strings, as a blithe female voice chippily announced: 'Radio Eireann. We present: *The Kennedys of Castleross.*'

A butterfly swerved across the cabbage patch and flattened itself against the netting wire, before eventually, through a series of frantic, valiant efforts, pluckily securing its freedom.

Doaty rose to her feet and brushed a few crumbs of dirt from her knees.

'I'm so silly. I really am. Do you know what I am? I'm a right silly goose. That's what I am – a silly old goose, Mr Coogan.'

Then she laughed and stared absent-mindedly at her trowel.

'I'd best be going in. The old dinner. Got to get the old dinner ready before the Procession, isn't it?'

Mr Coogan offered to carry her flowers. She waved him away good-humouredly.

'Ah not at all. Sure I'm still an able-bodied girl – isn't it? I'm still in the full of my health. Ha ha. Still an old girl in the full of her health!'

She turned on her heel and gave us one last wave, before disappearing through the back door. We stood there in silence, swamped by shadows doing their best to fit together, for all the world like broken jigsaw pieces. The church bell tolled thinly – the first of the day.

'Time to eat,' said Mr Coogan, emptying dead ash onto the undisturbed gravel. Then he crunched it into the ground.

'Let's see him straighten that,' he said icily, 'let's see the crabbit cunt straighten that out.'

I made no reply as I watched him pass. He stood for a moment behind his wall, before delivering a military salute with a mocking smile. When I looked again he was gone. Mr Coogan had once been in the army. They claimed he had attained the rank of Captain. But you didn't know whether it was true or not. It could have been something he had suggested himself, which then became a game that everyone played along with, whenever he saluted, calling him 'Captain'. I had a feeling it was that – just a game they'd agreed to play. As I left to go inside, I caught a glimpse of the 'Captain' at the window, staring out with thin compressed lips, a seam of wrinkles drawn tautly across his forehead.

My sister arranged her white lace veil, striking a variety of devout poses before the parlour mirror. Being a first communicant, and specially selected for the day, she had prepared her small wicker basket of rose petals. My mother was putting the finishing touches to a poster she had been labouring over for the greater part of the week, a crude oleograph of Christ rising triumphantly from banked piles of crimson glory. With his arms upraised, and a radiant halo crowning his head. Spreading from his toes in swords of light, fanned the rubric *IHS*. The picture possessed an innocent gaudiness I found attractive, with its hopelessly childish and simple *naïveté*.

'Wait until they see this. There's not many will have the like of this.'

My father grunted impatiently, returning his attention to a recalcitrant collar stud. His dry-cleaned suit lay spread across the sofa. She sat down beside it and, somewhat distractedly, smoothed its lapels.

'Wait until they see this,' she said. 'There's not many will have the like of this. Have you got your badge? All eyes will be on the stewards, remember.'

I climbed into my own clothes, grey trousers and a blazer, upon which my *Nineveh* essay medal was displayed – shining prominently on the left-hand lapel.

'Now we're right,' said my mother happily, standing back to admire me once more.

*The Kennedys of Castleross* had long since ended. Now across the airwaves organ pipes swelled magnificently as a microphone spurted and a priest began his address, in a faraway town whose name we did not know.

'*Aufer a nobis, quaesumus, Domine, iniquitates nostras.*'

'Take away from us our iniquities, we implore thee Lord,' my father loudly interjected, pressing my shoulder reassuringly, as though to suggest: one day, through perseverance, you could become as learned as I.

My mother approved his appearance tenderly, her two weathered hands folded across her apron.

'It's going to be some day,' remarked my father tensely, rotating his shoulders like a prizefighter, 'we just couldn't have got a better day for it.'

The Supreme Pontiff, the Head of the One True Church, waved from the polished fanlights, elaborately coloured standards hung from upstairs windows. My mother affixed her oleograph to the gable end of our house.

'Did you do that yourself, Mrs?' asked Annie Lennon.

My mother nodded, humbly.

'IHS,' said Annie Lennon, 'but don't you know what that stands for?'

'Of course I do – *I have suffered*,' replied my mother.

An expression of alarm transformed Annie Lennon's face. She inclined a conspiratorial head before ushering my mother nervously into the entry.

'Oh God bless us. Aren't you lucky you didn't put that in?' she said.

There could be no mistaking my mother's perplexity.

Annie Lennon went on to explain: 'It stands for Jesus Saviour of Men, daughter. *Jesu Hominum Salvator.*'

Almost at once she made as if to thoroughly disown the remark, dismissing it with a flippant gesture. Then she stepped back out into the street and went to her own statue, whose joined hands she polished assiduously. She was smiling to herself as she wiped each individual digit. I could see my mother staring at her, standing by her garish, inaccurate picture, which already had abjectly slumped from its tenuous moorings on the gable wall.

Mrs Coyle kept calling from inside the house:

'Are they on yet? Are they on yet?'

The arc of stars which crowned The Little Flower's head erupted abruptly into illumination.

Mrs Coyle called again:

'Yes, they're on. *No they're not!*'

The saint gazed upwards impassively, as Mrs Coyle squealed, *'Yes! That's it! Don't touch the plug!'*

Mr Lennon appeared with a large ball of blue glass, inside which The Virgin of the Snows smiled wanly and parted her tiny pale hands. It shone on the windowsill like an enormous fairy-tale marble. Mr Lennon lit a cigarette.

'Lucy brought it back from Lourdes,' he remarked to no one in particular, padding about as he apprehended it thoughtfully.

'I've never seen the beat of it,' remarked my father, abstractedly fingering his steward's badge.

Mr Coogan filled the doorway, handsomely attired in a grey pinstripe suit. He adjusted his tiepin and stared up and down the length of the terrace. By common consent his display had been declared as little short of 'pitiful', comprised as it was of an ancient, flaking Child of Prague, and just a handful of wilting flowers. Mrs Lennon said you couldn't expect much where there was no woman in the house.

Erskine Phibbs had assumed his post, his leather sole alertly poised.

In her fitted costume of dusty pink, Doaty Finn was a vision by the turnips. Mr Coogan sighed and his lips seemed to part without his even knowing.

'*Pink*,' I heard him sigh.

Doaty was wearing white kid gloves and you could smell her perfume as it slid past on the air. Mrs Lennon scrutinised her without respite. As Doaty strolled past her inspecting the glass, plying the cuff of her glove.

'Mrs Lennon,' she quizzed throatily, 'what on earth does it say on the little plaque?'

She coughed demurely before bending down to inspect the inscription. Mr Coogan coloured sharply and looked away. Mr James erupted into a bout of violent coughing. Doaty sighed, her white fingers spread on her upraised hip.

'The Virgin of the Snows. Isn't it just the last word, Mrs?'

'His sister got it in Lourdes,' explained Mrs Lennon curtly.

Inexplicably, Mr Coogan blurted out, 'That's a fine costume you're wearing. Did you get it in England?'

Doaty smiled shyly as she fingered a pearl earring.

'Oh. You really think so, Mr Coogan?'

She patted her coiffeured hair and lowered her eyelashes as she turned to Mrs Lennon.

'Mr Coogan loves pink,' she said in a heavy whisper. '*Pink*, Mrs Lennon!'

Quite unexpectedly then, she transferred her attentions to Phibbs, who was standing, mute, in the centre of his gravel.

'*Pink*, Erskine!!'

Phibbs made no reply, just remained there with his eyes flitting darkly.

Doaty said to Mrs Lennon, 'As we ladies know, pink is all about looking pretty in bloom. Isn't that right, Mrs Lennon?'

Mrs Lennon said nothing, just folded her arms in silence and glowered. It was as if all the ill-fitting shadows of the lane had somehow managed to come together at last, calibrated perfectly in the centre of her face, making absolutely no sound at all.

St Martin de Porres and St Christopher stood erect on the school roof proprietorially monitoring the town. '*O Sacrament Most Holy O Sacrament Divine,*' issued the hymn from the PA, interrupted intermittently by spurts and piercing whistles. The assembly had converged on the convent gates, the busy sisters swarming in and out of the building like woodlice. The boy scouts had gathered up at the front, flanked by the First Communicants with their wicker baskets crammed with luscious rose petals. Ladies in sea-blue robes and decorous lace veils stood side by side beneath the vast gold-on-blue ensign: *Legio Mariae*.

My father, as head steward, was in a state of grim unease, alternately pacing frenziedly with his hands behind his back and barking high-pitched instructions, it seemed to no one. The teachers and the clergy, in choir dress and copes, stood four-square beneath the canopy, under whose fringed gilt cloth roof reposed the monstrance which contained the Blessed Sacrament. To the front, a brace of altar boys determinedly swung thuribles. A huge silence descended like a billowing sheet as my father began:

'We are now ready to begin. May I say how heartening it is to see such an enthusiastic turnout. The Corpus Christi Procession is one of the highlights of the liturgical calendar. It is an event. A community event. Each part of the town is represented. Thank you. Thank you so much.'

The banners wavered a little and a soft hush of pride rippled pleasantly through the crowd. Mr Coogan squeezed my arm, as though seeking solace from a moment of extreme but very private trepidation. Then we were moving, surging forward before settling into a slow and reverent pace. Many of the procession were bearing hand-candles and printed programmes.

I heard my father again:

'Please ensure there are no more than four abreast. Thank you. We will be taking the appointed route through Water Street, past the creamery, round by Mackle's and thence to the square.'

The Blue Army rose and fell like an enormous but deadly quiet tidal breaker. The pipes of the organ swept from the PA as the choir and the cantor sang in an angelic falsetto from the Bank of Ireland steps.

The legend CORPUS CHRISTI had been spelt out on the tarmac in an arrangement of flowers, and it took our breath away as we rounded the meat factory corner. In Water Street small shoals of petals fluttered to our feet. Decades of the rosary were recited with dull monotony. In the dead heat, all you could hear was the rise and fall of the celebrant's chanting, the clink of the holy water vessel seemed to carry for miles. As I observed him blessing the abject heads of the kerbside penitents, their shameful eyes drew me back once more to the forbidden terrain of Nineveh, a city full of rumours where history's retribution loomed.

I saw my father in a rough grey robe, trembling between the columns of an alien temple.

'The city of Nineveh will sink into the dust. It will be as though it had never existed,' he wept weakly.

Try as I might, I could not chivvy the recurrent thought and as we passed the dry-cleaners, I felt myself sink into a swoon, clutching my silver medal as I watched the first flames lick the spars of the city's rumbling towers, the cries of retreating animals filling the air. I covered my eyes and by a supreme act of will once more regained the familiar streets of the town and our determined but rapturous, advancing throng. By now we had gained the brightly painted creamery, where St Michael the Archangel was waiting, surrounded by obsequious plaster acolytes. We were to be allowed no respite until we attained the main square of the town. It was there the holy sacrifice of the Mass was to be celebrated.

'You are a very special boy, John Cunningham,' I fondly recalled the catechetical inspector declaring before the class, 'and you have laboured hard to obtain this acknowledgement, this special medal of the Immaculate Conception. It is my fervent hope that you may one day choose to follow the Lord's path. To distinguish your town and fulfil your mother's wishes. Bless you, my son, you are a credit to us all.'

'You are the whore, not I, my son. You, my little soldier, the concupiscent transgressor.'

At times, her Home Counties etiquette and Methodist upbringing notwithstanding, Mrs Beggs could intimidate with a fatal, dread antipathy.

'You asked me to do it, did you not, John Cunningham? You made this request of Mrs Beggs on your knees. You pleaded with her, didn't you, here in the cloisters of her longed-for, hallowed temple?'

The brothel I had regularly frequented could scarcely have been so described. It was little more than a dingy basement, a damp bedsitter in which Mrs Beggs conducted her nefarious offices – mostly at weekends, when she travelled up from Sussex. She laid me out as though I were a corpse. Placing the rose, as instructed, upon my burning cheek.

*'Little Soldier. He likes the flower.'*

The ritual rarely varied, apart from the single occasion, in the grip of a near-delirium, I had prevailed upon her to sing 'Softly Softly'. Initially she had shrunk from the suggestion in derision, threatening, in fact, to terminate our acquaintanceship forthwith. 'Don't attempt to assuage your guilt through flippancy,' she had adjured me coldly. That hadn't been my intention at all, but I had made no reply and turned my burning face away.

No amount of time alone in the solitude of the cloisters could wash away the stain, or stay the taunting cries from the western gallery:

'Your father did it too, John Cunningham. Many times.'

Mr Coogan, protecting his good suit, was kneeling on his handkerchief, gazing upwards to the heavens with the pleading eye of a supplicant in agony. The old and the handicapped were wheeled up to the altar and arranged in military formation beneath a large banner which read: *The Town of Balla Welcomes Our Saviour*. They were attired in their best clothes and their wheelchairs looked splendid in their raiment of papal ribbons. As the priest administered his blessing the procession arose sharply and, at his behest, once again fell obsequiously to its knees.

'The heat,' groaned Mr Coogan, 'the fucking heat', pressing a finger awkwardly into his collar.

Doaty closed her prayerbook for a moment, leaning over to rest her arm on my shoulder as she directed her attention to a loosened ankle strap. Her proximity had the effect of dramatically quickening my pulse and summoning, unbidden, the phrase 'appalling rites'. In the course of my researches for my prizewinning composition, quite by chance a haunting engraving had come to my attention, a mezzotint whose scenes those words described with terrifying exactitude. It had shown a woman convicted of adultery being buried in the sand and covered in honey. The sneers of her tormentors were purposely exaggerated, as was the hatred that shone in their eyes. Her arms reached up in pathetic appeal, just as the locust-drone sounded afar. They would strip the lily-white flesh from her bones. Strangers would come upon a bleached crate in the sand and never suspect it had once worn the flesh of a beautiful woman.

'Thus will perish Nineveh's whores,' a voice had exerted its influence upon me as I sat there in my room, my pen in my agitation falling from my grasp. I prayed that loathsome image would depart, as I sat there, rigid, in the room's failing light. Ever so clearly seeing Mr Coogan in the desert, blithely puffing on his pipe as he remarked, 'It's a pity this had to happen, really, Doaty. But then, of course, you brought it on yourself.'

The locusts had already burrowed deeply, finding their way beneath her very soft skin. The bedroom was filled with their dread droning sound. Beyond the walls of the town I felt I heard the blast of a trumpet, the lumbering shift of the menacing hordes, lustfully converging beyond Noble's Garage.

Now, in the square, on this day of Corpus Christi, I prayed as I had never prayed before. And I found myself rewarded by being transported to a place of the cleanest washed marble, sacred cloisters from whose sanctuary I never wished to depart. My mother was there, and all my neighbours, and there was a palpable sensation of joy in the air. As there ought to have been, for I had just celebrated the sacrifice of the Mass. I swept down the aisle in my starched linen vestments and I heard Doaty Finn whisper softly to my mother:

'I always knew he wouldn't let you down.'

Mr Coogan was standing at the back of the chapel. He was holding his hat, blinded by tears of both empathy and vindication. He had once confided in me that as a youth he himself had considered entering the order of Melchizedek.

'Of becoming one of the holy infantry,' he had said, 'a captain, except this time for Christ.'

The consecration bell sounded three times.

'There's something so beautiful about it, isn't there, John?'

I started when I heard Doaty's voice.

'Over in England, isn't it, they don't have anything like this. You know where they go on Corpus Christi? They go to the pub, that's where they go.'

The cover of her prayer book was mother-of-pearl. The celebrant parted his hands.

'*Benedicat vos omnipotens Deus, Pater, et Filius, et Spiritus Sanctus.*'

'Amen.'

The leaden drone of the congregation seemed somehow to lighten, almost to come adrift from its source, then float off to heaven like some weightless, inexpressibly fragrant fragrance. I looked at Doaty. Her eyes were smiling from in behind her prayer book. I amost fainted.

'Well, that's it for another year,' said Mrs Paddy James as we turned into the lane.

'And do you know what, it was the nicest procession yet,' suggested Annie Lennon.

'Wasn't it,' agreed Mrs James, 'wasn't it a credit?'

'It's good to see everyone making the effort – isn't it, Doaty?'

'It is indeed. And the terrace definitely held its own. Isn't it?'

We rounded the gable end and, for a moment, stood wistfully by the gardens. Then the Jameses announced they were going inside. Mr Coogan leaned over the fence. Doaty's eyes twinkled. She fastidiously folded her pink costume jacket and draped it neatly across the gate. Her bracelet tinkled as she locked her fingers in a cradle behind her head, indulging in the most luxurious sigh. In a deft pincer movement she removed a thread from her blouse, directly above her swelling bosom.

'Well, Mr Coogan,' she said, 'that's it for another year.'

Mr Coogan drummed on the gatepost and replied, as though unconvinced of something, I thought, 'Aye, it is now, Doaty. It is indeed. All over now bar the shouting. Another year goes by, indeed it does.'

Mr and Mrs James reappeared, attired now in their everyday clothes and set to dismantling their altar. Mrs James went by with a candlestick.

'Mrs James,' enquired Doaty, 'are you taking your altar in already?'

Mrs James shuddered, her nose creasing: 'Do you know what it is – I think we're as well, Doaty. I wouldn't like any harm to come to the statue. You know yourself.'

'Oh,' replied Doaty.

Mr James stood by the Sacred Heart effigy and firmly took its head in his hands. His wife gripped its feet and together they gently carried it inside, taking great care when they reached the raised step. Erskine Phibbs came out, affecting obliviousness to proceedings. But every so often his covetousness would betray him, and his eyes would lift beneath his flattened cap. Doaty looked at Mr Coogan. Mr Coogan nodded, then looked away. Then she said:

'Mr James?'

Mr James chewed obsessively at his lip.

Doaty's bosom rose as she said, in a babyish voice, 'Mr James?'

She coughed a little and raised her small fist to her lips.

'Or should I say – Paddy?'

Mr James dropped one of the cloths.

Her tones were soft and low and heavy.

'*Paddy?*' Doaty repeated.

Doaty took a step forward and said, '*Paddy? Do you hear me, Paddy?*'

Mr James was absent-mindedly binding his wrist with a linen tie.

Doaty crossly lowered her voice. 'Don't ignore me, Mr James. I don't like that.'

'What's that?' he whimpered, 'what's that you say, Doaty?'

'Come here, Paddy. Come here to Doaty.'

My heartbeat gathered momentum as she observed him closely as he made his way towards her. She didn't move, just kept smiling. Mr Coogan stared off down the garden and once again whistled his faint little tune. Doaty released the softest of moans. Paddy James's lower lip quivered as Doaty addressed him intimately. Then – with no warning – she sharply snapped her fingers.

Mr Coogan cried out, in an alarmingly loud high register, 'The tea, I say! It's time for the tea!'

Phibbs looked away. Doaty coolly slipped on her jacket.

'You know what I think, Erskine,' she said, 'I think Mr Coogan's tired.'

Phibbs growled and turned his back.

'Are you, Mr Coogan? Tired from all the walking are we?'

Then came the moment I had been so fearful of, the one of which I'd experienced so many presentiments. The evening sun was flashing on the gold of her bracelet as she slowly approached me.

'And what about you, my little soldier? Are *you* tired?'

I didn't reply. I might have been standing on the shore of eternity. I felt her firm pink fingernails tracing smoothly along the length of my cheek.

'Flowers are nice, aren't they?'

The last thing I saw was Erskine Phibbs glaring murderously as Doaty brazenly crunched her high-heel into his gravel.

Tan water collected in the puddle hole. An abandoned bicycle lay on its side in the ditch. Mr Coogan's Child of Prague remained there, abandoned, his little orb like a rotting apple in his hand. Annie Lennon came out, her head cowled in a towel, impatiently scooping coal into a scuttle. My father stood by the window, gazing morosely at the sky of battleship-grey.

'And after such a good day,' he sighed regretfully, as the first rumble of thunder sounded far across the town.

'Would it be too late for you to get me cigarettes?' he asked.

I shrugged.

The car park now was a great lake, on its surface a devastated navy of rubbish. In the square the sodden banner strained heavily at its moorings. The altar had been taken down, torn posters dangling haplessly from wet wooden poles.

The shops, to my dismay, I found closed, without exception, so I was faced with no choice but to continue to the far end of town.

'You were lucky to get me on the day of the procession,' the owner informed me without raising his head. I thanked him profusely and turned for home. I took the short cut that led through the railway tunnel, a route as a rule I would studiously have avoided, rumoured as it was to have been the site of appalling rites in the past – none of which had ever been satisfactorily defined. But I knew very well this horrid aspect, for I had once been pursued by the Minotaur deep within its labyrinthine core, returning home late from Benediction one evening, and the feelings invoked by the tormentor of Theseus now returned to plague me with a fearsome vengeance. I remembered fancying myself fleeing through streets that were open sewers, carrion birds circling aloft in the sky. I shivered hopelessly now as a stone colossus fell soundlessly onto plains.

As I climbed the rank stairwell, the bronze head of a bearded monarch came to life before my eyes, but no word of learning or comforting wisdom was destined to pass those lips. It glared at me and erupted startlingly into harsh laughter.

I pressed myself against the seeping wall and remained there, petrified, beneath the arch of a doorway, as the hairs like needles stood erect upon my neck. There could be no mistaking the sound of laughter – pealing as it did, with blood-curdling clarity, from the far end of that suffocating gloom, where the deserted railway warehouse was located. The entrance to which – I approached it now with beating heart – swung effortlessly open, as though in express anticipation of my arrival.

As might be imagined, my entry into that forbidden place was tentative in the extreme and it required all the courage I could muster not to flee, this unnameable pit of the foulest odours, the birthplace of pestilence, concupiscence's home. My agitation betrayed itself in deep-drawn gasps and I felt I was certain to meet a dismal and solitary end. Then a broad flood of moonlight entered through a high curtainless window and I found myself – with a heart-stopping suddenness – gazing into the face of Paddy James – standing directly in front of me. In the extremity of my concern I considered myself incarcerated in the deepest seclusion of a castellated abbey, where folding doors slid back to reveal visions no human soul ought ever to entertain. An iciness of feeling pervaded my frame as a lamp was elevated and another familiar countenance loomed from the dark.

'My little brave soldier. Didn't I know you'd come?'

It was Doaty. I shuddered violently. But when I looked again she had already disappeared, gliding purposefully towards another figure, shrinking back with him towards a recess in the wall. I recognised Mr Coogan at once.

'Didn't it turn out bad?' I heard him say, patiently rummaging in his pocket for his pipe. The match flared – bodiless heads, powder-white, were illuminated sharply.

Not a sound was to be heard; apart from that continuing within the seclusion of that narrow world – not that of a distant bell, or bark, or even the faintest of cries from without. I looked up to see Mr James smiling. He approached me and decisively ran his fingers through my hair, as I fought with sensations of the deepest discomfort.

'Come here,' he said, 'Doaty wants to talk to you. Doaty wants to chat to her little soldier.'

A cry of panic escaped my lips and I flung myself blindly towards the door – to no avail. Mr James's grip fastened tightly about my wrist and I looked up to see Mr Coogan regarding me reproachfully.

'*Tut tut,*' I heard him say.

'Not a good idea,' Mr James whispered, as Erskine Phibbs tugged his cap down and nodded.

'No need for that,' Mr Coogan affirmed softly, turning his back and puffing quietly in the ash-grey light, 'no need for that, you see, at all.'

'Come here to me, pet. Come over to Doaty's.'

I knew – or so I succeeded in persuading myself – a facility which I was to develop considerably in my adult years – that I had no choice but to yield. Mr James resolutely steered me towards her and I stood before Doaty, I fancied, naked between flaming tripods.

'*Ah,*' she sighed, '*ah, my good little soldier.*'

Her blouse had been removed and I could see the stark pale flesh of her shoulders as she ran her hands up and down her pale freckled arms. Her fingernails began their familiar itinerary, ever so patiently mapping the line right down my cheek. Her arms reached down into the very well of my soul, elbow-deep.

'You see,' she explained, 'if you were to run, little soldier. If you were to do a silly thing like that –

'The town will know –

'The town would get to hear –

'Your father did it too, John Cunningham.

'Many times.'

Doaty softly chuckled, floating airily into Mr Coogan's arms.

Outside the night had grown stormy, and I had by now fallen into a state of complete dejection, heightened by their low and intermittent dialogues, splintered occasionally by lascivious cries and sudden peals of barbarous laughter. At the slightest sound or small surprise of the senses I would start, before relapsing into a melancholy even deeper than before. In the vagary of my delirium I saw myself harshly presented to the contemplation of an authority charged with the subjugation of monstrous and detestable creeds, whose exertions had executed the destruction of Nineveh, which was nothing more now than a smouldering ruin. I prayed my shame would remain concealed within – but even that was not to be. The figure that appeared in the doorway at length assumed a rigorous distinctness of outline and the aromatic fragrance which accompanied it revealed itself not as that of one's longings and transports, the odour of blossoms piled high on majestic blue-veined marble, but the ethereal issue of the extended limbs of a voluptuous enchantress, shamefully bare as they once more approached.

'Poor baby,' Doaty's husky voice whispered plaintively, 'poor little baby all alone in the dark. I brought this for you.'

It shocked me to see it was the softest pink rose. She cradled my head on her shoulder and I was wholly consumed by its gently unfolding texture.

'Do you like it? It's damask.'

The hostility which raged in my heart began to die, and I experienced that strange commingling of sadness and pleasure I would come to know so well in my sinful adult years.

The following day it was as though the Procession had never taken place. The storm the night before had wreaked havoc across the town. The creamery roof had literally been peeled off and the telephone wires were down in every street. It was late now, well after tea and a single street light lit the terrace. My father was still complaining about how long it had taken me to get the cigarettes, availing of the opportunity to provoke small, quite unnecessary confrontations, now that his coveted stewardship was over for another year. My mother said he shouldn't be smoking. He shook the paper and said he'd smoke all he liked, then glared at her in a manner reminiscent of Erskine Phibbs. Outside Mr Coogan's, the Child of Prague lay on its side on a bed of broken flowers. Doaty lifted it up and caressed its head in pity.

'Oh dear, Mr Coogan,' she said, 'the poor head's come off.'

Mr Coogan shuddered palely, looking away as he picked up the dead flowers.

'I must have forgot all about it, Doaty.'

'Yes, Mr Coogan, that must be what happened. You must have forgotten all about it.'

She smiled at him and he shuffled inside. I stared at Doaty as she whispered something to Mr James. Erskine Phibbs was standing by the ash pit – as if he had forgotten his gravel patch had ever existed. Doaty affixed some pins to the back of her hair and then came over and stood beside me. My pulse raced as her pink lips parted.

'It's all right, soldier,' she whispered, 'you don't have to worry. From this day on we'll all of us be together.'

It was after three o' clock in the Balla Arms when I was awakened by the kindly night porter, who informed me that he had received a message from the hospital – to the effect that I ought to contact them as soon as possible. As it turned out, the news proved positive. My mother had rallied in the most extraordinary fashion, I was told. She had always been resilient in that respect, I knew, and when I saw the renewed vitality in her eyes as I entered the ward, a spectacular joy gripped me. I don't know how long we spent together that night – talking about old times, inevitably returning to the occasion which had meant so much to her, the occasion of my ordination that day in Maynooth, 1970.

'When you joined the order of Melchizedek, my son,' she choked proudly, 'such a day of joy for us all.'

They were beautiful words and I delighted in hearing them.

'I am so proud of you,' she continued, kissing my hands, 'for all you have ever done is bring honour to your town. How are things in England, love? The world has become such a dangerous place. There were car bombs in Iraq – a hundred people have died. They say there'll never be peace there again. You will be careful, won't you son? But God will protect us – He always has.'

'I love you, mother,' I said, as the nurse arrived at my side.

'I'm sorry, Father Cunningham. She really must sleep.'

She died that night and I dreamed of her borne nobly aloft upon a bier, clutching a framed photograph of my ordination ceremony. She departed contented, I'm convinced of that, and never, thank God, got to hear of my unfortunate difficulties. Which amounted to very little, really, in the end. The talk of an internal investigation continued for some time but, eventually, as I'd long suspected, there was only one decision I could ever possibly have made, such was the extent of my guilt, in the face of continuing failure to subjugate my weaknesses. Even afterwards, I'd continued with my visits to Mrs Beggs, whose contempt for me by now was naked. The bishop said he'd be sorry to see me go – that I had done much work I ought to be proud of. They gave me some money and, with the help of the local council, I managed to secure a little flat in a small block – a kind of sheltered housing scheme, although strictly speaking I'm not entitled to it. But nobody interferes and I've attained, I suppose, some measure of contentment. Although inevitably there will be times when I miss the security, that sense of *communion* which is so much a part of the organised church. There are extended periods, however, throughout which I do not permit myself to darken a chapel door. When I'll pray by my window in the hope that he'll forgive me, the Sacred Heart who regards me ruefully with disappointment and pity. As I kneel there, once again, in a state of tortuous confusion, my hands tightly clasped and a rain of tears upon my cheeks. The countenance of Mrs Beggs slowly emerging from the murky interior, lividly painted as she lowers herself onto me, reproachfully informing me that she wholly approves of my abject state, tantalisingly pinning my silver medal to my chest, before flinging her head back to release the wildest music, like some fleeing animal plunging headlong into flame.

# The Talks

## Joseph O'Connor

### 1

His father had become steadily more fretful as he aged. The price of tinned soup, the poor quality of woollens. Snipegrass. The euro. Cancer among the neighbours. The inability of RTE newsreaders to pronounce certain sounds accurately. Unreliable taxi drivers. The immigrants to Dublin.

'I wouldn't mind, only there's so many of them. I don't object to a few. But now every shop you go into, there's a rake of them behind the counter.'

Peter Hanahoe gave no answer. He was concentrating on the road. The car was too hot and he was smoking.

'I don't mean to be prejudiced. It isn't that I don't like them.'

'I know.'

'They're grand people; it isn't that. Hard-working. Lovely manners. Family people, too: they're very good with their children. And you don't see them begging. I never have, anyway. Not like certain gurriers we have of our own. It's just – there's an awful lot of them suddenly. You just feel – I don't know –'

He waited for his father to say what you just felt, but he didn't say anything, only looked ahead of himself at the windscreen. The radio was playing quietly and the glass was beginning to mist. It was almost midnight. He was driving his father into Wicklow.

His father, a retired policeman, was treasurer of a walkers' club that undertook this arduous hike once a year. You started at Glenmalure at one in the morning, slogged overnight into the city, all the way to Dublin Castle, through Greystones, Bray, Killiney, Blackrock, the sleeping suburbs of the south side. It had been named the O'Neill Trek, after a patriot of old, whose absconding from Dublin Castle the walk commemorated – oddly, it seemed to Peter Hanahoe, by reversing the escape route he had taken. As though the walkers wished to re-imprison his ghost.

You couldn't trust a taxi-man to collect you at eleven. No one these days would honour a commitment; that was the problem with Ireland now: inconsistency, no integrity; people only in it for the buck, everyone waiting on the better offer. Peter Hanahoe had offered to collect his father. It would be a way of saying goodbye.

It was raining. He was forty-three. They were headed towards the Salley Gap. In his apartment was a coil of hosepipe he had bought the previous weekend, at the Garden Centre across the dual carriageway from his apartment. He had left it in its shrink-wrap for a couple of days. Tonight, at the apartment, he had opened it.

There was a card of powerful sedatives on the draining board in the kitchen. He had had them a couple of years, since breaking his ankle on ice. There was a garage he had the use of in the car park of the apartment block. He would wait until the neighbours had gone to work.

His father was staring at the facade of the Subaru's radio, which was blinking subtly as though trying to placate something. The midnight news came on but there was a crackle of static. It must be the mountains interfering.

'I suppose they feel lonely. Being so far from where they belong. They must have families over beyond, God love them.'

'Yes.'

'If only there weren't so many of them. We'll be sorry again we're finished. They're in the garage, the Spar; I see them through the windows of the takeaways. Jimmy Dunne has one working for him in the Post Office now. I don't know. I think they're after making a mistake.'

'Who is?'

'The authorities. Fianna Fáil. To let so many come in.'

'There's not so many, really, Dad. Not as many as in New York.'

'I know,' said his father. 'But New York is New York.'

'I suppose it is,' Peter Hanahoe said quietly.

'Exactly,' said his father. 'But who listens?'

2

Since the divorce, Peter Hanahoe, a statistician at a government department, had seen a great deal more of his father. His former wife, Marie-Therese, a lecturer at UCD, had been awarded primary custody of their twins. Peter Hanahoe had them every other weekend and for a month in the summer. It left too much time to be filled.

The time had proved difficult. The separation had been messy. Marie-Therese had moved on, had remarried, was pregnant. It was painful to think of another man living with your children. Other aspects were painful, too, but you couldn't afford to think about those. He had been prescribed daily Prozac for anxiety.

He found it difficult to sleep. He began leaving the hallway lamps on, then the light in the bedroom of his apartment. Solitude in darkness became impossible for him. He would find himself dazed on the balcony at dawn, looking down into the car park, at the trees and SUVs, at the workers in suits leaving early to beat the rush, at the trucks lumbering past from the ferry-port. He had returned to cigarettes after many years without them. His blood pressure, he had been warned, was in the pre-hypertension range.

He had made a fool of himself with a married colleague – they had been among a group of civil servants attending a conference in Galway – and had slept with a journalist acquaintance he had known since UCD days. The college acquaintance had made it clear that there might be something more between them, if they took a little time, got to know one another's lives. In fact their short affair, drink-fuelled and fraught, had ruined even the ghost of the friendship. She had asked him to stop calling. His indecision was too much. He didn't know what he wanted, or even what he didn't want. He was stuck in a moment he couldn't get out of. She advised him to seek professional help.

He missed Marie-Therese. Her companionship, her sparkiness, the sound of her walking around in the mornings. He missed their talks, their long, long talks, and the way she entered a room. On nights she worked at home, he would bring her a coffee in the study. There was something about computer light that made most people ugly, but not her, it made her eyes palely glow. The way she read a newspaper, quietly commenting on the articles, clicking her tongue when she disagreed with what was being written. The aroma of her shampoo, of an Italian moisturiser she used. Her kindliness. Seeing her with the children. Her sense of tact. And he missed her physically, which you were not supposed to say. But it was true. He missed her sexually.

They had been so compatible, he had always felt. Other couples sometimes hinted that their ardour had burned away. There were jokes about it in sitcoms. People phoned radio shows about it. He had several times heard such discussions in the car on his way to work, or on late-night radio at home. It caused sadness for many couples – he could see how it would. It had never happened to him and Marie-Therese.

Their bodies had changed, were not those of teenagers; but her jokey flirtatiousness, the fervour of their deep kisses, he had found as thrilling as ever. And there was an openness that had grown in the sexuality of their marriage; they had been able to talk, to say what gave them pleasure, to ask, to offer, to play. Sex had been part of their comradeship, their amity. At least, that was what he had always thought.

Once, overnighting on a work trip to Belfast, he had telephoned to say goodnight. He had had a few pints; she had drunk a little wine after putting the kids to bed. Neither of them had been able to put down the phone; they had talked for more than an hour. She had asked him to describe the bedroom at the hotel; told him teasingly that she wished she were there with him. Would he like it if she were? Was there a nice big shower? What would he do to her? What would he like done to him? His voice, she told him, sounded sexy down the line. It was a turn-on, she said, just hearing it. If he didn't stop talking, she might not be responsible. His voice was an occasion of sin.

Her soft, low laugh. Should she open her shirt? Did he think the British authorities bugged the phones in Belfast? What would they say if they heard this conversation? Would they be arrested for pervs? Would the tape be played in court? How about if she suggested something very bold indeed? Was he feeling sleepy now or was he game for a dare?

There were flowers on his desk when he arrived back to the office in Dublin. SILVER TONGUED DEVIL said the card.

Awakening alone. Eating breakfast alone. Coming back to the apartment in the evenings. The whine of the lift gliding up and down through the building, the slam of the fire doors on the landings. Bank Holiday weekends in the apartment alone, knowing the whole block was empty, its silence. He had never thought stopping being married would be so fierce; so violent. He found himself welling up at stupid movies.

Often of late, and especially in the mornings, he had the intuition that he would never again feel a sexual intimacy. What he felt about this loss was a kind of shocking grief. Before his divorce, it had never seemed that important, or, rather, so important that you didn't think about its importance very much. It was part of his life with her, lovingly or for fun, like talking; it was a kind of conversation.

He was *jolie-laide*, she used to joke, one of her favourite terms in French, though usually it was employed about women. It meant 'beautiful despite imperfections' or because of them, she said. In his case – and in her own – because of them. He had come to think of his whole marriage as *jolie-laide*, too. But that hadn't been enough to save it.

## 3

Since the divorce he had gained weight. He was uncomfortable in his clothes. A colleague at the Department, one of the new intake, had greeted him one morning with a sleepily amiable nod and the well-intentioned words: 'How's the Bigman?' He had never thought of himself as a big man. It seemed a sentence, a verdict. 'Grand,' he had replied uncertainly. It had disturbed him.

Catching glimpses of his reflection in the windows of shops. Wearing a darker coloured suit, even on warm Dublin days. Women didn't look at him – not that they ever had, much. But now they had a way of seeming to peer straight through him, as though he were street furniture, or weather.

He bought an expensive membership of a gym near his apartment but had only attended twice. His was not the usually stated reason for falling away – the ubiquity of beautiful bodies, the inadequacies of one's own. It was more that he could not deal with the other men in the locker room. Since the divorce, his facility for small talk had gone.

He did not like to be around people; it was the strangest symptom. He had come to find social life a crucifixion. Always he had understood that most conversations are about nothing, but are simply a communication of non-specific goodwill, the willingness to bond, at least temporarily, but it had never been a problem; he had accepted it. He had been one of those men able to construct a friendship around sport, though in fact he had never liked Gaelic, the parochial nonsense that went with it, and secretly he detested rugby and its guffawing devotees, and soccer with its charmless pundits. He was uneasy talking politics or Leinster House gossip, except with a few trusted friends, but most of those had sided with Marie-Therese. The phone in the apartment rarely rang any more. His mobile was hardly worth its rental.

The therapist he saw on Mondays advised him to keep busy. She had once been a nun, he felt sure. There was a thing in the way she talked, a mid-Atlanticism, an argot, that floated up a fog between them. She was 'not into value judgements'. She was into listening 'and hearing'. He found the usages distancing.

Everyone had 'stuff'. Everyone needed to be heard. Everyone had 'an Inner Child', she advised Peter Hanahoe; a core personality, a little version of the self; it was important to 'check on it' often. She gave him pamphlets, self-help books, invitations to seminars, information on training to be a therapist himself. Several of her clients had progressed to becoming therapists – 'progressed' was her word, a value-judgement if ever there was – so long as their own issues had been processed, of course, so long as their baggage had been dealt with. There was a sticker on her window, reading IT'S OKAY NOT TO BE OKAY. Often, he felt okay until he noticed it.

It cost fifty euro to see her. She smiled embarrassedly when he paid, as though the exchange was a compromise, something shameful or corrupt, when to him it was a safety, for the money allowed him to talk and not to feel invaded by her questions. Had he issues around trust? Had he issues around womanness? Where was he at, sexually? Had he tried reiki, or yoga? The increase in his weight: what was that about? What was going on for Little Peter? In some ways, seeing a therapist was not unlike making confession, though in those days you got a penance, not a bill. And the Redemptorists didn't advocate tantric masturbation to the sinners; and often you felt better having confessed.

Keeping busy was something that demanded a lot of effort; it was almost as exhausting as doing nothing. He kept up with contemporary fiction, an old interest from college, read the review sections of the weekend broadsheets, Irish and English, and magazines about art, and *Granta*. He had an aunt, a National Schoolteacher, who had published short stories in regional newspapers: she advised him to write; it was enriching. He bought notebooks, a new computer, but it was still in its box. He was not going to write. It was a ridiculous idea. There was nothing he wanted to say.

He ate lunch, alone, at the National Gallery restaurant. Sometimes, afterwards, he walked the park in Merrion Square, or went into the bookshops on Dawson Street. On those weekends when he didn't have the twins, he went to an exhibition or a reading. Always he went alone.

Lately he had found himself noticing the young. The boys seemed so confident, their clothes cool and expensive. The girls wore those crop-tops, those miniskirts and low-slung jeans. A colleague, a girl from Laois, had had a twenty-fifth birthday party in a nightclub.

He had been dutifully invited, most probably, so he felt, because to leave him uninvited would be rude or tactless, which nobody wanted to be. He wondered if they somehow knew about the overdose, the hospitalisation. It was still a small and gossipy town.

How freely they moved and touched one another as they danced. He was becoming his father, he felt. In work they dressed conservatively; here it was different, the boys wore vests and trainers, you could see the girls' nipples through their tank tops. The lyrics of the rap songs were lurid, misogynistic; but none of them seemed to care.

He had sat at the bar with the rest of the oldsters, drinking too-cold pints of Guinness and wishing you were allowed to smoke. They all drank vodka cocktails. He would never again kiss a girl's abdomen. At forty-three, it was unlikely. You had to face facts.

Very late in the night, they had insisted that he dance with them. They had applauded and cheered him; he had hated it. 'Fair play to you, Peter.' 'Go on, you mad thing.' 'Fatboy Slim, how are you?' One of them had taken a photograph of him on her mobile phone and emailed it around the Department as a joke. He had become the Good Sport you can never imagine weeping. The man who doesn't take himself too seriously.

'Fair balls,' slurred the birthday girl, badly drunk at the end of the night. 'I had you down as a dry shite. But fair balls.'

It had occurred to him to ask if she would consider coming home with him. But he was afraid of what she might say.


# 4

'Everything's all right with you, is it?' his father asked absently, peering at his guidebooks, riffling their pages.

'Grand. Yes. Well: how do you mean?'

'You seem a bit quiet.'

'No. Just tired I suppose.'

'That month you were off work? When you had that virus or whatever. Did they ever get to the bottom of it?'

'It was only a chest thing.'

'Was it asthma?'

'Yes. It was something like that.'

'The fags don't help asthma.'

'I know, Dad. They told me.'

'Would you not give them up again?'

'I will in a while.'

'The fags are the worst lads of all.'

## 5

A number of years previously, a senior colleague had taken maternity leave and asked would he take on one of her duties while she was away. It was something she felt might interest him, a breath of fresh air. He would do it very well, she thought. In the event, she had not returned and so the task had become unofficially his. It was to advise the Taoiseach's officials on which works of art might be exhibited at Government Buildings. The artworks were kept in various places around the city – some on public display, others stored by the Office of Public Works. It was a part of the job he liked and regarded as important. They changed around the holdings every nine months or so. He looked forward to it; felt involved in something good.

He enjoyed drawing up the lists, discussing them with the Taoiseach's officials. He gave it scrupulous attention; if anything, too much. He would clip essays on Irish artists from scholarly journals, photocopy reviews for the files. In the old days he had discussed the selections with Marie-Therese, too, whose post-doctorate had been on nineteenth-century landscape. It seemed valuable – how ridiculous, he was not sentimental, was uneasy about nationalisms, had always voted Labour or Green – but somehow it had seemed to him not entirely a sham: this image of Ireland as a place where art was respected. He had seen it as an idea to which most could give an allegiance, in that sense, a sort of presidency.

One afternoon, at work, during a session of the Northern Ireland talks, he had gone to a corridor in Government Buildings to retrieve a file of photostats he had left by the water cooler. Tony Blair was in the passageway looking at a Louis le Brocquy portrait. His bodyguards were at a distance, in the French windows that led to the garden. His glance met Peter Hanahoe's and he nodded towards the picture as though taken by some aura it transmitted.

'Very striking,' said Tony Blair.

'Isn't it,' said Peter Hanahoe.

'Who is it? O'Casey?'

'It's actually Beckett.'

'I thought it was O'Casey.'

'Yes, there's a resemblance right enough.'

'Forgive me; we haven't met.'

'Peter Hanahoe. You're welcome to Dublin.'

'You're with the Taoiseach's Department, are you?'

'Just a penpusher upstairs.'

'My wife's father was an actor. He liked O'Casey and Wilde. A lot of those Irish guys. I don't know much about Beckett. But I rather like the picture. Rather grabs one's attention as one passes.'

'He wrote *Waiting for Godot*,' Peter Hanahoe found himself saying.

Tony Blair looked at him.

'Quite,' he said.

## 6

'Marie-Therese rang the house,' his father said quietly. 'It was on Tuesday or Wednesday. I hope you don't mind.'

What was this? he wondered. Any mention of her name made him uneasy. It was always hard to know what to say to it.

'It isn't my business any more who she calls.'

'It was Mam's anniversary. You probably forgot.'

The gears ground lowly and he re-engaged them. One of the wipers was squeaking on the glass.

'I went up to the grave Tuesday,' his father said. 'I left flowers from you, as well. I like to see it kept right.'

His father in a cemetery with a bundle of chrysanthemums and a house-key to scrape off the moss.

'You might get up at the weekend. It'd be nice if you could. Or if you're passing in the meantime, just run in for a minute.'

'I'll try, Dad.'

'I knew you would. I told her you would.'

'Marie-Therese? What the hell business is it of hers?'

'No, your mam, of course. I told her you'd drop by if you were passing.'

He was uneasy when his father conversed in this way, because he did not understand it, found it vaguely embarrassing. He felt no connection whatever to that view of the dead. His mother was not listening to anything.

Shame flickered up in him, the guilt of the escapee. Soon, he himself would hear nothing. He realised – strange thought – that he was not afraid. If there was pain, which he doubted, he would endure it.

'There was something I wanted to say to you, Peter. About Mam and me.'

His father did not speak for a moment or two, and when finally he did, his voice was apprehensive, as though he had learned what he was about to say by memorising it from a book, but was troubled now the moment had come to speak it.

'You didn't talk about certain subjects, not in those days. But yes: I loved her. And she loved me, too. She was the most beautiful girl I ever saw. I mean a beautiful-looking person, as well as everything else. It was important to us both. In our marriage, I mean. To find the other person attractive. Do you know what I mean? I'm probably not putting it very well.'

'I know what you mean,' Peter Hanahoe said.

'The pill was great that way, you know, when it came in. Well, we didn't like to use it, because the priests were full of guff; but we thought, after all, it's our lookout what we do. I wanted to say that to you. To you and your brother. You were very much loved. You were children of love.'

They did not speak again for five or ten minutes. He couldn't think of any way in. Lately his father had been talking like this: focused on the past, on things that couldn't be changed now. As though some very simple statement needed to be made but could only be advanced in camouflage.

'A woman can lose her confidence in the house all day. It's better for women, now, when you think of how it is for them. No running to a husband for an allowance or that. If she wants a pair of tights, or a hair-do, or whatever. I often think, with your mam, if she'd had a little job, it might have given her an interest. Did you ever think that?'

'About Mam?'

'Yes.'

'I don't know. I suppose I didn't. She seemed happy enough at home.'

'A little job in a shop. She liked being around people.'

'I think she was happy at home.'

His father fell quiet again. Peter Hanahoe was grateful. He did not want to talk about his mother, or Ireland, or society, or progress, or anything else. Most of all, he did not want to talk about Marie-Therese and he felt that his father did.

There was a dinner party they had attended at the house of a friend. A Dublin literary journalist had been at the table, entertaining the company outrageously. Luas, Lapdancer, Nigerian, Café Latte, Immigrant, Gridlock, Asylum Seeker, Refugee, Property Prices, Sushi, Paedophile Priest – there were a couple of other words but Peter couldn't remember them all. Any piece of Irish fiction containing even one of these words should be banned, the journalist had declaimed. If you uttered the phrase 'Celtic Tiger' – if you even thought about that phrase – you should be imprisoned on an Aran Island 'with Mary Harney'. The phrase 'Mary Harney' should itself be verboten, but he was claiming a special exemption, the journalist said.

They were laughing, a bit drunk. It was good to be home. No one in New York conversed so freely and mischievously. It was the thing they had missed during their year in New York: the relaxed smart-arsery of Dubliners. It was the night everything changed. They'd been driving home from the party. Often, he was to wonder what would have happened if they had not gone to it, and if anything would have played out differently.

She'd been here in the car. In the seat where his father sat now. She'd been wearing a jacket he'd bought her in Manhattan: dark green with a belt, it was expensive. She was smoking with the window rolled halfway down, her hand trailing out with the cigarette.

There was something on her mind. It had better be said. There wasn't a right time to say it.

'Fuck off,' he laughed, when she told him what it was.

But Marie-Therese was not laughing.

She was moving out at the weekend. It was something she had to do. For a long time she had been unhappy; it wasn't Peter's fault. There was something she needed to deal with, something in her past. Since becoming a mother, it had sharpened. A while before meeting him, something had happened that had hurt her; she would not say what it was, it had happened in her second year at Oxford. She had thought she was over it, but in fact she was not. She could not get past it; and the marriage had become part of it, somehow, for there must be a reason why she had never been able to tell him and still could not do so now.

The separation might be temporary; she could not say at the moment. She was sorry for the deception, the lies. She did not know how it had happened, but she did not love him any more. She could not go on pretending. There was only one life. He was a very good man. He deserved better than she could offer. No, there wasn't any point in counselling.

He realised, through the pulses of drink-fuzzed shock, that he would always remember the words she was saying, and the thought had struck him as intensely strange, for most life-changing moments are only recognisable as such in retrospect, where this one had the scald of present tense.

She was talking about the twins, about rental agencies for apartments, the closing of their joint bank account, for Christ's sake, the bills. There would be no need for lawyers, at least not initially. The house would probably have to be sold. What had cored him was the extent of her preparedness to go. Clearly she had been planning for months.

They were drunk. There were tears. He should not have been driving. He was aware of not knowing what to say. He was holding her hand. A Garda car blurred by. Its blue light was flashing towards Wicklow.

They had somehow begun to kiss and it had quickly become passionate, probably, he thought now, because they had been drinking. He remembered unbuttoning her jeans, her fingertips on his wrist, the tremor of her body as she orgasmed. She had given him oral sex; they had driven home afterwards, paid the neighbour's girl who sat for them, locked up the house.

She had taken off her jeans and top when he came in from the gate and was sitting by the empty fireplace in her underwear. She had a joint in her hand; he did not know how she had come by it, but she offered it wordlessly, as though it was a token of something, and he took a deep, obliterating pull. Her mascara was smudged: she was cleaning it off with a tissue. Nothing was said for what seemed a long time. The television was on, but its sound had been turned down very low. They made love again at some point – he does not remember everything. She was kneeling, he was behind her, kissing the hardness of her shoulder blades, a position neither of them had tried with any other lover, they had often laughed, and she was coming very hard, and, then, so was he. And the mascara-stained tissues in the fireplace.

In the morning she told him, again, that she would leave at the weekend. What had happened last night was goodbye.

# 7

His father opened the glovebox and took out the map, while the wipers cut steadily through the drizzle.

'We're lost,' he said.

'We're not. It's down here.'

'We should've turned at the crossroads.'

'Then why didn't you tell me?'

'I thought you knew.'

'If I'd known, I'd've turned.'

'I couldn't see with the rain. I'm after forgetting my glasses.'

*'For Christ's sake, Dad. Do I have to do every fucking thing?'*

He drove on abruptly, headlights turned full, while his father examined the atlas. The newsreader came on at half-past midnight with a breaking story about a murder in Scotland. A mother, a successful businesswoman, had killed three of her children, for no reason anyone knew. Later she had turned the shotgun on herself. The police had to batter down the door.

He switched the channels quickly; a classical music station came on. Since the divorce, he found it unbearable when such stories were recounted. It frightened him, what they made him feel.

When he was married it had seemed that the world was somehow distant, that its tragedies and evils were at an unseeable remove, like the things beyond the gleam of his headlights now, as he gunned the heavy car through the mud. You regretted them; Christ, yes, you had a stake in the future; and the thought of having to explain them to the children you protected was grotesque; but you didn't truly dwell on such horrors too long, because people needed you not to. Since Marie-Therese had gone, the world had edged closer. Nobody needed him now.

Hedgerows went past. A signpost for Arklow. A line of travellers' caravans under dreeping trees. Pearls of bright rain in cold yellow halogen. It was then that he realised his father was crying.

He stopped the car. A donkey peered over a fence. Rain was spattering on the roof.

'I'm sorry. I didn't mean it. I shouldn't have spoken to you that way.'

'You're all right. I'm the one who's sorry. It just took me aback.'

'I don't know what's the matter. I've been finding it hard to sleep.'

'You're upset. It's Marie-Therese. I shouldn't have told you she rang. She asked me not to let on to you. She knew you wouldn't like it.'

'I'm taking this stuff Prozac. It's for depression, anxiety. I don't know. I feel knackered all the time.'

'She's worried about you, Peter.'

'It's lately that happened to her.'

'She mentioned – it's none of my business – but she mentioned, just in passing, that you didn't see the kids this last while now.'

'I haven't seen them in two months.'

'Well, you're busy.'

'It isn't that.'

'So, what is it, son? Is everything all right? If there's a way I can help you, or you want to have a talk for a while . . .'

'I find it a bit much,' he interrupted. 'Seeing them, I mean. I can't take it any more. Mooching around town, or a movie or something, then dropping them off at teatime like a box of eggs. They tend to get upset. Tom, especially. It seems hard for him to understand. Then that upsets Emma.'

'Kids need their father.'

Peter Hanahoe was silent.

'Would you not bring them over?'

'OK. If you're sure.'

'God, how would I not be? Bring them up to me at the weekend. I'll get in a tea for them. They can Lewis the piano.'

It was one of his father's favourite jokes about his grandchildren, that they played the piano standing up, like Jerry Lee Lewis. They would not be playing the piano this Saturday afternoon. They would not be playing at all.

'I'll bring them,' Peter Hanahoe said, and drove on through the darkness. You could see the moon through trees.

# 8

In the car park of the pub the walkers were circled around a brazier, their oilskins gleaming in the rain. They looked buoyed, expectant, like children on Christmas Eve. One of them was passing out sandwiches.

'Can you give me a dig-out with the stuff? I've one of the lads' rucksacks in the back.'

'Yes,' said Peter Hanahoe. 'It looks heavy.'

They weren't prepared for the wind, which rushed up against them like a wave, making his trouser-legs flap, and he shivered. Wind slapped his back like a hardswung pillow. His father introduced him to some of the walkers; there were jokes about the weather, their masochism. He felt like a parent leaving his son to school. It was good to see his father belonging.

It was nearly one o'clock. It was time to go. He felt he might break down if he stayed.

'I'll be seeing you, Dad.'

'On Saturday. Yes.'

'On Saturday. Right. Good luck.'

They shook hands rather formally, but that was all right. His father was not a hugger. Anyway, the walkers were watching.

'You're a good lad,' his father said. 'Thanks for tonight. I'd have been up the creek without you, that's the truth.'

'I just want you to know: everything is OK for me, Dad. Don't be worried about anything. All right?'

'Are you sure now, Peter? There's nothing going on?'

'You're not to go thinking anything bad. Everything is great with me. Everything is very clear.'

'You just look a bit stressed. I don't know. Not yourself. Would you come with me, do you think? On the walk?'

'No, Dad. I'm tired. I've work in the morning.'

'Wouldn't it be a bit of crack? One of the lads here could kit you out. We all bring spare kit on a night like this. And I'd love to have your company along.'

'I can't. There's the car. I wouldn't want to leave it.'

'Sure, what about it, when you think? Isn't it only a car? We could get a taxi down for it tomorrow in the morning. It would only take an hour. Would you not?'

They stood in the drizzle. The walkers were watching them. He was picturing the apartment, the coil of hosepipe on the table, the masking tape, the sedatives, the notes. He had written one for Marie-Therese, saying it wasn't her fault, he had always loved her, wished her nothing but the best, was sorry for having done such a violent thing, but life had become unbearable now. There was one for his father and one each for the twins, the latter not to be opened, he had written on the envelopes, before they reached sixteen. If they had forgotten him by then, Marie-Therese could destroy the notes. Whatever she thought was best.

'Starter's orders,' said his father. 'The lads are getting going.'

'You were a great father to us, Dad. I don't know if I ever said it. I know it was hard for you. All those nights you did overtime. You're a wonderful man, I think so anyway. I could never thank you enough for what you did.'

'God bless us, there's a spake,' said Michael Hanahoe. 'That beats Banagher now.'

'I mean it, anyway. So now you know.'

'Would you not come with me, son? We have to get on while it's not too bad.'

'Another time, Dad. Not tonight.'

'Well, there'll be other nights again. Drive safely. God bless.'

'God bless, Dad. Thanks for everything.'

He drove slowly over Wicklow, through the sleeping suburbs of the south side, pausing a few minutes by the harbour at Dun Laoghaire. Everything was quiet. The lighthouse beam glinted. He walked a way along the pier, down as far as the bandstand, where he smoked two of his last three cigarettes. The security camera at a garage captured him at quarter to four, buying chocolate and a bottle of water. Shortly before dawn, he returned to the apartment. He waited for his neighbours to go to work.

# Yesterday's Weather

## ANNE ENRIGHT

Hazel didn't want to eat outside – the amount of suncream you had to put on a baby and the way he kept shaking the little hat off his head. Also there were flies, and her sister-in-law Margaret didn't have a steriliser – why should she? – so Hazel would be boiling bottles and cups and spoons to beat the band. Then John would mooch up to her at the cooker and tell her to calm down – so not only would she have to do all the work, she would also have to apologise for doing all the work when she should be having a good time, sitting outside and watching bluebottles put their shitty feet on the teat of the baby's bottle while everyone else got drunk in the sun.

In the hotel foyer, she remembered, there was a tall man who handled his baby like a newborn lamb; setting it down on its stomach to swim its way across the carpet outside the residents' bar. And Hazel had, briefly, wanted to be married to him instead.

Now she grabbed a bowl of potato salad with the arm that held the baby and a party pack of crisps with the other, hoofed the sliding door open and stepped over the chrome lip on to the garden step. The baby buried his face in her shoulder and wiped his nose on her T-shirt. He had a summer cold, so Hazel's top looked like slugs had been crawling all over it. There was something utterly depressing about being covered in snot. It was just not something she had ever anticipated. She would go and change but the baby would not be put down and John, when she looked for him, was playing rounders with his niece and nephews under the apple trees. He saw her and waved. She put down the bowl and the crisps on the garden table, and shielded baby's head against the hard ball.

The baby's skin, under the downy hair, breathed a sweat so fine it was lost as soon as she lifted her hand. Women don't even know

121

they miss this, until they get it; this smoothness, seeing as men were so abrasive or – what were they like? – she tried to remember the comfort of John's belly with the hair stroked all one way, or the shocking silk of his dick, even, bobbing up under her hand, but he was so lumbering and large, these days, and it was always too long since he had shaved.

'Grrrr . . .' said Margaret, beside her, rummaging a bag of crisps from out of the party pack. This is what happens when you have kids, Hazel thought, you eat all their food – while Margaret's children, as far as she could see, ate nothing at all. They ate nothing whatsoever. Even so, everyone was fat.

'Come and eat,' Margaret shouted down the garden, while Hazel turned the baby away from the sudden noise.

'Boys! Steffie! Please! Come and eat.'

Her voice was solid in the air, you could almost feel it hitting the side of the baby's head. But her children ignored her – John too. He had lost his manners since coming home. He pretended his sister did not exist, or only barely existed.

'How's the job coming?' she might say and he'd say:

'. . . Fine', like *What a stupid question*.

It made Hazel panic, slightly. Though he was not like that with her. At least, not yet. And he lavished affection on his sister's three little children; he threw them up in the air, and he caught them, coming down. Still, Hazel found it hard to get her breath, like the baby was still inside her, pushing up against her lungs, making everything tight.

But the baby was not inside her. The baby was in her arms.

'Come and eat!' shouted Margaret again. 'Come on!'

Still, no one found it necessary to hear. Hazel would shout herself, but that would definitely make the baby cry. She stood by the white wrought-iron table, set with salads and fizzy orange and cut ham, and she watched this perfect picture of a family at play, while beside her Margaret said:

'God between me and prawn-flavoured Skips,' ripping open one of the crinkly packets and diving in.

The ball rolled past Hazel's foot. John looked up the length of the garden at her.

'Hey!' he called.

'What?'

'The ball.'

'Sorry?'

'The ball!'

It seemed to Hazel that she could not hear him, even though his words were quite clear to her. Or that she could not be heard, even though she was saying nothing at all. She found herself walking down the garden and she did not know why, until she was standing in front of him, with the baby thrust out at arm's length.

'Take him,' she said.

'What?'

'Take the baby.'

'What?'

'Take the fucking baby!'

The baby dangled between them, so shocked that when John fumbled it into his arms, the sound of wailing was a relief – at least it turned the volume in her head back on. But Hazel was already walking back up to the ball. She picked it up and slung it low towards the apple trees.

'Now. There's your ball.' Then she turned to go inside.

John's father was at the sliding door, his stick clutched high against his chest, as he managed his way down the small step. He looked at her and smiled so sweetly that Hazel knew he had just witnessed the scene on the lawn. Also that he forgave her. And this was so unbearable to her – that a complete stranger should be able to forgive her most intimate dealings in this way – that Hazel swung past the tiny old man as she went inside, nearly pushing him against the glass.

John found her hunkered on the floor in the living room searching through the nappy bag. She looked up. He was not carrying the baby.

'Where's the baby?' she said.

'What's wrong with you?' he said.

'I have to change my top. What did you do with the baby?'

'What's wrong with your top?'

*Snots.* Hazel could not bring herself to say the word; it would make her cry, and then they would both laugh.

But there was no clean T-shirt in the bag. They were staying in a hotel, because Hazel had thought it would be easier to get the baby asleep away from all the noise. But there's always a teething ring left in the cool of the minibar, or a vital plastic spoon in the hotel sink, and so of course there was no T-shirt in the bag. And, anyway, John would not let her bring the baby back to the hotel for a nap.

'He's fine. He's fine,' he kept saying as the baby became ever more cranky and bewildered, screaming in terror if she tried to put him down.

'Why should he be unhappy?' she wanted to say, 'he has had so few days in this world. Why should the unhappiness start here?'

Instead she kept her head down, and rummaged for nothing in the nappy bag.

'Go and get the baby,' she said.

'He's with Margaret, he's fine.'

Hazel had a sudden image of the baby choking on a prawn-flavoured Skip – but she couldn't say this of course, because if she said this, then she would sound like a snob. It seemed that, ever since they had arrived in Clonmel, there was a reason not to say every single thought that came into her head.

'I hate this,' she said, eventually, sinking back from the bag.

'What?'

'All of it.'

'Hazel,' he said, 'we are just having a good time. This is what people do when they have a good time.'

And she would have cried then, for being such a wrong-headed, miserable bitch, were it not for a quiet thought that crossed her mind. She looked up at him.

'No, you're not,' she said.

'What?'

'You are not having a good time.'

'Sure,' he said, 'whatever you say', and turned to go.

Margaret hadn't, in fact, asked the baby to suck a prawn-flavoured Skip. She had transformed the baby into a gurgling stranger, sitting on the brink of her knee and getting its hands clapped. The baby's brown eyes were dark with delight, and his mouth was fizzing with smiles and spit. At least it was, until he heard Hazel's voice, when he turned, and remembered who his mother was, and started to howl.

'Well, don't say you didn't like it,' said Hazel, taking him on to her shoulder, feeling betrayed.

'Sorry,' said Margaret, 'I was dying to have a go.'

'Oh any time,' said Hazel, archly. 'You can keep him if you like,' listening already to her housewife's camp.

Why not? She sat down at the table and threw a white baby cloth over the worst of the slug trails on her chest and lifted her face to the weak Easter sun.

'How's the new house?' said Margaret.

'Oh, I don't know,' said Hazel. 'You can't get anything done.'

'Five years,' said Margaret. 'Five years I have been trying to get carpet for the back bedrooms.'

'I know what you mean.'

'I mean five years I've been trying to get *to the shop* to look at the carpet books to start *thinking* about carpet for the back bedrooms.'

'What did you used to have?' said Hazel, then realised she shouldn't ask this, because it was John's parents' house, and talking about the old carpet was talking about his dead mother, and God knows what else.

'I mean, did you have lino or boards, or what?'

'I couldn't look at them,' said Margaret. 'I got down on my hands and knees and I got – you know – a claw hammer, and I prised them up.'

Hazel looked at the laughing children running after John, who was also laughing.

'The dirt,' said Margaret.

'John!' said Hazel, 'teatime. Now please.' Then she said to her sister-in-law, 'A friend of mine found amazing stuff on the Internet. Stripes and picture rugs, and I don't know what else.'

'Really,' said Margaret, and started to butter a round of bread.

John's father turned to them, and either shook his fist, or just lifted his hand – he had such a bad tremor, it was hard to tell. And this was another thing that Hazel could not figure out: what part of him was affected by the Parkinson's, or was it Parkinson's at all? Was his speech funny? Truth be told, she never understood a word he said.

'Hffash en silla?'

'Well, they're kids, Daddy,' said Margaret without a blink – so maybe it was just her, after all. They watched him for a while, poking at the flower bed with his stick.

'He used to love his sweet pea along that wall,' like the man was already dead.

Hazel said nothing.

'Will you take a bite to eat, Daddy, pet?' but he ignored her, like all the rest.

Hazel had a sudden pang for her little garden in Lucan. The seeded grass was sprouting, and the tulips were about to bloom. She had planted the bulbs the week they got the keys: kneeling on the front path, seven months pregnant, digging with the little shovel from the fire irons; a straight line from the gate to the door of fat, red tulips, the type you get in a park – 'a bit municipal' as her mother had said, squinting at the pack – that were now flaming red at the tips, like little cups of green fire.

'That's what I love about this place,' she said. 'This wonderful stretch of garden.'

'Yes,' said Margaret, carefully.

'John. Divorce! Now!' shouted Hazel, and he finally brought the laughing children to the tableside.

The baby didn't cry when she shouted. That was something she hadn't known, that the baby didn't actually mind shouting. Or maybe he just didn't mind hers.

Still, it was an advance.

'Who wants ham?' Hazel said to the kids; loading it on to the bread, helping out.

'I don't like ham,' said Stephanie, who was nearly four.

'No?'

'No I don't like it.'

'I don't like ham,' they were all saying it now, her big brother and her little brother. 'I don't *like* ham.' It was all a bit intense, Hazel thought, and accusatory.

'I think you are confusing me with someone who gives a fuck,' she said – changing at the last moment, of course, to 'someone who *cares* whether you like ham or not'.

John gave her a quick glance. The child, Stephanie, gazed at her with blank and sophisticated eyes.

'Maybe a little bit of ham?' said Hazel.

'I don't think so,' said Stephanie.

'Right.'

John picked an apple out of the pile on the table.

'A is for?' he said, holding it high.

'Answer,' said Stephanie. 'A is for A-A-Answer', and the children laughed, even though they didn't quite know what the joke was. They laughed on and on, and then a bit more, until they had used up every scrap of laughter they had.

'How do you spell "wrong"?' said Kenneth, the eldest.

'W-R-O-N-G,' said Hazel.

'W is for Wrong,' he said. 'W is for Wrong Answer', and they were off again; this amazing, endless sound, like a flock of friendly birds – and this time the baby joined in.

He was asleep before they reached the hotel. The weather had changed and they carried him through a wind-whipped car park that did not even make him stir. Nor did he wake up in the room, when Hazel prised him out of the car seat – so she lay him on the bed as he was, profoundly asleep, in a dirty nappy and milk-encrusted Babygro.

'He'll wake up in a minute,' she said. 'He needs a feed.' But he still didn't wake up: not for his feed, not when John went down to the bar for drinks. He slept through the remains of a film on the telly and another round of drinks, and he slept through the sound of his parents screaming at each other from either side of the bed where he lay. It blew up from nowhere.

'And you can tell your fucking sister that I don't want her fucking house.'

'No one says you want it.'

'Jesus, sometimes I think you're just pretending to be thick and sometimes I think you actually are thick. You can't talk about the carpets without her thinking what you'll put down once the old man is dead.'

'Oh you are,' he said, with his voice quite trembly. 'Oh you really are . . .'

'You fucking bet I am.'

'No, well done. Well done.'

'Oh shut up.'

'Carpet is it? I thought you were talking about my father.'

'Whatever.'

'I thought you were talking about my father, there, for a minute.'

'Well, I am not talking about your father. That is exactly what I am not talking about. You are the one who is talking about your father. Actually. Or not talking about him. Or whatever passes in your fucking family for *talking*.'

'You are such an uppity cunt, you know that?'

'Yes, I am. Yes, I fucking am. And I don't want your fat sister's fat house.'

'Well, actually, it's not her house.'

'Actually, if you don't mind, I don't want to talk about whose house it is. We can get our own house.'

'We have our own house.'

'A proper fucking house!!!'

Hazel was so angry she thought she might pop something, or have some style of a prolapse; her body, after the baby, being a much less reliable place. Meanwhile, the reason they needed a house in the first place slept on. His blissful flesh rose and fell. His mouth smiled.

The baby slept like he knew just what he was doing. The baby slept like he was eating sleep; his front stiff with old food and his back soft with shit. He slept through the roaring and the thrown hairbrush, and the storming of his father off to the residents' bar. He slept through the return of his father twenty seconds later to say something very level and very telling, and the double-fisted assault as his mother pushed him back out to the corridor crying that he could sleep in the fucking bar. He slept through his mother's anguished weeping, the roar of the taps, and the sad slosh and drip of her body shifting in the bath. It was, in fact, only when Hazel had fallen asleep, crawling for a moment in under the covers, that the baby decided to wake up and scream. Maybe it was the silence that woke him. Mind you, his screaming sounded the same as every other night's screaming, she thought, so it was impossible to know how much he had been damaged by it all; by the total collapse of his world and of the love that made him. Could anger hurt him, when he did not yet know what it was?

Hazel plugged his roars with the bottle that was still floating, forgotten, in the hotel kettle. She undid the poppers on his Babygro, as he sucked, and extracted him from it, one limb at a time. She reached between his soft legs to undo the poppers of his vest, which had a wet brown stain across the back, and she rolled the vest carefully under itself to keep the shit on the inside. When the vest was high enough, she pushed two baby wipes down into the nappy to stop the leak. All of this while the baby sat in her naked lap, with her left hand propping up the bottle and his eyes on hers.

The baby was huge – maybe it was because she had nothing on. He seemed twice as big as the last time. Hazel felt like she kept losing this baby, and getting someone new. She thought that she would fall in love with the baby if only it would stay still, just for a minute, but the baby never did stay still. Sometimes it seemed like it was all around her, like there was nothing in her world *except* the baby, but every time she looked straight at the baby, or tried to look straight at the baby . . . whatever it was, just wasn't there.

She was looking at him now.

She still clung to it, whatever it was. She still hoped and hung on. Was this enough? Was this the way you loved a baby?

The line of milk pulsed and bubbled as it sank down into the teat, and the baby started to suck air. Hazel pulled the empty bottle out with a pop and set him on her shoulder, holding him with her forearms now, because she thought there might be shit on her hands.

The baby was full, his belly taut. She would get some wind out of him, and then clean up. Meanwhile, the feel of his bare skin against her own made Hazel vague with pleasure. She brushed her cheek against his fine hair, and the baby belched fantastically down the skin of her back.

'Oh! so clever,' she said, dipping and turning around. 'Oh! so clever,' dipping and turning back again. She did it a few more times, just to get the weight and poise of it, with the fat baby against her fat chest, and her crossed hands dangling beneath his bum. Dip and turn, dip and turn. The baby's cheek a millimetre away from her own cheek – a hair's breath, that is what that was called. A hair's breath.

Outside, the wind had picked up.

*Rock a bye baby*, she sang in a whisper, *on the tree top*.

She was nearly out of wipes – she would have to dunk a hotel towel in the sink and use that, no matter who had to pick it up, or use it afterwards. God, this baby business brought you very low, she thought, and turned with a smile to the opening door.

They were shattered when they got home.

John drove like the road could feel his tyres; like the tyres could feel the road; like the whole world was as tender as they were. At Monasterevin, he reached his hand to touch her cheek, and she held it there with the flat of her own hand while, in the back of the car, the baby still slept.

When they pulled into the driveway, Hazel saw that her tulips had been blown down – at least the ones that had opened first. She wondered if the storm had hit here too, and how strong was that wind anyway – was it a usual sort of wind? What would she be able to grow, here? She tried to think of a number she could ring, or a site online, but there was nowhere she could find what she needed to know. It was all about tomorrow: no one ever described yesterday's weather.

# In the Form of Fiction

## AIDAN MATHEWS

Afterwards the two of them went for a coffee in a coffeeshop in Palo Alto. They sat together in a pine-wood carrel under the anachronistic television set, and one or other of them signalled to the waitress to mute the volume, which she did, so that the semi-omniscient narrator could hear them think.

Actually, the coffee shop was only two doors up/down, depending on direction, from the cinema, but you would not necessarily know from a reference to a multiplex called the Emerald that it was located in California and not in County Limerick, say, especially when the film they were watching was a Baltic movie with subtitles and many of the audience, statistically if not socio-culturally, were South East Asians. Not that I have anything against South East Asians. I make that disclaimer at the very outset.

Anyhow, she had a sorbet and he had lemon tea. We are back in the coffee shop. They were communicating quite well, he thought. But it had been subject-verb-object since the start. They had been able to set aside the three tedious stages of gnosis, agnosis and negotiation.

For the record I have nothing against Balts, either. In fact, I have never met one and I do not particularly want to.

'Actually,' he said, 'I'm going to have a cappuccino.' That was because saying the sentence gave him conversational access to an anecdote that came into his mind while he was squeezing the lemon into the glass. Otherwise there would be no intelligible transition, and connections matter. If you do not connect consecutively, you end up not shaving. You end up sleeping in your clothes. This is true.

'Would a cappuccino not keep you awake?' said Beth. She has to have a name, but it is/was not necessarily hers. Besides, pronouns panic at a certain point in time. They experience a vertigo not a thousand miles from Asperger's, a remote, immobilised, concussive, far-fetched focus.

'Only caffeine makes my heart beat faster now,' Peter said. There was the risk of a non sequitur here, but he might forget to say it later on. So he said it at this stage. Then he remarked, or perhaps he made the remark after he had bought and paid for the coffee, and brought it back to the table to avoid tipping the waitress, 'Do you know the Capuchins?'

'Uh, uh,' Beth said, which is to be construed as an amiable negative. Not that there was any negativity in the woman I think I am going to call Beth Ann instead of Beth, because Beth Ann is easier to say than Beth, and I have to name her a fair few times before the end of her say in the story, which is sooner than you might think. Not that I have anything against her. I respect her very much as a person, and have done so from the commencement of the narrative.

'Wait,' she said. 'Are they monkeys who look after paralysed people? They can brush their teeth. I don't know about the toilet so much.'

'No,' he said. 'They're priests with beards. In Ireland, they run parishes because of the shortage of priests.'

'Shortage of priests with or without beards?' she said. But that could just have been her sense of humour, dark and *demi-mondaine*. She had had two Hawaiian Anchor Steam beers at the cinema, one before the film and one during the intermission, which was why she had had to go to the toilet for most of the trial scene and two flashbacks. In fact, it was a bit disgusting to think of her mopping her bush with three or four folded perforations of Charmin toilet paper, with her thong down around her espadrilles and one or two corkscrew hairs embedded in the crusted cerise gusset. He was not going to think about that for one moment.

'Go on,' she said. 'I'm listening.'

Maybe she was Jewish or Mennonite. If she were, then rabbis and Mennonite elders have beards, so that she would logically draw a straight line, the shortest distance between two points, leading from religious life to facial growth. Not that Peter had anything against Jews or Mennonites. They are great when you get to know them, but the thing is, you never do get to know them. You are always made to feel like an outsider.

'The point is,' he said, 'they call their acolytes cappuccinos.' And to think that the cappuccino which got him to his paragraph had set him back three dollars, fifty cents. It was outrageous, and without waitress service, either. That in itself was a complete non sequitur.

'What are acolytes?' she asked him. Well, it was a question. *Asked* is appropriate. *Asked* is all right. Also it is vernacular. Creative writing classes go on and on about synonyms: 'You've said *road* already. What about avenue, boulevard, cul-de-sac, via dolorosa?'

'Altar-servers,' he told her. This, by the way, is elegant variation. You can find it on the Modern Languages Association style-sheet. It is no great mystery. 'Acolytes are altar-servers.'

'And altar-servers are . . .?' Beth queried.

The coffee was lukewarm already. He was going to bring it straight back. Peter felt momentarily yet momentously embittered and disheartened. If he were the president, he would press the button before any of the bodyguards could stop him. Besides, they would be looking at everybody except the president. So much for Central American Intelligence. It is a joke.

'Miss,' he said. Well, he said it out loud. You could say he called, but obviously in the vocal sense and not in the vocational. He didn't drop by. It wasn't Yahweh calling Samuel. Of course, the irony is that the waitress was no miss. She was a mizz. She had probably been shagged a thousand times. And was she going to service him? No way. That was because he had gone to the counter for the coffee, to circumvent the gratuity.

'You're always talking about priests,' said Beth Ann. 'You talked about priests before the film. You talked about priests during the film. Here we are, the film is over, the coffee shop is closing, night has fallen, and you are still talking about priests.'

'Well,' said Peter, 'the film was set in a seminary. I am just trying to orchestrate the thematics. After all, I am supposed to be a sexually inexperienced male who impersonates a religious vocation precisely in order to attract rogue females for the purposes of fellatio.'

'Are you going to be a priest?' said Beth Ann to Peter. I am building up to something big in an ascending series of disclosures and deferrals. Bear with me.

He needn't have bought the cappuccino at all. That was the last laugh, but his disheartenment lifted like a migraine, which is rather nice when it happens and even nicer when you put it that way. His embitterment, ditto.

'Yes,' he said. 'I am going to be a priest. I am going to be a priest unless, of course, some beautiful woman bewitches me with her toilette.'

He had intended to say 'talents' but the cross-rhyme between 'bewitch' and 'toilette' is very hard to resist if you have been born and bred in the assonantal tradition, and Peter had. Alternatively, he might have said 'mysticism', because of the cross-rhyme between its sibilant fricative and the tarter in-breath of 'bewitch', like the distant lash of a switch on a chatelaine's ass deep in a Transylvanian castle. Besides, what would Beth Ann know about mysticism? She had never even heard of the strict observance of the Capuchins. She needed a few lessons.

Period; new paragraph. Pause in projected public reading of same.

She had been thinking about what he said all through the *explication de texte* that ends with the words 'strict observance of the Capuchins. She needed a few lessons.'

In fact, by way of elucidating recurrent compositional strategies for the interested auditor/lector/reader, the whole business about the assonantal tradition had as its *raison d'être* the provision of a space of silence for Beth Ann in and by means of which to consider and to contemplate Peter's revelation. She was, after all, a fee-paying sophomore and not a postgraduate on scholarship from Dublin.

'From Dublin?' she said. She ran her tongue over her lips hungrily. That was the sorbet. Or was it a non sequitur?

'Yes,' he admitted, although it would be perfectly apparent to any discerning listener on the audio cassette, because they had taken such trouble over the accents.

'I thought you were from Limerick,' she said.

'That was the first draft,' he said. 'The only people from Limerick in the United States are illegal aliens, not postgraduates from Dublin on full scholarship.'

The prepositional revision is illuminating. Now there is less chance that anyone, even the discerning, will imagine that the scholarship was *from* Dublin rather than *to* an individual ordinarily resident there. A bit of a bursary from Baile Atha Cliath would go no great distance in a story set not a thousand miles from Silicon Valley where at any moment the president may or may not be running the palps of his fingers over the titanium buttons of the control panel while those awful obese American bodyguards are watching the wrong people, especially the Islamic lab attendants from the subcontinent. How our prejudices can disarm us!

'I think you're brilliant,' said Beth Ann. 'Here we are in the heartless heart of the fifth most affluent nation on the planet if we seceded from the Union. Everyone is fucking everyone else, even though the Pax Penicillin has proved to be a poignant phantasm with the advent of Aids. Everyone is getting their hole, which, as you explained in the cinema after I came back from the restroom, is an Irish idiom that indicates full coitus, and you, in the midst of so much radiant ass, are committing yourself to the most enigmatic vigil of all, the quest par excellence, the seeker's search for the sought-after.'

Her nipples had hardened like a nursing mother's under her Oxford button-down shirt. In fact, now that Peter looked at the garment again, its fabric seemed finer, flimsy, a chemise from Victoria's Secrets. He thought he had been feeling a draft.

'Unless,' he said, 'the Lord wants me to assume flesh, to incarnate my project, to enter the historical process in the community of two bodies.'

'I would love to give you a hug,' Beth Ann said to him. 'I would love to give you a hand-job. I only give hand-jobs on a first date. Blow-jobs and I spit on a second date; blow-jobs and I swallow on the third. I like an ascending series. An ascending series is more . . . eschatological than a mere narrative. It graduates what would otherwise be linear.'

'The shortest distance between two points has its own pathos,' he said. 'To start with a hand-job is to begin humbly. And humility is endless.'

'I feel really close to you,' she said. 'Now that you've told me you're going to be a priest, I can set aside the tedious stuff. I can set aside the gnosis, the agnosis, the negotiation. We meet, we greet. I come on to you, you come into me, we come in reverse alphabetical order, I browse some of your philosophy books to determine your patronymic while you evacuate the broccoli from the pizza, because how were you to know that I'm allergic, and then I go home because I really wanted to watch *Rebecca* by myself. It's so shallow.'

'Not necessarily,' he said. 'The Lord can use our superficiality to deepen us.'

'You are so Christian,' she said. 'I honour you. I honour your intention to become a priest. I would not disrespect you by making a pass. You could lick my pussy all night long, until you had lockjaw, and we would not be as close as we are, just sitting here in a coffee shop two doors down from the Emerald cinema in Palo Alto, California, where we've just seen a movie called *Seminarians*, a denotative title, as it happens, in that the film is actually about young men studying for the priesthood in the course of an investigation by the DA's office into bullying in the workplace that is spearheaded by the same woman who plays the lead role in that other film we saw last week about the mad president who wants to press the button while his bodyguards are looking at everybody else. I say *film* because *film* is more of an arthouse word than *movie* which is demotic, although *movie* is contextually accurate as current American usage. On the other hand, *film* is something I would say as a Jewish-American princess with pretensions.'

'Wait a minute,' Peter said. 'This is our first date. We have long since established that. Ergo, mention of another film/movie completely invalidates the premise, destabilises the confidence of the listener/ lector, depending on whether it's a public reading or a private reading and on whether the vocalisation is live or on audio cassette in an automobile. I could say car, but I am long enough on the West Coast to have acclimated; and that acclimation is reflected in, and revealed by, localised diction. Additionally, you cannot know about the mad president. That is between me and my pre-frontal cortex. My narrator is not omniscient. Nor are you. Accordingly, you could only know about the mad president if you had heard me talking in my sleep, and we have never slept together. Anyway, I never talk in my sleep. I take a half Mogadon every night. Finally and fundamentally, you are not a Jewish-American princess. You may be Jewish, you may be American, but you are not East Coast elite. Dream on, baby.'

'Well,' said Beth, a beautiful Hebrew word that means house and carries immediate connotations not only of an abode but of an abiding place, a base as in Bachelard's benign phenomenology.

'Well, what?'

This was Peter, but at a certain point you don't want to impede the forward impetus of the dialogue by interpolating redundant nominations, unless, of course, the repetition expedites a motive of biblical stateliness or of exponential ridicule, or both.

Her eyes had filled up with tears, or perhaps she was wearing contact lenses and he was smoking. Perhaps she had put the contact lenses in during the film when she went to the john.

'You know me as I am,' she said. 'There's no BS between us. We're like me and my girlfriends. I can even fart in front of them and not be embarrassed. We would just move on from there. I think I could pass wind in front of you this moment and not mind at all. That is the greatest compliment I have ever paid to a man.'

His eyes filled up as well. He was wearing contact lenses too, and had completely forgotten. That was not like him. He took off his tortoiseshell glasses, the NHS prescription spectacles he had inherited from his grandmother on the sad occasion of her sudden death at ninety-three, and put them away in the breast pocket of his reefer jacket.

'I love you, Peter,' she said to him.

'I love you too,' he said. 'But my name is not Peter. It is too obvious. It is a canard. Even fictional human beings have fictional human rights.'

'Beth is too breathy,' she said. 'And I've never met a Jew called Beth anything. But there you are. Besides, you might have been called Rocky.'

'Uh uh,' he said, which may be construed as an amiable negative. 'Peter is black comedy; Rocky would be farce. There would be doors opening and closing all over the place. There would be ithyphallic undertones to Rocky or subliminal cephalic resonances from the Judeo-Christian texts.'

'We have transcended the sexual,' said the woman, who obviously had no notion what cephalic means. 'If we can transcend things, surely we can transcend the names of things. We are so much at one on this page of the story that I could mop my bush with three or four folded pieces of Charmin toilet-paper, with my thong down around my espadrilles and one or two corkscrew hairs embedded in the crusted cerise gusset.'

'I found that disgusting the first time,' Peter said. 'I am not into body fluids.'

'Me, neither,' she said. 'That's why I said what I said about the fart. If I wouldn't be embarrassed to fart in front of you, that would signify a relationship amounting almost to stereoscopic simultaneity, or, in the expression of the Hebrew Bible which Christians continue to denigrate as the Old Testament when there is nothing old about it, to Oneflesh. No hyphen. Period. New paragraph.'

'Sir?'

It was the waitress, exactly at the mid-point. Nobody had anticipated this. It was the very same as the scenario with the president. You are always looking in the wrong direction of the story. It is a classic Hitchcockian manoeuvre.

'Please don't smoke in the non-smoking section,' the waitress said. 'The non-smoking section is for non-smokers. That repetition is redundant, but redundancy functions rhetorically as a form of ridicule.'

'I'm not smoking,' Peter said. 'Neither is Beth. Enough is enough.'

'I could have sworn you were,' she said. 'I could have sworn I smelled smoke. There's no smoke without fire. Besides, my eyes had begun to fill up and displaced my disposable contact lenses.'

Peter looked at her angrily.

'Why are you looking at me so angrily?' said the waitress. 'Have you something against South East Asians?'

'Your being South East Asian didn't even register with me,' said Peter. 'I thought you were Norwegian. Not that I have anything against Norwegians.'

'I may be a Norwegian national,' said the waitress, 'but I am racially SEA. I was airlifted out of Saigon when that city fell/was liberated, which is appropriate, in terms of my age-profile, for an anthropology teaching assistant who will celebrate/commemorate the twentieth five anniversary of her neo-natal separation from her birth mother in two weeks' time.'

'You see,' said Peter. 'The little shit didn't even bother Googling a Vietnamese patronymic for the birth mother. How long does it take to Google these things? It takes seconds on broadband.'

'He called her Ng in an early draft,' the waitress said. 'Imagine that.'

'You'd know he was prejudiced,' said Beth Ann to the waitress. 'There was a disclaimer at the very outset. And the Torah Talmud thing is that a character only disclaims the desires he/she/it admits to privately. Surely you've heard?'

'I was listening on audio cassette,' said the waitress. 'The quality is very poor, but they have obviously worked on the accents. The Irish accent is spot on. I would place it within ten miles of Limerick. Norwegians shop there regularly.'

'He didn't even bother to give me eyebrows,' Peter said. 'I don't mind saying it.'

'They'll grow back,' the waitress said. 'He put an ST in my lunchbox. He has a thing about periods. It's so creepy. It's so prurient and patriarchal. Did you know that the Barbelo-Gnostics in the second century AD used to drink menses instead of communion wine at their nocturnal Eucharists? Because I didn't, either.'

'AD is so in your face,' said Beth. 'He knows perfectly well that the polite thing nowadays is to say common era.'

'AD might be a *mea culpa*,' Peter said. 'Eyebrows is vindictive. You don't not think about eyebrows. They're staring you in the face.'

'I tell you what's staring you in the face,' said Beth. 'He has given me long axillary hair that is auburn, and all the fraternity jocks love to inhale it.'

'Wise up, woman,' said the waitress, who felt momentarily yet momentously disheartened and embittered. 'He has given me a cold sore. He has given me a period smell. I am supposed to have a whiff like the warm Mediterranean, and he thinks that is a compliment. He thinks that is the greatest compliment a man can pay a woman. Well, I can tell you this for nothing. I do not have a whiff like the warm Mediterranean. I do not have a whiff at all. Once upon a time perhaps, when we all lived happily ever after, I may have had a whiff. My mother, the Lord have mercy on her, as Norwegians say, had a nose like a bloodhound. But I have stopped having periods since the time I developed anorexia because my whole life is a complete non sequitur.'

'He wants me to undergo a real religious conversion after only three blow-jobs,' Peter said. 'In the second draft, he promised me hundreds of them. My grandfather used to call them gobble-jobs, which is Hiberno-English argot, but that is beside the point. I get three blow-jobs. Then I enter the Jesuits which takes fourteen fucking years before I'm ordained and rogue females find me irresistible again. By that time I'll have forgotten what it feels like to have an erection. The whole thing is completely unbelievable, as far as I'm concerned.'

'Peter. Beth. The South East Asian waitress. It stinks,' said Beth to Peter and the waitress.

'Do you know what I would do if I was standing beside the presidential button on the control panel at the heart of the military–industrial complex?' asked the teaching assistant. 'I would be tempted to press the damn thing. It wouldn't be the end of the world, as far as I'm concerned. It would certainly be better than having anorexia, a cold sore and a salty whiff of the Mediterranean for the rest of my life.'

'I was supposed to self-harm in solidarity with El Salvador,' said Beth. 'That is completely foreign to my family values. Besides, El Salvador was twenty years ago. Nobody gives a shit about El Salvador any more. He could have Googled the Sudan in a split-second.'

'Why don't we go home?' said the waitress. 'Why don't we shut the fuck up and go home? Home is a beautiful Hebrew word that means house and carries immediate connotations not only of an abode but of an abiding place, a base as in Bachelard's benign phenomenology.'

'Where is home and how can we get there?' Beth said. 'There is nothing outside the coffee shop except a multiplex called the Emerald which is two doors up or down, depending on direction, and in which the current programme includes a Baltic movie with subtitles called *Seminarians*, and where many of this evening's audience, statistically if not socio-culturally, are South East Asians. Not that I have anything against South East Asians, least of all those bi-nationals who have adapted to the rigours of the Norwegian climate.'

'I would not go to that multiplex if I were bursting to go,' said the waitress. 'Bursting to go is a Hiberno-English idiom that refers to bladder control. I have inhaled it by osmosis.'

'Why would you not go there, even if, as you say, your bladder control was precarious?' said Peter, who sensed a complete non sequitur.

'I went in there earlier,' said the waitress, 'because there are no toilets in this coffee shop. The doors advertising restrooms are facsimiles stencilled on beauty-board. So I went to the Emerald, because it would have taken me several pages of paragraphs to access the departmental john that is used by the anthropology TA's. There would have been no intelligible transition, and connections matter. There is such a thing as the subject-verb-object structure. The species arrived at it by dint of much travail. I object to being subjected verbally to anything else. Then, when I did go in, I found two corkscrew hairs embedded in the crusted cerise gusset of a thong. It was so disgusting.'

'That is not me,' said Beth. 'That is him talking. He has a thing about it. It is really gross. It is harassment in the workplace.'

'The specificity has a certain frisson,' said Peter. 'But he cannot even make a simple transition, such as I am making now, effortlessly, and without drawing attention in an attention-seeking manner, to my having done so. Remember when it took him three pages to get the trophy Oriental babysitter from the microwave to the tumble-dryer?'

'That was before my time,' said the South East Asian waitress.

'*Moi aussi*,' said Beth. 'It must have happened while I was at French class.' Her accent was really beautiful. She was the business.

'Listen,' said Peter. 'That is the first *explication de texte* for ages. We are not forgotten.'

'You're right,' said Beth. 'It is the first *explication de texte* for quite some time.' But she said it even better than he had, after years at the Alliance Française, not to mention the time-share in Ez.

'It is far too late in the day to bring in new cultural references,' said the waitress. 'That is Page One territory.'

'He is off the lithium,' said Beth. 'That is the long and the short of it.'

'He's been off the lithium since Easter Sunday,' said the waitress. 'He is off the periodic table. He has even been writing verse again.'

'Say no more,' said Peter and Beth simultaneously, as it happened. If that was gospel, it was very bad news. It could kick-start all the old stuff again: the gnosis, the agnosis, the negotiation.

'I am supposed to walk home from here,' the waitress said. 'I am supposed to walk all the way to Menlo Park. How am I going to manage in these shoes?'

Sure enough, she was wearing espadrilles, the very same as Beth's/Beth Ann's.

'He only knows espadrilles,' the waitress said. 'Espadrilles and court shoes and slippers with pompoms. He knows moccasins but he cannot spell the word and therefore avoids it assiduously. I am not asking him to be a foot fetishist. I am only asking him to do some basic research.'

'Me too,' said Beth. 'He has me rooming with an elderly psychoanalyst who eats hash brownies because of irritable bowel syndrome. It is all so unlikely and heavy-handed. When I get home tonight, if I get home tonight, in the comprehensive absence of avenues, boulevards, cul-de-sacs and *viae dolorosae*, I encounter a deer drinking from the deep end of the swimming pool. He/she/it is antlered. The tongue-tip radiates ripples on the heavily chlorinated and undrinkable surface of the water. Its slow, successive sips, in contradistinction to the cacophony of the actual swallowing of liquid from a stream/waterhole in such scenic areas as Yosemite wilderness, are dumbfoundingly silent. I am not to intervene to prevent gastric complications in a protected species. I am not to throw my espadrilles at it. I suppose I am to emit another whiff of the warm Mediterranean, forgetful of the fact that the cult black-and-white movie *Rebecca* is about to begin on PBS, and that nothing but caffeine can make my heart beat faster now.'

'But there has been absolutely no prior reference to deer,' Beth said, 'even by way of a natural decollation on the wall of this coffee shop or over the patented warm-air hand-dryer in the restroom of the Emerald. He has not even bothered his arse to invoke either *The Deer Hunter* or *The Yearling* or the classic Walt Disney cartoon *Bambi*, any one of which would have introduced the motif with an economy amounting to elegance.'

'There has been absolutely no prior reference to racoons, either,' said Peter. 'But I am scheduled to have an epiphany involving racoons at some stage. What happens is, I go home, I am seized by a sudden desire to launder my linen during the small hours, I act upon this impulse, I enter the basement facility and am solicited immediately by two Bahai Iranian/Persians who are proselytising on behalf of their syncretistic system after dark. In this aftermath of this importunity, as I air the freshened linen on the balcony of a high-rise student apartment, I notice a racoon among the garbage at ground level. He/she/it has jammed their snout in an empty aluminum can, and the jagged metal serrations have pierced the membrane of the eyelid and are fretting the cornea irreversibly. Now what has that to do with anything?'

'Local municipal ordinances make it very unlikely that careless waste disposal would result in such injury,' said Beth. 'Besides, it is much more likely to have been a skunk.'

'It is just the *ex nihilo* negligence of the whole thing,' Peter said. 'He does not give a damn any more.'

'On the other hand,' said Beth, 'it suits the priestly scenario. There is something solemn and sacerdotal about it. Whereas I have to go home and feed a fox. I kid you not. Not that I have anything against foxes. I make that disclaimer at the outset. I have never met a fox and I do not particularly want to. This fox comes into the kitchen and drinks pasteurised milk from the cat's saucer. But it must be a vixen, because there are cubs at the door. Now it is a whole menagerie. Yet I can smell zilch. Suddenly polyps have developed in my sinuses. Yet there is no hint of an antihistamine anywhere in the foregoing.'

'It is more than beastly,' Peter said. 'It is bestial. It is anencephalic, whatever that means.'

'We should do nothing,' the waitress said. 'The thing to do is to do nothing. Neither should we say anything. If we say nothing and do nothing, he will no longer have carte blanche to carry on as he likes. Our silence will silence him. There can be no *explication de texte* if there is no text to explicate.'

Her French accent was almost as good as Beth's. They had been locked in mimetic conflict for years, of course.

'He can still hear us thinking, is the problem,' Peter said. 'He still has a pass key to the paschal mystery of the pre-frontal cortex.'

So one or other of them signalled to the waitress to turn up the volume of the anachronistic television set over the pine-wood carrel, and she did. The president's voice was in perfect lip-synch with the movements of his mouth. He was surrounded by awful obese men, not that I have anything against obesity.

Pause. Period. New paragraph.

But this is what I love the most. This is the moment I have been waiting for. They are motionless. They are mute. Now and only now can I begin to hear the a cappella of the dust-mites in their eyebrows. Even in Peter's lack of them can I hear the sound of it, the soprano line and the solitary counter-tenor, where the follicles are multiplying minutely as I intimate them. I can even hear the doxology of the bacteria in his lower intestine, and the great Amen of the sperm awaiting Easter in the scrotal sac. Now and only now can I see the ultra-scans of the great-grandchildren of the South East Asian waitress. Now and only now can I touch her recessive genes with the palps of my fingers. Now and only now (and even then, only now and then) can I taste the molecular disturbance of Beth Ann's sorbet. Now and only now can I inhale by osmosis the warm salt-water whiff of the Mediterranean.

Now and only now. And even then, only now and then.

For I have made intelligible transitions and material connections. I have been involved in a character-building exercise. I have built characters. They are great when you get to know them, but the thing is, you never do get to know them. You are always made to feel like an outsider. But I am not going to think about that for one moment. It is a complete non sequitur. I do not want to end up sleeping in my clothes. I do not want to shave my clerical beard. I do not want to end up with an encrusted cerise gusset. It is/was not necessarily mine. Besides, pronouns panic at a certain point in time. No, I am not going to think about that for one moment, unless the Lord wants me to assume flesh, to incarnate my project, to enter the historical process in the community of two bodies who communicate quite well.

This is true. I do not object to being subjected to verbs.

They are, after all, recurrent compositional strategies. They are dark and demi-mondaine disclosures and deferrals which lead me by drives and boulevards and cul-de-sacs and *viae dolorosae* to the auditor/ lector/reader, to the paused button on the audio cassette, to the enigmatic vigil.

# Eclipsed

## Anthony Glavin

It was the grainy black and white footage of Bob Dylan talking to another skinny, older guy on the pub telly that brought it all back home to Conor that night. Landed him back in the Rathmines house he and Peadar had shared with the Gang of Four in the late 1970s, following which Peadar disappeared for ever. All of it back in a long-ago Dublin, before the city filled up with foreigners, or anybody under thirty had the kind of money Conor saw kids nowadays pissing away, literally so, after the late-night bars threw them out.

Someone had switched the telly in Kehoe's over to an English football match, which interested Conor even less than folk music. But now it had begun, other stuff flooded back: somebody's purple comb on the bathroom handbasin, or a pair of red shoes in the basement kitchen where the morning sun was briefly eclipsed each time the No 15 pulled up outside. Or, for that matter, the line he had done with a Russian spy who lived across town, their half-made plans to go to Amerikay, all those schemes and dreams you stow away in a previous life.

Conor was never into Dylan, but Peadar had all his albums, which he played on the bockety turntable in their bedroom with its acid-yellow, woodchip wallpaper and a green fireplace that smoked whenever the wind went west. Dylan was too hippy-dippy for Conor, who was into the home-town Rats and Radiators, but he hadn't money for music, so it was mostly Dylan and Dave Van Ronk who played, along with a Ry Cooder album someone had left behind when they moved out.

The house belonged to an old dear who lived with her sister in Dalkey, and whose nephew, a balding maths teacher, called round every month for the rent. It was a proper house too, had yet to devolve into a jumble of bedsits like the red-brick rabbit warren on the North

Circular Road, where Conor had first lived after he came up from the country. There his room had sat on a small landing onto which he used to toss tiny balls of paper for the landlady's crazed cat to chase out those nights it came in his open window. The cat was crazed because it could not get out of the house, only onto the roof, and it occasionally terrorised Conor coming home at night by springing in the dark from the front hall table up to his chest as he fumbled for the wall switch to the timer light that stayed lit just long enough for him to fumble again for the switch on each successive landing. The landlady, who kept two rooms on the ground floor, and who spooked Conor in a different way, asked him once about the balls of paper outside his door, but he just sang dumb. He began to dread going to the toilet at night however, knowing the cat was somewhere out there, and he took to peeing instead into a lemonade bottle which he emptied each morning down the roof slates into the gutter.

There was also somebody always knocking at all hours on his door to ask for a cigarette, so that autumn, when a fellow clerk at the ESB mentioned hearing of a shared room going in a Rathmines house, Conor moved out the following week. The new place was grand, but it took Conor a while to figure out his room-mate Peadar, even if they both came from the West, himself from Mayo and Peadar from Donegal. 'Are you going somewhere?' he had enquired that first evening, as Peadar stood at the cooker and spooned sizzling fat onto a chop. That someone their age wore a cap struck Conor as strange, never mind while making their tea, but Peadar just remarked how seventy per cent of body heat escapes out the top of the head. It was the kind of oddball fact he often came out with – something left of centre, but not so off the wall you could simply laugh at him. 'You'd do better just shelving those books, not opening them,' Conor would later advise Peadar, who worked as a library assistant for the Corpo, but that evening he merely nodded back.

It was cold all right in the house, along with the bone-chilling damp that most large Irish houses exuded before the advent of central heating. Sometimes they lit a small fire in the bedroom with a few pieces of coal from the bag they had bought between them, feeding the feeble flames with small bits of timber they picked up here and there. But all too often the wind would shift, and by spring a thin film of coal dust had painted everything from the window ledge to the picture rail.

It was damp and dusty, they hadn't much money, but they were young, and most of the time the world seemed young as well. The others in the house were all Dubs, the Gang of Four as Peadar used to call them. Fergus and John were both in the Bank, while John's girl-friend, Liz, along with Pauline, had recently qualified as nurses. There was usually also another housemate, a succession of guys and girls, none of whom seemed to last for very long in the draughty box room at the front. But the large front sitting room with its trellised bay windows, and downstairs kitchen with its small fridge crammed full of various foodstuffs all labelled with different names, made for a congenially communal arrangement that surpassed bedsits altogether. There was, of course, the occasional spat over who forgot to put their few bob into the cracked milk jug that served as a kitty for staples like milk, sugar, and tea, and a more serious row the time Fergus insisted the three pea-cock feathers Pauline had placed over the sitting-room mirror were dead unlucky indoors, but apart from a short-term box-roomer who repeatedly robbed from the fridge, there was little aggro in the house.

Peadar, like them all, was in his early twenties, only his thinning fair hair and library gig somehow made him seem older. Or maybe it was the banjo he was attempting to master at a time when everybody and his brother were trying to learn the guitar. Or the way he sometimes stayed in with a book on a Saturday night, instead of heading out to the pub or a dance. Indeed Conor often tried to roust him out, but after he met Sharon that summer, the two lads rarely saw one another outside of the house.

Sharon, who came from Athy, worked for a solicitor in Merrion Square, and lived in a house on Ailesbury Road, not far from the Russian and Chinese Embassies. 'I ought to move,' she told Conor the night they met, 'as I'm probably being slowly microwaved to death.' 'Sure, you probably work for the Rooskies yourself,' Conor attempted a Texan twang. 'I don't do dates,' she laughed later that night, after he asked might he see her again, 'only assignations.' It became a kind of running joke, long enough anyhow for Conor to introduce her to Peadar back at the house a few weeks later as his friend from the KGB.

It turned out that Sharon worked with a girl from the same Donegal village as Peadar, who told Sharon during a tea break that Peadar's mother had killed herself when he was still small. 'She didn't mean it as gossip,' Sharon added, when Conor said the problem with Ireland was everybody knowing what you both ate and shat. Of course Dublin was better that way than a Donegal or Mayo village, but Conor was still keen to try America, and he and Sharon batted the idea back and forth between them over several months. 'Would you go yourself?' Sharon asked Peadar during one such session at the kitchen table, after Peadar had made fun of his uncle in Chicago who said life over there wasn't safe with the blacks, and insisted his aunt drive everywhere with a life-sized inflatable doll in the passenger's seat. 'Ach, I don't know,' Peadar shrugged – as if for all his interest in its folk music, the place itself didn't really interest him.

It was Peadar at home one afternoon when the doorbell rang coming up to that second Christmas, somebody enquiring about the ad in the *Evening Herald* for the vacant box room. Conor had thought about taking it himself, as Peadar was invariably in their room if ever Sharon and he came back to the house after the pictures or the pub. Still, the landlady's nephew collected an extra fiver monthly for the single rooms, and while Sharon and he had fairly unbuttoned each other beneath the beech tree beside her house on Ailesbury Road, any keenness to go to bed with him was not so readily apparent as to justify that expenditure.

In a way it made sense to Conor afterwards, how it had been Peadar at home that afternoon – for who else in Ireland would have placed the guy with a full head of curly hair in the photograph? But that is getting ahead of the story as Peadar told it, seated on his bed later that night, trying to work out a chord progression on his banjo.

'There's a woman standing there when I opened the door,' he told Conor, 'holding a newspaper cutting, only her nose begins to bleed just as she says hello.' And not just bleed, but gush blood, down the front of her coat and onto the doorstep, before she finally managed to fish out a tissue and stem the flow. 'Keep your head back!' Peadar told her, but apparently that was an old wives' tale, or so the woman informed him in an American accent, adding 'You need to keep your head down instead.'

As it all flooded back to him that night in Kehoe's, Conor found himself resisting a sudden urge to tell the burly stranger on the adjoining stool what else Peadar had recounted. How he had brought the woman into the front room before he went down to the kitchen to wet a clean tea towel. And how when he returned it looked like she hadn't moved at all – had just sat there, stunned, like a starling flown into a window. And even stayed a bit dazed-looking, even after she tidied herself up.

'Large, slender hands,' he answered Conor, the kind of thing you might expect Peadar to say if you asked him to describe a bird. 'Long blonde hair,' he added like an afterthought, 'tied back in a ponytail.'

'How old?'

'Early thirties maybe? Kind of pretty too, in a washed-out sort of way.'

Peadar had offered her a cup of tea, but your woman asked instead for a glass of water. He must have shown her the box room too, though in retrospect her reason for calling seemed almost incidental. They chatted a bit about the house at any rate, before she finally put away the bloodstained cutting and brought out a photograph from her woven shoulder bag.

'She showed you a photograph?'

'Aye, a black and white photograph,' Peadar said, 'only she said "snapshot".'

'A photo of what?' asked Conor, as if Peadar might, and not for the first time, lose the track of his own tale.

But Peadar had only been gathering himself, for he put down his banjo and slowly began to describe what happened next. 'A photograph of herself as a little girl, nine or ten maybe, standing in a sunny field with her mother and younger brother, and this skinny guy squinting at the camera.'

'Is that your family?' he asked out of politeness, but the woman merely shook her head and held out her hand. Only something prompted Peadar then to take another look at the man.

'That's not Woody Guthrie?' he frowned, knowing full well how foolish the question was, even by his own standards.

Only it wasn't so foolish after all. Your woman did not stay for long – just long enough to tell of the long-distance obsession her mother had cultivated for Guthrie, whose songs she sang night and day, until finally she packed her two children into the family Ford, and leaving their father behind in Philadelphia, drove out to the Midwest. Once there, she followed the singer around for a year, working as a waitress in various cafés, and struggling to provide some facsimile of family life in a series of cheaply rented rooms. The following Christmas they drove back to Philadelphia, where her mother left her and her brother in the car outside an apartment building while she went up to see their father. 'None of us knew yet that he didn't live there any more,' the woman told Peadar – that he had died only weeks before of a broken heart, or so he wrote in a note left behind.

Peadar didn't tell all of it that night. The following morning he repeated that much for John and Liz, who asked had anybody enquired about the empty room. And that same morning Conor spied a drop of blood on the wooden hall floor as he left for work, a perfect circle with a dark-red sheen like nail varnish. But it wasn't until another day or two later that Peadar told him how he had shown your woman a photograph in turn, himself as a kid up in Donegal, only he likely said 'gassur' instead.

It was only in Kehoe's, however, that Conor suddenly wondered if Peadar's mother had been in that second photo too? Not that he had ever been entirely sure of Sharon's workmate's story. That Peadar's mother had died was true enough, as Peadar had once told, as part of another yarn, how the shopkeeper who doubled as village undertaker had pencilled a packet of firelighters and forty cigarettes on the bill he presented to Peadar's father for her coffin and removal.

For that matter, Peadar wasn't sure himself how much he believed of the American woman's story. At least that's what he said a few weeks later, after the household had got over the Christmas, and shortly before he took off for the States. He said nothing in advance of leaving, just left his share of February's rent on Conor's bed, along with a note saying Conor was welcome to the Dylan albums and a few bits of clothing he hadn't bothered to pack. It bothered Conor a good deal at the time, the lack of any farewell, and, if he were honest, how for all his own talk about America, it was Peadar who had pulled up stakes and gone over beyond.

Peadar hadn't seemed any different after your woman called, not that it would have been altogether easy to spot him acting odder. Nonetheless Conor had always linked her arrival to his departure – much the same way a picture of them, seated side by side in that front room, had lodged in his head for weeks. Either way, the woman never rang back about the box room, which was let to a lively London-Irish girl named Tommy for whom John fell in a big way, so that the land-lady's nephew had to advertise again that spring after Liz moved out. But all that was several months after Fergus had moved in with Conor, and just before Pauline went off to nurse in London.

Dylan was back on the TV, in colour this time and looking his age, but Conor had had enough for one night. The Romanian accordion player was still at his post on Grafton Street, only this time Conor tossed a two-euro coin into the battered case with its small hand-lettered sign:

*Music is Life.* But the past is not always so easily bought off, and he continued to think about Peadar on the No 32 home. There had been a letter from New Jersey a month or so later, apologising after a fashion for his abrupt departure, followed by a couple of postcards during Conor's last months in the house. Then, six years later, Peadar turned up on their answer machine one New Year's Eve, however he had found the number, wishing Conor the best in that same soft Donegal accent, but leaving no number for himself.

It was less than a five-minute walk from Raheny Village to the house. Leaving out the Pixies CD that Fiona, their seventeen-year-old, had asked him to pick up in town, he went upstairs and quietly undressed, as Sharon was already asleep in the other bed. Once settled, he gave himself over to the footage that played on yet inside his head, the afternoon sunlight on the red-brick Rathmines Town Hall, or the smiling face of the local butcher who insisted everybody needed a bargain as he threw in an extra chop. But nothing he saw there answered why it still felt like all of them had come closer then to something vital. As Sharon turned over in the opposite bed, he thought again of what the American woman had told Peadar as she got up to go – how 'loneliness is the worst thing of all'. And then just as sleep came, he saw again – or did he only imagine it, the kind of thing Peadar might easily have said – that just as she spoke, a passing No 15 shattered the shadow of the window trellis on the sitting-room wall a sudden, startled patterning of angular shapes, like a flock of birds taking flight.

# The Hardest Winter

## Breda Wall Ryan

The Travellers move into the sheltered lane under cover of darkness. They cut the headlights and crawl along in low gear, one van at a time, but Mam and I hear. Sound carries on the moors in November when the ground is iron-hard and the stars crackle. The first snow flurries whiten the higher slopes and I've driven the sheep down. I ease the stiffness from my shoulders. Muscles along my forearms stand proud from drawing firewood, cord after cord. When the Forestry put the price up I couldn't afford a winter's supply, so I helped myself. I heaved the logs through the breached fence by moonlight, loaded them onto the tractor-trailer, stacked them loose in the shed. It's state forest and I'm a citizen; I'm entitled.

'No New Agers are going to walk all over me,' I tell Mam. 'It's private property.' I whistle up the dogs.

'It's late, Kate,' Mam says. She jabs the fire with a poker so the flames jump. 'And terrible cold. Can't you leave them till morning?'

'They could have a couple of sheep in the pot or a few of your Leghorns in their bellies by then.' Those hens are squawky dirty things, always watching for a chance to scratch up the vegetables or shit on the doorstep. They can't look you straight in the face, so they give you one evil eye at a time. Mam loves them, but they give me the shudders.

'What harm the loss of a few sheep? They'll make nothing at the mart, and we'll get the headage subsidy regardless. They might as well feed a few children,' she says. 'Besides, a bit of company would be nice.'

'Don't go drawing them into the house,' I warn. 'They're travellers.'

'You used to like Mrs Connors, when she came up this way,' Mam says. '*She* was a traveller.'

'That was different.' The Connors used to camp in the lane every year at shearing time. Mrs Connors sheared cleaner and faster than a man and Seanie Connors would butcher a couple of the fat lambs ready for Mam and me to salt away in the barrel or smoke in the chimney. That was before we got the freezer. Mrs Connors used to sit with Mam by the kitchen fire in the evenings, our winter socks snaking off their knitting needles, while they debated the relative merits of oiled wool and washed yarn, or wondered when the young ones, me and Lizzie Connors, would outgrow our sulks. Mrs Connors wouldn't hear of Lizzie sleeping in my room for even one night, on account of travellers not mixing with settled people. 'Too knowing for young girls, those two, through watching the sheep and seeing what they shouldn't,' she said. 'They need marrying. That'd keep them out of trouble.'

'Mam,' I say now, 'the Connors were genuine. This lot are New Agers, playing at travelling, living off the dole and whatever they can lift.'

'It's an alternative lifestyle, Kate,' she says, all reasonableness, while I pull on my boots. 'They do things different, is all.' *Alternative lifestyle.* Turning my own words on me. 'The women might drop in,' she maunders. 'That's something I miss, a woman's company.' That rankles.

'What am I then, a man? Or maybe a sheep?' I slam the door hard so it bounces open again. She'll have to creak out of her spindle-back chair to shut out the cold.

The New Agers' vans are half-circled in the lane around three simmering fires. I want them gone by ten tomorrow. I make sure they see me noting their licence plates on my wrist and eyeing the sparking logs, four-foot baulks of spruce like the load in my shed. I warn them every stick, stone, beast and fowl on the place is counted.

'You've nothing to fear, Miss. We live and let live,' a man says. 'Anything I could help with around the farm? Mucking out, chopping firewood, repairs, perhaps? I can turn my hand to anything.' Eyes intent on my face, he adds, 'Payment in kind.'

He sounds like a BBC newsreader. I could do with help but I can't afford wages. I've been working the place on my own since Pop died.

Pop clung to the 1950s all his life. He didn't believe in taking the backbreak out of farming; buying tractors, he thought, squandered money.

'Any day now, Kate, the right man will come along,' he'd say. 'I'll be able to hand the place over, take things easy.' I'd been doing all the heavy work since I was fifteen but he ignored that. 'Farming', Pop said, 'is no life for a girl on her own.'

I wanted my name on the deeds; mine and Lizzie's. No man would get the place by shoving his hands up my jumper or stretching his legs under my table. The Connors married Lizzie off to a cousin in Manchester. I waited. I heard about the three-day wedding, then her new council house. Still I clung to the dream; Lizzie and me, running sheep. When word came of a baby and another on the way, that dream fell the way leaves fall from trees.

Then last year, Pop died. And I bought a tractor.

The traveller senses my hesitation. 'No wages, as such. Sawing firewood, for example, I'd keep one log in ten. That's fair.' He grasps my hand, shakes. It's a done deal. I should have kept my hands in my pockets. 'A week,' he adds, 'will see that shed logged.' He's scouted the sheds already, and the dogs never barked. He'll take watching.

'Four days, tops,' I warn. My boots ring on the frosted ground. I kick the yard gate wide, furious at being outmanoeuvred.

At seven next morning, he's at the door.

'I like to make an early start,' he says. 'I work eight hours a day. I'll take a couple of hours off later, bag a few rabbits. Unless they're counted?' He grins, but I don't respond. 'We have our own chickens,' he adds. 'They're in arks, they won't bother you.'

'What breed?' Mam pipes up. I stomp across to the woodshed, drag the sawhorse under the yellow arc from the yard lamp and start up the chainsaw. Sawdust mounds up like spilled sugar and the air is tangy with resin, but the whining saw sets my teeth on edge. I'm logging my third baulk when the traveller and Mam get through comparing Leghorns and Rhode Islands and Silky Bantams. He hefts his own chainsaw off his shoulder and waits for me to cut mine so I can hear.

'I would have done that,' he tilts his head towards the sawhorse.

'With two saws, it'll take no time,' I answer.

'You don't have a safety guard. Or goggles.' I ignore him. 'I prefer to work alone,' he says, 'so I don't have to worry about lopping off anyone's arm.'

'I'll feed,' I snap, pulling goggles from my pocket. 'But it'll take twice as long.'

When it gets light, I go in for breakfast and the traveller takes his to his van. Afterwards, we work on at a steady pace for another couple of hours until Mam brings us mugs of sweet tea to warm the cockles of our hearts. Mam has a daft saying for every occasion. We are low on milk, she says, and will I get a newspaper, too, while I'm in town?

I pull on clean cords and a half-decent jumper and tease out a few strands of fringe with a hairbrush. Mam says I look nice, so I push the hair off my face again. She wants me to look nice, in case I run into the 'right man'. We probably don't really need milk, but I won't find the right man out among the sheep.

'Anthony,' she says. 'That's the traveller's name, Anthony. He went to see the church window, but it's under repair. There's a woman artist fixing the stained glass.' She searches my face for a sign of interest. 'And he reads, Kate. He has dozens of books in that van.'

Before Anthony came, Mam dangled an ex-seminarian and before that, a vegetarian bee-keeper. Now she'll settle for a traveller husband for me. What she really wants are grandchildren.

'Is Anthony married, by any chance?' My sarcasm is wasted.

'No, not married,' she beams. 'He has his own van. Motor home,' she amends, pitching him hard. 'His sister and her husband and children are in the red van, and two friends in the rusty one. I asked him to come in for his dinner, but he declined.'

Declined, indeed. Like royalty. I keep silent.

'Oh, Kate, isn't he nice? Do you like him?' She has to ask.

'No,' I snap. 'He's trespassing.'

'Oh. I thought when you took him on ... the firewood ...' Her disappointment fogs up the warm kitchen.

In town I pick up milk and the newspaper. I need to order sheep nuts, but the Co-op is closed for dinner-hour, so I sit in the car and open the paper to while away the time. There's a feature on the new church window and the artist, Róisín Cronin, and three photographs. The window of lurid glass, fractured and set in lead strip, shows our seventh-century saint Spideoigín. She had spirit. Legend says she cut off her breasts and grew a beard to repel a lover, then founded a nunnery. The photo is double-exposed, so it's difficult to tell if the work is naive or just plain awful. In another, the artist, in overalls and standing on a ladder, smiles over her shoulder at the camera. The third is a close-up. Her visor is pushed up. High cheekbones and dark curly hair frame wide-awake eyes that gaze straight into the lens. I stroll down the back of Main Street to the church. I tell myself I have nothing better to do; she mightn't have Lizzie's eyes at all.

She's nibbling glass with pincers at a trestle, too far away to make out much, except that she looks better in the flesh than on paper. After a while, she saunters over. No mistake: Lizzie's eyes. I stare at the window so my feelings won't show as a leer, the way boys' eyes used to lick me on the school bus. It's too late to turn away, so I stand my ground.

'Are you from around here?' She flicks her tongue along her lips.

'Six miles out, on the lower slopes of the mountain.' She shields her eyes to take in the mountain looming indigo, the gullies snow-sugared near the summit.

'Must be peaceful. Remote. Solitude to do your work.' Her voice is melted chocolate.

'Sheep farm,' I tell her. 'Nothing for miles, except solitude and sheep. And a New Age camp,' I add, 'but they'll be moving on.'

She studies me so closely I have to break eye-contact.

'I'm going to the Summit for a bite to eat. Would you like to come? I'm Róisín.' She pulls off the leather work-gloves and extends a hand that is chamois-soft, the nails broad and cut very short. I wish I had worn work-gloves this past year. In the pub I tease out my fringe again while Róisín orders. We talk until the mountain fades into the dark and the street lights come on.

Back at the yard, the traveller has left a half-day's worth of logs cut and stacked. I wonder if he had any luck with the rabbits.

'I'm going out Friday,' I say, getting Mam's hopes up. 'To the pictures.'

'Anyone I know?'

'Daniel Day Lewis, Brenda Fricker, Colm Meany,' I answer. She sighs.

'Anthony,' she checks that I'm listening, then launches into a litany: his educated manners, his work that is fast and tidy; the woodshed is packed with sawn and split logs. 'He's good company, Kate. The Leghorns adore him. His nieces, too. You can tell he'd make a good father. You could do worse.' I slam the knife-drawer on my fingers, choke off a yelp.

I can't stay away from Róisín. Every day, I find a pretext to drive into town, so I can watch her welding the coloured wedges of glass together and share a sandwich. When the local lads chat her up, I seethe, though their wooing is as clumsy as mine. Morning and evening, I check the flock. I dread that first lamb that will end my freedom until late spring.

My luck holds. The lambs bide their time, snug inside the ewes. This is the coldest winter on record. The radio warns of blizzards but when I read the sky over the mountain, I know the snow will hold off for a spell. At dusk, I pack a couple of rugs so we can talk while the windows of the car fog up and ice-ferns grow on the inside of the glass. I can hardly steer for shivering and my chilblained fingers ache, but when

Róisín tugs off her gloves, her hands on my belly are smooth and toasty. We are opposites, I think, chalk and cheese. But Róisín says we are hot apple pie and ice cream; different but compatible. The second time I let her name slip Mam says nothing, just corrugates her forehead into the frown that ended Lizzie Connors' visits at shearing time.

Mam is planning pot-roasted mutton with rosemary and thyme. Her talk of crispy potatoes and gravy makes me swallow.

'Why don't you slip across and ask Anthony to eat with us?' she asks. The travellers are staying another week. Mam has Anthony mending sheep-wire, waiting for the lambing.

'I don't want him in the house.'

'The right man won't turn up twice in a lifetime, Kate.' Her voice has a new edge, a kind of panic. 'If you don't make an effort, you'll end up with all your chances behind you, having to settle.' When she married him, Pop was an old man.

'I won't settle.' I am adamant. She says she'll go ahead with the dinner anyway.

In the Summit, Róisín is holding two seats by the fire. I carry the beers over without slopping. It may be a good omen.

'I can't stomach another of Mrs Summit's deceased sandwiches, Róisín. Let's get a proper dinner.' I don't tell her where we're going. When I lift the latch on the crackling logs and the aroma of herby roasting meat, she stands still, enchanted. Anthony is at the stove, stirring glossy gravy. Mam welcomes us with whiskies.

'That'll stick to your ribs and keep your skin from cracking, Róisín,' she says and Róisín laughs. She can't read Mam's forehead. Mam keeps a good table, her roast is thick-sliced and tender. Anthony sees Mam's matchmaking is nothing for him to worry about. The talk is of Róisín's work and Anthony's way of life and how a sheep farm is a bind in a hard winter.

Anthony says I'm very quiet; am I worried about the lambing? I say I'm worried about having an amateur helping, more like. Then he says he'll manage. Only he's bothered about having to dress an orphaned lamb in a dead lamb's skin to trick a ewe into adopting it, like he's seen done on television.

'Skinning dead lambs, that's barbaric!' I say. 'A dollop of Vick's Vapour Rub on the ewe's nose will confuse her sense of smell so she'll take to the stranger. After suckling, her scent will ooze out through the orphan's fleece and they'll be right for each other.'

'You're a hard woman, Kate. But it's only an act,' Anthony says, like he's worked out some sort of cryptic clue. Mam is at the stove. Her hair is stabbed into a grey bun with the diamanté notice-me pin Lizzie and I used to play with. I can tell she's smirking from the set of her shoulders. I snap that Anthony needn't think I'm a pushover. 'I know that, Kate,' he says. 'We'll do the lambing your way.'

'Oh, for God's sake!' Róisín cuts in. 'Vapour rub and skinned lambs. Give me a break!' Her eyes glint like Mam's hairpin.

They talk about Leghorns and Rhode Island Reds and how stunning their plumage would look in stained glass. Róisín tells us about Vermont and Berlin and the Caribbean. We play a few hands of cards. I smile and smile and say nothing; I'm too happy.

Róisín thanks us for a lovely evening. She must say goodbye; she's leaving tomorrow to live in Spain. Her words are ice in my guts but I go on smiling. She muffles up for the drive back to town. Anthony offers to drive so that I can stay snug indoors and Róisín says, 'Excellent!' She flashes her eyes at him but he's not bothered. I say nothing, just keep on smiling hard, because what's the point?

'I asked Anthony to stay on after the lambing. He can do up the loft over the stable for himself, nice and snug,' Mam says. My smile collapses. She won't give up. 'We don't need that stable now that you have the tractor, but you can't carry all the work on your own.' I wait for her to go on. 'That's if he can handle working for two women.'

'Or three.' The words tumble out. '*Three* women.' Mam's eyes on my face soften. She waves to Anthony. He taps the car horn once and drives the threat of Róisín into the night, into the hardest winter on record.

'That won't happen, Kate.'

Róisín was never a threat to Mam's grandchildren. That was always me, wishing too hard with my eyes shut tight.

'I only want you to be happy.'

I was happy with Lizzie. She didn't want that.

'Give him a chance. He works hard. He's better company than the radio.' Mam gentles a few strands of hair onto my forehead. I leave them there. 'Can't you settle for that?'

# A Visitor from the Future

## Harry Clifton

When the call came, it was August. Half of Wexford was indoors, watching the All Ireland. Margaret was somewhere about the house, and Eugene was out in the fields, with their father, harvesting. Ann herself, in a tattered dress, was forking rubbish into the slow burn of an outhouse ashpit.

'It's somebody called Rebecca,' her mother said. 'From the university.'

A colleague of Rebecca's, at the last minute, had taken leave. His work was being parcelled out through the English department. Ann could have a large enough slice of it, Rebecca said, to keep her in Ireland for the time being. All was not lost. It was the first good news in months.

'I won't be going back to America,' she told her mother as she came away from the telephone. 'Not this year anyhow.'

She went back across the yard to continue with the burning. The dog leapt up and followed her. Hadn't it learned that everything must earn its place? That nothing, not even a spot of idleness in the sun, is free? She resented that about growing up here – the anxiety on the faces around the table, even their mother fussing endlessly, trying to deserve her keep.

'Whatever else,' her father said, when he took her under his notice, 'don't let them pick your brains.'

He meant the university. She had been sent away at sixteen to the Training College, and later, much later, had paid her way through doctoral studies in the United States. She would get an education, but no stake in the land. That had been made clear a long time ago, while they ate at the long table in the kitchen, sitting on old church pews. America had swallowed her last decade, in the basements of great research libraries, teaching composition at colleges in towns blanked out when the Arctic weather swept down, or the heatwaves blazed – a decade dreaming, like everyone else in her field, of getting back to Ireland.

She felt, at her ankle, the nose of the dog. Wanting affection. Searching blindly for a loophole in the iron law of necessity. Work to eat, eat to work, the reality she had come away from, in the United States. Was it the same here? She let her spare hand crawl through its fur, as it trembled with gratitude.

She could hear a tractor now, in the yard outside. Eugene, with the grain in the trailer, back from the weighbridge. She stayed in the dark, the ash smouldering, smoke in her face. Let Eugene not be making remarks. Her father would blast through the gate any minute now, in his own tractor. Eugene and himself would fall to repairs, in deadly intimacy, while the women waited in the kitchen with the table set, the elder wine set out, and Uncle Matty down for his meal from the room on the turn of the stairs, the return room, where he lived since they had taken him in, too simple now to understand. And the men would enter with their terrifying energy and cheerfulness, the meal would be served, and this time, for a while, she could look them in the eye and give an account of herself.

Three weeks later, she was sitting in Rebecca's high functional office with the Dublin mountains in the distance, across the Liffey. In between lay the city itself, the campus fields and the hard-edged architecture of faculty buildings. As undergraduates, they had sat in spaces like these. None of the windows opened then. Had the air changed in the meantime?

'You are not their mother,' Rebecca was saying. 'Remember that. If they don't show for classes, it's their funeral. You don't phone them, or chase after them. A letter goes out, that's all. They must prepare for the real world.'

Rebecca herself, who had refused to computerise, was not yet in the real world. The secretaries, two ladies of impeccable middle-class credentials, had created a protective zone about their head of department, filtering information, blocking unnecessary contacts, while she steered, like a child at a control panel, through cultural crosswinds to an unknown future.

'They will try to outwit you,' she whispered. 'They are up to everything electronic – or so I am told. Plagiarism, recycling. If you suspect it, send it on to the secretaries. They smell it out in no time.'

Rebecca wore a leather skirt, but her blonde hair had turned to ash. She was a thin, ravaged but still attractive version of the friend Ann had known as an undergraduate. But she had gone to Cambridge then, instead of America, and they had welcomed her, in this redbrick university, with a job on the spot. They still liked that here in Ireland – the tincture of Englishness, even as the American ethos swept in like a tidal wave.

'You were lucky,' Ann said.

'I was. But we have a new president now, from Harvard Business School. Expect developments.'

Ann was sorry to be downstairs, with the tutors. Up here, there would be the cabals, terrified or conspiratorial, she knew too well from America. Doors that opened and closed as if by magic, when the coast was clear. The microsecond of fright behind the eyes, before the bland unavoidable greeting. And the air, like an odourless nerve gas, eating away at freedom of spirit.

Consuela, a young Latin American woman, took her down to the tutors' office on the ground floor. An overheated room of a type she was familiar with through the years, with the Bible and Shakespeare on the shelves, a couple of dog-eared anthologies to plunder for class material, and a water-cooler refilled, once a week, by a franchised firm who threw in plastic cups. Gemma, an elderly tutor, gave her keys to a filing cabinet and a private letterbox for student submissions. Others, a decade younger than herself, were planning classes, telephoning their lovers, jabbing at the keyboard of the one computer screen.

'The bottom rung of the ladder,' Consuela said. 'If we ever get off it. I am, by the way, the union representative.'

Ann went on to the concourse. The students were flooding back to lectures. A dyed blonde generation, unconscious of itself. Why go to America, when America was already here? Wasn't it Mussolini who had said that, to the poor Italians in the thirties? She remembered the country she had grown up through and left – primary schools in Wexford, smoky little staffrooms, where women with closed faces looked her over, and her life in the stone house out by the Nore was an open secret. A lost world of old pubs by the harbour in Curracloe, the Volks that Zinc had sold her, the time she had been raped and told no one. The freedom, after years in the Training College. And these ones flooding past her – what had they to escape from? What lay ahead of them, to be terrified of?

At the start of September, she had taken a room on the turn of the stairs in a red-brick terrace behind the Liberties. A kitchenette, shower and toilet, an unusable easy chair (she bought herself a new one) and a single bed. A wall-telephone on the landing outside her door, left over from the seventies, rang dramatically in the small hours. Students danced on the floor above her head. She was back again in her young years, this time as a visitor from the future. If any of those students wanted to listen, she could tell them where they were headed.

Each morning, a bus took her across the Liffey, past the Phoenix Park to the grey outskirts and the university. Students slept through the journey, thanked the driver as they got down – a vestige of class solidarity, vanishing in the cool abstraction of campus sandwich bars, the wink of franchise and logo on glass and clothing, the long concourses of sponsored leisure where they sprawled all day, talking. She bought a coffee and sat for an hour, watching the tired academics at neighbouring tables, shuffling their papers for the day to come. Was there a clear space still where the spirit might breathe? Was this it, this precious morning hour before everything really began?

'When do we have lunch?' Rebecca said, on her way back to her office with a styrofoam cup of coffee.

'This day next week?'

'Knock on my door at one.'

In grey unheated rooms, the students sat waiting. Their faces were neutral, passive. Had they chosen her course or been forced into it by pressure of numbers elsewhere?

Always have a plan B, Rebecca had said. Whatever you ask them to bring, they will forget. They never buy books, they all copy from the one text in the library. Welcome to the post-literate age. A few tried to look invisible, others ostentatiously arrived late, others were names on a sheet, never to be seen. Part of her mind apprehended them, nonetheless, as aspects of generational passing time. There were long silences. In time, Rebecca had said, you will become very comfortable with long, uncomfortable silences.

'You see,' she told each group, 'I too started out in rooms like these, went to America, now I'm here again . . .'

She heard herself, in the acoustic wastes of the seminar rooms, the wind loud on the panes, laying down an anecdotal ground on which they might read books together, discuss texts. Reading, they would see

Ireland again – as it had been, as it might be. But which Ireland? Hers, where objects were solid and real, where people were continuous with themselves, and everything could be named? Or theirs, weightless and discontinuous, where day and night, work and play were interchangeable, and money was no object?

'Modernism', a young man told her, 'is when you are sad about disintegration and chaos. But postmodernism, like today, is when you're feeling OK with it, and it's absolutely fine.'

At lunch, she sat over a sandwich in the cafeteria with the life-scarred like herself. The housewives, tired from childrearing, in search of an afterlife beyond domesticity. The adventuresses, whose erotic energy had burnt itself out in art and love-affairs, intensities and impoverishments, anxious now for a late consolidation. With these she talked freely, of a life they had all come out of, in Ireland or elsewhere. Her lost, damaged life in America, that theatre of failure and experiment, could declare itself.

'These children,' she asked them. 'Are they really rich?'

'They all have cars, if that's what you mean.'

'And are they, as we used to say, alienated?'

'Put it this way. They are eating lunch alone in their cars, and waiting between classes, even as we speak. What do you call that?'

She had sold her own Volks to be in a place like this. Everything had had weight, solidity, value. The fat books on the library shelves, the ideas with real meaning, the angers that turned political, translating themselves into action, marches, shouts. But what of this neutral, free-floating vacuum where she sat now, chatting about nothing, her hand touching window-glass to remind herself she was real?

'I had a boy in class this morning. He said if I murder you here and now, and they catch me out in the corridor, they have nothing on me, for I am no longer the same person I was when I killed you.'

'Comforting. I wish you a happy year.'

When her afternoon classes were finished, she checked at the office for anything left in her box. Gemma was there, slaving away at essays. A doctoral candidate asked Consuela about the world upstairs he aspired to enter. Could they use a staffroom for their consultations? Would the piece-rate for essay corrections go up a cent or two? Would they get paid for writing assessments? The stale air, the drained human energy at the end of an institutional day, the cleaning-staff vacuuming intellectual detritus off the corridors – she had walked away from it half her life, into the sub-zero freshness of nights in the middle west.

The city buses sat at the campus terminal, their engines idling. A few students, a staff member or two, dozed on the seats. She leant her face against the cool pane as the bus moved off, through a night of static and moving lights.

'Capitalism,' Rebecca was saying. 'Red in tooth and claw.'

They were eating lunch, a week later, in one of the franchised places on campus, looking across the city through giant panes, with the Dublin mountains beyond. Someone very rich had endowed all this – the minimalist decor, the Chinese women at the checkout, like yellow dots in a Mondrian abstract. Prices of stocks and shares flowed past each other, on a coloured screen. Would his name live for ever, that businessman? Was that what he wanted? What, anyway, was the business equivalent of for ever?

'We in the English department teach them the liberal version,' Rebecca said. 'But this is the real thing.'

They were pecking at salads, sipping at mineral water. Existing, as both of them knew, on next to nothing. The abyss of history had closed beneath them. As recently as the eighties, she had queued with her plate, in a student fug of eating and smoking, meat and vegetables, cream cakes sweltering in their own juices, as if the generations gone before them, lost and underprivileged, demanded to be fed retrospectively, by proxy as it were, through the sons and daughters who had made it through to the clear air of a liberal education.

'They will pay their own fees soon,' Rebecca said, 'if this new man has his way.'

'The things some women did in the States, to earn their fees . . .'

'I can help you to get back there,' Rebecca said instantly. 'I can write you a reference, if you like. Here it's so provincial . . .'

'On the contrary here it's international, there it's provincial.'

Rebecca began to praise, in a fulsome way, the university Ann had taught in. It had some excellent people – an eminent Dante specialist, a Bible scholar and, of course, unbeatable sports facilities. All right the social life, apart from a strip club downtown, died at nine in the evening, and you had to be part of a church or people couldn't place you. But wasn't there a famous bookshop?

'And if I wanted to stay here?'

'I couldn't promise anything. Of course you know how much we appreciate what you *do* do . . .'

Ann remembered that bookshop. It had thick beige carpets, air temp-erature control and distant, tasteful music that stayed in your mind long after you had forgotten the beautiful editions on the shelves that were somehow substanceless, unreal, as the food there tasted unreal and the neo-classical palaces of art were unreal in that different Midwestern air devoid of history. Was that the air everyone here was beginning to breathe? Once, browsing there, she had overheard a man talking to the shop assistant. His marriage had broken up, he was travelling west. He would winter in Texas or New Mexico, change his name, his work, get a new life. The terrifying openness of American space, where everything was possible and nothing was for ever – what did Rebecca know of that?

But Rebecca didn't want to get into particulars. She went on in a more general way.

'Every day, this new man demands more – the plan for next year changed, the jobs we do enlarged. Sell yourselves, he says, set out your stalls. Have open days, use your best students as advertisements. By the way, Ann, have you any exceptionally good ones we might use?'

She thought of the young man who had explained to her the benefits of postmodernism, and was changing his name. Could he be called exceptional? Or was he an image of her own infatuation with the young, her excessive desire to give them the benefit of the doubt? Would he evolve as she had, to be at odds with everything? Or merge, as her own generation had done, into contented invisibility?

'It depends what you mean by exceptional . . .'

'I mean marks,' Rebecca said decisively. 'Marks, marks, marks. Mark positively, Ann. This is a numbers game, remember.'

A week ago, Ann had slipped late into a conference. Rebecca and her colleagues sat with closed faces to one side, while on the other, a group of postgraduates presented papers. She recognised them, the young men and women who toiled in the tutors' office on the ground floor, who lived in cubbyholes all over Dublin – dressed and lipsticked now, for this ritual. The girl from Eastern Europe. The boy bringing up a baby on his own. In toneless voices they read incomprehensible texts, after which Rebecca or one of her colleagues asked a single question, not expecting an answer, simply to express superior knowledge. Ann had intervened, passionately, at one point. The whole place had stared stonily at her, and she had realised again, that truth had nothing to do with what was happening here, that this was a sifting, at an ideological level, of the willing and the intellectually complicit.

'What do you think?' Rebecca said, looking at two colleagues at a neighbouring table working on policy. 'Are they lovers?'

'They look the right age.'

They left their trays at the disposal bins and walked slowly downstairs. A young and beautiful Irish woman, in a short skirt, walked ahead of them into the grey November afternoon, clutching business folders. Was that the new happiness? Was her own and Rebecca's liberal torment a thing of the dark past? Had they sacrificed their best years for nothing?

In December, Margaret collected her off the Wexford train at Enniscorthy. They drove the nineteen narrow, slow miles to New Ross behind haulage, the trees and fields bare on either side, the road wet with leaf mould.

'You're seeing it as it really is,' Margaret said, 'not through American eyes.'

'What about the stone house?'

'It depends on commissions. I've a baptismal font in Bunclody and two headstones in Graiguenamanagh. I do it bit by bit.'

The stone house had been bought between them years ago, in another wilder life. It looked out from the woods onto the tidal reaches of the Nore. Lacking money to make it over, they had camped rather than lived in it, between times at the family home. Margaret, a stonecarver, got by on small commissions. But no great wind had blown through her life to change things. She still ate, half the week, at the family table.

'Mammy bakes, day in day out. She'll be at it even now.'

'Does she ever relax?'

'Uncle Matty's in the home. He'll be out for Christmas Day.'

Neither of the sisters had anyone in their lives. There had been men, there would be again. They took them when they wanted them, showed them the door the morning after. Thank God for the stone house, to bring them back to. Nothing bad had happened but that one thing with Ann. In the States she had taken people with trades, not grey intellectuals. Home had formed her tastes.

'Eugene's in there already,' Margaret said as they rattled into the yard. 'Waited on hand and foot.'

He was sitting in the kitchen, dandling his baby, looking absently through pebble-glasses at a television screen, while their mother scurried between the Aga stove and the table. Earning her keep, as he always said. He smiled with delight when he saw his sister, and started in at once.

'Do poets make a good living these days?'

'Only when they're dead.'

They had fought all through childhood and still tussled. Once he had made her a metal bird, a thing of strange beauty and energy. Then he had gone to agricultural college and drifted a while in London before coming back to marry and farm with their father. The spark, whatever it was, had turned to ashes.

'She had a letter in the *Irish Times*,' he laughed, pointing at their mother. 'Did she tell you that?'

'About Haughey,' the mother said timidly. 'What he has done for artists.'

'You mean like Margaret?' he jeered.

'Some day she too may benefit.'

The letter, short and sensible, the work of an intelligent country-woman, had been pointed out to her by colleagues in the common room, all of whom disapproved of Haughey, as a matter of course. Those, she noticed, who made a living off the backs of poets and artists were the most hostile to the life of art.

Her father came in, on a wave of energy. As they ate, she wondered why her mother was so afraid of him. They were ahead of their time, the pair of them. They had gone on a delegation to Romania in the communist years, to study the farming methods. In New Ross, he ran the farmers association, while she had formed a local history group. Yet the energy in the house was male. Her father, young for his age, sat there like an idling motor, even now in the slack months. Only Eugene, sure of his place in the scheme of things, was completely relaxed.

'Zinc was asking after you,' her father said sincerely.

Eugene jeered.

That night, she lay between cold sheets in the guest room. Five miles west, the lights of New Ross lit up the horizon. When they went to Romania, Ann had brought Zinc back to bed in this very room. Young Matty he had been called in those days, to distinguish him from Uncle Matty. Zinc was the name she had given him later, when he started his own garage.

'I hadn't a chance to change the sheets,' she had told him.

'I like dirty sheets,' he said.

The week before Christmas, snow fell. The whole country turned bright, as far as the Barrow. The low rolling hills, the big fields Eugene and her father worked all year. The dog clung to the wall of the yard, out of the bitter wind. She drove slowly into New Ross, on icy roads, to drink coffee in the hotel and go through texts for the coming semester. At the dockside, a ship that took summer visitors upriver lay at anchor. In the old days, Margaret had sung, played guitar on that ship, for pin money. Foreign men had loved her, there had been upsets, she had threatened once to throw herself into the water. All that was over now, the iron laws of age and necessity had made themselves felt. She moved carefully about the family home, not getting on the wrong side of anyone.

'No one will ever get Zinc,' she said to Ann. 'That man is far too careful to be caught.'

Nevertheless she met him, on a crowded Friday night at the hotel bar. His hair was greyer but he still wore his leather jacket. He drank with her, laughing his high incredulous laugh, as if nothing had happened in between and his easy-going, almost feminine approach to life was the answer to everything. You were always the aggressor, he said, as they sped out along the banks of the Nore in the small hours. She spread him on the bed and rode him, for old time's sake, on her sister's cold and borrowed sheets. We have male souls, Margaret had said to her once. We should have been born men.

On Christmas Day, instead of game or venison, they ate a great pike Eugene had caught in the Barrow. Uncle Matty had been brought over for the day. His meal lay broken in pieces on the plate before him, while he stared peacefully into space. He was living entirely in the present now.

'I'm going to Ross,' he said.

'You'd go to the moon,' Eugene cut in, 'if there was someone to take you there by the hand.'

'Hettie's raving again,' her mother said. 'Did you know that, Eugene?'

Eugene, as a boy, had tormented Hettie, their unmarried schoolmistress – slipping, with other boys into the male toilets when she went to the female side. Lifting the lid, looking along the space between, till her bottom appeared.

'And then she dropped it,' he said breathlessly, as if the years in between meant nothing. 'Hapes of it!'

That was his childhood, Ann knew. His moral horizon. Dandling his baby, he would stare into a future that repeated his past, completely at ease in the wheel of recurrence. She could feel her father, a man of few words to whom everyone deferred, looking at her. For once, they were of one mind.

At nine one January morning, she sorted the disability circulars and doctors' notes from her box. Gemma, clinging to the few teaching hours that gave her identity, ticked and annotated essays no one would look at again. Consuela, at the screen, formatted flyers for a lesbian literary conference. A young man, instructing a numbed student in Anglo-Saxon grammar, looked up and smiled at her over-solicitously. A rival.

'You see what they think of us,' Gemma sighed. 'Tea and sandwiches in the common room, but no invitation to the Christmas party.'

'We can't say we weren't warned,' the charming young man said, who already had his foot in the door for next year.

'They hire you in the autumn and kick you out in the spring,' Consuela said. 'Like seasonal migrant workers.'

Upstairs, in a cold sterile room, her group was already waiting. A blaze of women's leggings, in dialogue and competition, across empty space. Blonde hair, artificial suntans. A figure or two, sprawled at the back against the radiator. As she set out notes and attendance sheets, in that first indeterminate silence, her young man came up.

'My name is no longer John O'Dwyer,' he said. 'It's Ahmed Ali. I wonder, could you note that.'

Slowly, things got under way. She wanted to talk, she told them, about Ireland as if it was an island somewhere in the middle of the Atlantic, situated between the Old and the New Worlds. They would wander in mind and spirit, over the next nine weeks, with the émigré Irish writers who had gone in either direction. And they would find, not surprisingly in the light of twentieth-century history, that the island they were on was edging ever westward. As she went on, the friendliness and the suicidal emptiness of America opened again before her. She warmed to the fate of those who had gone before her, and those still there, for whatever reason, vanity or necessity. And it seemed to her they had left the hard life of their own land, with its tangible essences, for a glamorous afterlife over there, where they were dead without knowing it. That was somehow terrible, wasn't it? And the poems they wrote there, the novels, were like messages in a bottle, drifting back to the land of the living. Did they agree? Was that too extreme? Only the scratching of pens on paper answered her. Like a dream, the hour passed.

'And we will look at those poems and novels,' she said as the class broke up. 'But you must buy them, do you hear?'

She made her way upstairs, to the common room. There were staff and colleagues there, drinking coffee, talking window frames, patio extensions, car insurance. Habit had dried them up, the attrition of day-long meetings. They dreamed of weekends, of a conference somewhere exotic, a few summer weeks picking over the bones of a dead poet, in the air-conditioned basement of a sun-baked library somewhere in the United States.

'Our visiting writer, I see, has arrived,' one said. 'A bit rude I thought . . .'

'That's their business I suppose.'

'What is their business?'

'To shake us up. Disturb us.'

'Someone should try to attend his lectures,' Rebecca said. 'Don't let him die of loneliness.'

Sometimes Ann felt she was participating, however unwillingly, in a mass crime against the spirit. Like all mass crimes, it happened quietly, off the record as it were, with a functioning office structure, and the knowledge of what to think and say and what not, and to whom and about whom. Power and fear, masked as affability. The correct texts on everyone's shelves, their pages uncut.

'We're all dispensable,' Rebecca said to her suddenly. 'Don't give too much of yourself in here. Don't waste your best energies.'

The day went on. The grey weather moved up from the south-west, across the Dublin mountains and the Liffey, and beat in rainy gusts on the windowpanes of the cold classrooms where she taught. Everything was easier after the first tryout of new ideas. You repeated yourself more and more automatically until, after four, the last group trudged out and you went down and bought yourself a cup of tea and talked in the office with the other underdogs.

The elderly Gemma was talking over an essay, point by point, with an indifferent gum-chewing girl. Discarded lunch-packets littered the office. The doctoral students ate at their desks, the cleaning ladies swept up the remains. Consuela, on the wall, had warned of reduced correction rates, the need to assert rights. A Bible lay open on the table – consulted for phrases. A young Romanian woman spoke softly into the telephone to her lover. Would she be lucky, Ann wondered, and marry some local academic, live happily ever after . . .

'There are the ones ahead of you, whose jobs you envy,' the charming young man said to her. 'And the ones snapping at your heels, who you have to watch. It's dog-eat-dog, isn't it?'

'There are too many of us,' Ann said.

'To hell with the higher life,' he went on. 'Give me a house, a car, a regular salary – I'd be perfectly happy. Have you tried the business schools? The night schools? They might be good for the autumn.'

It was night outside, with the lights of the waiting buses and the after-shine of rain on the campus pavements. The freshness of the world came back to her, the damp air, the smell of the earth – the shock of reality. She was back on the banks of the Barrow, one summer afternoon, sunbathing nude with Margaret, in a secluded spot, while the river oozed coldly beside them, through old roots. A moment of perfect peace. You could feed on it for ever. And to think it was the wet grass that had brought it back. She would call Margaret for a long talk about nothing, or the weather.

'Kissy kissy, darling,' an out-of-work actress spoke into the wallphone on the landing. 'Keep warm, won't you darling, for me . . .'

The actress knocked on the door. She often knocked, in the small hours, looking for milk, sugar, emotional succour. We should get to know each other, she said in her throaty voice, her face ravaged by bad nights. We should all get to know each other, all us women alone in this house. She too would be gone by summer – another figure sitting at the bottom of the stairs, with a mountain of plastic bags, a box of compact discs, waiting for a taxi to take her away.

'I've had nothing but bad luck in this place,' she burst out savagely on her way out. 'I can't wait to get the hell out!'

The weeks passed. Between the rooftops, spring came in. The feeling of lateness, of extended evening light. The branches she could see through her back window put on watery blossoms then hardened again through March to a complex of green points. In all this there was lightness, the lightness of a small northern country undergoing its seasonal changes, a world away from the blaze of extremes, of heat and cold, she had known in the middle west. Hadn't the best things in civilisation come from little states like this, extending themselves to infinity?

The classes came to an end. Was there no wine, no farewell? Did everyone drift away, indifferently? She had put the best of herself into these sessions, her strange sense that the country she came from was levitating into a weightless, valueless space where everything equalled everything else. These things – disintegration, discontinuity – are not threatening but good, the best of them told her. Tomorrow we will change our names, invent ourselves again.

'Yes,' she said, as the essays came in. 'I know. You are no longer John O'Dwyer. You are Ahmed Ali.'

Already, there was a new appointment. Rebecca, with averted eyes, introduced her to the charming young man from the office downstairs, as if they had never met. A product of the Catholic mid-century, he had done his doctoral work, like herself, in the United States. He could be relied upon to keep the channels open to certain green power-centres in Japan, South Africa and the Western world, and to keep alive the flame of grievance and victimhood.

'I know Ann,' he said eagerly, grasping her hand. 'We've had great chats downstairs.'

One day in April, Rebecca gathered the rest of them together. The elderly Gemma, the young man, unshaven, with the baby on his lap, the women from Eastern Europe, desperate to stay. There have been changes, she said. We are learning, through our new president, that certain things are no longer necessary, including, I regret to say, yourselves. And that the rest of us must work ever harder, to sell this place to a new generation. Which is not to say we do not thank you, of course we do, for all you do here. But next year, only those will continue who give the students, who are after all our clients, precisely what they want.

'If anyone needs to talk to me afterwards,' Rebecca said, hyperventilating in the silence, 'I'm always in my room.'

In the office of the department, the secretaries were tying into bundles the essays received from students after the seminars. Staff breezed in and out. Sandwiches, from the latest meeting, teetered on plates on the edge of filing cabinets. Consuela, pointing at a pile of essays, was arguing.

'They are treated like slaves downstairs,' she was saying. 'The dirt they are paid, for correcting these things!'

The secretaries eyed her, with a mixture of curiosity and circumspection, before slipping into official mode. She might think, they said, of passing on those comments to the head of department. Or putting them in a letter. Or could they themselves pass them along? Rebecca herself put her head around the door, and withdrew. Ann collected her pile in silence. She was on her way back to America.

The blossom was everywhere. The trees on the campus were airy with it, the ground on which it lay was weightless as she walked away. The mountains were deep blue, and the rumour of the city came up through the deep cut the Liffey made in its lower valley as it passed, flat and slow, full of angled dripping oars from the rowing clubs, below the wall of the Phoenix Park. She would get off there, with her essays, and do them out of doors. There were trees there, greening spaces, red-brick terraces across the river, where her college years had been lived. Children played by the little lake, and their parents watched them, the men and women who once had been her contemporaries.

The summer was coming. The wheel of recurrence turned.

She was going south again, through the lives, the houses. Sandymount passed in the train window, and Booterstown, Dun Laoghaire. The sea to her left was white and quiet, on a midweek morning. Other people's working week. Then let it be so. Beyond Greystones, the land stretched flat to Kilcoole and Wicklow, where the line turned inland to Rathdrum. South of Mount Leinster, she was again in her own country, of rolling barley fields coming to a head for the first mowing. At Enniscorthy, Margaret was waiting.

'Matty died yesterday.'

'It was time he passed along.'

They talked over tea, in a cafeteria up the town. Beaten people, eating bad food, in a fug of their own making. She had always preferred Ross. So Matty was gone – a person like themselves, possessed of unusual powers and empathies. A friend of cattle-dealers, better with their animals than the local vet. A folk-healer, a carrier of collective memory. There would be a big crowd, out of nowhere, at his burial. Like themselves, he had led a nebulous life, patched together from this and that, never marrying. And yet, the world had found space for him, given him a room to return to at the end of his days. Around her, people with pinched narrow faces fed themselves obsessively.

'Why is Enniscorthy so sad?'

'Too many people with no future.'

They motored slowly on the narrow road to New Ross. There would be no phone calls this time around. No voice would call her back across the yard, as the dog shrank out of the way, and the men, so terribly certain of themselves, meshed and unmeshed the gears of a tractor-engine. The room at the turn of the stairs would already be swept and aired.

'Any sign of you making a few bob?' Eugene would warm to his theme, as soon as he saw her.

His beaten metal bird was the best of him, if only he knew it.

# Room 303

## Carlo Gébler

They hired a car at Belfast International and drove through the winter darkness. Anna was silent and he was both irritated and relieved.

At Madigan's Travel Inn he parked badly, straddling one of the white lines painted on the tarmac in the car park.

Anna opened her door and looked down. 'Ah, Liam, still as good as ever, I see.'

Her accent was English, with a hint of Ulster. This was all that remained, he thought, of the time they lived here as man and wife, that and whatever was in the graveyard.

'And you, Anna, witty as ever, I see.'

They got out. He lifted his old canvas holdall and her new black suitcase from the boot. He locked the car and they set off, the wheels on her case rumbling as he pulled it behind.

'Pity Henry's has gone,' she said.

This was the old family hotel that once stood in the centre of the town. After he met Anna at Queen's University and brought her home to meet his parents (she was billed as his English girlfriend, and his Catholic parents were not exactly delighted), she was put in the guest room while he went into his old childhood bedroom. It was impossible to creep over at night to Anna, so he took a room in Henry's and on stiff linen sheets they made love on long summer afternoons.

Later, by which time his parents were dead, when he and Anna were living in the town and working as teachers, though he'd begun to broadcast too, they would often go to Henry's for Sunday lunch, taking Ciaran, their son. The dining room had red turkey carpet and a booming grandfather clock. They loved the floury potatoes and the plates heaped with moist lamb and the rhubarb pie with thick custard that had a pliable yellow skin. The elderly waitresses always asked if you had enough and if you said no brought more.

Several years later, by which time he and Anna had left and gone their separate ways – he, along with his new wife, Geraldine, to Edinburgh and a job in radio, and Anna to London and work in a school in the East End, Henry's sold up; the hotel was knocked down and a bank put up in its place. The Madigan's hotel chain, seeing an opening, bought the old pork factory outside town and put up one of their trade-mark Travel Inns. This was the long low building they were now approaching. They negotiated a ramp and came out beside the swimming pool tacked to the end. On the other side of the glass he saw a wheelchair passing, the occupant a girl in a bikini, and three more wheelchairs by the poolside, all empty.

'Wish I'd my togs, I'd love a swim,' he said.

'Not I,' said Anna. 'My hair and Mrs Chlorine don't get on.'

Two doors slid back and they stepped into the lobby. Another wheel-chair passed. They crossed to the desk. There was a clerk behind with yellow curly hair and a big Adam's apple.

'Good evening,' he said, 'my name is John.'

'I booked two rooms,' said Liam.

'Name?'

'Cotter.'

John squinted at a screen Liam couldn't see.

'I have the booking,' said John, 'but it's just one room, a double.'

'Can't you switch us to two singles?'

No, John explained. Madigan's was completely full on account of the Irish Paraplegic Games which were taking place that weekend and so were all the town's B and Bs. The nearest place to get a bed was Belfast.

'If you want I'll try and book you something,' he concluded.

Before Liam could reply, Anna spoke: 'I'm not going to Belfast,' she said. 'If you want, go ahead but really, the blessing of the graves is tomorrow at eleven and do you really want to go off now and come back?'

The idea of the drive to Belfast, an evening on his own and then the drive back did not appeal. On the other hand, what if Geraldine dis-covered he was sharing? He could forestall that, of course, by ringing her first. That was a good idea. Then he had another thought.

'What about a discount?' he said, 'seeing as Madigan's is at fault?'

'I'll ask the manager.'

John went into an office behind the desk.

'This is why you've gone so far, of course,' said Anna. 'I'm so English and repressed I wouldn't think of asking, let alone have the courage.'

She was dissembling but he didn't care. It was more important they agree protocol.

'If the phone rings in the room,' he said, 'let me answer, will you?'

She turned and smiled. Her long hair was fair and wavy, her eyes grey. She had a large nose and a cleft in her chin. She always said it was the face of a Victorian governess – presentable but not pretty – and that accounted for her frank and sometimes acerbic manner. It was the only way to get attention.

'Christ, yes,' she said. 'Think what Geraldine would think if I answered?'

John came back.

'How'd twenty per cent be?' he asked.

They each filled in a registration form and handed these to him.

'Ah, Mr Cotter and . . . Mrs Cotter,' he read.

'We were married, once,' said Anna.

John handed Liam a plastic card for their bedroom door and the lights.

'Room 303,' he said, 'third floor. The lift is over there.'

Liam dropped the luggage and stuck the card into the unit by the door as John had explained. All the lights came on. Room 303 was big and square and there was a long curtained window, a sofa and armchairs, and a wide low bed with a brick-orange-coloured fitted woollen cover.

'I can't believe this,' he said. 'I telephoned. Spent hours speaking to someone.'

'Hours, really?' She said this in her reasonable voice.

'All right, minutes but I emailed.'

'Of course you did. You are so very punctilious.'

'Yeah, I am, aren't I?'

They hadn't even closed the door and already there was friction. But he did not want to fight. No, he definitely did not.

'You seem a bit touchy, suddenly,' she said.

'Me?'

'Is anyone else here? Yes, you.'

She'd now switched to acid mode. That was Anna. She could change tone in an instant.

'Of course I'm touchy.'

He closed the door.

'You're criticising me,' he said, though he knew self-pity, even diluted, was the worst posture to adopt with Anna.

'That sounds like something Geraldine would say,' she said. ' "Anna's always criticising you, Liam. Why don't you tell her to jump off a cliff?" ' Anna said this in a Northern Ireland accent. It was surprisingly good.

'She never says anything about you, actually.'

'Really, I'd have thought she couldn't stop gabbing about me.'

'Well, there you are, you think wrong.'

The shade of the standard lamp in the corner was touching the wall. She pulled the lamp free and tilted the shade level.

'I must say,' she said, 'I'm disappointed and annoyed. To quote our old friend Oscar, the only thing worse than being the subject of tittle-tattle is not being the subject. Don't you agree?'

She took off her long fitted coat and hung it on a rail in the cupboard.

'Let's get settled in,' she said.

Liam sat on the sofa, his bag, unpacked, at his feet. He heard Anna behind throwing things into drawers. He heard her combing her hair. Then she spoke: 'There's a mini-bar. Shall we get sloshed?'

He shook his head. 'No thanks,' he said.

He heard the little gasp as the pneumatic seal broke and the fridge door opened.

'On the wagon, are we?'

'No. I take the odd glass of wine, but that's about the height of it.'

'Oh,' she said, as if this information was highly significant.

'No, it's not Geraldine, she hasn't stopped me.'

It was actually ageing that had made him more abstemious but he didn't want to tell Anna that. She'd only mock.

'Did I say anything?'

'You don't have to. I can tell what you're thinking.'

She appeared in front of him, holding a bottle of white wine, the glass misty with condensation.

'Let's conduct an experiment. What am I thinking?'

'I've no idea,' he said.

'South African Chardonnay!' she exclaimed and then, reading the label, she went on, ' "It has an austere but attractive style." Well, Liam, that's you all over. Chardonnay was your tipple, wasn't it? The elephant me. Forget nothing you see.'

She handed him the bottle and a corkscrew and sat on the sofa beside him.

'Let's test if you really can read my mind. I'll think of something from our past and you guess what it is. To make it easy we can both hold the bottle.'

He had twisted the prong into the cork but had not pulled the cork out yet. She grabbed the base with two hands.

'I don't want to do this,' he said.

'Go on.'

She closed her eyes. 'I'm thinking. It's travelling down my arm and across the bottle and up your arm.'

He closed his eyes: 'I see Larne . . . an Orange arch . . . flags . . . it's Twelfth week and we're fleeing . . . to England . . . to your parents.'

'That's it?'

'Not quite, I see Scottish bandsmen, lots of Tennent's lager and vomit. And that is it.'

She let go of the bottle and he pulled the cork with a pop. He went to the mini-bar, filled two glasses and brought them back. They toasted one another and drank.

'You were right to think it involved driving,' she said. 'I was remembering our honeymoon. You parked somewhere in Connemara, overlooking the Atlantic. I wore a tweed skirt, a bit formal for '75, and you put your hand over and you stroked my knees. "Your lovely knees," you said, "your lovely knees." Don't look so shocked. I don't just remember the bad things. I remember the good things too. They're inscribed, you know where. Drink up.'

They both emptied their glasses and he refilled them.

'I'm going to try reception again,' he said.

She snorted. 'Why? I'm not going to jump you.'

'No, but I think, probably . . . it's for the best.'

'You're frightened of me.'

He denied this but she said he was lying because the corner of his mouth was quivering: 'It always does when you lie, as I found out.'

He called her bitter, unforgiving and twisted, but in a light joshing way.

'All things considered, I think I'm remarkably generous,' she said. 'Plus, after everything, we are having a civilised drink.'

They each emptied their glasses and he refilled them. This left the bottle empty.

'But then,' she continued, 'why wouldn't we be civilised? So much life lived together. Three years courting . . . fifteen years married, eighteen years in all and that's more time together than we've been apart.'

'Yes, I suppose,' he said carefully. He was not certain where this was going but he feared that when he got there he wouldn't like it.

'And we had a child.'

This was the first mention she'd made of Ciaran since they met at the airport. The cloudy fuzzy feeling in his head vanished and he became horribly lucid and his heart began to beat in his chest.

'We're the only two people in the world who had the child we had. That surely means something. That surely means we should be able to rub along. Wouldn't you agree, Liam?'

He was relieved to discover this was the point she'd been driving at. He nodded agreement and, as he did, he felt his heart slowing.

'I'm having a bath,' she announced. Anna took her glass into the bathroom and turned the taps on. She came back, stripped off her skirt and blouse and hung them up. Liam rang the desk to see if there'd been a cancellation. There hadn't. Anna went into the bathroom and closed the door behind. He rang Geraldine. The answerphone was on.

'Oh, hi,' he said. 'Little me speaking. Got here, met Anna at the airport. We had an awful dinner, and now I'm in my bedroom in the hotel. I'm going to have an early one. I'll ring in the morning. I love you. Good night.'

He put his black suit trousers in the press and hung the matching jacket in the wardrobe. He put his underwear in a drawer. He plugged in his charger near the bed and attached his mobile phone. He sat on the sofa again and waited. Anna came out of the bathroom in a towelling dressing gown. She sat at the dressing table and began drying her hair with a dryer.

'Are you hungry?'

'No.' He never did feel like eating when he had drink taken.

'I'm sure room service can send something up.'

'I'm not hungry,' he said.

She lifted her glass and waggled it at him. It was empty.

'Will you do the honours?'

He considered. He'd had half a bottle. Was another half going to do him any harm? No, he decided. He opened a second.

Two glasses later, by which time Anna was sitting beside him on the sofa painting red varnish on her toenails, she said, 'Why did you leave me?'

'Oh no.'

'What?'

'We're sitting here, having a nice chat, haven't argued . . .'

'Exactly,' she said, interrupting. 'There'll never be a better time to answer the question.'

He diverted her with talk of the Relate counsellor they saw when their marriage began to go wrong, a woman with bad breath, who at first seemed to side with Anna but then switched to Liam. Anna laughed and asked again, 'Why did you leave me?'

'Can't we talk about something else?'

'Oh, come on, this is too good an opportunity to turn down.'

'I don't mind.'

'Turning it down?'

He nodded.

'You've been looking at me in a funny way,' she said abruptly.

'What sort of a way is that?'

'Amorously.'

'What?' She'd changed tack so suddenly he didn't know where he was.

'You're looking at my breasts,' she said.

Her robe was slightly open and now she mentioned it her cleavage was showing.

'Actually, you're staring.'

It was only because she'd drawn his attention to her chest that he was looking in the first place. She was so unfair. He'd forgotten that.

'Do you remember, I mention this strictly in the interests of recollection, what you would do?'

'Do?'

'With just your thumb you would rub the top of the nipple and you would rub and rub and it produced what you called the thimble effect.'

'I think you should stop now.'

'Very apposite that, the thimble effect, but then, given your way with words that's only to be expected. You tell it how it is.'

There was a moment of silence. He could hear the lift mechanism in the distance.

'Sometimes you'd stroke both. That gave the two-thimble effect.'

'Please stop.'

'This reminiscence is too much?'

'Yes.'

'Why? Is it arousing feelings you'd rather not have? Are you feeling guilty? Or do you fear too much of this and you'll betray Geraldine?'

'Neither,' he said.

'Interesting answer.'

His glass was empty. So was hers.

'There's a third bottle,' she said. 'I know. I checked. Go on.'

They'd had two glasses each from the third and were talking about ageing.

'I'm considering a nip and tuck,' she said.

'Unnecessary.'

'My jaw has always been my weak point,' said Anna. 'It sags, which is strange considering what a mobile mouth I have.'

He said she should let herself age naturally and she replied this was exactly what a man would say. She wondered if he had any idea what it was to grow old and he said he had some idea. He had the bottle by the neck, the base on his knee. Anna snatched it from him suddenly and shouted, 'Conch rules.'

In William Golding's *Lord of the Flies*, which they both taught when they were teachers in two different schools in town, the boy holding the shell can't be interrupted while talking, and in their marital arguments the same rule applied with a nominated object. In their case this was usually a bottle.

'I haven't heard that . . .' said Liam.

'Since we divorced,' she said, finishing his sentence. 'Why did you leave me?' she continued, and handed him the bottle.

'I felt I was in a play all the time, and you were the aggrieved leading lady, unfulfilled, talented, thwarted, and I was the cad who always let you down. Hence the weary "Oh-God-he-is-so-disappointing" tone you had all the time. I'd had a bellyful, so I ran.'

He handed her the bottle.

'Aren't you leaving Geraldine out? You'd been seeing her before Ciaran, and I had averted my gaze and told myself, he'll come to his senses. She's young, but she's not his wife and he and her don't have a child and Liam and I do have a child, and we love our child and we're a family and he won't throw that away. That's what I thought and then

Ciaran happened and then you thought, I don't have to stay. We're not a family any more. I can split. Our tragedy was your excuse to skip off, isn't that it?'

He took the bottle back. The stem was warm from her hand, he noticed, yet the bottom, where the last of the wine slopped about, retained a glaze of condensation.

'Ciaran's death didn't kill our marriage. It just meant what would have taken five years took five minutes. It was already over and only for that was I able to go with Geraldine. Got it?'

Without waiting for the bottle she said, 'Has Geraldine seen the cold and utterly selfish side you've just shown me?'

'Conch rules prohibit extraneous argument,' he announced. 'What Geraldine sees or doesn't see, has no bearing on the subject we're discussing.'

Anna wrenched the bottle back.

'Why did you lie to her when you left a message?'

He looked puzzled.

'I was listening from the bathroom when you called home earlier. You didn't imagine I wouldn't? You said you were alone and going to sleep. You were a liar when we were married and haven't changed.'

He decided he would ignore the last point and answer the earlier charge about his character. 'For the record,' he said quietly, 'Geraldine does not see the cold or selfish side as you call it. Our relationship is good and warm and free from rancour.'

She declined the bottle and gazed at him instead.

'I shouldn't have said what I said,' she began, quietly, 'about what Geraldine sees. I shouldn't have eavesdropped either. I apologise, unequivocally.'

She had made another of her miraculous but also bewildering turns. It was one of her best techniques in arguments.

'Aren't you impressed?' she continued. 'Don't look so serious. I want another drink, please.'

He put the last third of the bottle into their two glasses.

'We have to drink to something,' Anna said.

'I'd drink to forgetfulness,' he said. 'I'd like a neat surgical operation that could take out a bit of my memory, that's what I'd like.'

'But you are what happened to you,' she said.

Her voice was filled with passion and he wondered whether a stranger listening would think she was drunk or inspired. He could no longer tell himself but that was drink for you: it robbed you of judgement.

'If the past was taken away you'd be different because it wouldn't then be there in your memory exercising its influence.'

'I wouldn't mind,' he said grimly.

'I don't want to forget even the worst things,' she said, 'not you understand that I think about them very much. I've got them in a box and sometimes . . . when I'm feeling strong . . . I lift the lid and take a peek inside and then . . . wham, I slam the lid down.'

'Don't you wish it never happened?'

'Oh yes, a new life . . . to be a different woman . . . these are some of the options I've considered over the years. This was on the couch, having my head shrunk. But, in the end, I decided I wouldn't have any of them because what I learnt . . . with a lot of agony and difficulty . . . was something I never thought I would learn. Only wish for what you can have, only try to fix the things that lie within your power to change . . . and make good the relationships you have . . .'

'Yeah,' he said, amazed she could have said something so complex and considered after what she had to drink, '. . . interesting what pain teaches.'

'That said,' she added, 'those impossible wishes, they haven't gone away you know.'

It might be dangerous, he decided, to let her talk about these, so to curtail her he found his polishing kit, and began brushing waxy polish into the soft leather of one of his good shoes.

'Always had a thing for clean shoes, haven't you?' said Anna.

'Still have.'

He watched the leather going dull from the polish, and then, after further work, the shine returning.

A few minutes later, she said, 'It's the quickest way to judge a man's character . . . how clean his shoes are . . . isn't that what you used to say?'

'Yes.'

'It's what your father said, right?'

'He did.'

'And he got it from the army?'

'Plus being a cobbler's son, plus running a shoe shop all his life.'

'You and I, both, were the first in our families to go to university.'

'Yes.'

'That probably drew us together.'

'Proles unite,' he said and laughed. 'No, the attraction wasn't based on class. It was your long legs and generous disposition, sorry.'

She stretched her legs out and admired her painted toes.

'I don't know about my pins but the disposition remains accommodating.'

He scrutinised his shoes, both now done.

'There . . . what do you think?'

'Can you see your reflection in the leather, Private Cotter?'

'I don't know.'

'Give them to me.'

She took his shoes and peered at them.

'Not bad, Private, not bad, lad,' she said in her sergeant-major voice. She slipped her bare feet into the shoes and began to stomp around the room.

'I'd forgotten how huge your feet are. I'm swimming in these.'

'I never could understand,' he said, 'with my feet being as big as they are, why I didn't grow more.'

'Your mother didn't feed you?'

'No, she fed me.'

'They say foot and cock size are related. Is that true?'

'No idea.'

'Pity.'

She took off the shoes and looked inside them.

'Church's shoes,' she said. 'Someone's doing well for himself.'

'They were a present.'

'From Geraldine, for your radio series winning that prize?'

He said nothing though it was true and he tried to keep his face still but he couldn't. She saw.

'My powers of deduction remain, as ever . . . wonderful. You've gone peaky again.'

'That's another reason I left,' he said, boldly.

'My female intuition.'

She handed him back his shoes.

'Right. What hope had I against that?'

'None actually.'

'So I fled.'

'Which makes me my own worst enemy, driving away what I could not stand to lose.'

'Don't be so hard on yourself,' he said.

'If I'm not, who else will be? Well, actually, you were for a while, I shan't forget that.'

'No.'

'But now I'm older and wiser. And forgiving.'

'Yes.'

He went into the bathroom. He ran the cold tap, wet his hands, which were stained with polish and began to soap them.

'It's time for our nightcap,' she called.

'We've had a bottle each.'

'One and a half, darling.'

'Let this be our last,' he shouted back.

He dried his hands and fixed them each a large vodka and tonic.

'I am going to feel terrible tomorrow,' he said, when he handed her a tumbler, the floating ice cubes banging against the glass. 'Can't metabolise,' he continued. 'Well, not like I used to.'

'Ah, the ageing process . . . has very little to recommend it.'

From age she segued to her break-up with her last boyfriend, Mike. In his car one day he told her he had another woman, a white Zimbabwean, with two children. After making his confession Mike thought the conversation was finished and drove Anna back to her flat in Tower Hamlets. But Anna insisted there was more to discuss. She refused to get out of his car. Mike drove to a police station, and, taking the keys, ran up the steps and disappeared inside. He had left his Filofax on the dash. Anna flipped to M – 'The girlfriend's name was Mimi and like a whore she was listed by her first name' – and proceeded to write in pen, over the pencil entry, Miss Slut, 26, Whoresdale Road, Flabby Fanny, near Gonorrhoea Corner, Brothel Town, Cuntland. Mike and two policemen appeared. Anna was pulled from the car and Mike drove off. When she got to the end of the story, which had made Liam chuckle, she said, 'what do you think of that?'

'You're barmy.'

'Good story though.'

It was. He had to admit that.

She finished her glass and asked for one more, promising it would be her very last. He made another round of drinks.

'Thank you kindly,' she said, taking the glass.

'It's what I'm good for,' he said, sinking down heavily. He would have to drink this one slowly. He suddenly felt quite drunk.

'Which is what?' she said.

'Mixing drinks.'

'Oh, that and a few other things,' she said.

The belt of her robe had come loose and he could see her belly button and her stomach, which was quite brown and still surprisingly flat. He wondered if she'd undone the belt deliberately but decided he was wrong, deluded. That was the way with towelling gowns; the belts just came undone.

'Cheers. Longevity,' she said.

'Forgetfulness, oblivion.' He clinked her glass with his.

'But think how much you'd lose.'

'You're repeating yourself. You've said that already.'

' "Your lovely knees," you said. Do you remember . . . on our honeymoon?'

Her voice had a thrilling undertow of passion.

'I wouldn't want to forget that moment, would you? You wouldn't, you couldn't. That would be a crime, wouldn't it?'

He said nothing.

'Could you forget the way the little hire car smelt of cough sweets,' she said, 'the churning Atlantic spread out all along the horizon and the way the side windows steamed up, and then what happened next? I pulled out your cock . . . and when you came there was just the faintest taste of the Branston pickle you'd had with your cheese in the pub for lunch . . .'

He revised his opinion about the belt. It hadn't come loose. She'd undone it.

'I can't,' he said.

'What?'

'Sleep with you.'

'What?'

'I can't possibly sleep with you.'

'Why not?'

'For old time's sake, is it? The so-called mercy fuck? You are incorrigible.'

Liam started to laugh, nervously, then, with more and more gusto, and after a while, he noticed, she was laughing with him but her robe was still open.

He woke. His head felt heavy. He opened his eyes. He was on the sofa, his feet tucked in under one armrest, his head jammed under the other, and his body curled between the two. There were rumpled blankets, which he had found in the cupboard, lying over his body, and a pillow from the double bed – where Anna lay sleeping – under his cheek. He sat up carefully. He felt sluggish but not as terrible as he expected given what he had had to drink. He'd had several glasses of water and two Alka Seltzers before he lay down the night before and they had taken the edge off his hangover. He needed to pee though. He padded to the bathroom. His pee came out in a long colourless stream. He drank more water. He closed the door, ran a shower and got under. As the water streamed onto his face he felt better. Over the next few minutes he edged the control along the blue line until the water was cold. He felt better still. He turned the control the other way, washed his hair in warm water, dried himself and dressed in the good trousers and shoes, the shirt and the vest he had brought. It only remained to shave. He went back to the bathroom, and began to lather his face using a brush and a geranium-scented soap in a wooden bowl.

'Morning,' he heard.

Through the open door he saw Anna, her head on the pillow, looking at him. He would need to be extremely careful after the way things ended the night before.

'Oh,' he said.

'Is that all you can say? Where's good morning? What ever happened to old-fashioned civility?'

She had only opened her eyes and already she was on. He felt irked. Before he could stop himself, the words came out.

'I don't know,' he said. 'You tell me.'

'I think someone's a bit shirty this morning. Someone didn't get his beauty sleep, perhaps?'

'No.'

In the mirror he saw his face with its beard of soapy white. With long strong strokes he began to pull the blade upwards, intermittently running his razor under the hot tap to clean the head.

'How did you sleep then?'

'Fine,' he said.

'You slept fine on the sofa? Come off it.'

'No, it was fine.'

'You'd have been much comfier in this lovely bed, you know.'

'Honestly, I was fine.'

'I'm waiting, you know.'

'For what?'

'For a pee,' she said.

'I thought you always said your bladder was cast iron.'

'Yes, I did, didn't I? I'd forgotten. When we made love in the morning, I never needed to pee before and you always did.'

She sat up in bed.

'You know, that's what's so great about spending time together, like this, you discover all these little nooks and crannies from the life you had forgotten.'

He ran the blade carefully over his upper lip.

'I'm sorry, I can't wait.'

She threw back the covers and stood up. She was naked. At first he was surprised by her bareness but that quickly gave way to curiosity. The skin was a little looser here and there and the flesh a little plumper but this was unmistakably the woman to whom he had been married and with whom he had had a child, and fifteen years on, the sense of reconnection with what had once been so familiar was unexpectedly pleasing.

She came into the bathroom behind him and reappeared at his side.

'I'm not waiting a second longer,' she said, quietly.

'I haven't finished.'

'My need is greater than yours.'

Pushing him with her belly she shunted him out of the doorway and into the bedroom, then closed the door.

'You're impossible,' he shouted.

'Is breakfast coming?'

'Yep.'

Before bed the night before he had filled in the form and hung it in the corridor on their doorknob.

'Full Irish?'

'Naturally.'

The lavatory flushed and the door opened. Anna stood at the sink with a towel around her.

'Can I use your toothbrush?'

She took the brush from his bag.

'Can't you use your own?'

'I want to use yours.'

'Why?'

'Because.'

She brushed and came out of the bathroom rubbing her tongue over her teeth and came up to him.

'You've got lather on your face.'

'You booted me out of the bathroom, in case you've forgotten. I didn't get a chance to wash my face.'

'I'm a rotter, aren't I?'

'Not always.'

'High praise from His Majesty.'

'I'm not bitter,' he said. 'I don't believe in abolishing history. You could be marvellous . . . the rows were dreadful but when we made up after, I admit it was always . . . wonderful.'

He wanted to touch her cheek but before he could make a move she had taken the razor from his hand.

'Let me wipe your face. You don't mind me wiping your face?'

She tossed the razor into the sink and then, using a corner of her towel, she carefully wiped the lather from his chin and his ears.

Then she stepped closer to him. She was almost touching.

'There, you're all dry and smooth.'

He could feel her breath and smell the toothpaste.

'We have a two-thimble situation,' she said.

He heard the lift rumbling through the walls again.

'There's no better cure for a hangover,' she said. 'We always agreed on that, didn't we? And my mouth's all fresh. I'm ready.'

'For what?'

'For kissing of course.'

They fell on the bed. She unzipped his fly and a moment later he was inside. Anna gave a small sigh and tilted her pelvis towards him in a way that was both totally familiar and utterly unique to her. A sense of recognition, similar to when he saw her naked but far stronger flooded through him. He wanted to enjoy the sensation of being inside her, the taste of her mouth, the slope of her shoulders, and the re-establishment of contact with everything else with which he had been intimate for such a long part of his life, but after a few moments he felt the ability to savour receding. Carried away by desire, there was only one thing that mattered now. He was aware then of knocking on the door. Hell, he thought, breakfast.

'Hang on, just minute,' Anna called feverishly. 'Come on,' she whispered. She reached between their legs and cupped him tenderly just as she would have always done when they made love in the past before his climax. A moment later all sense that he was in a particular place at a particular time vanished, and with his mind's eye he saw a great white light. A moment later again he came and then immediately after he felt the delicious post-sex weariness.

The knocking resumed.

'Yeah, coming,' Anna called.

He fell off her, stood and zipped himself up.

'Coming,' he shouted.

He opened the door and found himself facing John, with his curly hair and big Adam's apple.

'The breakfast,' he said, 'I have it.'

He carried in the tray, which looked heavy, and set it on the table. Anna, now sitting up in bed, her shoulders bare but the rest of her body covered, called over, 'Good morning.'

'Shall I open the curtains?'

'Please,' Anna said.

While he fiddled with the drapes Anna mouthed at Liam, 'Tip.' Liam located his wallet, found some coins and threw the wallet on the end of the bed.

The curtains swished open to reveal a sweep of lawn with fir trees behind planted as a windbreak. The sky was grey and the cloud low.

'Not a bad day,' said John, turning.

Liam pressed the coins into John's palm.

'Thank you,' he said. 'Now, the plates are very hot. Enjoy breakfast and have a fabulous day.' He turned and stopped. 'You're the parents of the Ciaran Cotter lad. "Have a fabulous day" . . . at the blessing of the graves. I'm sorry, I don't know where that came from.'

Anna smiled beautifully.

'You know the only thing that would offend?'

'Ah, Anna,' Liam began, hoping to stop her.

'Pretending it never happened, sweeping it all under the carpet . . . you know . . . the new orthodoxy . . . Whatever you do, don't talk about the dead or the Troubles . . . that's what I can't hack.'

As John, mollified by this, left and closed the door behind him, Liam's mobile rang and, before he could stop her, Anna had picked it up from the bedside table.

'Hello.'

From the look on Anna's face he knew who it was.

'I'm in Liam's room now,' she said, 'about to tuck into the Celtic equivalent of the ploughman's lunch, the full Irish.' She added the reason they were in Liam's room was because the dining room was full of people in wheelchairs on account of the Irish Paraplegic Games. It was a lie of such simplicity, delivered with such fluency, he knew Geraldine wouldn't doubt it.

He took the phone, went to the window and stared out at the fir trees. As his long, anodyne conversation with Geraldine unfolded, he was aware of Anna behind. She had made herself a bacon sandwich and then she was taking something from his wallet. That was a strange thing to be doing and then, appalled, he realised what she was doing.

'I've got to go now, Geraldine,' he said. 'I've got to eat the breakfast and get ready.'

But she wanted to know exactly when he would get back and exactly what he wanted to eat. He could sense anxiety behind the solicitude. She hadn't liked him coming to Ireland and meeting up with Anna. She wanted him home and she needed to know he was absolutely and uniquely hers. All of this was in her tone.

'I'll be home about eight,' he said.

Anna was moving across the room, her food in one hand, the clipping in the other.

'Pasta and a bottle of red,' he suggested. 'A nice night in.'

Anna disappeared through the bathroom doorway. The door closed. The lock snapped inside. Jesus, he thought.

'So I'll see you later,' he said.

'Tell me you love me.'

'I love you,' he said.

'Me too, I love you,' said Geraldine.

The line went dead. He shoved the phone into his pocket and hurried to the bathroom door and turned the handle. The door wouldn't open of course. He put his ear to the wood. On the other side he could hear Anna sobbing quietly and hiccuping, as happened sometimes when she cried. He knocked on the door and asked Anna to let him in. She refused. He pleaded. She wouldn't budge.

'I'll break the door down,' he said. After threatening this for several more minutes, he convinced her he meant it and he heard the lock turn. He swung the door open. Anna stood at the sink, a wet flannel pressed to her face. The yellowing cutting lay open beside the basin, with its headline in bold: 'Scenes of grief at funeral of local boy'. The bacon sandwich she had made lay nearby. It was untouched.

'You're a masochist,' he said.

She patted her face dry, reached for her foundation and began to smear it on.

'I suppose you thought threatening to break the door down was going to make me less upset?' she said finally.

'So you read it? Well, first you took it, and then you read it?'

'Yes, I read it. "The whole town came to a complete standstill," she began, quoting the opening paragraph, "on Thursday last for the funeral of the IRA bomb victim Ciaran Cotter, killed while caddying with the Northern Ireland Employment Secretary, Lord . . ." '

He picked up the clipping.

'Yes . . . all right . . . I know what it says.'

He folded the clipping carefully. The paper was dry and powdery and he took particular care to crease it where it had always been creased.

'Why in hell's name did you take it?'

'Saw it in your wallet . . . when it was lying on the bed . . . saw it sticking out . . . and I couldn't stop myself . . .'

He found his wallet, put the clipping behind the bills where he always kept it, pulled on his jacket, and put the wallet in the inside pocket. He found his black tie, went back to the bathroom, and stood beside Anna in front of the mirror and began to put his tie on.

'You should have stopped yourself, you know,' he said.

'How could I?'

'Exercise of willpower.'

'There are some things willpower won't ever override. This was about him . . . our son . . .'

'You'd read it before.'

'At the time, I must have, I don't remember, one doesn't remember. Pain . . . grief . . . is such a huge overwhelming thing. It cancels everything else out. But I must have. I mean I had to have because as I'm reading it just now I find just the second before I read it I know the next word that's to come. It's all in my head.'

She put on her black dress and they sat down at the table to eat. The food was cold but he cleared a plate. Anna ate only a piece of toast. She talked instead about the cutting and then she said, 'Can I tell you something?'

Some terrible confidence was coming but he couldn't stop her now.

'When I heard the explosion I was at home, it was Saturday, and I thought it came from the direction of the golf course and I remember thinking, "Could it be?" and then thinking, "No, they wouldn't put a bomb on a golf course, would they? Not even they'd do that." Then I heard the sirens. "Oh yeah, there they go," I thought. And then I thought nothing more of this terrible calamity, unfolding in this miserable town until a police car came and stopped outside the house. I remember looking at the police car and thinking "That's strange" but still not connecting it to me. And then I watched the policeman getting out in his flak jacket and thinking "I wonder who he's come to see?" I still didn't think it was me. And then I watched him dive back into the car and when he came out he had his hat . . . his fucking hat . . . and he put it on and straightened it. And at that moment I knew he had come for me and that the news was the worst. The hat told me that.'

'I see that.'

'Can you see it? With its little peak and its harp and crown badge and the leather band inside the rim, shiny from wear?'

'Yes,' he said simply, and yes, he could see it, oh yes he could.

'And can you imagine what that moment was for me . . . I'm not saying it's worse than your worst moment . . . but for me you can see . . . how awful it was . . . that moment when I knew before I knew.'

'Yes,' he said.

She began to cry quietly. He put his hand out and she took it.

'It's very good not to be completely alone.'

'I have to agree,' he said. 'I can't say I'm keen on it myself.'

He pulled his chair towards her and she pulled hers to him. Then she leant against him and he felt her wet hot face against his neck. That was when he remembered the way she talked the night before about wishes that didn't go away. He should let her have her say. He could at least do that, couldn't he?

'If God came down and said, "Anna, whatever you want, have it", what would you say?' he asked.

There was a long pause. Gradually, the sobbing stopped.

'Well, obviously, I would ask to get into the coffin . . . that would be the thing I would ask of God if he came down and granted me a wish. Just to get in there. But not with Ciaran as he is now. No, obviously, of course not. This is a fantasy. It would be Ciaran then. And not even Ciaran then. It would be Ciaran dead, of course, but Ciaran whole not blasted and mangled like he was . . . but he would be dead and yes, he would be actually cold. I mean, I'd know he was dead because I know he is dead. I'm mad but I'm not that mad. And I would be in there, down there and I would hold him . . . hold that dead body. I never had the chance, you remember, to do that . . . you protected me by not letting me touch the corpse. Obviously, this is a completely unrealistic fantasy. I mean, I say this is what I'd ask God but of course even he couldn't give me back the boy as he was unblemished without interfering with the past which even God, I think, couldn't or wouldn't do. So what I'd ask for . . . instead . . . you see I've given this a lot of thought . . . what I'd ask for . . . Christ I'm suddenly . . . I'm suddenly embarrassed.'

'Don't be.'

'Why should I trust you . . . why should I expose myself?'

'Oh . . . what's coming is more . . . revealing . . . than wanting to get into the grave? What could top that?'

She sighed.

'I'd ask God for a radio transmitter. It would be in Ciaran's headstone . . . and . . . back in my flat in Tower Hamlets I'd have the receiver permanently on. And any time . . . day or night . . . I could tune in and hear the sound of the rain falling . . . the rooks cawing in the trees . . . you know how they're always cawing in the graveyard . . . and the sound of the wind blowing in from the Lough. That's what I'd ask for . . . which I think is very reasonable, don't you agree? I don't think God would mind, do you? It's not a lot to ask?'

She sat up and dried her eyes.

'We did something,' she said, 'that no one else did . . . we made a child and that . . . that made a special bond . . . between us . . . you see that don't you?'

He realised then that the moment of intimacy earlier, which was botched and hopeless anyway, was irrelevant to their future. This was the moment when he made the decision. Here was the fork, the empty road one way, the other with Anna standing in the middle, going the other. So, which was it to be? The words came out without his even thinking them.

'Yes, I do see that,' he agreed.

He packed his bag and washed his teeth carefully. Anna finished her make-up and packed her case. They pulled on their coats. They both stood side by side in the middle of the room looking around in case they had left anything behind.

Anna was saying something but he wasn't listening. He was thinking about what had just happened, what she had said, what he had said in reply, and what this meant. His trajectory, his life, was about to go in an entirely new direction. Or was it? Suddenly, he was uncertain.

'Did you hear me?' she said.

He hadn't and he shook his head. 'Come again,' he said.

She looked into his eyes and he looked back into hers and he saw she believed she had just confirmed their understanding. And he knew for certain he had started on something he previously believed was impossible. The prospect was as thrilling as it was appalling but it was too late to go back now.

'Let's go.'

He took his holdall and her suitcase. They walked out, leaving the door open, and made their way down the corridor to the lift bay.

# Red Tide

## Desmond Hogan

Tonight is the night of the Red Tide – Saint Valentine's Day. Nutrients from inland, with the change of season, after rainy weather, light up the combers, blue and white.

For some days patisserie windows have been full of pralines – cakes composed of mousse, caramel and pecan nuts. Earlier there were boys on skateboards on the boardwalk in Bermuda shorts with busbys or traveller's cheques on them, carrying bunches of Greek wild flowers. Groups of old ladies in owl-eye glasses, in the ruby lake of Mickey Mouse or the lemon of Donald Duck, paraded by the ocean.

An elderly man in a Borsalino hat passed a shaven-headed Chinese boy, with a birthmark on his face like a great burn, who was staring at a flock of plovers, and I thought of shirts I'd worn in London as if they'd been women I'd known – a long-sleeved terracotta shirt with sepia roosters, a short butterfly-sleeved vermilion shirt with coral-grey swallows.

'How do you get to Amsterdam? You take a bus through Ranelagh.' I had this dream shortly before I went to Amsterdam for the first time.

I went with Rena. We were going to travel south from there. In London before setting off we went to an Andy Warhol double-bill and all the beautiful naked young men inspired a greater intensity in our lovemaking.

We stayed with a Dutch couple we'd met while hitch-hiking that summer in north Connemara. In the window of the corner café, despite it being late September there was a Santa Claus with a hyacinthine beard with little acorns on it.

The couple gave us kipper soup for supper, and the following morning we had breakfast cake. On our one full day in Amsterdam we purchased two dozen or so postcards of Jan Mankes' paintings and drawings to send to friends. A few self-portraits of Mankes. One in a tiny Roman collar and smock, with a wing quiff, against a lemon landscape. Hair sometimes brown, sometimes amber. Eyes sometimes blue, sometimes brown. A woman in silhouette tending geese. A woman with head dipped in a gaslit room. Salmon-coloured roofs. An old person with a nose like a root vegetable. Birds in snow. An art nouveau, besequinned turkey. A landscape breaking into water. A bunch of honesty. A mouse in the snow. Geese with their beaks to heaven. Goats looking as if they're wearing clogs. A rattan chair. A nightingale. A kestrel. A thrush. An owlet. A reading boy. Birch trees.

It was as if these cards and their images by a painter who'd died young, held together before being despatched on a day when cyclists held golf-size umbrellas, composed our lives as they had been together.

In Paris we slept near the statue of Henry IV on Pont Neuf.

Then we hitch-hiked south. We had an ugly row when we reached the warmth but then a truck took us and brought us as far as Marseille where we both had our first sight of the Mediterranean, cerulean-ash.

The grapes were translucent, hands reaching under them. The hills of Provence at evening were like little stone walls, Roman ruins.

A truck driver with a moustache took us to Monaco where he put us up for the night in an apartment looking to the sea, gave Rena a T-shirt with Gerd Müller of Bayer Leverkusen soccer team on it.

Our first day in Italy we had pasta in a workers' café in the suburbs of Milan, given to us by a blonde waitress in black.

In Venice Rena's face, with her silver-blonde hair and starling's egg-blue eyes, was reflected in glass just blown in a little canal-side glass-making place. Her life, her anxieties were in those reflections; a French schoolboy's cape, autumn leaves in Dublin, mustard-coloured leaves lining the long avenue.

We did not stay in the Excelsior Hotel on the Lido. We slept in a large cement pipe but we took advantage of the cordoned-off beaches around the Excelsior. Last effigies of beauty on those beaches in the faltering sunshine of fall-boys in hi-waist bathing togs.

On the way back we took a tram through the narrow streets of La Spezia, then walked by the apricot, papaya, yellow ochre-coloured houses of Portovenere to the rocky place where the Harrow mutineer Lord Byron used to swim.

Perhaps it was the light or lack of sleep, but I saw a child there, a little boy in a blue-and-white-striped T-shirt.

Rena went back to Dublin from London. I stayed in a house in Hanwell with a reproduction of Arthur Rackham's young Fionn on the wall.

Later in the fall I ventured to Italy again. Mustard-coloured leaves were reflected in the front mirror of a truck heading towards Florence.

In the Uffizi a Japanese girl with bobbed hair, in a long skirt and high-heels with bevelled undersides, paused in front of Botticelli's young man in a skull cap holding a honey-coloured medallion.

On a day trip to Siena I sent a postcard reproduction to Dublin of a self-portrait Dürer did at twenty-two, red-tasselled cap, carrying field eryngo in his hand. Eryngium in German means Man's Fidelity.

I saw the turbanned Ancient Egyptian Hermes Trismegistus in a pavement mosaic at the entrance to the cathedral.

In Viareggio, where the drowned Shelley was cremated with salt and frankincense in the flame, the sky was grey, there were tankers at sea, gold lace on the combers. I swam at the beach there. The grey lifted shortly after Viareggio.

In Rome the skies were cerulean. I paused in front of Pope John XXIII's pilgrim door, I saw the statue of a young early Christian shepherd with corkscrew curls, I saw a mural Mussolini had commissioned depicting Odysseus embracing his son Telemachus, I sat in the sunshine near the persimmon throat of a fountain, I listened to Bob Dylan's 'A Satisfied Mind' under the statue of Giordano Bruno. That statue spoke years later. I read somewhere that he'd said: 'Through the light which shines in the crocus, the daffodil, the sunflower, we ascend to the life that presides over them.'

One night when I slept in a train by Rome's pre-war brown station I was beaten up and everything I had robbed. I had to return to England with a document the Irish Embassy gave me and some money my father sent me. An English girl on the train gave me a jersey of kingfisher blue. The sea was harebell blue at Folkestone. I was stopped by the police. The English girl stood with me. Back in Dublin at Christmas I found Rena was having an affair with a boy with a Henry the Eighth horseshoe beard.

I started teaching in the new year in a school where a boy brought an Alsatian to school one day, where a prostitute used to come into the yard and sing a Dublin courtship song: '. . . And I tied up me sleeve to buckle her shoe.'

At Easter Rena and I were travelling again together. We had a camera, and in Cork, outside Frank O'Connor's cottage, where a woman neighbour had chased an anti-Parnellite priest with a stick, we were photographed, and little boys, many of them, arrived out of nowhere and posed behind us, cheering. It was as if they were cheering on my own stories. The roll of film was lost.

The previous Easter we'd stayed in a cottage one weekend in Ballinskelligs with a photograph of a young man in a zoot suit, kipper tie, wing-tip shoes on the wall.

The following weekend, Easter weekend, I returned to Kerry alone and swam in olive-drab underpants in the turquoise water at Clogher Strand.

In the summer we camped near a cliffside barracks in Duncannon in County Wexford and mutually flirted with the soldiers.

Rena had gone to school in the West of Ireland, a school with a picture of a Penal Day's mass on the wall and bits of information from an erudite old nun there were always breaking through her conversation. 'Lord Cornwallis who suppressed the Rising of 1798 had previously lived in Yorktown – New York.'

Near Enniscorthy we picked up a boy in a tiger-stripe tanktop and hipster jeans and he slept in the tent with us, and after I'd made love to Rena my hand touched his chest.

Some weeks after our trip to Cork bombs went off in Dublin and shortly afterwards Rena went to California.

In October 1976 I went to California from Dublin to see her. In the evening at San Francisco airport her eyes were the blue of a bunch of chicory. She wore a long scarlet skirt surviving from Connemara days. I gave her an old edition of a book by Kate O'Brien. Inside was a motif of swans.

The following afternoon on a boat in San Francisco Bay she asked me about death, mortality. She'd joined a religious group.

We hitch-hiked north together, staying in a motel in Mendocino. I'd been working with a street theatre group in Dublin.

She wore a honeycombed swimsuit. The whales were going south, a *passeggiata* on the horizon. There was a great palm tree on the beach, maybe the last one north. The distant whales, the morning ultramarine of the Pacific were framed by rocks on either side of the beach as if it was a theatre scene.

She returned to Dublin the following May. The last time I made love to her easily there was an image of Mexican forests in my mind. At a party in Dublin, in front of everyone, a girl accused me of impotence and after that I couldn't make love to Rena any more. She went back to California.

Years later in Southern California a boy in a lumber jacket with mailbox pockets would explain the nature of schizophrenia to me – people say things or do things that have no connection with their emotions, with what they feel.

In the summer in southern Egypt, near where some of the Gnostic Gospels were found – Coptic priests in flowing black robes among the little white houses, iron Coptic crosses nearby in the desert – I swam in the Nile, despite the fact I was warned that there were insects in it which could get into your blood. The Nile was an earthenware-jar cerulean.

I was feeling dead after the attack in Dublin. I walked out into the night in southern Egypt. There were great palm trees against the stars and distantly a man on a camel moved in the desert. In the desert night there were strange sounds, almost songs, half chants by male voices. There was nothing to distinguish the scene from two thousand years ago. That night I decided to live.

Next morning I went for a swim in the Nile again. There were a few little boys in nappy-like garments paddling. No other swimmers.

On the way back north I visited an Irish poet on a Greek island whose address I'd been given in Dublin. On his hall-stand was a Spanish hat.

There were dances on the island in a dance venue that was covered but with open sides. Young men in glove-fitting jeans and girls in white party dresses stood around. The instruments were shot-gold and the band played the summoning mariachi music of a village afternoon gala. Priests drank coffee on tables that were covered in chequered red and white.

Sophisticated Americans, in bush shirts belted below the waist or cheesecloth peasant dresses, came to dinner one night and everyone dined on the patio. The Americans showed little interest in me. When they were gone the poet said, 'Tomorrow you'll be gone and nothing I say will make any difference.'

On the wall there was a signed black and white photograph of Anna Akhmatova. He'd met her in Taormina in 1964 when she'd been awarded the Taormina Prize. Before I left he gave me a book of her poems. I saw dolphins on the Aegean on my way back to the mainland.

In a café in Belgrade there was a bunch of marigolds beside a bottle of white wine in half wicker.

Rena's voice returned with some information the old nun had given her. 'J. F. Gravelet, the French tightrope-walker Blondin, stood upon his head, wheeled a man in a barrow blindfold and cooked an omelette on a stove on a tightrope across the Niagara Falls.'

A raven had lived near the convent and once stole one of the nun's habits for its nest. Did I know what ravens' eggs looked like Rena had asked me on a boat in San Francisco Bay? Remarkably small for the size of the bird, pale blue or pale green, with dark brown spots and ashy markings, but sometimes just pale blue.

It's like painting a bunch of marigolds I thought years later in southern California, to keep the light, to make something. It's to accept the gravity of marigolds; marigolds on the station platform of a small town in County Galway; a bunch of marigolds on a shelf in a café in Belgrade on a fall morning.

There are frontiers beyond which a person can't go, frontiers of shatterment. My friend vanished into a village of condominiums and caravans in northern California. Often in the British Library in London, placed in a book, I'd come across a card for the religious group she'd joined, an emblem of laminated pink rosebuds on what could have been the silver of an old man's hair.

# Waking in a Strange Place

## MARY LELAND

Through the dark the lights that mark Askeaton gleam in a cluster made golden by distance. The fields are visible only by their depth of mist. The trees hold patterned stars hung in dimming stencils against a sky softened by ambient town glow. Maeve imagines she can see the castle's gaunt, serrated gable, that she can hear the river rushing past its bawn. The night around her is not silent. The land has its whispers, its calls and signals, its sudden flurries of sound or hidden movements. Up here among the trees the undergrowth of autumn has quietened with her disturbance. As the darkness thins its life returns, a quick harsh startling cry, a gasp as if of quickened breath, the gust of something passing close, unsuspecting, unalarmed, so furtive has been her own bedding into the lap of the hill.

Preparing for this night she had not thought she could sleep. It is a little adventure, something she has dared herself to do, a promise made which now she has to keep. An intruder, she huddles in her nest of fern and rock, cloaked in her rug as through the centuries many must have lain in the fields, among the rocks, on guard. Maeve is an intruder. Yet the night embraces her, the smells rank and damp but not unfamiliar. She is almost comfortable as images prowl their way into her idling mind. She is not the first to find this cranny, to set her back against this stony slope, to look westwards through the dark, imagining the castle's keep and barefaced high defiant walls.

Thousands have gathered here, half a thousand years ago. These are the presences which haunt Maeve, hearing from her lair the tumble of the stream a mile away, feeling more than seeing those unbidden images which, even at home, reading herself to sleep, can file between the pages slipping from her hands and which now, here in the wintry dark, have a vitality and insistence she seems unable to repress.

Random as they are, they penetrate some slanting crevice in her mind. They have their own particularity, voiceless yet potent. They seem immediate to this occasion, to her vigil on this hillside, to her waiting half-asleep for the keeping of a promise. It is as if her mind is trying to catch its breath, or to retrace, somehow, the steps taken by others before her.

There is no comfort in remembering, because she does not remember now, that only six hours ago she was among friends, cheered by their own sense of mission and of daring as they struck out one by one for their posts among the trees, along the hillside, above the plain. Instead her mind envisages a meeting on a rough-hewn road, the clasping of hands across the sweating rearing backs of impatient horses, the illicit joy in the keeping of a tryst, the sealing of a covenant. Where is this coming from?

'Mind yourself out there,' Beth had advised when they talked of this vigil. 'Waking up in a strange place can do things to your head.' Ironic but not indifferent, Beth has not joined her. Friends can protest in different ways as much as for different cause. And Maeve knows that friendship is a balancing act; it takes skill to distinguish between intimacy and confidence. Beth may be her intimate friend – certainly she was once – but Maeve has not confided in her, for example, about Hugo except, once, to describe him lightly as 'a gentleman caller'.

Maeve shudders to the chilling of her flesh as she rouses herself, the late November dawn disturbing her drowsing watch. Waking as if her mind were itself webbed with the stranded smells and colours of a memory, she shrugs herself more fully, more gratefully, into consciousness. No longer dreaming but stretching uneasily on the bracken the stiff actualities of her discomforts shred the phantasms of the night. She reminds herself that up here on the heather and the stone it is easy to believe in the ghostly steed with silver shoes said to rise from the lake below, a legend cantering into these oak cloisters and vanishing in a vapour, soundless, vague as a comet.

She has quenched her torch, knowing before she slept that two hundred yards away another torch will answer any signal, and further on again another and another. The leaves rustle as she moves. She lies for a while content in the darkness, almost warm, almost comfortable. The taint of her dream dissipates in the stench of fern and flattened grass, the fuzz of lichen. She is wholly herself, yet there is a trace somewhere in the way she breathes of something other, a death, a solitude. She has been close to a man's dying. The worn leaves which shatter as she moves remind her of his fragile flesh, the rustle as his skin slipped from her clutch. Was this the resonance, somewhere within her mind, stirred by these conditions of watching, waiting, flicked like a torch into a dream of hope and disaster? Yet no beacons have marked her companions among the trees; in this dawn she expects no other flare than the one she seeks low to the east, her comet.

Awake, alone, she remembers how that month the heavens shone. The hospital was built beyond the city and from its windows to the east and north she had watched for the asteroids, the sprinkling of flaring dust through the galaxies. All the light was behind her, the effluent light which dimmed the skies, and from the railed roof she had watched the stars falling, falling, into nothingness. Those hours had been a postponement. She knew it even then. She knew it when Beth had arrived at her side, staring upwards too in friendship's sharing of the post of sentinel. Then in a gesture Maeve would always remember, even though it was made in this darkness, Beth pushed the flat palm of her hand hard against her eyes. It was what those Somali women, those Rwandan women, those African women did to dry the tears of starvation and of grief, familiar through television. A brushing aside of despair.

'They want you now,' Beth had said. 'You must go in. He's asleep. I left him in a good place.'

Maeve was trembling. 'They want me to let him go. To let him not wake up. They say – let nature take its course. It's killing me, Beth!'

In the silence Maeve felt Beth's dry hand rest on hers where she clutched the railing.

'This isn't about you. It's about him.'

Beth's voice too was dry, a surface dryness as of clothes inadequately wrung out after washing. She said, 'I was reading something, an article in a magazine. A memoir. It said that there comes a time when a dying man has to die as a tired man has to sleep. Col is tired, Maeve. He has fought and struggled from the beginning of this. You know what it has cost him. He has nothing left to fight with. He has to rest. He has to sleep.'

'That's what the doctors said this evening. But it means I'll be killing him!'

Beth said nothing. She had been with Maeve when the consultant had beckoned them away from the bedside, had brought them both to sit in a grubby little room, stained and littered with cigarette butts, a drooping curtain holding back the sun. This death, they learned, was now inevitable. It could be easy, in his sleep, a slow natural closure. Or he could be allowed to recover from this last procedure to live for – what? Four, five days? – until the fluid in his remaining lung drove out the last thin breaths. He would drown. Almost a week, it seemed to Maeve. What would he have wanted to do with that one last week? Who could say?

The consultant drew a diagram – very legible, he must be used to this, thought Maeve. All the hospital needed from her was the permission, the DNR – do not resuscitate. She felt as if she couldn't breathe, as if she herself were drowning, the walls of her chest constricted, her bra crushing her ribcage, the blood drumming, her brain adrift and floating.

Beth had asked the questions: Would he wake at all? Would he know? Would he suffer? 'He mustn't know he has been defeated,' Beth said earnestly to the doctor.

'Did you tell him that his voice box wasn't affected, that he would be able to speak once the tube is taken out? That he would be able to drink?'

Yes. He had been told, reassured; the irony was that it was true that the operation itself had been a success. But he couldn't live, things had gone too deep, too far, too late. It was too everything. The consultant was speaking to Beth but his words were for Maeve. Col would not know. He would not suffer. Now it was up to her how her husband died.

She had gone to the roof. A coalition of sister, brother, mother and friends were all keeping watch in turn, on the children at home, on Col in the hospital, on Maeve herself as she waited. But now it was night, a night of stars and glorious debris, on such a night as this. Maeve felt Beth's hand on her skin. She remembered that faint flicker of jealousy once when he had said how he loved to see Beth, who brought with her, he said, the wild suggestion of otherness, alternatives, a world, a way elsewhere.

That was because, the illness confirmed, its fatal nature accepted at last, Beth had bounced into Maeve's sitting room one sunny day and said the time had come, at last, for some decent old-fashioned unprotected sex. 'I'm looking forward to the menopause,' she had said as they laughed. 'Honestly! There's a great freedom in knowing the worst. We have to take advantage of it!'

They had taken advantage. Maeve made all those arrangements which had been so possible then, arrangements about leave of absence and sick leave and – oh, everything that could be done to lighten the burden of knowing their future. They had gone to Mayo and walked the long slow beaches, the wind blowing salt and sand into their eyes and hair. A school of dolphins had spun like black question marks between a high sky, a glittering sea. A sunset had splintered the horizon with scarlet and gold, the islands molten in the glare. Famagusta and Tyre, he had said, ever the teacher; black Cyprus.

These things will continue, he had said, no matter what we do, what happens to us. The sun will set, the dolphins dance, the islands melt on the horizon. There will always be a sea, a lake, a hill, a moon rising, a comet appearing from somewhere and going somewhere else.

It puts us in our place, he had said, that 'always'. It gives pain a perspective. But he coughed, and could not draw breath, and then came the hectic heat of an ambulance and the hospital and the summons to his deathbed. 'What they don't understand,' Maeve said to Beth as they watched the stars from the roof, 'is that he doesn't want to die. They are telling me to let him go. To kill him. It isn't that I don't want to do the best for his sake, that I don't want to let nature take its course. It's that I'm the only one who truly, truly, knows what he wants – and he doesn't want to die. He could have died before now – but he doesn't want to!'

In the pocket of her summer skirt was the message he had written. Beth had brought in pens, spiral-bound notebooks so the pages could be easily torn off. His swelling pallid fingers replaced his voice: go thy way, he had spelled out carefully. Eat thy bread with joy and drink thy wine with a merry heart, for God hath already accepted thy works.

Beth had given it to her. It was for Maeve, Beth said, when Maeve arrived at the bedside, before Beth went off to see to the children. Just before he slept, Beth said, Col had written this. For Maeve. Maeve had looked down at the sleeping man, her husband. She heard the swish of Beth's departing sandals on the hospital floor, the twirl of her cotton dress with its big red and yellow poppies, the kind of dress, she knew, he would love to see through the haze of his drugs. Or his dreams.

On that evening Beth had taken the children to see the equinoctial moon rising over the Burren. There was wind but the dunes were high, their slopes sheltered. They would picnic on the terraces of rock among the harebells. All blues – the intense sky, the stone, the flowers, the long, thin-fringed sea, all blues until the first primrose gleam heralded the moon. Early, this was still August, but Beth had promised him an equinox and was providing one. For these were the permanent things, the sun setting and the moon rising. These were the things which would go on for ever, like an eternal promise.

'It's the sense of possibilities I love about Beth,' he had said to Maeve sometime or other, someday or other, a day forgotten – how could she forget the days? – except for this. 'And her stories – remember that time she was in America? The story about Mexico, when she went there with that man? Who was it? I love those stories!'

And what about the stories I could tell you? Maeve had not said this but her little smile of acknowledgement was not complicit. Or what about, she thought, that terrible time when Beth wanted to get pregnant, and we talked about nothing but ovaries for weeks? And then we talked about abortions?

There on the roof the little letter rustled in her pocket while the stars exploded gently through the night. He was sleeping, dying, his white face turned into the white pillow, a tube of pale green plastic coiling from his mouth, his hands white and flaccid on the quilt, the skin patched with the bruises of his last agony.

What was that hymn – Those dear tokens of his passion still his dazzling body bears. Maeve could remember the cadences; the short 'still' like a gasp, how could it still be so? Still – then the long 'dazzling' the rising 'body' a four-beat, then the double-beat on 'bears'.

It was, it had been, a dazzling body. Now its bones were hangers for its skin. She would never again see Col upright, never see him walk towards her with the intention of love. Ordinary love, receptive but with excitement always a possibility in the way they enjoyed one another. His body had been handed over to others, shrouded in white, in green, hidden from her eyes, tendon-thin beneath the sheets, touched only by professional intimacy. Their last lip kiss had been outside the operating theatre. She had bent to take off his glasses which exaggerated beyond bearing his frantic eyes. 'You want to do this,' she had whispered. 'It's going to work. I'll be here when you wake up, I won't leave you.'

He said, 'Take care of the children for me –', and then the sheeted arms had reached from the door to take in the trolley and he disappeared, the moisture of her kiss still on his mouth.

When the consultant had finished talking to them in that dimmed, smoke-smelling room he had taken both her hands in his, hearing her whisper: 'But he trusts me?'

'This is not a betrayal,' he said. 'This is your covenant.'

The unexpected word swung between them. As Beth turned to lead Maeve away the doctor put out his hand in a gesture of complicity. Beth had been working in her casual way in Maeve's garden before coming to the hospital; when she took her hand from her pocket it brought with it a litter of gathered roseleaves, mottled and dry, some already dust, brittle yet aromatic, falling like dust to the floor.

On the roof the two women watched the sky. 'Is there a God?' Maeve asked.

'I'm telling the children that there is,' said Beth firmly.

'But if there is a God, how can he let this happen?'

Beth kept her eyes on the stars. 'Because he can let this happen,' she said as if she were convinced. Only conviction could calm the sundering agony Maeve was suffering, Col was enduring, the anguish they had seen coming from a long way off and could not deflect.

'I was telling the children about the stars, about the theory that people are made from stardust, not Disney stardust but debris, atoms, nuclei. The ancestral stars. They liked that.'

In this dawn Maeve searches for that last exploding star, the comet that would show in the east as it had appeared all these last cloudless nights in the north-west, low down, caught in the angle of the telephone wires crossing the stable-yard and the furthest trees of the avenue. It had been a friendly presence, a dim but distinct white flare. It had kept her company when walking the dogs along the beach. 'I've been walking the comet,' she had said accidentally to her daughter when belatedly answering her telephone message.

'The thing is,' she added as she explained how to find it, 'it's almost better not to look at it directly, even with the binoculars. If you look slightly away from it, at a nearby star or just a patch that seems empty, then you see it best, sideways on.'

She had said to Hugo that if he liked he could come to her house to see the comet glowing in a sky undiluted by city lights. For months he had hovered outside her life; not the first suitor, but perhaps the most persistent. He was not much interested in the stars, he said, but if she joined him at his house she could watch it by the sea.

But Maeve was secure now: in her adult children, in her profession, in her possessions, in her widowhood as sturdy as her house.

'I have my own sea,' she said.

And there it is, nearer than at night, a pallid nimbus in the sky where soon the sun will quench its flame. Maeve changes her focus and squints between the marked trees, those to be felled now indistinguishable from those to be retained, the numerals repeated in a puzzle the workmen will be unable to decode. An oak wood, a pine martin saved. Into her mind run the unwelcome images: the Siberian tiger, the elephant, the Russian bear, the dolphins, the oak forests. The Lottery is €6 million this week. If I won the Lottery, she thinks, I could help so much. Yet I have never bought a ticket.

The comet fades against the shadows of the holy mountain whose shelves have been excavated for a car park and lavatories. Maeve's mobile telephone buzzes to warn her that her replacement will arrive within the hour. She packs slowly, thinking of the masts on all the mountains. The bracken is cancerous; as she relieves herself in a cleared patch she feels like an animal, close to the wet earth, confident of its odours, its messages. Covering over her mess she thinks that this will confound a fox or two and sees, before she rises from her crouch, the round pockets of a badger's set between the roots of the tree she has made her latrine.

Like her, the badgers relieve themselves outside their lair, covering the spoor with earth and leaves. Good housekeepers. They think themselves so secure! Deep in the forest, under the trees, safe from invaders such as Maeve. Or have they, by now, grown that consciousness of inherited danger, of being prey for the sport of another species? Or like witches, condemned for the contamination of their blood? For this is all we want, she thinks: shelter. This is our instinct. It's me, my house by the sea, to which I may or may not invite my gentleman caller. All I really want is shelter. However we house ourselves the instinct is the same, security from weather and from woe.

Driving homewards the occult presences of the night hover at her wincing shoulders. How dreamlike much of her past life has been! Anguish is ephemeral. Even the nights when the boys pushed their squirming bodies beside her in her bed, half-awakened from their own dreams and seeking only the reassurance of her warmth, the bulwark of her body – there is no feeling left of this, only the knowledge that it happened. Yet she has this comfort: whatever went wrong in her life, the children went right. That was a covenant too, she can tell herself.

Beth has become little more than a friendliness on the periphery of Maeve's life. Her retreat began once she had understood that no one was to have a grief like Maeve's, once she had learned that she was not to say how like Col the boys were becoming, or at least not in Maeve's hearing. But now Maeve remembers what they had once shared. Even if they had shared more than Maeve had wanted, she wonders if she has got the balance just a little wrong. What is it that lasts? What are the imprints of our lives? Skin on skin, lip on lip, the abrasions of sex, the sunderings of hope – these cannot be stored. Endurance leaves only a residue. Where now is the clutch of grief, the embrace of shared sorrow, those half-hidden sobs in the night? Where now is the passion of success, the prizes, the trophies of acclaim, the winnings they all praised, the sunny photograph? Or the delight of a picnic, of a gift, of a holiday? Ephemera, although a whole life. What are our lives to anyone? Even to ourselves they are only what we remember of them.

On the car radio Sinead O'Connor sings: 'You don't see me – but I see you.'

It's all too random, Maeve decides. The songs change before she re-tunes to the BBC: 'Do you know how much I miss you – No you don't, but I do . . .'

Who is you? Col, her children, Beth. Perhaps even Hugo. It's time to make her life conform to its potential. She feels a need, a longing, for maleness. For its smells, its strengths of body or of mind. She knows better now than to expect both together. Sometimes out walking she would pass a pair of lovers and the tang of aftershave would startle her senses and remind her of the smell of known breath, of the obligation to shirts and ties and polished shoes, even of the camaraderie which acknowledged her but did not include her. She had liked that exclusion, she had needed to feel that there was a male world.

Driving she passes stubble fields striped with after-grass. Tractors clog the narrow roads as she weaves down from the hills, a collie pounces from a gateway, a cycling postman salutes her. The last blackberries glisten among the hawes along the ditches. The ploughed acres look as if they have been combed and plaited like entries for the Dublin Horse Show. Her dream jerks back into her mind – what was it – horses, the mire of a riverside, silver on the lake? No, there was something more. A hand-clasp. A tryst.

She steers towards a scooped hedgerow and stops the car. She lets the dream seep back as far as it can, as far as she can re-dream it. As far as that meeting on the road, that hurried, threatened yet exultant grasp of hand in hand even as stirrup clanged against stirrup in a surge of sweat. And beyond that tryst the thought, somehow, of Col, his living face now as hard to recall as those of the mystic phantoms of her reverie. If she squinted a little she could re-figure it, like the comet it could best be seen sideways, out of focus.

And yet she is keeping her own tryst, surely, in these mountain vigils, in her walks with the comet, in her campaigns for the dolphin and the Russian bear and the oak woods and the unsullied shore? Isn't this, she asks herself, her covenant, her pledge? Has she kept faith?

Driving on again she decides that tonight she will return Hugo's telephone call, still hovering on the answering machine at home, the red light blinking.

# Isiah

## FRANK MCGUINNESS

I can spot a time waster instantly, but Isiah had the kind of face a man like myself can fall for in a big way.

It is lean, like Giotto's saints, and the eyes, though narrow, really do pierce when I look, as I will, straight into them. If they are brave and look back, taking up the challenge, then they hurt my head if I stare too long, so I am inclined to avoid giving too searching a gaze.

There is a type of man who takes advantage of this – what would I call it? – fear, nervousness, cowardice. Whatever you like. I should by now have their number.

There are marked shared traits. They are usually straight, short-haired, sometimes they smell as if they had just shaved. They are usually married with just one child but now lead lives separate from the wives they profess to adore, wives who put their careers, usually in the arts, before their husband's. They live in apartments too expensive for their pockets. To compensate for the mess in their financial lives, their flats are almost monastic in their domestic order, neat piles of folded grey and blue socks stacked beside many pairs of similarly check-patterned underpants in their wardrobe's top shelf.

I should at this stage of my life, at this stage of the game, really be able to smell danger, but that night sitting in the restaurant, surrounded mostly by strangers I disliked, my lamb fragrant, the shellfish to die for, I did not get any whiff off Isiah, not the slightest whiff, though I placed myself beside him.

There is something about spending your childhood in Jerusalem that compares well with being a bullied schoolboy in Donegal. Many centuries after my release from the asylum of primary school and its sadistic domini, I met another victim of their regime. He was begging

215

for his bread in Finsbury, London. I pitied him enough to throw a tenner in his cap. He told me what had happened to two older boys, both brothers, who'd crucified us on our way to that kip, keeping up the tradition of what was done inside it.

Jack and Robbie Dole were now serving at least twenty years in a maximum security joint. For murder. Murder so imaginatively gruesome that it still bore the shit-smeared hallmarks of their reign of terror, the precise embroidered scabbing of the compass point. I could have immediately identified who did it. I would still have kept my lips sealed, for they would have sewn them together before blasting my head open, should I have squealed. They would have tracked me down, I know it, for if they had a single virtue in spades, it was patience. To those boys death by a thousand cuts would have been too quick – a sign of Chinese softness.

The beggarman kept gibbering on about the Doles, even though I'd heard the full story. I remembered why he would be obsessed by them. Perhaps they were the reason for his instability. They one day promised to give him a hiding he would never forget because he supported Spurs. He blurted out that his football team was Everton. They looked at him and said nothing for ages. (Their timing was impeccable and had they gone into our business, might have done well as actors, something in a soap.) Both touching his knees, Jack and Robbie whispered simultaneously, all the worse for you. They really hated Everton. Piss spurted through the poor boy's trousers. No one laughed, they knew better. He sat all day over a pool in which they would rub his nose, spitting into his ear, dirty dog, dirty dog, dirty. I could see us, me and him, squeezed into a fleshly ball to divert the worst of their laces, studs, kicking boots, lying on the ground beside the playground wall. We shared one secret, I guessed. When we heard of a weeping wall we thought of the same school-yard and us stretched beside it. Still and all it was far from the first weeping wall, it was far from Jerusalem we were reared, but not Isiah.

Isiah was a man who had never been in a physical fight. That's what I would have guessed. In the business world of film-making he could have played with murderous impulse, but to lash out would have been considered unseemly by him. Absolutely not his cup of vinegar. His English father gained him a British passport, so he was never conscripted. Besides, there are other ways to serve the state.

This was the kind of information he could drop, probably intending it to be picked up as significant clues, were one to decipher the secrets of his expensive existence. Who paid all his bills? I admit that as the night journeyed on, the wine aiding and abetting us, the food giving solace, secrets were not what I desired from Isiah.

I am a fool for a man who can talk intelligently about Russia. Isiah told us stories about his grandmother, the pogroms, the bribery, the luck of the flight from Siberia, the kindness and savagery of that woman whom he once believed sang the whole journey from Vladivostok to Moscow, creating the continent with music flowing from within her, leaving home for ever, taking with her nothing but love for the country that hated her. That was why she'd always professed an astonishing devotion to Stalin and all his works, eventually driving each of her beloved sons from her house as they could not summon an equally ecstatic faith in the dictator. She died cursing them as they crowded around her deathbed, a copy of the *Communist Manifesto* held so tightly in her fingers that to remove it they would have had to break her hands. A terrible end for a working woman. They buried her with the book that disfigured their youth. No one wept at her funeral. Only tyrants pity the end of other tyrants and Grandmama had been just that – a tyrant, now in the sack with Uncle Joe in some paradisical socialist state whose subjects were just the two of them in their doctrinal purity. Isiah was sure they would each be plotting the discredit of the other and hell in this heaven would be the knowledge the other had survived despite all the diabolic odds. But I guess there was a fondness for the old biddy. He claimed he alone kissed her dead flesh and he closed her eyes.

Did he inherit her eyes I asked him?

It was the first time that night he realised I was serious. That he had a fight on his hands. He lit my cigarette, and I noticed the perfection of his fingers, the nails so clean they might have been scorched of any impurity, the arcs equally pure, the slight touch of varnish. In return for my thanks he gave a slightly shy bow of the head. Isiah was not immune to the compliments of other men, but at that instant I did wish he had served in the army, even for a short time. It might have roughened him a little and made him perfect, which was what he was not.

Even in his dreams he would not have claimed to be perfect, particularly not in the one he confessed to me in front of this company. Isiah was walking through the crowded streets of Jerusalem, moving expertly from pavement to road, dodging people and traffic, feeling in his nostrils the burning smell of salt caked by the sun that he always associated with that city. For some reason he was carrying a can of blackberries.

Then he was in a bus snaking down the same thronged street he'd just been in. People pressed in against him, something strange about them. He could swear each and every one, Jew, Arab, Christian, man, woman, child, all wore thick glasses. Without knowing how, he was suddenly back on the pavement watching the bus ten, twenty, thirty paces away. He had left the can of blackberries behind him. It was now he recognised that this was Dawson Street, Jerusalem transformed into Dublin, and he was looking into the window of Hodges Figgis Bookshop. He saw many faces staring at him through their spectacles and then they melted clean away, first the frames, then the glass, then the flesh. He turned and saw the red and black explosion of fire. Rooted to the spot, the bus chaffing all the air, he could not move as the multitude around him screamed and ran in every direction.

Isiah asked us if he had said too much? This was dinner, hardly the time for such visions, was this putting anyone off their food and drink? The silence he received encouraged him to explain why he was paralysed by what had happened.

Out of the blue he realised in his dream that it was he himself who had planted this terrible bomb. He had removed limb from innocent limb of those unfortunates in the wrong place and at the wrong time. Through the smell he could see and hear nothing but he knew he was to blame for this atrocity. He would only have been able to forgive himself if he had remained with those about to die and gone the way of all fragile flesh, those he had blown to the four winds.

He looked at his hands. They were as he expected, stained. Stained as if he had spent hours scouring through the fruit in the silver can, smoothing it into pulp so that when it did its filthy work the bomb would travel through each sinew and bone, each fibre and smell, even through the very hair of everyone around him, obliterating all sign and substance, smearing them with the fatal evidence of their proximity to himself, the killer.

As he told us of the nightmare, I noticed his fingers, playing in a circle as if he were stirring sugar into something poisonous and foul, so long did he keep up the motion. It was as if Isiah were casting a spell or performing some other unholy rite to protect himself from the black magic he had unearthed through the telling of the tale. Everyone else concentrated on those haunted eyes, filled with the sadness of the lives lost in the dream. I could not stop noticing his beauty, the kind mouth, the fair skin, when he spoke of bloodshed, how well it became him, though he was innocent of any crimes, yet even how in sleep he bore such guilt for what he had not and never would do.

He eyeballed me – I knew he would. He said, you would understand this fear, you come from so near the Irish border, dear old Donegal, you must have seen what bombs do.

I didn't answer. I knew this was not an attempt to make allies. No, this was something else. This was not for public consumption, although everyone at our table heard it. He was too cautious a man to put his hand on my knee even out of sight. Still and all, I knew. This was a love letter.

Or was that the wine talking? He certainly tried to ply me with the stuff. I resisted as I knew he wanted me to do.

Isiah likes to be standing, holding his own, while all about him are holding each other. I admire that in a man. I do of course indulge guys, leave them their fantasy that they are the strongest fuckers in the joint. But those I intend to seduce I do not spoil. They must prove themselves cut from my rock. In any good match of Gaelic football or hurling an essential is the ability to confound the opposing bastard. Hit the *sliotar* so hard it could break a man's mouth, or right into the eye and leave him half blinded. The Irish fight dirty. We are soldiers of destiny. From our lovers and our enemies we expect stamina. Isiah was beginning to falter in that respect.

He showed an increasing desperation to get me drunk. He ordered more wine, brandies, port, Calvados, even Irish whiskey. All around us the assembled mob was falling like flies, all too ready to break into song at Isiah's request. Tribal songs, sixties songs, songs from the barricades and finally he asks for a Donegal song. I could not oblige, for I know only one, in the Irish language, and it was a love song. Tonight it would not be appropriate. He pleaded, they pleaded, but I had begun to binge on iced water and was not playing the part of the drunk with sufficient panache. I wish I could say I lost all vestige, all respect for him when he tried the oldest trick going. But the offer was so simple, so sincere, I was compelled to believe him if only in passing – well, I blush to remember it – he offered to put me in the movies.

Of course it was not as ludicrous as that. He gave it a more political slant. Why didn't we do a documentary together? Something along the lines of an Irishman in Jerusalem. A man from the Irish border walking along the borderlines between Jew and Palestinian. My northern background would be a godsend to such a programme. With his television and movie contacts we could get the necessary funding. Or the necessary, as he abbreviated. I would love to visit the Holy Land some day, but first I needed to find a toilet.

Others had begun to leave the restaurant. The drink had not yet turned any of us sour. Taxis were called. Kisses exchanged. Love universal. Couples left. Isiah and myself, him knowing he was a little drunk, hence the nonsense about the film. He apologised. Said he regretted it as soon as the words left his mouth.

I began to watch that mouth closely, a mouth whose resistance to another man's tongue made it all the more certain I would invite his rejection. I knew then how this evening would end.

It was safe to drink into oblivion and Isiah would be my trusted, disloyal companion. From that sweet mouth between those soft lips poured words of flattery and precious endearments.

> O thou afflicted, tossed with tempests,
> And not comforted, behold Jerusalem,
> I will lay thy stones with fair colours
> And lay thy foundations with sapphires.

He knew he had in some powerful way placed himself beyond the pale of my hungry fingers, starved for the touch of beauty. I was determined he would enjoy himself absolutely in my company, even if that joy casually decreed my own dissatisfaction.

So I asked him about his wife. Tell me about your wife. She must have been someone very special. Wives are always very revealing. They say so much about the men they left. And who would love Isiah? A foolish virgin to run away from such a lovely man. Not a virgin – never that. There is at least one child involved. He let me ramble on, ignorantly staggering through the path of his life, falling from door to closed door. Rattling all his lonely windows, until I came to a halt where his child stood.

This he could not talk about. Something to do with the law. Custody, custody, yes – custody, he nodded. He left me a gap where I could understand and sympathise but my childish heart was cruel and I did not oblige. Rest assured he loved his child. Above life itself. I respected that cliché. Maybe I believed it. It was now very late and I'd drunk a lough of water. So I said that silence here was for the best. Safest. But allow me if I might, allow me in the whole of my health, Isiah's health, may we toast the child's continued good fortune, as we had raised our glasses so frequently to all the others throughout this entertaining, revealing evening. *Sláinte. Sláinte mhaith.* Revealing. What did I mean precisely? Enlighten Isiah, he ordered. Maybe another bottle. One more won't hurt. Just another.

And so it came to pass we did drink another back in his apartment. For his stay in the exile of Dublin, Isiah's driver is Lithuanian. He is wide and dark, handsome, and though he never smiles, he looks on his employer with a gentleness in his fierce Baltic eyes. He picks us up at the Mermaid and deposits us at Brighton Vale, the upstairs apartment Isiah rents near the Dart Station at Seapoint.

As we drive to Isiah's abode, drunk and disreputable, Isiah calls on his manly servant for a psalm. The hard fucker opens his mouth and sings in his native tongue. The words of that unheard language may sound strange, but not so much as the high voice that pours forth from that man's throat. Sweet heart of Jesus, font of love and mercy, our boy soprano's sweetness might have ripened in the chapels of our child-hoods, but here is a grown surly savage, who'd kick the lining out of you as soon as he'd look at you, singing like a lady in Isiah's car without embarrassment, without anger.

Perhaps I am wrong. Perhaps he is angry. As I've said this man is a driver. Each night Miss Lithuania brings the boy home. Safe and sound. And they must go inside for a nightcap. A last summary of the day's events. A shared joke or sorrow. And perhaps a song, a comforting verse of the Bible. This is how Isiah knows the man has an unforgettable voice. Because he pays the bills, Isiah can tell Lithuania to go home when he's had enough of him. Enough to drink. Isiah will hit the sack telling the driver, finish the wine, the brandy, the port, whatever is on the kitchen table, knowing not a drop will be touched unless it is in the presence of the lord and master. Isiah, I think, would approve of serfdom. And tonight the alcohol is laid out for our and not his relish.

The Lithuanian is annoyed. He barely gives me time to get out of the car. He drives off hissing whatever is Eastern Europe for fucker. Maybe it is queer. I simply bow and let him drive off like a creature of the night. Just now I could drain Isiah's blood, for he is not looking to fetch keys from his pocket nor is he apologising for his foreign friend. He is already snug and safe inside his apartment. I stand outside wondering if this bastard liter-ally wants to freeze me out of his attention. Is he too scared to venture any further into our amusement arcade? Shut the door behind us. Fall into bed. Kick his shorts from his blue stockinged feet. Slip out of his wine-coloured shirt. And stop then. I will never have sex with Isiah. Is it because he knows he is utterly safe with me that he leaves the door open?

I walk in. I look about his rented apartment. The first thing I notice is the gigantic window that watches the blackness. It eats the night. In it I catch a glimpse of myself. Jesus the sight, the shock before morning sobers. I notice how adroitly Isiah can avoid the mirror of the window. He dodges his reflection so accurately it is as if he has frequently choreographed these steps before. They may come spontaneously to him but I doubt it. Still, he is the director – that's how he made his name in film before turning to the more lucrative trade of production. He is a rich man who does not need to take stock of himself just right now, and he can get away with it. Still and all, I am glad to be soon rid of each other. We both deserve better. I do confess what intrigues me most is how he will convince himself he's not a queer and how I will encourage him.

He pours brandies. I shake my head. He produces a fine bottle of port. I simply look at him. He tells me he suddenly needs the toilet. He puts a hand to his cock and smiles. He runs off. He comes back with a cheap bottle of red wine. Australia. Jacob's Creek. I start to hum the opening bars of 'Waltzing Matilda'. He laughs. He opens the revolting piss – he may as well have peed into it. He gives me the wine. I allow it to sit, poisonously, at my feet after I've flattered Isiah by presenting this filth to my nostrils and not vomiting into the glass. He is delighted by my fortitude. Then I stand up, I whisper, I should be going home – the Dart is close by, what time does the first one run? He is shocked. Have a drink for Jesus sake, have a drink, tell me what the theatre is like in this town?

The theatre in Dublin depends on the goodwill of men and women who seek solace in its guillotine. Those who choose to work in that obstinate business of putting on plays will lose their heads, their hats, their shirts. They believe they will make money, make a living out of the passion for the stage they share with those who have passed away, who never will be, who never have been. All they believe in are fresh air, winds, strong gusts, great blasts of freezing hurricanes, typhoons of snow, washing away all that had existed before.

Isiah laughs at the sheer sweep of my belief in the death of dramatic art. He laughs, he mocks my metaphysics. He says, I just want to know that if I were putting my mind to it, if I were mad enough to invest, how the fuck do I make money out of plays in this town? Will the theatre provide me with an opportunity to make a few bucks, a few euro, some yen?

This is when I long to slap Isiah hard along the beautiful teeth. The delicate mouth. Smear red blood on his blue eyes. I want him to reel from my fists' blows. Hit Isiah again and again. Watch him stumble and stare in disbelief, as if he had never known another man beat him into submission. I could have no pity for him. I would tear the buttons from his shirt. They are white, the buttons, the shirt is purple, and he would turn the purple of his bleeding nose to me, suggesting by gesture of supplication I taste his blood.

If my hands now found themselves between Isiah's trousered legs, I would meet no resistance. Just at this moment – I would remind Isiah my cock is not for selling. Instead I'd say to him, fetch razor and I'll leave you clean as a new pin. He might want to indulge me. Play the game. Say I'd like that. Like to be shaved smooth as the fingers up my arse my wife sought to win me with when we were young and fresh, ready to believe in an almighty cure for the two of us, a cure to heal our fragmented world, the alcoholic world, the narcotic world that eventually divided us.

But no, that does not occur. We sit looking at each other. He repeats, I only want you to tell me what the theatre is like in this town. You must be in the know, he flatters me. You've made a few bob. Your name is known in America. I know for a fact, he continues, that when there was an attempt to place an advert against the war in Iraq in the *New York Times* and *Washington Post*, I know for a fact, he stresses, that you were one of the people approached for ten thousand dollars and I know – my spies in Dublin told me – you did not even deign to answer the request of your fellow artists against the war. That is what my spies in Dublin informed me, he smiles.

I smile back, I say had you listened to your spies in Jerusalem, you would have known you have been flirting with the wrong man. I am not the playwright, I am a simple primary schoolteacher. I thought there must be a mistake when you phoned me up. My name is in the book but the man you're looking for, the man with the same name, the man I'm frequently confused for, I am not that person. Sorry.

He laughs and begins to remove his black tie. I see his throat, he shakes his hair, I see his neck. There is an intense patch of red there. I try to describe to myself what that red reminds me of and I think it is the colour of polish my mother used to shine our front doorstep. Cardinal red, that is its name but Isiah is not a cardinal. He is a visitor to Dublin, come to produce a film about the life of John Henry Newman, who was a cardinal of the Roman Catholic Church.

It's fallen through, the film, he tells me. Nobody gives a fuck about Newman. He's learned the hard way to distrust Irish lies. They are full of shit, Irishmen. They promise much and deliver nothing. Why in the name of fuck did he believe any of them? Because he wanted to. He downs another slug of wine and he moves to the glasses of brandy. He smells them, asks me if I want mine, I say no. He drinks both.

Through that magnificent window in Brighton Vale the sun has begun its fearless ascent over Dublin Bay. He starts to take off his shirt, Isiah, then thinks better of baring his nipples, and puts it back on again, so that I begin to think he could be flying himself, that the shirt is part of his purple, beaten flesh. As the sun rises I would like it to transform the colour of Isiah. But he falls asleep. And the sun, it moves between blue and yellow. That's the colour of Saturn seen through a glass brightly.

Bright would be the underclothing of Isiah were he undressed in his living room in Seapoint, so near to the resurrection of the sun, the crucifixion of desire as I realise I really don't want this greedy fucker and I'd like to be heading home. Were the bastard dancing, doing his Salome act, I would, I admit, wait for him to discard more clothing. I wouldn't mind a quick flash of his cock.

It is circumcised beautifully, measured accurately to the specification laid down to ravish excellently the whore of Babylon. Not a half, not a quarter, not a tenth, not a centimetre or an inch or a metre wasted. Were the aforementioned whore to put that precious pink into her mouth, she could suck from it the salvation of his wife, but because I love him as much as she does not love me, as she too left him, I tell him it is time for this encounter to end, I must be going home.

Generous to a fault, he offers me his stash of drugs – the pretty colours, all of them white or dirty. Do not depart from me you accursed Irish bastard. You liar, he laughs, I should report you if as you say you teach children. All right! I'll pour myself another glass of Jacob's Creek, and I do. I say to him, Isiah, I have no condoms, do you?

Isiah replies he does not either.

The sun over Dublin Bay is no longer yellow. Rather it is an agitation of brown. A disturbance of rain solidified into light. It shines on me and Isiah. But we do not care any longer. We sit apart, warned by the morning, thanking Yahweh we can never meet again. He begins to scream for his mother. I do not move. Then he starts to scream for his uncle. He starts to chant his name, Isiah, Isiah, Isiah, then he attacks me, confusing me for – who does he confuse me for? It is someone he believes is going to fuck him. He is crying for his mother and his father and his child.

He cites them as protection from my rapacious hold on his virginity. I refrain again from giving him the hiding he richly deserves, for this I now realise is what he's looking for and sorry, sir, no cigar – not from this boy.

Through the window of that apartment in Brighton Vale I realise it is now clear morning. I look into the sky. All right, I've had a little something. Better to touch the merchandise than to touch the man. I see jewels and tapestries in the shape of red unicorns, green wedding dresses and gifts of cheap china, rough amulets and hard beautiful amber set in the rings of old maids' fingers, they who went abegging, never having known that when the truth was told they could not cook and did not deserve either a husband or a bride.

That is when I decided it was better never to marry man or woman. I decide to leave this establishment. I leave him with his trousers around his ankles, his underwear is untouched. I open the door and hear it close behind me. A ghost's touch. Perhaps Isiah is dead by his own hand? By my hand? Day is breaking all over Ireland. Men are lying in clean underpants blaming women for their cleanliness. How those women hate men. Perhaps it is the way the sun hates the earth. Hates the way it bends over and asks for the penetration that gives it, that continues its life. I refuse the sun's inclination. I do a runner. I do not look back and I do not listen. I do not want to hear Isiah's weeping. I call upon the Lord, I ask mercy for Isiah. I smell the brandy in his rancid breath. I dread the consequence of mercy. He is caught up in his life. His marriage. His child. Better for him to have been like Jerusalem.

> Sing o barren than that didst not bear,
> Break forth into singing and cry aloud,
> Thou that didst not travail with child,
> For more are the children of the desolate,
> Than the children of the married wife.

Poor Isiah, I pity my friend. Jesus, it's tragic the way you've let yourself down. I'm doing a runner away from you and yours. So should you have done, buddy.

# Inside

## BRIDGET O'TOOLE

I am a hostage. I'm scared. I don't know how I got here but there was violence. I remember a lot of fighting. I'm very scared. But I must not panic. I must keep my head. I need to work things out.

This room is dark. I've tried the door and of course it's locked. There's a bed in here, that's all. There's also a window but it has a sort of shutter on the inside, a solid board. This is also locked. I reached up and there was a keyhole.

It's very hot. They've taken my clothes and I'm wearing some kind of tunic. I can't see it but I can feel it coarse against my skin. It smells bad, sweet and sickly.

I sit on the bed. There's just one cover. I'm on the edge of the bed keeping my feet on the floor. My feet are bare. I keep them on the ground because it feels safer.

I'm trying to think. Where was I seized? Jack and I were at the airport. We were going to Morocco for a late summer holiday. There was some kind of a row at the airport. My head aches trying to think about it.

Jack must be here too. They wouldn't have taken me without him. Someone will negotiate for him. But what about me? Who do I have value for? I don't have any. I have no role, no profession. And of course no children.

I listen. At least my heart has stopped thumping now. There's no sound at all from outside. No voices, no footsteps.

Who will they negotiate with? The government will surely try to get Jack freed. Perhaps as his wife I can be part of the deal. I would never have wanted that before. I'm an independent woman. But I'm scared now. For being of no value they might kill me.

I lay back on the bed and I must have fallen asleep. I wake up terrified but force myself to be calm. Things look a bit different now. A tiny sliver of grey light has appeared round the edges of the window board. The keyhole shows very clearly. It's too high for me to look through so I move the bed to the window and by kneeling on it I can squint through to the outside. I'm excited, but all I can see is part of a white wall opposite and a door. A large black bird flies past. It looks like a crow. I don't learn anything. The wall and the door, which is a faded red, and the crow could be anywhere.

But while I've my eye screwed up to peer out, fresh air comes to my nostrils. It smells wonderful. Just ordinary, but of the outside and of the very early morning. I put my nose to the keyhole and breathe in as if I can draw life from it.

I can hear noises in the distance. Voices. They don't seem to be speaking low or secretively. What is this place? I hope someone will come to speak to me but at the same time I dread it.

I make sure I have my feet on the ground. I pace about, my stomach sinking as sounds come nearer. Then the door is unlocked and bursts open and a boy comes in, puts something on the ground and unlocks the window board. Light crashes round the walls. He goes quickly to the door again. He makes sure not to come near me. It's as though he's frightened of me. He must be about twelve, black-haired, dark-featured. He locks the door after him.

The bowl of food he's left on the floor could be anything – rice, wheat, couscous. I look closely and it smells like porridge. Anyway I won't be eating it. They tried to poison me last night.

Now I can see out of the window. It's barred. What is this place? The bars look as if they've always been there. It's no makeshift arrangement but some kind of regular holding centre.

I see now the thing I'm wearing is a dull green, some kind of regulation garment like a uniform. The bed cover is the same kind of green. The walls are cream, plain and undecorated and the floor seems to be lino made to look like wood.

There's not much to see through the window, just a wider view of the wall and the door. But now I see it's a mural, a lighthouse and headland has been painted in white on a reddish brick background. It reminds me of somewhere. The door looks as if it's never open. A few long grasses grow at the base of the wall and there's a small patch of green which could be the corner of a lawn. I'm having to stretch up to see all this so I move the bed again and kneel on it, staring out. Nothing moves, but I don't give up. Something has raised my hopes. It may be the daylight or the ordinariness of the wall and the door and the grasses at the foot of the wall. Even the painted lighthouse suggests human activity.

I won't go so far as to say there's a hint of normality; I'm in a locked room looking out through bars.

Nobody comes. The food is cold now and I'm hungry but I won't touch it. Last night they tried to make me drink a sweet-smelling red potion. I tossed it away. I think that's what's spilt on my garment. Now it's sticky and vile-smelling.

Jack comes into my mind and he seems far away already. He's in another life. But surely he is here too and he must be worried about me. I must try to make contact. I can't risk calling his name but I decide to sing to him. Something he'll know is me, that will lift his spirits, nothing wistful. I'm scared but I open my mouth and I sing Blanche's song when she's singing in the bath.

> 'It's a Barnum and Bailey world
> Just as something as it can be.
> But it wouldn't be make believe
> If you believed in me.'

After the first line I was confident. There's just my voice, strong and loud. No one comes to stop me. I carry on louder with the bits I remember,

> 'Without your love
> It's a honky-tonk parade
> Without your love . . .'

Now I hear knocking and banging in the distance and yelling but I don't hear Jack. 'Without your love . . .' Someone crashes against my door and tries to open it. 'Without your love it's a honky-tonk parade', then the door unlocks and in comes the young boy. But now it seems he's not a boy at all but a girl wearing a blue dress with a belt. She's looking very flustered. With her is a large-boned fair woman in the same kind of dress but a darker blue. She starts to yell at me in a loud Australian accent.

'Be quiet! You can't make that noise! You're disturbing other people.' She comes right into my cell and pushes the bed back into place. 'You must calm down now, Jeannie.'

So she knows my name?

She and the young dark one have a whispering session, something about 'seeing Ahmed'. As they leave, the dark one turns nervously to me and puts a finger to her lips as if to say 'hush' to a child.

Well, I know how to get their attention now, but do I want it? And who are the 'other people' who must not be disturbed? One thing, they don't seem to be planning to kill me. Not yet, anyway.

I've discovered something absolutely amazing. They've got that stolen picture here! The one by Munch, *The Scream* I think it's called with the woman on the bridge screaming in anguish. I found it when I was moving the bed out again. It was hidden in the corner wrapped in a tunic like mine only torn and dusty. It has been put in a different frame. This is a cheap, would-be gilt – totally unsuitable. I feel very shaky. It's amazing to have discovered it but what should I do? Who knows it's in this room? I want to tell the whole world but of course I'm silenced. I wrap it up again and hide it under the bed.

Now there's a problem. If I want to look out of the window I need to move the bed but then I risk exposing the picture's hiding place. It seems to be the picture or the outside world. I will have to move the bed and the picture along with it. Ha! For an hour or so I had been beginning to think there was a horrible simplicity to the life of a hostage. Now it's getting as complicated as the outside world.

Then I have a great idea. I hide the picture under the mattress. But first I take a good look at it, keeping it hidden from the door. Oh I know how it feels, that scream. It's the whole person and the sky like blood and the bridge. The whole world is in desperation. I've known that scream all right. Now, though, it calms me. The whole business steadies me, finding it, recognising it, working out how to hide it. The only thing that feels wrong is looking at it alone. Is that to be its fate, to be looked at in secret by some rich collector?

All this has stopped me feeling so scared. But now there are voices outside the door and somebody knocks. I don't answer. It's sheer mockery to imprison me and then knock on my door.

It opens and in comes Big Australian Bully with a tall dark man – Middle Eastern I think – and the little dark Nice Girl. Something in the body language of the three of them tells me the tall man is important. One of their leading figures, I assume. He looks serious. His fanaticism is well under control. His question is like the knock on the door.

'How are you feeling today?'

'How do you think? Confined, imprisoned. I don't want to be here. I am of no value to you. I want to be let go.'

'On the contrary, you are of value. All here are of value.'

He starts muttering to Big Australian. I speak again. 'Where is my husband? I want to see my husband.'

They mutter again and he states, 'You will see your husband.'

They turn to go and with the same serious expression he says, 'I hear you like to sing. You may sing but quietly, you understand?' His two companions smile but not at me.

After they've gone I lie on the bed with clenched fists pounding the mattress. I am furious at my own docility. I have allowed his presence to overpower me. I should have argued, persuaded, even pleaded. But I allowed myself to be drawn into the spell of his authority.

I take out the picture and let it do the screaming for me. The frame bothers me. And the painting itself seems oddly smooth in texture, almost like a reproduction. I'm puzzling over this when Nice Girl comes in without knocking. Seeing the picture she gasps.

'Where did you get that?'

I tell her. She holds out her hand gently and I give it to her.

'You must not have,' she says, so I snatch it back. Out she goes, returning almost at once with Big Australian who must have been told to be nice to me because she's very sweet and reasonable.

'This is not supposed to be here. It has been decided it isn't suitable in a place like this. I'll find you a better one.'

She takes *The Scream* from me and they both leave, saying, 'Lunchtime soon.'

*How odd*, I'm thinking. *Lunchtime?*

Nice Girl comes in a little later with a small glass of the red poison and some water.

'No thanks,' I say firmly.

'Then you will not be allowed lunch,' she says trying to look fierce.

'I don't give a damn,' I say, 'I'm not drinking that.'

After she's gone I sniff the red stuff. It's the same as was spilled on my tunic all right. No thanks.

I look forlornly out at the white wall and the once-red door and the grasses. I need to go to the bathroom. I'm quite uncomfortable by the time Big Australian comes bursting in.

'Dr Ahmed says you have to take your medication.'

'I need the toilet.'

She has brought another glass of water and a large white tablet. I make a show of swallowing this, tossing back my head but depositing it in my cheek.

'Good girl. That wasn't so bad was it?' I've heard that before.

She takes me across the corridor to the toilet. I flush away the tablet. It is when I am returning to the room, midway in the corridor a smell hits me. Something I've known before. Reminding me of another place and a distant feeling.

I lie on my bed and think about the 'medication'. I'm imagining some strange, dark chemical process whereby Ahmed rearranges and sedates our minds. But it's all very unconvincing and science fiction-y because at the same time my thoughts are whirling in a panic at another possibility and one that is far more likely.

What kind of a place is this?

There's a squeak of wheels outside the room, a loud knock and a cry of 'Tea!' The door opens and I see the lady with the tea-trolley. There is the large shiny teapot, the jug of milk, the cups and saucers and the tin of biscuits.

'Yes please,' I say and gaze at this familiar sight.

'Sugar, darlin'?' she asks, and now I know where I am. She hands me a cup of tea and there are two Bourbon biscuits on the saucer.

I don't want her to go. I need to know exactly which place this is. But I would feel a fool showing that I don't know. So I can only say 'Thanks' and she goes, taking certainty and knowledge with her.

If I am where I think I am it's even more urgent that I get out. Sheer panic assaults me when I realise the truth. All the rest of my thinking was fantasy – or was it? Now my mind starts to play back along with the fantasies. The smell in the corridor is a hospital smell. The tea-lady is the hospital tea-lady. But they could have arranged all this to deceive me.

When Nice Girl comes in again I ask her directly, 'Are you a nurse?'

'No, not exactly. I am in training.'

*Training, training. As what?*

'Do you expect to become a nurse?'

'Oh yes. And you must help me.'

'How can I help you?'

'By being a good patient and taking your medication and being calm and good.'

I don't want to spoil her prospects but when Big Aussie comes in with the replacement picture I behave like a proper mental hospital patient.

'This is much nicer,' she says, showing me something mostly brown with a flat pond and ducks and reeds.

'Take the disgusting thing away!'

I scream and throw it across the room.

I've surprised her, I think, because all she can say is 'Well!' and she leaves the room locking the door noisily behind her.

For a moment I remember the exhilaration of madness, the power it can give you. But I'm not mad. Not this time.

Now I'm even more anxious to know how I got here. And my mind has accepted where I am, linking together 'Dr' Ahmed, the smell, 'lunchtime', the tea-trolley. But it won't quite abandon the idea that I'm a hostage and these people are my captors.

Lunch comes. It's brought by the tea-lady. 'Do you not have a locker?' she asks, standing there with a plate of stew in her hands.

Then she puts it on the bed and leaves, saying I need a locker. It's a comforting thought. I'll be given a locker and there will be a jug of water and a glass on top and some pieces of fruit and then inside a few personal items, underwear and a towel and a notebook.

The stew is unmistakably Irish. Plenty of potatoes and a few bits of unknown meat. I'm hungry and eat it all.

There's a gentle knock on the door. Nice Girl comes in. She's Nice Nurse now. She approaches tentatively. I see her looking at the rejected picture on the floor. Its frame has survived the fall. It's the same kind of ersatz gilt as they'd put on the Munch.

'I need a locker,' I say.

'I will tell. Of course you must have.'

She seems reassured by my demand. 'But now. Your fingernails.'

'What?' I look at my nails for the first time in what seems like ages. 'They're not very long.'

'No, but too sharp. It will be nice. You see.'

She sits on the bed. 'Come.' She has a pair of nail scissors.

'Why do I have to have my nails cut?'

'See!' She shows me the back of her hand and the arm above the wrist. 'You did.'

There are red scratch marks, some quite deep.

'I did that?'

She nods.

'Oh I'm sorry. I didn't know. I thought you were bad people trying to imprison me.' Of course I'm sorry but I have no recollection of this and it's as though I'm being blamed for what I've done in someone else's dream.

'No, we are good people. This is a good place. Now.'

While shame and forgetfulness have brought down my defences she takes me by the hand and sits me on the bed beside her. Very carefully and gently she takes my fingers and clips each nail, talking soothingly as to a child. 'There, this is a pretty one, this is a little tough, I think,' and so on. At first I am stiff and flinch but then begin to relax. I look sideways at the dark eyelashes against dark skin and the brow puckered in concentration. I am almost sorry when the job is done.

'There, Jeannie. Not wild cat any more.'

'Thank you. Tell me, what is your name?'

What she says sounds like Chimaera.

'Ah that's a pretty name. Don't go, I want to ask you something.'

'OK.'

'Why am I here? Do you know?'

'Because you are sick. You need to rest.'

'I can't remember coming in. What do you know about it?'

'Your husband. He was worried.'

'But why?'

She's looking awkward now.

'Chimaera. Don't you think I have the right to know?'

'You tried to run away. At the airport.'

'Really? I tried to run away?'

'Yes, I believe you tried to get on a different plane. Then you got angry when they wouldn't let you and you had a bad fight with the people at the airport.'

'OK don't tell me any more.'

'You wanted to go to America.'

I remember nothing of this. She could have been making it up. But in some distant part of my mind it does remind me of something.

How tiring this is! As she leaves she says, 'You are nice to let me do your nails. Later I help you have a bath and I will see you get a locker.'

*And a chair, an armchair in the corner*, I think, with sinking heart.

I try to process Chimaera's information but it hardly seems connected with me. I lie on the bed and look at the sky which is absolutely pale like an empty page. I take another look out at the wall opposite, the door and the patch of grass. I wonder what's round the corner. It would be good to see trees and water. I feel the world has been taken away from me even though really it's me that's been taken away from it.

Later Chimaera takes me to bathe in a room with shiny yellow walls and a high window. She becomes quite playful, pretending not to hear my commands about the hot and cold taps. Her hair is getting in her face and eyes, she's indiscriminately splashing and laughing. For the first time in weeks, I notice another person's mood.

'You seem happy,' I say and she tells me she is going off duty for ten days. 'You won't be here when I come back,' she says and it's a little while before I realise what she means, that I am part of a timetable in the real world.

I am given a clean nightdress. It's a washed-out pale blue and softer than the one I've been wearing. It's quite easy for Chimaera to give me my tablet now. There are sheets on the bed. I try not to think about Jack because I know I have embarrassed and hurt him. I fall asleep easily.

I wake and remember where I am and that Jack is not here. They don't board up my window now. The morning sun shines on the wall opposite and I see that the lighthouse is not painted on at all. It's just that white paint has flaked off and left behind a shape that looks like a lighthouse. I feel worse now. This is not the scary adventure I thought it was but it's still frightening in its own way. Also when the door knocks and someone comes in, of course it's not Chimaera. This one has mousey hair and a plain face. She seems very offhand, her English perfect when she asks if I want toast this morning. I say 'Sure' but that what I really want is paper to write a letter. Toast comes but no paper. I take my tablet. I remember what it's like in a place like this: they will bring you porridge, tea and tablets but you may wait for ever for a piece of paper.

I look out and the sun is very bright now. It dazzles on the white part of the wall opposite. I see the red bricks clearly, they have weeds and moss growing between them. Some familiar-looking birds are pecking about on the patch of grass. I feel stupid when I remember what I thought this place was. And yet there still comes into my mind the idea of something sinister. It's true that I've realised about the white paint and that no one has actually painted a lighthouse. But the red door is still strange. It's always closed. What is it hiding?

Maybe she's not so bad, the English one. She brings paper and when I ask 'Pen?' sarcastically, she says, 'Oh sorry', and lends me her own.

I try to write to Jack. My writing is very shaky and I find it extremely difficult to form sentences. It's as if my mind is racing too much and at the same time is far too slow to catch up with itself. It's like two totally unmatched ponies trying to pull a cart.

The letter is quite short. I fold it up and put it under my pillow. Now the day lies ahead of me with the huge task of requesting and eventually, I hope, obtaining an envelope and then finding some way to post it. The odd thing is that as soon as I've hidden the letter away I completely forget what I've said in it. I don't bother to look. I just know I've begged him to get me out of here.

Then Big Australian comes in. Breezes in, I should say, with to me meaningless enquiries after my health. Why is she still here if Chimaera's gone? I wonder. She's pleased with herself. 'Look what came for you!' she says and hands me a package. She fusses with my bed and finds the letter.

'I need an envelope,' I say, turning the package over in my hands.

'Please,' she can't stop herself saying as she leaves. 'Please, may I have an envelope?'

I recognise Jack's writing of course, and his style of neatly reusing old envelopes and the address label on the back.

He's sent me a new nightdress, a bought one. It's pretty in a summery, flowery way. I unfold it and see that it has short sleeves and a high neck. It smells of fresh cotton. I suppose he couldn't send my favourite, an old jellaba torn under one arm, or his favourite, the skimpy black. There's a letter, a note rather. It's pretty skimpy itself with only two real sentences, 'I hope you are feeling better', and 'I'll come and visit you soon.'

Australia comes back quickly with an envelope. 'Nice surprise?' she asks, indicating the package.

I'm trying not to cry because he hasn't said he misses me and there's nothing about rescuing me. So I don't speak and so she goes out again, saying, 'You know your door's not locked now so you can go to the bathroom. But don't go wandering off because we can see you from the nurses' station.'

I feel like a child. The grown-ups have left me in the care of strangers.

A few minutes ago I was trying not to cry and now I can't. I lie on the bed. It's morning but I'm exhausted already. I fall asleep, reminding myself that Jack has always been 'a man of few words'. And so very very normal.

The tea-trolley wakes me. After it's gone I leave my door open and listen to it trundling and squeaking away and then to the other noises of the ward. There seems to be a communal area beyond the nurses' station because every so often screams of laughter come from that direction. It's high-pitched and sometimes desperate but I envy the laughers without wanting to join them. I'm sitting on the bed with the door open when a very tall, fair-haired woman about my age appears outside. She wears a vivid pink nightgown and is sliding along the wall opposite, pressed against the wall and shrinking as if from blows or threats of blows. Her whole body signals distress. She's acting out the despair I sometimes feel the way Munch's picture did. I'm paralysed but I feel I should help her. By the time I get to my feet and look out she's gone.

I drink my tea and put the letter in the envelope and address it. Of course I have no money for a stamp and it bothers me that I'll have to ask someone to post it.

The tablets must be making me drowsy. I sleep again and dream that I am strong and wearing my clothes and I'm conducting an orchestra. I'm in control but all the time I have to listen hard to know what they're playing. I wake to the sound of Ravel's 'Bolero' quite near. Then there's someone shouting and the music is the bit where it's so unmistakably yearning. Abruptly the sound is gone and a wail of anger is followed by Australian nurse's voice saying, 'I told you, Jennifer.' I look out and see a young girl being shepherded along the corridor towards the communal noise. I look both ways, hoping to see the one in the pink nightie but there is no sign of her. I'm feeling very shaky and upset now and when I wonder how soon before I will get out, I feel completely helpless.

There are noises outside my window. There's a loud clattering, a sound of wood hitting wood and men's voices. The door in the wall opposite is open! They are hauling deckchairs, lots of them, out of the darkness and leaning them against the wall. The canvas is bright and colourful against the faded paint. Then they are carried out of my sight. The door is left casually open.

There's a lot going on today. Visitors come. I hear voices in the corridor and groups of people pass, talking in even, normal tones or in tones slightly buffed up into cheerfulness.

I wait in the room for Jack. I have tidied the bed. My newly cut nails still have an edge to them as they press into my palms. Perhaps if I go for a walk I will meet him. I hope there won't be anyone else with him.

I wander down the corridor past the nurses' station. There is no one there. Sunlight is coming into the building. Long windows have been opened and outside them on the edge of the garden are the deckchairs and women sitting in them. Some wear dressing gowns in different bright colours. Others wear their clothes. They all have sun hats on. They call to each other and laugh. They know each other's names.

The sun is very bright out there. I see that the garden has a large lawn and flower beds.

I don't want to be seen. I don't know anyone. I go back to my room. It seems almost dark here now. The sun has left the wall opposite.

Jack doesn't come. I hear other people's visitors leaving. Outside my window the red door is still open showing a dark emptiness.

When my door opens it's two nurses, laughing and wheeling in a bedside locker. One is the English nurse from this morning. There are red streaks in her hair now.

'Thanks,' I say. 'I need a stamp for my letter. Please.'

'If you want to give me the letter, I'll post if for you.'

'Do you recognise her?' asks the other, giggling.

'Sure, why wouldn't I?' I take the letter from under my pillow and hand it to her. 'Thanks.'

'Do you like her hair?'

'It's OK.'

'Ahmed won't approve,' and they leave, still laughing.

I have a locker now but nothing to put in it. Then I remember the pen under my pillow and open the drawer of the locker and put it in.

A little later, on top of the locker there is a plate of ham salad which I have not touched. I'm very restless. I wish Chimaera were here.

I wander into the corridor. Once again the nurses' station is empty. I hear Red Streaks and the other laughing in someone's room. This time they're getting a response. I come to the French windows. The deckchairs are all empty now. A fallen leaf is lying on one. There are cigarette ends on the ground between them. I walk out past them to the lawn. It's sunny still but now the trees make long shadows. The grass feels lovely under my bare feet. I walk to the trees and shiver because it's nearly autumn and my arms are bare. I look back at the deckchairs. Their colours are blurry and jumbled together like in some warm Impressionist painting. And the flower beds glow, all yellows and deep reds. I go to look closely at the flowers and smell them and I hear bees making that rich, comfortable sound. There comes a moment of sudden joy and my eyes fill with tears. But then I sneeze and a nurse passing the windows sees me. She comes out looking cross until she notices my tears and puts an arm round me.

'You're cold. You'll catch your death. You can't come out here without your clothes.'

'I haven't got my clothes,' and I encourage my tears a little.

'Oh, we'll see about that. You must stay inside now.'

When I get back to my room, the patient in the pink nightie is there leaning on the wall near my door. She shrinks as I approach.

'It's all right, I won't hurt you,' I say.

'I know.' Then she comes close and whispers, 'Do you want to come swimming?'

'Swimming? Where?'

'Here. Look.'

She starts to slide along the wall, moving her arms and legs together as if in sidestroke. 'Come on, it's lovely!'

I lean against the wall beside her and stretch my arms along it.

'That's right, you've got it!'

The floor is shiny too.

She no longer looks wounded but is beginning to laugh. 'Come on! Keep up!'

Now I'm laughing too. It's a conspiracy of the mad. We are both gasping with laughter and breathless as we move along the wall.

At the end of the corridor we come to a closed door. 'That's where they put the men,' she whispers, 'I'm glad *they're* locked away.'

'Well, I enjoyed that,' she says, quite formally as if we'd just taken a turn round the grounds together. She puts out her hand as if to shake mine, then changes her mind. 'I must go back to the sitting room now. I have some knitting to attend to.' I want her to stay and speak to me. She has ended our encounter too quickly.

But back in my room I lie on my bed and smile at the thought of our crazy swim. Outside there's a clatter and bang as the deckchairs are put away and the door closed on them.

I look back over the day. It's true that Jack did not come. But I have obtained a sheet of paper and written a letter, and I have requested and received an envelope and arranged for the letter to be posted. I have walked in the garden and swum in the corridor. I will soon be getting my clothes back. Tomorrow I will start to negotiate my release.

# In the Lovely Long Ago

## VINCENT BANVILLE

The first time Lucy Swales saw Henry Morton he was aureoled in sunlight, his sturdy frame backlit by a golden glow. It was a day in high summer, the air wafting hot and close above sliding river murmurs where it skirted the boundary of the garden. Lucy had been eating ice cream from a silver dish and was holding her spoon, this way and that, to break the shafts of sunlight into dazzles of brilliance, when Henry came to shoulder his way into, not alone the confines of her childhood, but the whole of her life from that time on.

Diffident, he had sat himself down in the wrought-iron garden chair, anchored in his brown suit of coarse spun cloth and his sensible brogues. Bolt upright, he smiled at his host and hostess, Lucy's parents, a handsome young man of nineteen, shy enough, but conscious also, probably, of the effect he wished to make. The impression he had made on fifteen-year-old Lucy, if he had known it, was instant: she fell hopelessly and irrevocably in love with him, with his chestnut hair that gleamed like the well-polished mahogany table in their dining room, with his well-spaced brown eyes, with his noble nose, white teeth and the dimple in his manly chin.

Up to that time the only man in Lucy's life had been her father. She was his only child by a second marriage, although he already had two grown-up daughters by his first. Lucy, when she thought about it, felt that no other man could ever measure up to her father's charm and grace and ease with life; he was frail and old, but he dressed with a certainty of vision that showed taste and style, and he always wore a fresh flower in his lapel. He treated her with unfailing courtesy, and he was forever prepared to listen to whatever she might wish to confide to him, staring intently at her until she was finished and then nodding understandingly as though what he had heard was of the greatest importance.

Lucy's mother was much younger than her husband. She was a remarkably striking looking woman, her beauty being of the classic variety that appeared to need no grooming or attention to detail. Lucy had never seen her with a hair out of place: she radiated a surface that was shell-like in its unruffled perfection, her aspect being of the remote, and she spoke only when she absolutely had to. The longest speech she had ever made to Lucy had been in the form of a small homily on the occasion of Lucy's going away to boarding school on the advent of her fourteenth birthday:

'Remember, my dear,' she had counselled her, 'that you come from a well-to-do family . . . We never, just never, let ourselves down. We do not indulge in silly tantrums or base recriminations. Anger is vulgar. Don't believe the romantic novelists who insist that it serves to make a woman more beautiful if she loses her composure. Rather, it coarsens the skin and gives rise to unsightly flushes. Forgive, without necessarily forgetting. A time will surely come when one will have the opportunity to get one's own back. You will remember that, my dear, won't you?' And her mother looked at her with her own beautifully composed face, the make-up exactly applied, neither too discreet nor too emphatic, and with the smile that never quite reached her eyes playing about her carefully outlined mouth.

They lived, the three of them, in Swallowfield, a large manor house situated on the bank of the Suck River in the County of Wicklow. The townland was known as Grange East, and it was here that Charles Swales had come in the early part of the nineteenth century to set up his brewing business. He had begun in a small way – being a Catholic he had to be discreet – but business had boomed and soon the whole neighbourhood was involved. By the time that Lucy's father, the grandson of the founder, had taken over, things had evened out and it was obvious that, whereas the mill would always provide a living, it would never expand into the vast industry that at one time had been envisaged.

In her early years Lucy had been a delicate child and, because of that, she had not been sent away to school. Instead she had endured a succession of governesses, stiff corseted ladies mainly who smelled of mothballs and lavender water and who tried to teach her dry old subjects like mathematics and science in the specially arranged classroom off the parlour. By the time she was fourteen, she had shrugged off any predisposition towards illness and had become strong and sturdy and even a little tomboyish. She loved to wander in the fields and woods, and to follow the passage of the seasons as it was reflected in the differing shades and aspects of the countryside. Autumn was possibly her favourite time, when the great old oak and beech trees flamed into hues of russet and gold and a companionable sadness permeated the chilly air and was personified in the stately fall of individual leaves.

Now, to her delight, she found that Henry Morton was coming to work for her father in order to learn the brewing business. He was the son of a friend of the family, the youngest of five boys, and it was felt that in brewing he would find a secure niche for himself in the field of business. They were a Quaker family, a fact that in Lucy's mind added to the air of fascination that Henry held for her.

He moved into the house and the neighbourhood as though he had been born and bred to it. It pleased Lucy to hear her father say, 'That young Henry is a marvel. He gets on right well with the men – he can be firm with them, mind you, but he can laugh with them also. And he's picked up the business in no time . . .' There was a touch of wistfulness in her father's words for, although he doted on her, she knew that he regretted not having a son.

Her mother too, that remote and distant woman, seemed to find Henry's company more than bearable. Although of a different religious persuasion, he always journeyed to mass with them on Sundays, being particularly solicitous where her mother was concerned. He liked to perform little services for her, like handing her into the family Austin Princess, carrying her prayer book, placing her kneeler in a central position in the church, and even turning the pages of her hymnal on occasions when she was feeling particularly languid.

When Lucy visited the malt house Henry would bring her up to date on all that was taking place. He was inordinately proud of the knowledge he had accumulated in such a short space of time, and took great pleasure in showing off his grasp of the most intricate of the malting processes: he would set Lucy's head spinning with accounts of how the mashing was completed by separating the wort from the spent grain by filtration; he would recount for her the role that the hops played in imparting a tartness to the brew that it seemed was much sought after; he talked of mash tubs, brew kettles and something called a Saladin box; and finally he would prevail on her to sip one or two of the finished products, over which evil-tasting concoction she would exclaim with the proper amount of reserved delight.

She always experienced an initial shiver of unease upon leaving the light to venture into one or other of the buildings. The smell of the wet, germinating grain she found to be as strong as ammonia, and in the kilning rooms the air was so hot that it caught at one's throat as palpably as an encircling hand. When Henry appeared, however, sometimes in his brown suit and at other times with a leather apron looped about his neck and tied at his waist, the dark depressing atmosphere of the place dropped away and her spirits lifted.

Two happy months went by, with Henry becoming more and more confident in his chosen profession and growing ever more popular in his employer's kind regard. For Lucy, there was no need to rationalise her love for him; it was not something she had to think about, nor did she have to stoke its fires with understanding of small deficiencies or forgiveness of thoughtless indiscretions. Henry was unfailingly kind and considerate to her; he never kept her waiting no matter how busy he was; when he went up to the city on his rather infrequent visits to see his family, he always brought her back some small gift: a tortoiseshell comb, slabs of Cleeve's toffee, an autograph album with a shellacked cover and shaved like a heart, a novel by Annie M. P. Smithson; when the hunt was on he would stay back with her for a good part of the way, and once, when she fell, he took her home perched in front of him on his own horse. When they walked through the woods he talked of his childhood, of the big house in Rathfarnham with the polished parquet floors, of the large garden which contained an ornamental pond big enough to sail a boat on, and of the head-high privet maze in which he delighted in getting lost, thus causing consternation in the rest of the family. He talked of his Quaker faith – 'We are called the Society of Friends,' he told her. 'In the evenings it is the custom for the whole family to gather together to hold silent contemplation, and to await the coming of the Inward Light.' Without seeming to make any great effort, he took her whole existence and filled it with the trepidation of awakened feeling, so that the length of her days was warmed by the excitement of being in his presence.

Eventually the time came for her return to school, but she accepted this parting as a necessary imposition. Even then, still at that early age, Lucy was already conscious of the need not to make a scene. She was prepared to be compliant, in the firm belief that by adopting such an attitude she would be rewarded at a later date. All through her life she was to hold to this conviction, believing as she did that people who made a fuss caused themselves and those about them unnecessary bother: an outward placidity of manner, she was convinced, was the best defence against the world's shocks, and inner turmoil was all the more delicious when kept to oneself. She would not, and at a later date could not, see the sense in being obstructive or difficult; her life, as she saw it, would be far-like, closed in the face of others' observation, but brilliantly orchestrated in the hues of a peacock's tail in the depth of her own secret contemplation.

On the evening before her departure she walked with Henry through the great banks of pine that clothed the south flanks of Monkscadden Hill, the ground under their feet yielding and turf-like and the air chill about them like a penance. Henry was wearing a long, beltless overcoat and a plaid scarf loosely folded about his throat. He always walked resolutely, and Lucy imagined his fists clenched tightly in his pockets and the bunched power of his leg muscles as he placed his stout boots firmly against the earth. Always, when she was with him, she marvelled at the solidity of his presence. He never exhibited any sense of uncertainty and gave the impression of being completely in command of any situation. She prized this intrepid vision of him, for she knew that in her moments of solitude it would serve to bolster up and vitalise her own confidence in the correctness of things.

They spoke little on their walk, but their silence was the companionable silence of thoughts and feelings shared and understood. They had already agreed that they would miss one another, but the knowledge of their coming separation only served to bind them closer together. In the months ahead they would exist quite comfortably; they would talk and laugh and behave like reasonably contented people: in no way would they give the impression that they were pining for one another; but at the same time they would never be out of one another's thoughts, and if they needed consolation all they would have to do was to conjure up a familiar gesture, or a favourite phrase, and once more they would be warm and secure again, each with the other.

When they came out from under the shelter of the trees the light was beginning to fade along the tumbling currents of the river and in the hazy distances of the fields on the other side. As Lucy gazed into Henry's strong features and saw her own happiness mirrored there she experienced a swooning fall in her mind, a dislocation as it were of time and space: it was as if she had been granted a glimpse of her life as one complete and finished entity, from its opening to its close, and the immediacy of it took her breath away. Never again, she knew, would she doubt the expectation of wish fulfilment and, although still young in years, she became, in that moment, aware of the depth and breadth of her own femininity. It was an awareness, she felt sure, that would bloom and prosper, and a true manifestation of her woman's capacity for enduring, no matter what the odds.

'Thee I love,' she breathed, but whether she said it aloud or in her mind she could not tell. All around her the evening was spread out: whispering to her in the swish of the river water, welcoming in the muted scent of honeysuckle in the hedgerows, raucous in the cawing of the rooks in the tall trees, and loving in the steadfast regard of Henry's smiling eyes. No matter how far in time or distance she would travel from this moment she would hug this evening to her heart: it would be a link in the necklace of good things that had and would happen to her, a benefice to savour in the coming reality of her boarding school days.

And she needed moments like that, for there was a basic coldness to the tenor of her life at school. It was present in the physical aspect of the buildings and the rather shabby gardens, in the chill smooth caress of the white bedsheets and in the clammy touch of a succession of grey mornings broken open by the clamour of shrilly insistent bells. Mother Mary John's was a Catholic private school for the education, rather than the edification, of well-to-do young ladies, a place so regimented that the fear of breaking a rule, of being singled out from one's fellows by the premeditated or otherwise naughtiness of daring to challenge authority in any shape or form, was the paramount motivating force of every girl's behaviour. One tiptoed about its echoing corridors, forever on guard; conversations were whispered, with much turning of heads and anxious glancing about; laughter was a mere titter, quickly stifled. Even the most outspoken and tomboyish of girls were muted into conformity by the long list of dos and don'ts, and the nuns were experts in the art of pursed lips, disapproving sighs and pained sorrows. The ideal was a staid drabness, and individuality was frowned upon. Once a week only was the student body allowed to bathe, long ranked files of girls in linen shifts tripping shiveringly through the early morning and, as silence had to be maintained, even the relief of a muffled scream as goose-pimpled flesh encountered the blue-black bruising of icy water was denied them.

The interest was filleted from the various subjects they pursued by the uncompromising necessity to learn things by rote, the nuns being as much a prey to the rigidity of the system as their charges. Spontaneity amounted almost to a sin, and the salmon-leap quickening of the mind that should accompany the awakening of the learning process was sadly lacking.

To combat this regime of embattled narrowness Lucy took to embarking on flights of fancy: at first little darts and shifts that transformed prying glances into expressions of caring, disinterested gestures into signs of tenderness, and the odd word of praise into a hymn of eulogy. Then she began to extend her imaginings into the rarefied air of sustained daydreams: long trailing visions of Swallowfield, suffused in sunlight; vistas of the land, the river, and of the bulked pines that blackened the slopes of Monkscadden Hill like a beard. In her fancy she drifted as a benign ghost among all the scents and sounds and places she knew and loved so well: she stooped with her father to pluck a forget-me-not for his buttonhole; she sat with her mother before her vanity mirror and contemplated the slow rise and fall of her arm as she brushed her shining hair; and she journeyed with Henry through all the hours of his days as he performed his daily tasks.

Determinedly she endured the time of her separation from all that she loved, and it would have come as a great surprise to her fellow schoolmates and to the nuns if they had stumbled on the fact that she was in any way discontented. It was not in her nature to be outwardly restive; her mind possessed the ability to situate her on the point of always being about to move into sunlight – the shadow, certainly, hovering, but retreating rather than encroaching. She allowed herself deliberately to acknowledge the possibility of unhappiness, but only as an impetus to her to avoid its clutches at all costs. The consequence was that she achieved an evenness of temper and disposition that allowed her not merely to survive but to enjoy herself while doing it.

There were excursions, of course, to interrupt the circumscribed routine of school life: walks along by the sea, and in the People's Park where once she had the giggling pleasure of seeing and hearing an earnest band of musicians play Sousa marches in competition with a thunderstorm; educational tours in the cool brown silences of the National Museum; dawdling strolls through the still-life section of the National Art Gallery, and more hurried trots through the portraiture section where the reclining nudes caused the shepherding nuns to blush and the girls to smile surreptitiously at one another.

In April her father wrote to the Superioress, Mother Columbanus, giving permission for Lucy to go and spend a weekend at Henry's family home in Rathfarnham. She was even to be allowed to wear her own clothes, instead of the mouse-grey school uniform. Henry himself came to collect her, looking serious and grown-up in plus fours and a tweed hacking jacket. The nuns fussed over him, their pale anxious hands fluttering like moths and their eyes furtive in the immediacy of his restrained masculinity.

Outside, in the crisp air of the bright spring day, he behaved with the same gravitas, manoeuvring the large Morris Cowley motorcar through the gates and out onto the main road. With his black-gloved hands placed symmetrically on the steering wheel, he stared straight ahead of him as he drove. Lucy was in awe of him and answered his few queries as to her health and comfort in monosyllables. She had spent so much time recently in the company of her own sex that the pure animal presence of a man was as overwhelming as it was welcome. Out of the corner of her eye she watched his sure movements as he operated the gear lever or turned the wheel; there was the neutral scent about him of clean linen and well-scrubbed flesh, and when he turned his head once to smile at her the sunlight limned the clean cut smoothness of his jaw line and winked along the sheen of his hair.

They drove by the sea road and then turned into Mount Merrion Avenue. The houses, set back from the road, looked clean and eminently respectable. When the car reached Churchtown they were already in the country, a row of tramway cottages seeming to form the boundary between the urban sprawl and the more relaxed rural setting. In Nutgrove Avenue Henry had to pull in to allow a large omnibus to pass. It was crowded with men in flat caps and dark homespun clothes who grinned cheerily at Lucy and waved orange and green favours at her. The road here was potholed and rutted, and the huge vehicle groaned and staggered like an ocean liner in a stormy sea. Lucy feared for the safety of its occupants, but they merely cheered all the louder at each lurch of their conveyance.

In Rathfarnham village the shops were doing a thriving Saturday afternoon business. People walked as much on the road as they did on the pathways, and Henry had to be careful not to crush a number of them who seemed to be daring him to run them over. Lucy occupied herself by reading the names over the shopfronts: there was a Smallwood and a Greenfield, and an O'Shaughnessy and a Redfern;

a public house was owned by Hannigan & Son, and a grimy looking nook with a cobwebbed window proclaimed itself to be 'The Empire Hardware and Drapery Emporium'.

It was with relief on both their parts that they got out onto the open road once more, but they had only gone a short distance when they were halted yet again, this time by a most singular occurrence. Led by a military figure on a white horse, and blocking the road from one side to the other, came a crowd of marching men all attired in blue shirts and grey flannel trousers. Most of them were also wearing black berets, and they walked in jerky procession, their faces set and serious as though they were bent upon some grave endeavour.

The dust from their progress rose at the edge of the road where the car had stopped and filtered in through the partly open window. Lucy had to place a cologne-scented handkerchief over her mouth to ward off its acrid taste. The afternoon had suddenly become darkened for her by the appearance of these men, and by Henry's obvious hostile attitude upon seeing them. He sat, frowning at his gloved hands on the wheel, the thrust of his jaw exhibiting his distaste. Timidly Lucy asked him who they were.

'They call themselves the National Guard,' Henry told her. 'They have grown up in opposition to the government of Mr de Valera and are led by the ex-commissioner of the Civic Guards, General O'Duffy.'

'Was that him on the white horse?' Lucy asked.

'No,' Henry said, more abruptly than seemed warranted. He seemed perplexed, ill at ease even, and Lucy decided to drop the subject. Instead she commented on the dust that was still sifting in, and urged him to drive on.

They soon came to some silver-painted, wrought-iron gates, and Henry drove in between them and then along a winding driveway whose gravel crunched under the wheels of the car. When the house came into view, its castellated appearance gave it a medieval air: in Lucy's imagination it might have been the refuge to welcome home a Crusader from the Holy Land, or a merchant prince upon his return from Samarkand. The grounds surrounding it were beautifully tended and the pond that Henry had told her about had a small island in the middle of it, which contained a pagoda-shaped building that just cried out to be explored.

Inside, the house was vast, with a wide sweep of staircase and high-ceilinged, echoing rooms. Henry and Lucy were conducted through a scalloped archway by a girl only a little older than Lucy who wore a maid's uniform in a rakish manner as though she had only borrowed it for the occasion. The woman who rose to greet them, Henry's mother, was dressed in a floor-length, brightly patterned gown. She was tall and must have been in her early sixties, yet she had the clear, unblemished skin of a much younger woman. Her thick grey hair was worn in a plait that hung down her back and it compounded the impression she conveyed of someone who had taken on the sober lineaments of age much too quickly.

She took Lucy's hands in hers and led her to sit beside her on a mustard-coloured sofa. Tea was ordered and brought, and Lucy felt more at ease when she had something to occupy her. She sipped from a china cup and told her hostess about her life at school and of how exciting it was to be able to spend the weekend away from it. Mrs Morton listened with every evidence of interest, prompting her when she hesitated and giving her the confidence to feel at home.

Later, having bathed and rested, Lucy came down to dinner in the easy skirt and jersey jacket she had been given for her seventeenth birthday, but had not had the chance to wear up to then. She felt quite the sophisticated young lady, and Henry bolstered her sense of well-being by holding her chair for her and bowing her into it. Mr Morton had not yet arrived, but his aged father was already seated, a bony, crouched figure who disconcerted the rest of the company by removing his false teeth and placing them on the table beside his plate. He wore tails, and a shirt so rigidly starched that it remained immobile like a breastplate while he moved about behind it.

The only other guest was a stout, dumpy woman in horn-rimmed glasses who smoked hand-rolled cigarettes ceaselessly. This was Miss Penelope, and it transpired that she was a friend of Mrs Morton's. She ran a shop in the city that sold flowers, plants and handicrafts, and she had opinions on every subject under the sun and showed no hesitation about airing them.

She was in the middle of a diatribe about the conditions of the Dublin working classes when Henry's father came in and took up his position at the head of the table. To Lucy's amazement she found that he was the same man she had spied earlier in the afternoon on the white horse leading the rabble of blue-shirted marchers. Then he had been dressed in a military-style uniform, but now he was attired more soberly in black evening wear and bow tie.

250

She glanced at Henry, who also happened to be looking at her. He gave her a barely perceptible shake of the head, which she took to be a warning, so she said nothing of the earlier encounter.

After the meal the men retired to another room, Miss Penelope went off trailing clouds of smoke, and Mrs Morton invited Lucy to take a walk with her in the garden. The way was lit at intervals by gaslamps on the tops of metal poles, the light from them aureoled in starshine. Tightly cropped ornamental bushes lent a sculpted appearance, their serrated edges vivid against the surrounding dimness.

'We do live a quiet life,' Mrs Morton told Lucy. 'It's in our nature, you see, as well as in our beliefs. We pursue a serenity of spirit . . . in all things. Sometimes for the men it can be difficult. They tend to seek outlets for their . . . well, passions, I suppose.' She paused, as though about to impart a confidence, then seemed to think better of it and strolled on. Lucy watched her, thinking of Mr Morton mounted on his white horse, leading his makeshift army, and wondered if her companion was also thinking of him.

A little later, as they were moving along by the glimmering pond, Mrs Morton spoke again: 'We're very pleased that Henry is getting on so well. He's very taken with his work. It's so good to have him settled. He is settled, isn't he?' She stopped and gazed into Lucy's face, but before the girl could reply she went on: 'He's very fond of you, my dear, very fond.' She sighed. 'But you're so young. Hardly more than a child . . .'

'I'm seventeen . . .'

'Yes, seventeen. I was married myself at eighteen, you know. I sometimes wonder if it's the right thing . . .'

'The right thing?'

'To get married so young. There is so much to be learned, so much possible heartbreak.'

'Henry and I have an understanding,' Lucy said carefully. 'From the moment we met there was a communion of minds. We didn't even have to talk about it very much. It just seemed right . . .'

'Yes.' Mrs Morton nodded her head, but there was still a faraway look in her eyes. 'There's nothing more to be said, then, is there? We will let time take its course. If it's to be, then it will be.'

The rest of the weekend passed in a haze of pleasure for Lucy. On the Sunday she and Henry went riding, and that evening they took a skiff and rowed out to the island in the middle of the lake. The pagoda was merely decorative and contained no furniture, and when they went inside their voices echoed eerily in the cone-shaped interior. Henry told her a little of the history of such structures, remarking that they were of Buddhist origin and that in the beginning they were meant as funeral mounds erected over the relics of kings and holy men. 'They're also believed to be architectural diagrams of the cosmos,' he went on, 'and the Japanese still refer to the four corner columns as the pillars of the sky.' At Lucy's look of wonder, he suddenly laughed and told her that theirs had been built by a jobbing carpenter who needed the work, and that it had no historical significance whatever.

As they rowed back in the twilight across the stillness of the lake, he thanked her for not mentioning how they had seen his father leading his band of protesters. 'We don't approve of it, of course,' he said, 'but he won't be swayed by us. It's harmless on his part . . . play acting . . . He doesn't realise how dangerous the times are.'

His words sent a shiver of apprehension through Lucy, which only evaporated when, later that night, she took part in the family's hour of meditation. As she beheld the composed faces of her companions: Henry, his mother and father, the aged grandfather, and Miss Penelope, the flower lady, she experienced once more a feeling of the rightness of things; this was how life should always be, a quietness, a softness, a tranquillity of mood and aspiration, an unspoken acknowledgement of the basic natural harmonies. She was old enough, if not in years then in sensibility, to know that pain can never be totally kept at bay, but she vowed that when it came she would be ready for it, would damp it down and balance it out against her carefully nurtured store of remembered happiness. As the April evening gathered in about them she experienced the blossoming of a strength whose intensity half frightened and half exhilarated her; nothing truly wicked would ever succeed in breaking through the membrane of this new determination of hers to escape the constricting bonds of depression and despair. She felt sure that this must be the awakening of the Inner Light that Henry had so often told her about, and she knew that she would hold it steadfast no matter how ambiguous or stormy the way ahead might prove to be.

Little did she know how soon this strength of character of hers would be tested, for in late May, just before her summer holidays, her father died. He had shown no signs of being ill, but when he had not returned one morning from his daily walk a search party had gone out looking for him and had found him lying, composed as though in sleep, in one of the meadows on the lower slopes of Monkscadden Hill.

Lucy journeyed home with her head held high. All around her the countryside exhibited the sights and sounds and odours of early summer. There was an expectancy of growth in the air, people worked in the fields, cherry blossom was knitted through the trees, and near Grange East station a young colt galloped across a meadow in an excess of high spirits, his mane and tail streaming in the wind of his progress. Her father was lying in the big bed in her parents' room, his eyes closed, his face peaceful. He was wearing his best suit but, as soon as she came in, Lucy saw that something was missing. She went back down to the garden and picked a sky-blue forget-me-not, and when she placed it in her father's lapel she felt his presence smiling at her from every corner of the room.

After the funeral there was a period of mourning, and Lucy and her mother spent long hours together, either sitting silently in the drawing room or walking briskly in the garden. Black did not suit Mrs Swales – she was a butterfly who needed all of her adornment to soar. She took to wearing a veil and withdrew even further into herself, behind the veil, behind her facade of distanced melancholy. Lucy had often wondered about the relationship between her mother and her father: they had always treated one another with unfailing courtesy, but the little intimacies that usually exist between husband and wife had been sadly lacking.

Now, however, her mother behaved as though the staff of her life had been removed and, when she took to her bed and adopted the role of an invalid, Lucy was only mildly surprised. Sitting propped up by pillows, pale and lovely like a barely breathing anemone, suited her: she had never more than tiptoed through life, her resolve as insubstantial as gossamer.

Lucy gave up school and stayed at home, pretending a sacrifice that was in fact no sacrifice. When her father's will was read, it was found that he had left substantial bequests to his two grown-up and married daughters, but the rest of the estate to Lucy on condition that she looked after her mother for the duration of her life. With the help of the family solicitor, a Mr Lawless, Lucy arranged that Henry should run the business; for four years she paid him a salary, and on her twenty-first birthday they married in a civil ceremony that was later ratified in church when Henry converted to Catholicism.

In time Lucy gave birth to a daughter, and then to a son. The times in Ireland were turbulent: there was a lot of disorder in the country and during the Economic War, when the government of Mr de Valera refused to pay Land Annuities to Great Britain, there was much hardship. Henry found it difficult to import badly needed hops, and an attempt to find a substitute ended in failure. Also part of their land was commandeered to resettle Dublin tenement families, and the more disruptive of these people brought drunkenness and violence to the area.

Lucy, however, in the radiance of her inner strength, was never idle. To make money, she contacted Miss Penelope and made an arrangement with her to supply her shop with fresh vegetables, flowers and potted plants. When the brewing business failed, she encouraged Henry to turn his hand to market gardening and this side of things boomed when war spread its miasma across Europe.

In the midst of all their activities, Lucy and Henry always contrived to spend some time together each day. They still found one another's company more desirable than anyone else's, and the depth and resiliency of their love grew with the passing years. In spring and autumn they took long walks together, usually to the top of Monkscaddan Hill where the land spread out around them and in the distance they could see the sea. They both loved the feel of the wind in their faces, the smell of the earth and the sight of growing things. Their happiness was not something they had to analyse or work at, it evolved from the simple pleasures of touching and kissing, of always being considerate towards one another, of sharing joys and sorrows equally. They talked of their family and friends: of the unchanging aspect of Lucy's mother and how the fragility of her loveliness seemed to thrive on, the further she isolated herself from life; of how Miss Penelope had been imprisoned for a month because of her championing of women's rights; of the sickliness of their son and of the rude good health of their daughter. As evening darkened into night, they would walk home hand in hand, and the dipping swallows, returning in spring and leaving in autumn, epitomised in physical form the lightness of their hearts.

On a day in high summer and in his fifth year, their son, Malcolm, lost his tenuous hold on life and quietly faded away from them. They buried him in the family plot beside Lucy's father and sowed forget-me-nots on his grave. Their daughter, Maeve, then became the focus of their lives; she was a lively girl in whose nature Lucy's placidity and Henry's certainty manifested themselves as cornerstones of her personality. Because of Lucy's unwillingness to send her away as a boarder, she was educated at home and in the local school, and her deftness at drawing and sketching made them happy to have her trained as an artist.

Eventually she did leave home, to live and paint in Italy, and, when Lucy and Henry went to visit her where she lived near Florence, they found her sunburned and contented and living with a fellow artist who quite obviously loved her as much as they did.

When Henry was forty he developed a wasting illness similar to Parkinson's disease, and, although he lived on for a further five years, he became steadily more debilitated and, in the end, inclined to ramble. His former sturdiness deserted him and he had to be wheeled about in a wheelchair. During their last summer together, Lucy would sit with him in the garden, the line of sunlight, as it crept beyond the meridian, measuring out the length of each day. Quite often Henry imagined himself back in his youth, when he had first come to Swallowfield. He talked of the brewing, and of the good feel of the grain running through his fingers. He sniffed the air as though searching for the very odour and resonance of that long ago time. It became obvious to Lucy that the collapse of the business had had a greater effect on him than she had ever anticipated or known.

It pained her to see him so frail and weightless, the spark of life dying in his eyes, a little more each day. He had been a truly good man; a man who had been content to spend what life had been allotted to him on the smaller stage of family solidarity and the pursuit of minor joys. She had never known him to complain: on the contrary, he always seemed grateful for what each day might bring, taking an even course in the face of disappointments and rewards. Once only had she seen him weep, on the death of his son, and that in a natural, unfeigned manner without fuss or commotion. Among their friends and acquaintances, she knew, he sometimes gave the impression of being stolid and unimaginative, but this was because he had no interest in the triviality of much of social life. He distrusted role-playing, spoke what he felt, and gave his opinions as he saw them rather than as other people might wish him to see them.

To her he had been unfailingly gentle and understanding. He advised her when he saw fit, yet always in a kind and positive manner. It was she who ran the house and, after the failure of the brewing, the business end of things, but many of the more important and successful decisions taken were his. He refused to take credit and when people congratulated her on her business acumen he would smile and bask in the reflected happiness of her accomplishments.

Autumn was gently feeling its way into the last reaches of summer when he died. They were sitting in the garden and she was half dozing when she heard him make a sound. When she opened her eyes she saw that he was looking at her with the lucidity of someone whose mind was completely unencumbered by doubt or dismay. She cocked her head interrogatively and he smiled and said, 'I was watching you sleep and thinking how little you've changed since the first day I saw you. Do you remember? You were holding a silver spoon and the sun dancing on it made me think that you were the keeper of light.'

'And was I?'

'Oh, yes.' Miraculously the shaking that had afflicted his head and body had ceased and he was able to look at her with all the old assurance. 'That day you lit up my life, and you've been doing it ever since. We've had such happy times.' He paused, and she saw what an effort he had to make to say, 'Promise me that you won't grieve. It would be such a negation of all that has gone before . . .'

Lucy looked at him, and saw his life ebb away like a curl of smoke in the wind, and she was content that it appeared so effortless in the end for him. Inside herself she felt a flutter as though part of her had gone with him, up over the trees and far away, to be always by his side.

He was buried with their son and, after the funeral she went alone on their favourite walk to the top of Monkscaddan Hill. It was the middle of the afternoon and the air was so clear that she could see for miles. The earth looked burnished in its cloak of autumn and the swallows were writing their usual farewell against the sky. She stood for a long time, her mind full of sunlight. She knew that her own life was far from over and that she still had things to do. Herself and her mother would grow old together, needing one another as they always had, not in a tactile sense but on that distant shore of sense perception where minds meet without knowing or caring why. Her father would be there also, and her son who had barely nudged against life like a daylong butterfly. And her beloved Henry, so straight, so young, so manly. 'Thee I love,' she whispered, embracing them all, and the light trembled all about her like the dazzle from her silver spoon.

# Another Glorious Day

## MARY DORCEY

When I wake in the morning, if it is the morning, I don't know where I am or who I am. I think, I know, that I have been asleep. And now am awake. But where I have woken to eludes me. And the identity of the I who wonders about it escapes me completely. I cast my eyes around the room searching for a sign, for any indication as to my whereabouts; the time of day or the day of the week. Any concrete fact will do, to provide a foundation on which I can build. A stepping stone against the torrent.

A foothold.

I see a medium-sized pleasant room, some good furniture, a dressing table and chair, a tall window with curtains slightly parted. On the wall at the end of the bed I see what might be a large red and yellow parrot sitting on a wooden perch. Is this likely to be the case? I don't know. Apart from this parrot it appears to be a conventional, well-kept house, wherever it is. Possibly, I am fortunate to be here. It may well cost a great deal to maintain. And who does all the work? I must ask one of the nurses. Why did I say nurses? It is a hospital? Have I any reason to say that? It looks too relaxed for a hospital. A very good carpet and that picture of the little girls with the cat under the table, where have I seen that before? I am beginning to feel hungry; at least I think that's what the feeling is. How long is it since I've had anything to eat? Is there a bell I could ring for attention? I don't see anything resembling a bell.

'Unregarded age in corners thrown.' Where does age come into the puzzle I wonder?

Is there anyone else here who is hungry? Is there anyone else in the house? Is there any way of knowing? Perhaps I'm mad? Perhaps I'm in an asylum of some kind? Have I any means of determining this? I must calm myself. Study the situation. See what I can say for sure. I am lying

257

down, yes. I am wearing a nightdress, yes. I am warm, yes. There is a clean sheet pulled to my chin. A clean pillow under my head. There is silence around me. Is it complete? Can I hear anything? Yes, I hear a clock ticking faintly. Where? I can't see a clock. I am lying on my back with my head on a pillow (yes, a clean pillow I'm glad to say), I'm looking at a ceiling. It is high and white with one large grey cobweb in the far corner (the kind I would have knocked clear with one sweep of the brush). Though as yet there is no spider in evidence. 'Weaving spiders come not here, hence you long-legged spiders, hence.' Hamlet, I think.

It is remarkable and at the same time irritating somehow, that Shakespeare has a line to suit every occasion.

When I turn my head to the right I see a smooth wall and hanging on it a large painting in a dark frame. It shows a woman in a yellow cardigan holding a green umbrella. Is this what seemed before to resemble a parrot? I think I remember this painting. Granny used to have it in the sitting room. Is Granny alive or dead? Why did I say that? Who is Granny? Not mine surely? I must try to find out from someone. But who? Is there anyone available to ask? Perhaps it's a hotel or guesthouse. The wallpaper is good; there is a nice chest of drawers and a wardrobe. Should I try calling out? Will anyone answer?

Is it wise to call when I have no idea who might respond?

The light is so sharp it hurts my eyes. I close them for a moment or two. I think. When I open them again I recognise the same daylight making its way across the room. But the light of which day, I wonder? I wish someone would come and tell me, I must at least have the date and the year. Still the ticking of a clock.

Through the window I see a grey sky, white clouds, and below that yellow flowers in a garden. Is there something familiar about it – that garden? There is a cat or, at least, I see a cat walking through tall grass. A black cat. Is this a clue? Who owns a cat? Someone I know? I can't remember. There were cats somewhere else. Black pussy – that's what she was called; black pussy. She must be hungry. I should go home and feed the cats. How am I to manage it? Can I get up unaided? I wonder is there anyone looking after us? Should I call for assistance? I don't hear any sound of life at all. Where could it be? A hospital, a nursing home or a hotel perhaps. Could it be a quiet country house? There is some very good furniture. And the windows are beautifully clean.

A lot of work for someone with a very tall ladder.

Although, now I come to study it, the carpet is a little bit shabby. I never had enough money to replace carpets when they needed it or curtains. I had to wait. But I had sufficient for my needs. Adequate always. I had a hard life. You must remember, Sara; I have had a hard life. Who is Sara? Someone I love. I remember that I have someone I love who comes to see me. More than one person. There is a boy and a girl. I hear the telephone ringing. I hope someone answers it. I don't think I can get up. I'll try. Why is it so hard to stand up? I must ask someone what is wrong with my knees. They don't bend properly and I can't straighten my back. Is the phone still ringing? I should call someone. Will anyone come if I do? Who? A nurse? Perhaps I'm better off without a nurse. I don't think I need her services at present. And I can't know what kind of nurse. Nurses can be very difficult.

'Are you all right, Maeve, would you like another cup of tea?'

I hear a voice calling from somewhere in the house, above or below me I do not know. And who is Maeve? And why does she not answer? I'm sure I heard someone calling her before. Is the voice approaching or receding? I cannot tell. Silence now again. What was I thinking about when I was interrupted? I must concentrate on the important questions, or at least the most immediate. Where is this? Where did I come from? Am I alone? Some memory is stirring. What was I doing before this? I have a pair of spectacles in my hand. Reading glasses? When did I pick them up and from where? Were they under my pillow? I think I was studying the environment. Making notes. Mental notes. On a low table beside the bed I see a telephone and a photograph in a silver frame. I peer closer but I can't make out who it is a picture of (of whom it is a picture?). I see only that it's a portrait of two young women standing on a flight of stone steps. Good-looking girls, with intelligent faces and good clothes. The kind of girls I would have liked for daughters if I'd had daughters. I wonder why I had no children. I can't think of any reason now. I must ask someone. Daughters, the word rings a bell, some memory is stirring at the edge of my vision. I must wait quietly so as not to frighten it off. I've learned that this is the best way to trap them. Stealthily as one might hunt nervous animals, waiting silent in the long grass until they gather courage, draw closer and at last thrown off guard, come within my grasp.

No sign of the spider as yet.

'Maeve, were you calling? Have you finished your breakfast?'

A woman with a wide moon-shaped face looks round the door. She is smiling. The glass in her spectacles twinkles in the sunlight, which gives her face an impish look. She says my name in a loud clear voice as if doubtful that I can hear her although she is standing now at the foot of the bed. Would you like another cup of tea, love? Oh, it's such a relief to see you, I say, I was getting worried. I thought I was all alone in the house. Not a bit of it, she says, sure we never leave you on your own.

'Oh that's very good news. I wish I'd known that before. And how are you? How is everyone at home?'

'We're all grand, Maeve, all your family and mine.'

'Thank God for that. I was afraid everyone must be dead. There wasn't sound or any sign of life. I thought there must have been some general catastrophe and that by some awful chance I had survived.'

'There's not a bother on any of us.' She has a slight country accent. Somewhere near my part, I think, Tipperary or Limerick perhaps. Munster anyway which is reassuring. Irish by birth, Munster by the grace of God – who used to say that? She comes closer. She has short blonde hair and arched eyebrows. She is wearing some kind of yellow flannel-like jacket with square pockets and a long, wide zip. I cannot make out whether she's dressed for indoors or outdoors.

I return her smile.

What day of the week is it? I ask to gain a little time. It's evident from her face that she expects me to recognise her and I'm not sure that I do. Though there is certainly something familiar about it. What day is it I find the safest question. Hearing it people seem to assume that I know all the other things I'm not asking. If I make myself patient whoever is talking to me will, sooner or later, fill in the gaps. Do you want another cup of tea love or will you just not bother? my nice friend says. I recognise this as one of our little jokes. It seems to be a lovely day, Kitty, I reply, and suddenly, like Excalibur, the sword in the lake, her name has risen from the depths in one gleaming piece – Kitty! Kitty O'Neill.

'Did you have a little sleep?' she asks me.

'I think I must have, Kitty, yes. Where am I at present, may I enquire?'

'At home in your own house. Where else would you be?'

'My own house! Are you sure? Well that's extraordinary. I had no idea of that. I don't recognise it at all.' I put my hands to either side of my hips and push myself, groaning aloud, upright in the bed so that my back is propped against the pillows. 'I've been watching the sunlight shining on the grass and the little birds, sparrows, I think. They have amazing courage,' I say to make conversation. 'They swoop down to collect tiny crumbs of bread taking their lives in their hands.'

Not that they have hands, of course.

Kitty is standing now in the doorway, one foot in, one foot out. I have decided that the jacket is indoor wear so it's likely that she intends to stay for a while. 'I have to go downstairs to answer the telephone,' she tells me. 'Will you say some prayers until I come back?' She disappears as suddenly, I think, as she appeared. Silence follows. Has she left the house? No way of knowing. I look out the window into the garden and see to my surprise what might be a squirrel, some creature with thick greyish fur and a bushy tail, sitting on a tree branch. 'Sometimes my heart hath shaken with great joy, to see a leaping squirrel on a bough or something in a field at evening . . .' Can it be a squirrel? Unlikely. Is it evening? Possibly. It's gone from sight now so I may never know. And who wrote those lines? It's possible an answer might be supplied to this, at least.

Was it suggested to me recently (by whom?) that I should say some prayers? And when? Well, no time like the present. 'Hail Mary full of grace the Lord is with thee, blessed art thou among women and blessed is the fruit of thy womb Jesus. Holy Mary Mother of God . . .' Now, how does the rest of it go? Something about sinners. 'On Raglan Road on an autumn day I saw her first and knew that her dark hair would weave a snare that I would one day rue, I saw the danger yet . . .' There's no need to feel sorry for him then – he saw the danger. But he was always a morose fellow skulking about the canal. Who is it lives on Raglan Road now? A quiet street where old ghosts meet. There were eight in the family. Someone was telling me about them just this morning. What are their names? If I could get the first one I'd know the rest. I have to take a running jump at it. I wonder does anyone of them know I'm here. Have I any way of contacting them?

I don't know where I am myself so how could I direct anyone else?

Patrick Pierce, of course, I say aloud in excitement. The answer to some question I was struggling with has just arrived unbidden. I can't remember what the question was.

My nice friend is standing by the window shielding me from the sunlight.

'Kitty, what terrible thing has happened in the world? There's something at the back of my mind. A catastrophe of some kind? Was it an earthquake in India yesterday?'

'Did you say any prayers, Maeve? I thought I heard you.'

'Yes, I think I probably did. On Raglan Road on an autumn day . . .'

'That's a poem, Maeve, not a prayer.'

'Is it? Well, I don't suppose God will mind. He'll take my great age into account.'

Kitty is folding clothes beside what looks like a chest of drawers at the far end of the room. 'Why is it do you think,' I ask aloud, in reference to some news I can't recall, 'that some of us lead lives of such calm and security while others by a mere accident of geography are fraught with every kind of danger?' Kitty's head is lowered and she offers no solution to this. Instead after a moment she informs me that Jezebel is making her way along the corridor. I ask who Jezebel is when she's up and dressed? She sounds a very unlikely visitor to this respectable establishment. A large striped animal (black and silver stripes on greyish background) leaps onto the bottom of the bed. When she reaches my face she gives an angry cry and shows the extraordinary interior of her mouth – crimson and furrowed.

'Whose the bold pussycat stayed out all night?' Kitty says. I stroke her head and she purrs, and kneads my shoulder with piercing claws. 'Isn't it nice to have one free spirit left in the house?'

'Do you hear the phone, Maeve? I must go down and answer it.'

Down where? I hear nothing but then, that means nothing.

There is something stirring at the back of my mind, some disaster that has happened in the world. Is it the war I wonder, still raging? Not any of the wars I remember, some other one. But there is always a war.

My nice friend with the blonde hair and the matching glasses comes back into the room. That was your eldest son Kevin, she tells me, he rang to see how you are? 'I hope you told him I'm bothered and bewildered?' I answer, having found something sharp in the bed that turns out to be a pair of silver-rimmed spectacles.

'I said you're as fit as a fiddle.'

'Kevin, was it? I wish I'd known that when I was speaking to him. I would have asked him about his work. I hope I wasn't rude to him?'

'Not a bit of it,' Kitty says, 'you were clear and concise as always.'

'I am a very foolish fond old man and to deal plainly, I fear I am not in my perfect mind.'

Kitty tells me not to be worrying about my memory; it's better than hers. I'm a mine of information, she says. I was telling her only this morning, it seems, about the Spanish Civil War, and Franco and the Communists. She is straightening pillows behind my head and pulling back the covers. I see a blue cotton nightdress and two very thin white legs (mine?) protruding from it. She says I was talking about the Second World War yesterday when there was rationing of meat and sugar and the Russian Revolution and the White Army. I am holding onto the bed head with one hand and with the other I grasp Kitty's sleeve. Hey ho and up she rises.

'You're a true scholar,' she says. 'My head is like a sieve.'

'We'll have to be careful to put nothing in it or we'll make a terrible mess of the floor.'

We both laugh when I say this.

I like to see Kitty amused because it must be very dull work taking charge of me.

'I might as well stay in my dressing gown if we have only ourselves to please, Kitty?' She is standing in the doorway holding a tray in her hand. She asks if I can manage for myself while she tidies up below. 'Have you forgotten that Sara is taking you out for tea this afternoon because it's her birthday?' she asks. This comes as complete news but is all the more pleasant for that. 'The jewel in the crown, that's what we call her,' Kitty says. I wonder of what or whom does the crown consist. I decide not to ask or maybe I have asked because Kitty says, 'Your other children, all six of them.'

'Six! Now don't tease me, Kitty – how could I possibly have had six children?'

My friend sets down the tray and comes back into the room. She is proffering one of several small white garments outstretched in her right hand. 'What do we put on first?' she says. 'Underwear. I suppose that's why we call it underwear.' She says she'll get me started and then I can carry on. It's good for me to do as much as I can, so that I don't lose the habit. That sounds very sensible.

'It's very good of you to take so much trouble to explain everything. I must be a terrible trial?'

'Not a bit of it, Maeve. You're an angel.'

'A very earthbound angel, I'm afraid.'

I'm sitting on the edge of a bed. Why? With my feet in large (outsize in fact I would call them) slippers, resting squarely on the floor. What follows next?

The sunlight coming in through the window hurts my eyes. I don't know what day it is or where I am. I close my eyes and count to five. I open them again. Where does this go, for God's sake? There is a piece of white cloth in my hand, which seems to be composed of straps and pockets. It looks like a noose to hang myself. Or a bridle perhaps. To be led like a horse. An extraordinary object. Does it go over the head? Or around my waist? And this? What is this damn thing for? Do I put my feet through these holes, I wonder? That can't be right. Maybe I should wait until I get some help. Is there anyone in the house besides myself? Surely they wouldn't leave me alone. I don't think I'm in a fit state to be left alone. I don't know why. My brain is tired I think that's what it is. Now if I put this round my waist and then pull it up, it seems to make sense. Then I could put these straps up over my shoulders. Oh, you silly old fool why can't you remember? What is wrong with my head? Old? Why did I say old? I should call for help. 'Is there anyone there? Does anyone hear me? Am I all alone in the house?'

'Maeve, I'm coming now, don't panic . . .'
    'Oh, Kitty, at last, there you are. I was getting frightened.' In the mirror I'm holding I see a face reflected, an old woman's face with white hair and red-rimmed eyes. Theatrical looking. I don't know who she is and think it better not to ask.
    'It's like keeping order in a mad house, Kitty.'
    'What is?'
    'Managing my brain, effecting the smallest action . . . I seem to be completely vacant today.'
    'Indeed and you're not. Sure, you're a walking encyclopaedia,' she says. 'Now that would be a sight!'
    'Would you like me to give you the facts about yourself the way Sara does?' Kitty asks, and begins in the voice of a quizmaster: 'Maeve Kieley, née Roach, born in Waterford 1920, seven brothers and sisters. Moved to Donegal aged eight. Moved to Dublin, Pembroke Road, aged fourteen years. Moved to Seapoint, Dublin, on marriage to Michael Kieley. Six children, all surviving.' All this would be very interesting if I knew whom it concerned. But I don't like to interrupt with more questions.

She is fastening the buttons of my dress, at the cuffs and the collar, and she says I am just myself again. I wonder who I was before.
    'With your hair brushed you're beautiful. The contessa – isn't that what we call you? And you'll wear your coat with the fur collar because it's cold and because it suits a countess.'

'Who calls me the countess?'

'We all do because you're just like one.'

'The Hag of Beara, Kitty, I think, would be more like it.'

I put down the hairbrush I am holding in my hand. It has a silver back and short black bristles. 'I think I must need to make a visit to the toilet. I haven't been since yesterday.'

Kitty tells me I was there only half an hour ago.

'Are you sure? I don't think you can be right?'

'Come on now like a good girl. Stand up. Hold onto my arm. You're very steady once you're on your feet.'

We are passing the bathroom door. I see clean towels, green, two hanging on a rail. The blue tiles on the floor look newly washed. 'I think we get on very well, don't we, Kitty?' I say.

'It's because we have so much in common. We were both widowed young,' she says, 'and raised our families on our own and know all about worry and heartbreak.'

'And facing facts, Kitty,' I say. 'And not to kick against the inevitable.' We are making our way laboriously down the stairs. I ask if she knows that O'Neill is one of the great names of Ireland. We are moving one foot at a time and then another foot. And there are four legs to organise on a narrow staircase. The ancient Irish aristocracy, I tell her. Does she know about the Wild Geese and the Flight of the Earls? Kitty doesn't know or doesn't want to talk about them now. She is concentrating on getting down the stairs in one piece. That's what she says. I have to get you down in one piece. When the children were small I was always afraid one of them would break his neck on these stairs, used to dream of a bungalow, I tell her.

'Now, almost there. You're a great girl.'

'Hardly a girl any more, I'm afraid.'

'Do you know how old you are this year, Maeve?'

'Well, now I was hoping you could tell me that.'

'How old do you feel?'

'Well, I'm not sure. I feel very well. But I don't think I'm young. I feel mature. About fifty. Am I right?'

'Here's the birthday girl,' someone says. I am coming, step by step, down a steep staircase. You are standing in the doorway. The sun is forming a halo around your hair.

'Oh, Sara, what brings you here?' The birthday girl someone says, again, I don't know why. You kiss me on both cheeks and put your arms around me. Are we all ready to go? Kitty is pulling on my gloves. They have jammed at the wrist. 'She needs to wrap up in this cold weather.' You are pulling a hat over my head. Or are you taking it off? 'She doesn't like wearing it so it's always a battle.' I can't imagine that I would do battle over the wearing of a hat but you are both laughing so I laugh too.

'Don't be impatient with me now. Remember I didn't ask to lose my memory.'

The door is thrown wide. Ready steady go. I step out. On one side is a green hedge with yellow flowers on or is it a yellow hedge with green leaves? On the other a blue gate and a huge open sky, full of light. Which way are we going – in or out? If I wait someone will tell me. 'And watch the chocolate!' Kitty calls after us. Why is chocolate to be watched I wonder? It seems to have threatening properties that have escaped my notice.

There are two pairs of shoes going down the path, two black and two red. Mind your step. I think you must be unsteady on your feet today because you take my arm and hold it tightly. 'What will we do with the drunken sailor early in the morning,' I say.

Concentrate. No singing until we're at the gate.

When we reach the street we pause for what I don't know. A bird with red breast feathers is perched on the gatepost. What are we doing now? I ask. 'We're resting.' My hair or is it my hat is caught in a twig as we pass the hedge. You reach out to untangle it. 'Lean on my arm and use your stick on the other side or you'll fall over.'

'And on my leaning shoulder she laid her snow-white hand.' But it can't have been snow white if she was walking through the Sally gardens, can it? He was always a bit of a poseur, Yeats, but we liked him for it, I say. We used to pass him in Merrion Square. You are holding open the gate and I am inching my way through. I don't know why we are moving so slowly but it seems to be necessary.

We pause for a long time at the kerb and then progress again in our snail-like motion across the road.

'What day is it?' I ask. 'Thursday! Are you sure? I thought it was Sunday, love. It's doing an excellent imitation of Sunday. Are you sure now you're not trying to fool me? I rely on you.' A seagull is standing on the harbour wall. The sun is gleaming on its yellow feet. By the light, I think it must be an afternoon in autumn. A vague picture comes into my head – a woman and a child standing by the harbour wall. They are breaking a loaf of stale bread into small pieces to feed the birds. What day is it, I wonder? I must make enquiries. How are things in the great world, I ask instead. 'Is this terrible war still raging?' 'Yes,' you tell me.

'Isn't it extraordinary,' I say, 'that with all the advance in technology we can do nothing to alter human nature.' The wind is blowing a cold sun over our hands and knees. I see the shadow come and go. Someone I love is walking beside me with her arm through mine. I know the voice but her face is hidden from me. She is bending down now to tie her shoelace, I think. Is it one of my sisters? Or one of my daughters?

A cargo ship is passing behind the island. 'The sky is clearing, it's going to be a lovely afternoon,' you say.

'It's a lovely afternoon, already.'

You look at me with a puzzled (why?) and what seems a tender expression. You ask me if I know who you are today, am I quite clear? You turn your head towards me and I see that you're my daughter Sara.

'Sara, of course,' I say. 'That which we call a rose by any other name would smell as sweet.'

'You didn't recognise me for a while because of my hat.'

'It's a very impressive hat,' I say.

'Do you think I've changed much over the years?' I study your face. There are freckles on your cheeks, above your lip and above your eyebrow, one, two, three, four, and five. Your eyes are sea-green. 'Yes,' I say looking at the freckles, 'a little bit I suppose. Just enough.'

We are standing beside a green car. A little black dog is sitting on the back seat. Where did the dog come from?

'That's Charlie of course. Will we get in now and begin our drive?' You open the door and help me to sit down. 'Put your bottom in first and then swing your legs round.'

'We could do with a giant shoehorn, couldn't we?' I say.

Rain in slow drops is falling on the windscreen; the sun is catching in it, obscuring the view. You turn on the windscreen wipers. They travel to the very furthest edge of the wide screen and then all the way back again, back and forth, in a sing-song motion. Something is stirring in my mind about a child walking on a pier. She is carrying a cowboy hat in her hand. What day is it, I wonder?

'I think they should announce the day of the week when they're reading the news on television. There must be a great many people who need to know,' I say.

You put your hand on my knee. 'Are you all right, now?' you ask, 'are you feeling safe?'

'Well, I'm a bit through other, today, as they used to say in Donegal.'

'It comes and goes, the confusion doesn't it, like clouds over the sun?'

'A lot of cloud,' I say.

The little cat shifts position. Her claws dig into my knees, tearing my stocking but I don't want to give her away. 'Isn't the car a wonderful invention,' I say, 'it gives such extraordinary freedom. Do you remember in the old days waiting in the rain for a bus? I don't suppose you can remember that far back. Have you any memory of your father, at all? How old were you when he died? Six! Oh that was much too young!'

It has stopped raining. You switch off the wipers and turn to look at me. You are wearing black sunglasses. They give your face an unfamiliar aspect. I close my eyes and concentrate on your voice that doesn't change. Unaffected by the seasons or fashion.

'How are you getting on with Kitty these days?' you ask.

'Oh, very well, I think. Is there a reason why I wouldn't be?' I ask. 'Although, I have been worried about her,' I say, 'she seems to have some trouble in the family.' You put your hand on my knee and squeeze it as if to get my attention but I am already giving you my full attention. 'Watch the road, love,' I say.

'If you have any problem, of any kind you must tell me, you know that, don't you?' You pronounce this in a very emphatic tone. I see the anxiety in your eyes but I don't know what the cause is. 'I hope it's not taking up too much of your precious time all this managing of my affairs?'

You smile and kiss me.


The sun is so strong I can hardly open my eyes. I think it must be summer. The island has come into view from a strange angle. It seems to be drifting out to sea as if someone has cut it loose from its moorings.

Crushed shells, extraordinarily bright; red and blue and yellow covered the little beach. The children used to love them.

'If only this could go on for ever. I feel perfectly safe and content sitting here. With the sun shining and the little black cat asleep on my lap,' I say.

'Dog,' you correct me.

'Well, whatever she is,' I reply, 'she's a marvel. So good and so intelligent. And she makes such an effort to please you. But she doesn't want you to know it's an effort.' I stroke the soft hair that grows on her muzzle and she opens her eyes and looks at me sadly.

When I raise my eyes again the sky is filled with movement, white and silver birds. Or is it the shadow of the clouds blown across the hills? 'I wish your father could see this,' I say. Something is making a sound like small pebbles thrown against the glass. What is? Rain? 'He didn't want to die, you know. No man ever wanted to die less. He couldn't bear to leave you all. How long is he dead now? Forty years! I am horrified to hear this. How can that be?' I demand. I stare at you in astonishment. I see from your expression that you are not joking. 'But what age are you then?' I gasp at your answer. 'I thought you were still a teenager.'

There is a girl in a blue frock on a blue bicycle near a high white wall. A grey van goes past us at great speed. The car is buffeted as though by a strong wind. You are telling me about your childhood, about sunny days on the beach, about picnics and outings and trips to the pictures. There couldn't have been a better time or better setting. 'Did we go all the way to Glendalough?' I ask. 'How did we get there?' You tell me that I filled the car with children and drove you. This must be an exaggeration surely? Petrol, perhaps, not children.

A flurry of blossom, pink and white (spring?) is blowing along the black tarmac of the road ahead. I remember the smell of the tar melting on a hot day as we walked to the beach. And did I have anything to do with this happy childhood? I ask in connection with something you have been telling me. 'You were the platform on which everything else was built.' The little black dog licks the back of my hand with a small rough tongue. She looks at you enquiringly and back again to me.

'I know I tried my best. That's all anyone of us can do, Sara,' I say, 'I couldn't make up for your father of course because he was devoted to you. But he had more free time than I did. I had so much to do. I don't know if any of you realised that.'

The water is choppy, dark grey with purple streaks across it, beautiful and cold. The wind is rising, I think. You're not lonely at all, these days? you ask.

'Oh not a bit. There is some very pleasant friend who comes to help me in the house. I don't know who she is but she knows me. She seems to have some little difficulty, though. Some trouble in the family. I'm concerned about her. And she needs do things slowly. I think she might be hard of hearing.'

'Kitty you mean.'

'Yes, Kitty. Why did I forget that? She must be one the carers. Isn't that what we call them? A silly name, I think, carers. But that's not their fault. For the most part, they are very good people; kindly and considerate.' I see that the gorse is in full bloom on the hillside, buttercup yellow. It used to stain our fingers when we tried to pick it.

'And they are tactful,' I say, 'they take pains to conceal from me the fact that I'm a prisoner in my own home.'

I have saddened you now.

We round a bend and suddenly the whole sweep of the bay comes into view at once, a beach and hills and trees and white houses. You stop the car at the side of the road. Your face is pale when you turn towards me. 'I'm sorry they've started to lock the front door,' you say. 'I've spoken to them about it but it's an insurance thing – standard procedure. You never do anything foolish or careless but they don't know that.'

'Well, if they think it's necessary I don't mind,' I say, 'and you know sometimes I can be very confused. I don't think I should be on my own too much, unsupervised.'

'You're not; there's somebody with you all the time.'

'Oh that's a great relief to hear. Because my brain can be unreliable, you know. It comes and goes you see, the forgetfulness, for no reason I can think of.'

The clouds are flying along the sky and the waves are flying almost as fast below them. 'It would be a fascinating condition if I was well enough to study it,' I say.

You put your hand on my shoulder. It feels warm and soothing.

'Are you tired, love?' I ask you.

'I'm fine, I just worry about you a little.' I turn to look at you. It's an effort to concentrate. But I see that you are pale and there is a furrow between your eyebrows. 'Cease thou thy worrying, as Shakespeare would say. There is nothing to be concerned about. I'm splendid most of the time. And after all, at my great age I can't expect to be perfect.'

I count one, two, three bridges over the railway. Stone I think brought from the quarry in Victorian times. The boys used to ride to school along the disused railway.

'The mind is a mysterious organ, isn't it? Or the brain should I say? Was it Boswell or Swift when asked about the purpose of life, said a chicken is the egg's way of making another egg. Confusion worse confounded.'

I close my eyes. The words of a poem stir in my memory, 'Better to sleep than see this house now dark to me . . .' I open my eyes. 'In my own case I could quite happily forget about purpose if I had the least idea what my function is.'

'Don't worry about it,' you say. 'You remember everything you need to. There's only so much room on the shelves, you see.'

'Oh that's a comforting idea,' I say. 'I hope it's true.'

'Imagine a big house with all the precious things stored in the basement. You can't always get down because the stairs are worn but when you get hold of the ladder you find everything is just where you left it.'

When they were all growing up there wasn't a basement to store things in. Never enough room to put anything away for long. I see a tall man walking past on the pavement. He has a shaven head and thick black beard. He looks as if his face is upside down. I must make an effort. I must pull myself together. I must not keep asking questions.

'Anyway, I'm perfectly content now, sitting here with you. Perfectly safe and perfectly happy.'

'Good,' you say. 'That's what I like to hear.'

I read the names that are written on the gates along the roadside: 'Seaview', 'Seacrest', 'Seamount'. Does it make more or less work for the poor postman? I wonder. 'We joined the navy to see the world. And what did we see? We saw the sea.' Some child used to love that song.

'And tell me, how is life treating you these days?' I say, to change the subject, whatever it was. I would like to ask about your career but I'm not sure what it is. 'And your work – does it bring in much in the way of money?' Enough, you tell me and smile.

'I play the violin in the symphony orchestra.'

'Oh, isn't that wonderful.' I am delighted by this news. Although there is some faint picture in my mind. A girl by a window, a violin in her arms that is almost bigger than herself.

'It doesn't pay as much as I'd like but I like it so much it doesn't matter.'

I say that sounds like a tongue twister. 'But I think you're very wise, to be following a passion.' You are wearing a plain silver band on your ring finger. Does this mean you've become engaged without my knowing? But I remember then something of your situation and I put out my hand, touch the ring and say, 'Engaged to life.'

You glance at the driving mirror and then open the door on your side. 'I have to get something from the boot. Will you be all right for a moment on your own?'

'Yes, love but don't be too long will you?' The little dog jumps out after you, wagging her stub of a tail. There was some other dog with a thick-fringed black tail like a fan, long ago. We always had spaniels at home.

'Only a minute. Just sit here and keep your eye on me and you'll be perfectly safe.' I see you standing at the side of the car. You are walking backwards so that your face is turned towards me. You are smiling. Now you are behind me, almost out of sight. Your back is to me now. I try to turn my head. Suddenly, you have disappeared. A cloud must have gone across the sun blocking everything out.

My face is cold and my hands. There is a strange pressure in my chest.

A tall man with a shaven head and thick black beard is walking along the footpath. He is carrying a silver-topped walking stick. Why am I here? I wonder. Am I alone? I have the feeling that I shouldn't be alone. I can't remember why. I wonder do I know any of these people? Where am I? How long have I been here? Are there any clues? It's obviously some public place. There are people about and a lot of cars. There are houses and gardens with high gates and tall dark trees. Menacing looking. I wonder how I got here? Where was I before this? I can't remember anything before this moment. Where do I live? What is my name? Do I have any family or am I quite alone in the world? The wind is growing louder. The sea is purple, the waves look mutinous. 'My grief on the sea, how the waves of it roll . . . ' There are so many people passing on the road and none of them seems to know me. Have I to drive home? Do I know how to drive? I remember the handbrake start, the three-point turn. I didn't start to drive until I was forty, after Kenneth died. The hill start was the most difficult thing of all to master. Is there any possibility that I could manage it now? How far have I to go? Did I come with someone? Where is she? I'm sure it was one of the girls.

Who are the girls? What am I talking about?

That man has a strange air about him. I don't like the look of his cane. And his smile has something ominous in it. He is talking to a young woman in a black hat, a hat with a wide brim. I cannot see the face. Where am I? I wonder, and what am I doing here? The place looks completely unfamiliar. What time of year is it? What time of day? That path leading towards the sea looks vaguely familiar. How do I get home from here? I have no idea. Where is my home? If I knew my address I could ask someone. Come on, you silly old fool – just think now, think! What is your address? Name and address – old fool! Rank and serial number? Keep calm and think. Think! Someone must have brought you here. Who was it? Think! If you sit here quietly whoever it is will come back. You must keep calm. Say a prayer, that will help you to stay calm. 'Hail holy queen, Mother of mercy. Hail our life, our sweetness and our hope. To thee do we cry, poor banished children of Eve, to thee do we send up our sighs, mourning and weeping in this valley of tears . . .' I close my eyes and count to ten. I open them again.

Someone I was with was here and is gone.

Who was it? Someone I love. I know that much. Someone I love who loves me. If she loves me she will come back to find me. If I wait calmly she is bound to come looking for me. I must control my fear. I must try to organise my mind. If one of the children got lost long ago we told them to wait quietly until someone came looking. Just stay still. Don't cry. Someone will find you. Not lost but waiting to be found. Somebody who was here was telling me about a lake, a place we used to visit together. When was that? Why did we go there? And who was telling me about it? Something is hovering at the edge of my mind about a lake at evening. 'She stepped away from me and she moved through the fair, and fondly I watched her go here and go there, then she went her way homeward with one star awake, as the swan in the evening moves over the lake.' Where is she now?

I close my eyes. I count one, two, three, four, five, six, seven, eight, nine, ten seconds before I open them again. Dark purple clouds are gathered over the mountains. It looks like rain. My hands are cold and my feet. I am hungry, at least, I think that's what the feeling is. Who am I waiting for? What am I waiting for? 'Turn then, most gracious advocate, thine eyes of mercy towards and after this our exile show unto us . . .'

The wind must be rising; I hear it knocking against the windowpane. I look up. The door opens. A young woman in a black hat is standing looking at me. She is holding a small black animal in her arms. She gets into the driving seat beside me. She puts her arms around my shoulder. 'I'm back now,' she says. 'I'm here. Everything is all right.' Her face is smiling broadly as if there's nothing whatever the matter with the world.

I reach my hand and grasp yours.

'Oh Sara, I was never more pleased to see you. Your arm is trembling or is it mine? I thought there had been some terrible catastrophe,' I say, 'and that by some awful chance I had survived it.'

You kiss my forehead.

'Where is everyone? I've been sitting here on my own for hours.' You put your arm around my shoulder.

'I'm sorry,' you say. 'Your old friend Tom Mulcahy passed by and I stopped to talk to him.' You are speaking very softly and looking into my eyes. 'I was watching you all the time and you were looking at us.'

'Was I?' I fix my gaze on the black tarmac of the road ahead. It seems to be the only constant feature. 'I don't remember any of that, at all,' I say slowly, 'you can't imagine what it's like. I was terrified.'

You place a small shivering bundle on my knee. It feels warm and soft.

'I know,' you say, 'hold Charlie and he'll help to calm you.'

Your arm is around my shoulders. Your cheek is close to mine. You are speaking very gently as adults do to children. Do you have children? I wonder. I don't think you do.

'You must be patient, Sara. It's the most terrible sensation. My mind is a complete blank. I don't know where I am or how I got here. I can't remember anything at all. And nobody can help me.' You reach behind you and take a red and green plaid blanket from the back seat. You wrap it over my knees and under the small dog.

'I'll help you,' you say. The dog sits upright on my knees balanced precariously. She is panting. A small red tongue hangs from the side of her jaw. 'And Kitty when we get home again.'

I close my eyes and open them again slowly. Nothing seems to have changed. Nothing has become familiar.

'Oh yes, let's go home. Because if you don't mind, love, I'm very tired. Have we far to go?'

'Just down the road,' you say, 'we only stopped to admire the view.'

'My home is down the road!' I say astonished. 'But I've never been here before!' I try to make myself be patient. To wait for this mad confusion to clear. We are evidently at cross-purposes.

'You've been living here for sixty years,' you say with unsettling calm.

'Sixty years!' This is the most appalling news. 'I must have been in a dream the whole time then because I don't remember anything about it. Who lived here with me? Children? Oh, you'll have to stop telling me, Sara. I can't take in any more now. It's all a complete shock, I didn't know I had ever been married. I'll just have to take your word for it.'

I look around me, searching for any recognisable object or person. The trees and the houses and the gardens look equally strange. They might belong anywhere. There is nothing visible that means anything. If I live alone here how do I manage? Surely I'm not fit to be trusted to my own devices. You seem to imagine I'm quite sensible. Should I tell you the truth? But you look so pale and tired. I know you have your own worries. I can't remember if you have anyone to cook a hot meal for you when you get home. You seem exhausted. I am exhausting you. If only I could remember facts for myself. I must put a brave face on things. I must not be a burden. I must not be a worry to anyone. Especially my children. I will try not to be a nuisance. I will do whatever you tell me to do. I think I do that anyway.

You start up the engine and pull out onto the smooth black road.

'If we say some poems, will it help?' you ask.

'I don't know,' I say. 'I was going over a poem in my mind while you were gone. Something to do with a lake. "The Lake Isle of Inisfree", I think. Music has charms to soothe the savage breast, they say, and so has rhyme and narrative. I don't know why.'

'I think your brain is held together by poems and songs, isn't it?'

I am keeping my eyes fixed on the white line that divides the black tarmac of the road. It seems to be the only unchanging thing. What will become of me, if I go on like this? I will end in the mad house. How will I bear it? If I can't remember anything I'm helpless. And if I'm helpless I can't defend myself.

A soft drizzle is falling on the windscreen. You take a bar of chocolate from the glove compartment and break off four squares.

'Have some,' you say, 'as much as you like.'

Sunshine in a narrow shaft pierces the side window. It lights the air between us. It glistens on your hands that are holding the steering wheel and on the side of your face. The chocolate is delicious. It melts in my mouth.

'Aren't we extraordinarily fortunate in the weather, Sara?' I say. 'What they have to endure in other countries! The poor people in Pakistan at present, I can't stop thinking about them.'

The little dog leans forward from the back seat, panting with excitement. Her breath is moist and warm. She is resting a confiding paw on my shoulder.

'Charlie loves you,' you say. I have no way of telling if this is true but it's a very pleasing notion. Her paw is resting on me for support, I think.

'Do you know, Sara, I count my blessings at night and Charlie is one of them. And I think too I'm blessed in my health. I have the usual aches and pains, of course, but mercifully, I can still rely on my brain. You are smiling now I'm glad to see.

'I always had a good memory, though I say it myself who shouldn't.' Some picture comes to me, a picture of children on a stony beach. And a story about a sword rising from a lake. 'When I was young, someone used to say that there was no resource like a well-stocked mind,' I say, 'and do you know, I think they were right.'

The windscreen wipers are washing back and forth in their singsong motion. On either side of the road the hedges are ablaze with gorse. It must be April or May. I turn to look at you.

'It would be the very worst thing, wouldn't it, to have any condition that affected the mind.'

You are looking straight ahead concentrating your eyes on the road.

'Yes,' you say.

'You must take me out and shoot me, Sara, if anything ever goes wrong with my head. Promise me that?' You are still watching the road attentively.

'Yes,' you say. 'I promise.'

You lift your left hand from the gear stick and take hold of mine. 'But before any of that,' you say, 'can we have our tea first? We're on our way to Avoca, you know?'

I put another square (the last, is it?) of the delicious, dark chocolate into my mouth and lick my fingers.

'Of course, who wouldn't remember that name?' I say. ' "There's not in this whole world a valley so sweet . . ." Thomas Moore made sure we could never forget it even if we wanted to.'

You pass a white paper tissue to me. 'Wipe your fingers,' you say, 'and blow your nose.'

'Vie did the viper not vipe her nose?' I ask. 'Do you nose the answer?' I touch your nose with the finger of my glove.

'Because the adder 'ad 'er 'ankerchief,' we say in unison and then we both laugh aloud, delighted by our joke. 'Because the adder 'ad 'er 'ankerchief.' I see a woman standing at the side of the road facing us. She is leaning on a wrought-iron gate. The full skirt of her red dress blows out in the breeze. Some friend of ours, it must be because she smiles as we go by and lifts her hand to wave.

'I think he must have written it on a day like this, Sara. In sunshine and in shadow. A glorious day.'

# North of Riga

## Eoin McNamee

In late 2004 the Latvian workers started to arrive. They came in Opels and Skodas with blacked-out windows driven by blond young men wearing Saxon T-shirts, sweeping into town at night like angels of dark itinerancy. Each car contained one or two blonde girls wearing scarves and hats. The men left to work offshore. The Latvian girls went to the harbour. Aldra asked them about themselves. They said things like my name is Kirstin I come from Riga. My name is Mikela I come from Riga also I stay here to make some money and then I go home. They asked Aldra if she knew where Riga was.

'I am good with facts,' Aldra said, 'Riga is a city on the Baltic.' She told the retired fishermen that Riga was a city on the Baltic inhabited by blonde women who spoke in the present tense.

Aldra's parents and their friends were veterans of minor social movements. Crusties and travellers. They wore combat jackets and rigger boots and smoked Golden Virginia roll-ups. They drove adapted Commer vans to festivals of sustainable living. They put Aldra's hair in plaits with beads in them and self-diagnosed her as being within the spectrum of autism. They thought of themselves as apostate.

At 9 a.m. she went to learning support. At 12 a.m. she went to the library. At 1 p.m. she had lunch with the retired fishermen in the British Legion. Sometimes they brought things from the sea to show her. Sea anemones and urchins and mussels. Sometimes she listened to epic conversations on the subject of being old and ruined.

The Latvian girls started small businesses. They sold flowers. They set up a fish stall. On the road that climbed out of the town there was a disused lorry weighbridge with a small office attached. One day Aldra saw a sign on the office. *Coiffeuse*. There were lilies in a vase on the

279

window. Aldra went in. There was a small mirror on the wall with a wooden chair in front of it. There was a young woman standing by the chair. She had blonde hair in complex plaits and blue eyes and she kept her back very straight.

'My name is Sarah,' she said, 'I am coiffeuse.'

There was a blue plastic brush and a pair of electric clippers and a pair of scissors sitting on a tray beside the mirror. There was a card of steel combs hanging on the wall with a price for each comb written in pencil beside it.

'I'm Aldra,' Aldra said, 'don't go near the braids.'

'Do you think there is business for me, Aldra?' Sarah said.

'I don't know,' Aldra said.

Nobody went into the Coiffeuse for a while. Then one of the Scania drivers went in. The Scanias brought frozen processed fish inland from the plants at the harbour. They had to change down gears at the bottom of the hill opposite the weighbridge so they were able to see what it was. She gave them old-fashioned cuts. She gave them quiffs and south-backs and put Brylcreem on them. The truckdrivers were pleased. They liked to drive late at night and listen to country music and the haircuts gave them a lonesome authority that they considered themselves to be entitled to. Then teenage boys started to come, leaving with No 1 and No 2 haircuts which gave them a gaunt beauty like old pictures of Eastern European skinheads. Even though their hair was short they bought steel combs.

At the end of the evening Aldra would fold the towels for her and brush up the hair. She could see that Sarah was sad and proud and also dangerous. Her skin was so fine you could see the veins very clearly. The vascular system it was called. You could imagine it circulating, cool and salty. Often she saw Sarah looking at her braids. When she saw that look she thought of a wolverine standing under a pine tree in a cold snowy land.

'I like routine,' Aldra said, 'it is a feature of people like me. They don't like change. Your hands are always cold,' Aldra told her.

'I have bad circulation,' Sarah said, 'the feet are cold also.'

Aldra had told the retired fishermen about Sarah but it was too far for them to walk. One day Sarah closed and locked the door and they went down to the British Legion. When Sarah had finished stern patriarchs gazed unblinking from leatherette banquettes. The retired fishermen's wives came next. Sarah showed them magazine photographs that she had pasted into a book. The paper was old and yellowed. The photographs were of beautiful Eurasian women with high cheekbones and hair arranged in the manner of people like Veronica Lake and Jean Harlow and the retired fishermen's wives saw something of themselves in the photographs. Sarah did their hair for them and afterwards they carried themselves like people from a long time ago.

On the third day of December Aldra saw an old BMW with blacked-out windows drive down the hill and park in the square. No one got out. The car made Aldra think that there was a vendetta going on. That evening she helped Sarah to sweep the hair up and fold the towels. It was already dark outside, wintertime, headlights going past. Sarah had turned off all the lights except the one at the door. Aldra saw the BMW stop outside. A man got out. He had a moustache and his hair was cut short on top and grew long at the back. He had the darkest eyes that Aldra had ever seen. He pushed past her in the doorway as if she wasn't there.

Sarah turned around. When she saw the man she started to smile and took a step towards him. Then she stopped smiling. The man closed the door behind him. He took a long knife out of the inside pocket of his jacket. He said something in a stark northern language to Sarah. She started to speak back but he shook his head. He said something else. Sarah stared at him. Aldra could hear the Scanias climbing the hill. The man gestured with the knife again. Sarah's hands came up to her neck. She started to unbutton her blouse. She did it very carefully as though the blouse was very old and fragile. When she had finished she took the blouse off and put it on the back of the chair. The man gestured with the knife again. Sarah reached behind her. She undid her bra and dropped it on the floor.

Aldra looked at Sarah. She could see the indentations that the bra straps had left on her ribcage. She found herself thinking about the sea creatures the retired fishermen brought to show her, the bivalves, the fronds and frills combing the ocean for nutrients. The bra lay at Sarah's feet. A carapace of wires and catches and hard indented nylon. Outside the Scanias changed down for the hill, the high-pitched diesels like wolves howling on the timberline. The man turned away from Sarah and walked out of the door. Aldra heard the BMW pull off. Sarah stared after him then turned to Aldra.

'Get out,' she said.

It started to get cold. Arctic air massing in the north. Cold fronts sweeping down. There were seabirds in the air that no one had ever seen before. Skuas. Petrels. Aldra did not go back to the Coiffeuse. Sometimes the BMW was parked outside it. Aldra didn't know anybody she could tell about what had happened. About Sarah standing naked to the waist in the dim light like a roadside Madonna. The boats were fishing up near the Arctic Circle. You could see it in the deckhands' eyes. The frozen ports. The icebound seas.

The men of the town had begun to go to Sarah to have their hair cut. She gave them crew cuts and buzz cuts and angular fringes. The temperatures had been minus zero after dark, but now they were minus zero during the day. Aldra went down to the harbour to see the deep-water trawlers coming in. The water had turned a milky colour which meant that it was ready to freeze. An icy vapour rose from it and the trawlers emerged silently from this vapour like ghost boats. There were snow flurries in the town.

The boys continued to go to Sarah. They started to sharpen the metal combs and carry them as weapons. The lights in the Coiffeuse were always on. Sarah cut hair into the night. Aldra dreamed about the Coiffeuse. Cut hair blowing in plumes from its windows like snow.

The boats started coming home empty. The warm currents had failed and the fish had gone to other feeding grounds. They tied up in the harbour and ice formed around their hulls. To keep the plants going the Scania fleet had to bring in frozen fish from other ports to be processed. It was no better inland, the drivers said. They told stories about driving at night on the empty, salted roads, gritter trucks looming out of cold fogs, yellow hazard lights flashing, with an air of roadside carnage. The fish came in frozen slabs which had to be laid out on the factory floor to defrost. The Latvian girls did this as though they were setting out the pieces for a solemn national game. Once or twice Aldra saw the BMW in the square but she couldn't tell if there was anyone in it.

At the end of three weeks the roads and pavements were frozen. The boats were tied up and iced in. The retired fishermen inched along the pavement on aluminium frames. Their lips were cracked and their eyes were red. Their haircuts made them look severe and birdlike. Their wives caught glimpses of themselves in shop windows and saw the faces of sad, dead actresses.

After four weeks of this Aldra walked across the town. It was night. There were no cars. The cold was like a weight. The town seemed to have acquired the dark spaces of a larger place. The small churchyard seemed like a haunted cathedral cloister. Solitary men walking home along the esplanade cast the shadows of sinister boulevardiers. At the bottom of the hill she saw a single Scania revving its engine hard to try to get up the icy road. The lights of the Coiffeuse were on. Aldra walked in. Sarah was sitting on her own at the wall. Although there was no heating she was wearing a sleeveless white blouse and black pencil skirt. Aldra walked across the room and sat down in the chair in front of the mirror.

Sarah came up behind her. Aldra could see a gleam in her eyes and the two pointed incisors just visible on her lower lip. She started to unfasten the braids. Her hands were cold. Everything about her was cold. She undid the braids rapidly and shook out Aldra's hair. She lifted the blue brush and started to brush. In the cold room her breath came out as vapour as she worked rapidly and it seemed that the vapour formed in a swirling mist about Aldra's head and her hair was longer than she remembered and Sarah brushed it out until it seemed to reach the ground and then she lifted the scissors and started to cut. Aldra shut her eyes as the scissors flew about her head and outside the Scanias tried to climb the hill and their engines howled like the voices of cold northern witches.

As she worked she told Aldra stories about the place she came from. She told Aldra about an island in the sea off the harbour of her town. The island was made of human bones and during the summer families had picnics on it. Outside the town she said there was a forest of ten thousand trees. Under each tree a dragoon was buried. They had red uniforms and ornate moustaches. They each had a bullet hole in the forehead and they had been placed on their backs so that they could face the stars. Sarah seemed to think that these stories showed that mercy was abroad in the world.

When she was finished she led Aldra to the door and closed it behind her and turned out the light.

They found the BMW the next day. It was parked behind the diesel tanks at the harbour. The man with the dark eyes was in the driver's seat with his long knife in his chest. The body was stiff with frost and there was no surprise in his frozen cadaver gaze. He had been there for days they said. They went to look for Sarah but the office was locked and the Coiffeuse sign was gone.

They asked the Latvian girls where Sarah was from but they didn't know.

'She didn't come with us,' they said. 'Nobody knew her. She was from somewhere else. Far away. North of Riga.'

After that night Aldra sat at home listening to the sound of the Scanias climbing the hill. She brushed her hair two hundred times exactly. Her hair had grown out long and silvery and she parted it in the middle. She brushed it two hundred times with a blue plastic brush, waiting for the thaw and wondering if she too lived in a town of the dead.

# It's Not About the Money

## MARY BYRNE

Chantal had a voice exactly like a drag queen, and one of those blonde bouffant hairstyles that went with it. A baroque version of what was once known as a French pleat, I believe.

She came to us on some kind of transfer scheme. It was that or get pre-retired, and at her age she couldn't afford that, any more than any-one else. At the interview (it wasn't an interview, she'd been parachuted in over his head) our boss told her she wasn't bad looking at all. Already nervous, she nearly jumped a yard off the ground when he then asked her if she'd ever been through analysis.

'Oh la la!' she said, in that double-pitch of hers, when she came out to the coffee corner. She was in a bit of a state, but braving it out.

I did my best to reassure her: he was like that, he said the same to everybody, he was bull-goose loony. We called him 'Madame' behind his back. We asked each other, 'How's *she* doin' today?' when we wanted to know what mood he was in. We could do it in front of him without his knowing who we were talking about. The difficulty was not to crack up with laughter.

Chantal raised her plastic cup of hot sugared and lemoned water that pretended to be tea.

'Here's lookin' at you,' she said.

Chantal joined my office, where there wouldn't have been enough of us if they'd sent in ten Chantals. Ours was one of the less obscure offices of the Préfecture de Police in Paris, charged with filtering endless streams of stressed-out, nervous immigrants. Most had insufficient documentation. If they produced all the paperwork, we found another document that was needed and managed to keep them coming back and back until an earlier in-date document was now out of date and so they had to start again. Of course there were also the over-confident ones who leaped out of flash, double-parked cars, jumped the queue and tried to pull the wool over our eyes. Sometimes they sent an envoy to do it. Sometimes it even worked. But generally the wannabe immigrants were in the asking position, we had all the power. You became immune to the misery of it all, after a while.

Chantal, a spinster farmer's daughter from a forgotten corner of Normandy, brought it all to the surface again:

'What's the cattle-crush out front for?' she asked me that first day, during the lunch break.

She was referring to the steel barriers, erected every morning by our 'bouncers' – doormen and security men – to keep the wannabe immigrants in line.

Even I had a sense of shame, as I replied, 'Hail, rain or shine.'

'May the Lord look down on them,' said Chantal. We were unused to hearing anyone make that kind of remark these days.

'That's not all,' I explained. 'They start queuing at two o'clock in the morning because we only handle so many each day. They relay each other for toilets and coffee.'

'What must those busloads of foreign tourists – what must *the world* – think of us?'

Chantal first started seeing the shrink because she was being harassed by our boss. Either she was particularly raw-skinned, or the rest of us had just turned into the fat cows he accused us of being. It was well known that he referred to our office sniggeringly as the 'gynecea'. From the Greek. 'Fat cows!' he would say, under his breath. 'Whores!' When angry with one of us, his favourite question to her was 'Got your period today?'

Some months after she came, Chantal started seeing a shrink once a week. Because she didn't fully believe in him, really, she also read, on the side, any books of psychology she could get her hands on, or understand, as a kind of double check. In one of the books she came across an anal-hoarding sadist. It was demonstrated that Himmler and Hitler had been such individuals. Chantal said it described our boss perfectly.

We all liked it, so the name stuck.

Work was his god, the office his church. He insisted that everything be done exactly as it always had been in the past. We weren't even allowed to move a desk or a chair or a plant. Every morning he whipped the bouncers downstairs into a frenzy of viciousness (he had a different method of needling men that I needn't go into here) then he came up the stairs and started on his gynecea.

Apart from him, our office was woman only. An accident, they pretended. However, the bigger office in the city centre – where more important things were done, like stamping a residence permit because a decision had been made elsewhere and transmitted – was mostly full of men. Me and my colleagues had long since given up wondering about all that. They only gave us women the vote, for God's sake, in 1945.

Each morning he came up the stairs and goaded us to speed up. Every day it was something different: the queue was around the block already, the préfet was coming on a visit, the traffic police were getting antsy, a row had broken out about placement in the queue. Whatever it was, it was our fault.

After six months of this, Chantal announced she was giving up the shrink. I asked why.

'Said I was maybe giving off the wrong signals.'

'Wouldn't believe you, huh?'

'If what I said was true, then it was so outlandish that I must be encouraging such torture.'

'What'd you do?'

'I unpacked myself from his over-comfortable chair. I stood up. I said, "How much do I owe you?" '

Shortly afterwards, one Friday in May, Chantal was due to go on holiday leave.

As if he were jealous of her time off, or angry that his favourite boxing-bag was escaping, the anal-hoarder gave her a terrible gruelling that morning.

She seemed to be taking it, except that by eleven o'clock she got into a row with a wannabe. This was unusual for Chantal, and she should have known better – it was a European wannabe: white, articulate. The anal-hoarder was prowling behind her. She exploded.

'Paris is full of immigrants – full! Bad hotels are overflowing with them! The hotels are so shitty they frequently burn! We have so many immigrants we burn them alive!'

The black and brown wannabes shied back, startled yet slightly amused.

The white wannabe stalked out, threatening letters.

The anal-hoarding sadist told Chantal to go to the doctor, the chemist, anywhere only get out.

She went next door and was given a tranquillising injection. She came back after lunch determined to finish out her day and go on holiday. 'Like an ordinary Christian,' as she said to me. She looked strained. Her French pleat was mussed, something I'd never seen before.

I put her on a back desk.

When he saw her not only back but at an unaccustomed desk, he barked, 'Either you're well enough to work or you're ill. Get on the front desk.'

This was the hot seat. People he considered particularly slow, 'having their periods' etc., were put here and personally supervised. This made everyone nervous, and provided a particularly effective wannabe filter.

Chantal seemed to be standing it quite well, considering. After lunch, the anal-hoarder stuck to his office.

Then at three o'clock or so, the computers froze, and all hell broke loose.

Chantal was assailed by people desperate to get their paperwork before the weekend. An Italian couple were getting married. A German woman had an acting role to start immediately, without her the play couldn't go on. An ailing Serb lady needed her daughter to help her in and out of hospital. And that was just the Europeans.

The anal-hoarder came out from the back like a king to his court, studiously straightening up the cord railing that kept the upstairs rabble in line.

'What's going on?'

She explained.

'Take a look at yourself,' he said to her. 'You're ageing, fast.'

This was his tack for those he considered past their periods.

Chantal suddenly swung into action. She dived into her handbag and came out with a chemist's paper bag of medication which she waved at the wannabes.

'The whole country's on tranquillisers,' she said. 'You could do with them too,' she turned to him, 'although you might be in need of something stronger. Strait-jacketing, maybe.'

She turned to the wannabes again. 'It's a wonder any self-respecting foreigner would want hand, act or part of such a country.'

We all grinned. This was the truth. But it was all the anal-hoarding sadist needed.

'You're suspended,' he said. 'Out. Now.'

Chantal's lower lip was trembling as she grabbed her stuff and left.

She was pre-retired with less pension than she would've got, but she was delighted not to have to look at him ever again.

She decided to leave the city altogether. 'I'm baling out. They say you're only free when the kids have finished university, and the dog is dead,' she smiled. 'You could say that's about where I am, now.'

She headed for Normandy and had a look at various heaps, eventually settling on one. She came back to Paris and sold her small studio for a modest sum – 'It's a helluva lot more than I put into it,' she said.

I helped her load the hired van and we drove out to Normandy during the full fury of the 60th commemoration of the Allied landings.

It was not a good idea. Roads were blocked and deviated and security was at its most tense, as heads of state from far and wide made their way to Omaha Beach and the rest of it.

'Did you time this deliberately?' I asked her.

'Was so busy packing boxes I never even noticed.'

We got closer to her chosen place, and deeper and deeper into a forgotten country of little stone villages and small fields and wild hedgerows and farmyards of hens and geese and ponds of ducks. It all looked as if it hadn't changed for several centuries.

When we finally juddered up the last narrow little path – you could hardly call it a road – I was shocked.

The place was in ruins. It was a collection of stone buildings arranged in a U around a yard. The side she planned to restore first consisted of a little house attached to a barn. Both had a very deep roof, covered in artistically rusting corrugated sheets. The rest had no roof at all. Oh, it was picturesque, all right. But it was a disaster.

She showed me round, knowledgeably. Off to one side was an old mill, and a reed-ridden field that even I knew in winter would be water-sodden.

We unloaded and dispersed her stuff in places we thought waterproof. She set up a tent hastily, before nightfall.

I almost felt guilty, leaving her there in the middle of nowhere, on her own.

'Go on. I'm a country girl at heart,' she said.

And I drove the van back to Paris and my job with the wannabes.


With one thing and another I didn't get out there again for months. I hired a car and drove out in boiling heat one August day, the car loaded with city goodies for Chantal. In the left lane, look-at-me sports vehicles sped past, headed for Deauville.

When I left the traffic behind and got to her place, I had time to take in the whole place again. It hadn't changed a whit. The tent was still under a lean-to. However, I glimpsed two caravans.

An elderly lady in waist-length grey hair came out of a barn towards me, walking on crutches.

When she started to speak the voice was the falsetto of Chantal. You'd have heard her three fields away. 'Oh la la!' she said. 'Have I been having a time of it!'

She was gabbling so much I stopped listening and just looked. Gone the French pleat. The hair was only yellow at the bottom now. She was wearing stained tracksuit bottoms and a tanktop. Her face was brown, her skin wrinkled without its smoothing make-up. But she looked more youthful, even happy.

She was collecting plums for the visiting architect and had fallen from the tree. She had broken several ribs.

'Without the neighbours I'd have been jiggered,' she said.

She showed me around. She'd bought a beat-up old white van. There was a caravan under a hayloft and another in the house itself. One served as kitchen and the other as bedroom. There were umpteen cats, two dusty Appaloosa ponies, and a donkey. The Appaloosas whinnied whenever we were in earshot. 'I can't resist giving them treats,' she admitted. In another meadow two huge drays raised their heads and lumbered towards us, curiously.

'Guy couldn't feed them, nobody wanted to buy them. Was contemplating selling them to the factory for meat. So I couldn't resist.'

'And the donkey?'

'My favourite. Everyone has a donkey here,' she said. 'They keep the grass down.' She had a number of hectares, some of them rented.

Her hands were still black from picking blackberries the day before. Blackberries weren't good this year, she said, because of the drought. She had invited some people around for dinner to meet me, and was planning a barbecue. 'Although I don't usually eat meat,' she added.

She even had a garden. She was soaking nettles in water to use against unwelcome insects. Tall blue-green absinthe plants leaned against the wind, for the same purpose.

The evening was pleasant, bucolic. The sun sank red behind Chantal's ruins as we drank *cidre bouché* and gnawed on bones. There was talk of the price of firewood (hot on the heels of gas and oil), the profitability of growing cereals (50 hectares didn't produce sufficient revenue for a family). Maize needed prodigious amounts of water just to produce one kilo. Things like that.

This gave me time to study Chantal's guests. Most were wily-eyed peasants with rough hands and plump wives. The older ones talked of the war, as if this were expected of them. One old lady had thrown a broom at a German soldier who came looking for butter and milk. *'Nichts lait, nichts beurre,'* she had told him.

When at one point the question of our work came up, we both sighed and told them a little about our boss. We said he was a *connard*. The old lady with no fear of Germans said he sounded like a right *peau de hareng:* a right old herring-skin. We got a great laugh out of that.

One member of the company was different. For one thing, he wasn't a local at all, but where he came from was a bit vague. I never got his name right, either. There was a double name and then a nickname like Mimi or something awful. He sat across from me. He had dark lumpy skin and wore a leather tie with a turquoise stone in it. His greasy hair was held in a ponytail by another leather tie and turquoise stone. He smoked roll-ups. He appeared to be on the dole. He did odd-jobs. He sculpted with stuff he found on tips. Had I seen the horse he'd made for Chantal? I recalled a rusted effort inside one of the barns. I'd seen guys like this all over the Mediterranean.

When it was all over, people helpfully washed dishes and left them to dry on one of the various oilcloth-covered tables Chantal had laid out over the yard. I was surprised to see Ponytail stay behind when the others left. He didn't have a car either, apparently.

Chantal showed me to my quarters in the bedroom caravan, told me where best to pee and how to block the door against cats, grass-snakes, foxes –

'Stop!' I said. 'I'll be wanting back to my seventeen square metres, if you tell me any more!'

Then she and Ponytail retired to the tent on the sheltered side of the house.

I lay awake for a long time thinking about all that.

In the morning, Ponytail had to have hot chocolate, while we had coffee from big heavy bowls. He wasn't after the calcium for his teeth, I reckoned, because one or two were already missing. Others looked ready to follow.

It was hot. Chantal had no electricity yet, and flies came and went and laid eggs in any dead meat left lying around. The cats deposited dead mice or else came with live ones and consumed them whole before our eyes – tails, teeth, and all. We walked lots. Around the locality, Parisians repaired their roofs, clipped their hedges and generally prepared to batten down the hatches for winter. 'You'd wonder', said Chantal, 'what amusement they get out of their holidays at all.'

Ponytail said he drank pastis in the evenings. I discovered he drank it at any time of day, forcing it on anyone who dropped in to see Chantal. Sometimes he even bought a bottle from the travelling grocer, in case he'd run short.

One evening, he took us to a bar he liked to frequent – what he called a 'decent drinkers' bar' – in a nearby village. 'Le Novelty' it was called. There was a giant Union Jack on the back wall. It was a favourite haunt for tourist Brits.

Luckily for us the Brits weren't there that day. But Ponytail could talk of little else, and the bartender was equally enthusiastic. He looked at Chantal, and said, 'I hear the table groans with food over in your place.' He gave the impression that his bar specialised in English speakers. 'There's X from Scotland,' he said, 'and Y from Wales, and –'

Suddenly a local man at one of the tables spoke up: 'A bird in the hand is worth two in the bush,' he announced. 'I'm sitting here and no one to even ask if I have a drought on me.'

On the 15th of August in the village there was a huge fête to commemorate the war. Film of elderly people recounting their war was followed by folk dancing and storytelling – much of it extremely lewd. Then a sound-and-light show at the old chateau recounted how village and chateau had been torched by the Germans on the eve of their departure. *On this very day, sixty years ago.* I'd seen various rehearsals with jeeps and men in uniform in Paris, but somehow all this brought it closer to home. Here, the noise and dust were more real. The show ended with the arrival of a fleet of old American vehicles belching black fumes and teeming with young people, the women in light frocks and ankle socks, the men in army uniforms. All smoked cigarettes and tapped hands and feet to Glenn Miller. This was followed by fireworks as good as any in Paris. We Oohed! and we Aahed! and made our way home on foot, with cricks in our necks.

I got into the habit of going out to visit Chantal often. I suppose I envied her in a way.

Ponytail was more often absent than present, especially when I came. He was very friendly with the son of a British couple who owned a manor house in the region, an idle young man in his early twenties whom I earmarked straight away for a junkie ('God silence your viper tongue!' said Chantal). Ponytail was helping the Brits with work on their house, he was sculpting for them. The parents were rich, early retired. Their main activity was studying the French. 'They're always whining,' Ponytail informed us. It wasn't a complaint, he was studying them studying us. 'When she goes shopping, she complains that the French're either over-eager to do the hard sell or they just ignore you while they concentrate on stylish layout. It could be tomatoes or designer goods – doesn't matter.'

It had taken the Brits several years to come up with their big theory about the French: *It's not about the money*. The French were sex and food addicts, hedonists if you wanted to be polite about it. They were terribly focused on remaining secular. They were frequently revolting. They were always arrogant. But throughout all of that you had to hand it to them, because while the rest of the world was hell-bent on getting rich or being rich, the French still preferred to talk about 'decent' wages and quality of life. *It wasn't about the money*.

Chantal and I stuck to our more earthly pursuits. Her house had clearly become a sort of halfway house where all dropped in and many stayed to eat. I never saw anyone bring her anything, but imagined there must be some arrangement between them. A man came and pared the donkey's hooves. Four rounds of dark nail with a half-moon of paler substance, sat on the flagstones before the house. The locals sat and watched and said nothing. I learned about aphids and compost and that anything you planted on the feast of Sainte Catherine would grow.

When I was there, I wished I was back in Paris, and when I was back in Paris I could think of nothing better than being out in the country again.

We went mushrooming in autumn, as work began on Chantal's roof. This was a huge affair, and I didn't dare ask how much it was costing or if she'd have anything left over. Ponytail was spending more and more time with the Brits. That way he avoided getting involved in any of the work on the house. They'd lodged him in an empty wing of the house. But occasionally he graced us with his presence and came smelling of pastis and roll-ups. He told us about the arguments he'd had with the Brits over William the Conqueror. 'They think they invaded France!' he chortled. The young man, his new friend, was called William, which led to further chortling. Ponytail had done his homework: sixty per cent of the English language came from either Norman or French – and they weren't the same thing, he reminded us. Nobody, not even the Allies, had managed to bomb the Conqueror's chateaux to bits. The Conqueror had built the Tower of London. The Normans had gone on the Crusades. There were people with names of Norman origin in Sicily and the Middle East.

And so on, and so on.

After the roof, Chantal attacked the house itself. She had the walls sanded to bring out the stone, and this is where she got a big surprise. One day the workmen came running to say there was a 'problem': they'd have to stop sanding in order to strip a wall that seemed to be covered in tons of plaster. 'Could be anything under there – maybe the wall's in trouble,' they said helpfully. The wall was seriously bulbous.

I wondered why the architect hadn't gone into the question, but kept my mouth shut.

Chantal wanted everything out in the open and upfront. 'Let's strip it and know the worst,' she said.

So they went through layers of plaster until they came to stone. It took ages. I was there for the start of it, but then I had to leave again.

'Anyone that hasn't got a layer of fat on them now, is fucked,' a customer remarked to the cheese vendor as I hovered in the market one early winter day. I was waiting for Chantal to collect me. I had abandoned cars for the leisurely train.

A bitter wind blew through the cheese vendor's hair. She checked her clients for offence-calibre, and giggled.

When we got to the house, I was astonished. Inside the main living room was a chimney the size of the entire wall. The stone was beautiful. The corbels were sculpted.

'Why on earth would anyone want to hide that?' I asked.

'Nobody knows anything,' she said. 'I've checked high and low. You'd be forgiven for feeling paranoid.'

She had other problems too: the new phone number she'd been given turned out to be a former fax, and she kept receiving faxes from advertising computers to which she couldn't reply.

'Day and night,' she said. 'It's Kafkaesque. I have to unplug the phone to sleep. But if I forget, I'm done for.'

Telecom refused to help, all they could do was change her number again.

There was also trouble about a septic tank she'd had installed by a local, without taking account of the new European rules and regulations and permissions and technical considerations.

To cap it all, the next-door farmer was after her land.

'Sometimes,' she eyed me carefully as she said it, 'I think there's a jinx on me.'

It got so bad that I worried for her, and having little else to do, I went out there for Christmas. We chose pigments, and painted wall after wall. Then we sat before the huge chimney and with giant tongs fiddled with logs a yard long in the great fire. I had to admit Chantal had made a great job of the huge room with its high-beamed ceiling. She hadn't gone too precious on it, but had left a certain rusticity, all the better to set off the antiques she was collecting all over the region. She'd even got good at beating Parisian dealers to the choicest items. After Christmas we continued 'the hunt' as she referred to it. On good days, she'd say, 'Bagged plenty', on bad days, 'Nothing bagged.'

It even snowed and the electricity blacked out. We spent a whole evening by candlelight, eating food produced on the fire. Chantal was in her element. She had found catechism benches somewhere and cleaned them up for the kitchen table. As we sat there with friends or neighbours, she'd suddenly say, 'Who made the world?' then answer herself, 'God made the world.' Then, 'Who do we call God?' Even the locals didn't remember such basics. Some of it contrasted oddly with the antiques and the rest.

It all contrasted utterly with our poor wannabes in the heart of the city.

The following summer, Chantal came to Paris more often. She came for specific events like the *Fête de la Musique* on the longest day, and later she came again for the 14th of July. I wondered what it all meant. I found out that Ponytail was looking after the garden and the animals in her absence. 'I didn't leave him a key,' she added, 'he has no business inside the house and there's the insurance to think of. Anyway, I'm paying him for it, he's strapped at the moment.'

In August we went back to Normandy together and found things a mess. The garden was parched and yellow. More dramatically, even the animals were dry. Nobody had seen Ponytail for days. A neighbour had only noticed the situation hours before, but had done little other than water the animals.

'I need to have this out with him,' she said.

Inside the house, there was a dreadful smell. She seemed more worried about Ponytail than the smell.

'Must be the septic tank,' she said lightly. 'I'll put a dose of "Urgent" in it.'

Because we hadn't found out where Ponytail had gone and because I'd always wanted to see it, I dragged her next morning – protesting – off to a local hunting fête, where horses, dogs and men were blessed from the altar and long polished horns were sounded during Mass. Something else struck me too: here was another, utterly non-peasant side of local life. Pedigree dogs and horses were not only pure-bred but impeccably groomed with shiny backsides and evenly trimmed tails, unlike the dusty Appaloosas in Chantal's back field. The men and women mounted on them were beefy, well-fed and sleek, in utter contrast to the specimens that frequented Chantal's place. Their gear was their best, for the festival, green outfits and black outfits and grey and stunning red with matching hats, feathers and sometimes a white fur trim. They walked and talked with the confidence of people who were afraid of nothing and owed nothing to anyone, the kind who could train or whip a horse or a dog and buy or sell a bishop or a gendarme. It was a whole side of local life I knew nothing about, and that Chantal chose to ignore.

We wandered and talked throughout the day, but I couldn't distract her from the problem of the missing Ponytail.

Finally we decided to brazen it out, go over to the Brits' house and ask for him. As we left the hunting festival we stumbled on a mountain of backed-up traffic. We were forced to make a huge deviation. The gendarmes directing the heavy traffic were polite but unrelenting: you kept moving and you went where they told you. That was all.

'I wouldn't have the courage if you weren't with me,' Chantal said. 'Anyway, the longer we stay away from home, the better chance the smell will be gone.'

So we rattled over there and up their avenue in the yellowing van.

Here was utter contrast to Chantal's abode. Lawns and flowerbeds had been landscaped, then neatly manicured. Windows shone.

'Not a hair out of place,' said Chantal.

The doors and shutters were a Laura Ashley green.

'Very British,' I said.

The Brits, it turned out, weren't interested in her problem.

'Our son William has gone missing,' they said, in their impeccable lounge. There seemed to be something else, but they didn't want to talk to us. Ponytail seemed much less important than a son.

Chantal was silent as we drove back to her place.

'What do you make of all this?' she said finally.

I couldn't help her, didn't know how deep she was in, but it was clear that she thought Ponytail must be involved with the Brit's disappearance somehow.

After a day of agonising and doing everything in our power to reduce the smell, which seemed to have settled in the kitchen of all places, we went to the gendarmes.

They questioned Chantal for a while, then sent us into another office. A higher-up gendarme came in, removed his kepi from a sweating forehead, and said,

'The news is bad, I'm afraid. Car accident.' He watched us for reactions. 'Mr Bacasse was killed instantly. 'Bout an hour from your place.'

So that was his name, I thought. It sounded foreign.

Ponytail had had his last pastis and hot chocolate. They hadn't contacted Chantal because she wasn't family. In fact, it had taken them a while to track down his family. He seemed to be out of contact with them. They turned out to be in the middle of Paris. I asked him to repeat the family name.

'Greek,' said the gendarme. 'Greek, from Barbès.'

I was briefly reminded of our wannabes.

By now the entire house was pervaded with the awful smell. It had seeped into all the rooms, attached itself to the upholstery. Even when we showered, it seemed to remain on our skin.

I dug out sleeping tablets for her and for me.

After a fitful night I got Chantal out of there as best I could. I arranged for the farmer neighbour to look after the animals and the mail, and took her back to Paris with me. The problem of smells and septic tanks I left for another day.

She actually made me go with her to Ponytail's funeral. I don't know what we expected, but there wasn't a funeral as such. They'd had him incinerated. In a small whitewashed courtyard in Barbès – not unlike how I imagined Greece – his ashes sat on a windowsill in a grey plastic urn. A sad and motionless black-clad mother sat on a wooden chair, surrounded by a huge extended family. They were having a *mechoui*, more to feed the multitude than to celebrate anything, least of all Ponytail's passing.

We were received and entertained by an older brother of Ponytail. He had organised everything. 'For the mother, mostly,' he said. Of the adults of our own age, he was the only one who spoke to us in French. No one talked of Ponytail. The brother talked of his own retirement, slated for six months' time. He would go to Greece, where with a tomato and a piece of bread you could feed yourself. 'Hope she lives long enough to take her back,' he indicated the silent mother. A Greek was not like a Frenchman. 'If you're hungry,' he said, 'another Greek will feed you. There's solidarity over there, there's none in France.' He was a member of one of the redder trade unions. He'd been working at Renault when the riots broke out in '68. The riot police wouldn't go in there: 'The CRS didn't dare.' The first thing he'd do if he were prime minister of France, would be to close down all these charitable organisations and give everyone a room and access to sanitary facilities. 'We don't want charity,' he said, 'we want treating like human beings.' Their own house – a collection of small houses surrounding the yard – had started life as a squat. Little by little, the family had grown and invested the abandoned shells. No one knew who owned them. The town hall had to do something about housing people. They were helping them with the paperwork to purchase it.

It all seemed to bring some peace to Chantal. She stayed in the city for ages, even met up with the older brother occasionally for chats in cafés about the way the world was going. She was amazed that she could like the city again, in love with city life as for the first time, astonished to see how swollen the immigrant population had become. When she said, with a wry smile, 'You people not doing your job?' I knew it was time to talk to her about going back.

I took a late-autumn week, with the anal-hoarding sadist's approval. We trained it out there. The van was still rusting in the station lot where we'd left it. We had to get a garage to jump-start it.

The house looked abandoned, but the animals were glad to see us.

Inside, the smell was still there, but fainter. We threw open the windows. 'The bloody tank, I suppose,' said Chantal. 'I'll put a dose in it.'

The house was chill too.

'I'm going to light the fire,' Chantal announced. 'That's what I missed most in Paris.'

The fire was difficult to get going. 'Chimney's good and cold,' Chantal said, working away at it like a professional. 'Always like this, the first fire of the winter.'

The smoke began to fill the room. She still didn't panic. 'That's funny,' she said, 'it's never done that before.'

She opened the door. 'Create a draught,' she said. 'I forgot to have the chimney cleaned this summer.'

Even when there was a rustling noise in the chimney she still didn't panic.

'I've even had birds and their nests falling into it.'

Then it happened.

A foot fell into the fireplace.

We shot to our feet and recoiled. We recognised it as a foot because there was a shoe, and even a sock, but the bones and the rest of it only became clear after a lot of 'Oh la la!' and dragging it out of the embers with the mercifully long tongs.

Then of course a foot begged the question of a body.

And sure enough, when we got the courage to look, the rest of the body was still up there. Stuck, so to speak, between heaven and hell. Chantal blessed herself and went to the phone.

It took some persuading. No one would believe her.

She pressed the loudspeaker button. 'You pulling my wire?' a policeman asked. 'The other one has bells on it.'

Chantal was somewhere between laughing and crying. I took the phone and explained. As I hung up, it struck me that maybe her ambiguous falsetto didn't help.

When coroner, gendarmes, firemen and all the others who eventually turned up had done with us and 'it', and had taken 'it' away, Chantal poured us both a stiff glass of *goutte*.

'It was the Brit,' she said, huddling up to an electric radiator.

'What?'

I thought she might be losing it again, like the day the computers crashed.

'It was William, Mimi's friend.'

We both studied the now-empty fireplace.

'They're expecting me in town tomorrow. To fill out a report.'

She was still amazingly calm.

'They reckon he came to burgle the house,' she said quietly.

I burst out laughing. 'With all the dosh they have, and the Laura Ashley paint?'

'Not the parents, the son. The gendarmes said burglary was quite common in unoccupied country houses.'

'There you are!' I said, overenthusiastically. 'Yours is occupied!'

Next day, we went to the gendarmerie.

One unoccupied night is enough, they told her. The British boy, as they called him, would have needed the money for drugs. The antiques were always saleable, no questions asked. Paris dealers were always interested.

They'd examined his mobile phone messages. He'd got stuck in the chimney. He'd phoned Ponytail for help. They surmised that Ponytail had hightailed it off to get help from someone like himself, but unused to the car and preoccupied, he'd gone straight through a dangerous crossroads. Nobody suggested he was running.

What shocked me most was what Chantal said next:

'I keep imagining William there in the chimney, waiting for Mimi to come back. I think of his dawning realisation that Mimi has betrayed him. Just imagine his thirst, the fatigue, the hunger, the thirst, the terrible need for the drug . . .'

I took her out of there. Again.

I helped her sell the place – the price was rock-bottom after all that had happened and the greedy farmer got it for a song, horses and all. I arranged for her to sign it all in a Paris notary's office. Before that I went out there and got a dealer she knew to take the antiques. He was keeping them in a warehouse until Chantal decided what she wanted to do.

'Let it go,' said Chantal when it was done, as if I were the one selling. 'Like I let go the anal-hoarding sadist, and Mimi and a whole host of stuff.'

She never talked about young William in the chimney any more, but she started going into churches more often, lighting candles. Things like that.

Back in the office that winter, old Herringskin, as our boss was now known, became unbearable. He was pushing more of our buttons than ever before, pushing everyone equally. You'd be forgiven for thinking he missed Chantal.

At my instigation, we struck. We got out and demonstrated on the street with the wannabes. He tried to fire more of us for incompetence, but it was too late. We sued for harassment. Chantal came in with us. We all got a small stipend.

But it wasn't about the money. We were happier at last and free at last and Chantal's voice came down an octave and we could look at ourselves in the mirror again.

# A Russian Beauty

## Sebastian Barry

I don't remember her name, but she was very beautiful.

I have to admit to a certain amount of uncertainty in general about this story, because not only were the most important parts of it only told to me, and I didn't witness any of the main events, but it was told to me many years ago. And as everyone knows, stories shift in the mind as the years go on, they are infected by dreams, altered as the poor mind turns in its cradle of bones.

Though she wasn't my type, as they say, she was very beautiful even at forty, and she must have been achingly beautiful in her heyday. Beautiful the way a model of the seventies would have been, because she was a model of the seventies. Not in London, but in Russia.

I don't remember her name, not because she made no impression on me, indeed I have thought of her and her story a thousand times since the early nineties; but because it has simply vanished. So maybe I can call her Nadia.

She was my translator while I was lecturing at the Gorki Institute. That sounds quite grand, or at least romantic. But it didn't turn out that way. It was just me blithering away to an oddly buoyant bunch of students that looked more like schoolchildren than anything else. But they were strange years in Russia and everyone was undernourished. You'd be lucky to eat anything palatable. I ordered chicken one day in a café, and what came to the table may well have been chicken one time, but now it looked like roadkill. Like a chicken that had been run over a few times, and left to lie in the ditch of a road; and in the rain at that.

I looked around and the Russians were tucking into similar plates of chicken. They ate like grateful wolves.

In those days there was absolutely nothing in the supermarkets. You went into the supermarkets and there was just nothing; to Western eyes at least. Maybe the Russians could see things on the shelves that I could not.

It was terrifying.

But there are many different kinds of terror. There is the terror such as we had ourselves in the North of Ireland; there is the terror, the interior terror of incest and child abuse. There is the terror of shifting memory. There are a million terrors that go with life. Even a leader that professes to be fighting terror, sometimes is himself causing terror. It must be a sort of human background music. From terror we come and to terror we must return.

At a party in Moscow though, the editor of a famous Russian journal said to me that we were all children in the West. We hadn't endured one tenth of what they had in Russia. We were babies in history. I thought of the Irish famine and the general history of oppression, the First World War and the second, and so on, but I said nothing; she needed it to be true and maybe it was.

Nadia herself took a very bleak view of Russia and Russians. She said Stalin had killed everyone of any worth. He had left only the sick and the mad, she said. It was a phrase that stuck with me, of course. The sick and the mad. At first I thought she was excluding herself, the way she said it, as if maybe she had miraculously come through, not sick and not mad. But of course I was wrong. Not mad, maybe.

Nadia was married, or lived with, a famous film director. He was about thirty years older than herself. He had made a famous film in the fifties with Innokenty Smokdunovski, the great Russian actor. They lived in a better than most apartment in Moscow. She brought me there once. Her old film director was like one of the Irish poets I had known years before, rather grizzled and bad tempered and appealing, called Arthur Power, who had been a friend of Joyce. I thought maybe he was Arthur in a new guise, which was comforting. Arthur was long dead.

At any rate, they lived there together, he on the glory of the fifties, she on the glory of the seventies, when she had been a famous model – the most beautiful of them all, her husband said. Oddly enough he had the same family name as one of Stalin's henchmen, but no relation, apparently. It is hard in a country to know what names are as common as Smith or Murphy. You know the way Americans sometimes ask, do you know Pat Murphy in Dublin? As if there were only a few. The Pat Murphys of Ireland are legion.

The door of their flat was fortified with steel. It had been recently done. Nadia said that they lived in terror of the new gangsters that were roaming about. If they thought you had anything of value, they would break down your door, kill you, and take what they wanted, and no one would ever catch them. It was dangerous in Russia in those times to possess anything, or have the reputation of possessing anything.

By that time there really was no one to catch them. The army was being fed in their compounds, but the police were suffering somewhere in their offices and barracks. It was the time just before Yeltsin stormed the Russian White House with his tanks. I saw that happening on the television news back home in Ireland later, and wondered about Nadia. Hoped better times were coming for her. But maybe she didn't have any better times left.

She had been very popular and in demand in her heyday, and of course her husband was a celebrity. Somehow or other he had managed to assuage the various regimes, from one leader to the next, without wholly compromising himself. He was not a radical, and he was not a collaborator. He was just a living man, an artist, and liked the peaceful life.

One time they were in Italy together. It was an embassy dinner of some sort, which embassy I don't remember, perhaps even the Russian embassy itself in Rome. One of Brezhnev's sons was there, or maybe his only son, I don't recall. It was only recently I read that Brezhnev's family was often accused of feathering their nests while their father was in power, especially his daughter. But whatever embassy it was, it was inclined to honour his son, and he was the guest of honour at any rate.

There were place-settings assigned, with the names of everyone there that Rome night, and at the last minute there was a change of plan. The places were all changed about and as it happened Nadia found herself sitting in the chair that had been first assigned to Brezhnev's son. So, everyone set to, I suppose, and ate their dinner, and talked – that old lost talk of the seventies.

One of the curious coincidences about all this was that one of the reasons I had come to Moscow to lecture to the Gorki Institute was that it would give me a chance to see Innokenty Smokdunovski – now quite an old man – on stage at the Moscow Arts. He had played in Dublin and I thought he was one of the greatest actors alive. And wanted to see him acting again. But that is neither here nor there. Apart from the fact that it sort of bound me to Nadia's husband; if not spiritually, then at least at the level of the ordinary weave of things, how things answer things and are plaited into things in that mysterious and yet quite common way.

The last morning I was with Nadia she was showing me her favourite church in Moscow. It was a part of a monastery. It was evening, a yellow light sat in the winter trees. Moscow for an Irish person was like a skating rink. An Irish person was always in the wrong shoes and had to walk very slowly and carefully, like an aged man.

There were a few old women begging at the door of the church. A different yellow light seeped out of the open door, the yellow of candles, bare bulbs, and golden icons. Yellows mixing in the air outside, and the desperate, terrifying hands of the old women outstretched.

Nadia had reached the portal of the church, but suddenly she stopped and leaned against the old stones. For a few moments her eyes looked as old as the old beggars, older, ageless.

Are you all right? I said.

Yes, yes, fine, she said, please, give me a moment.

Are you unwell? I said.

I am unwell, she said.

Maybe something you ate? I said, thinking of the chicken.

Yes, she said. Yes. Something I ate.

Then she told me her story under the darkened church wall.

Some years ago she had gone to her doctor with severe pains in her belly. He had prescribed various remedies, but it had done little good, and the pains persisted. Then her husband brought her to a very famous doctor. I don't remember his name of course. The famous doctor gave her a diagnosis that astounded her. Terrified her. She wept for three days she said.

I wept for three days, she said.

The diagnosis he gave her was poisoning. Not food poisoning, but a very particular poisoning used by various secret departments of government. It would be a slow-moving poison, maybe of many years, in order to put the victim at a distance from the poisoners, but that would more than likely kill the victim – like a long-distance rifle shot, only different. Could she remember, he asked her, any instance in her life when she might have been put in the way of such poison?

She went home to her husband, she said, and told him. He held her in his old arms and they racked their brains together.

Then it occurred to him. The dinner at the embassy in Rome all those years before. Brezhnev's son, and the change of places at the last minute. Her in the place meant for him.

You would have eaten the food originally meant for him, her husband said.

They went back to the famous doctor and told him and he shook his head gravely, the way doctors do in all languages and countries when the news is as bad as it can be.

Probably then —, said the doctor, naming a particular poison. It was a poison known to be used by the KGB itself, but also other foreign secret services. Brezhnev's son perhaps was as opportunistic as his sister, I don't know, and anyway there are always a thousand reasons for doing away with people in power, or near power. Actually, she said, the famous doctor was visibly upset, because he remembered her from her heyday – he may even have been sweet on her, she thought, when she was a beautiful girl in the magazines of Russia.

What was the prognosis, I asked her, suddenly feeling, under that church wall, that I was not only asking her, but asking the whole country, because we in Ireland are accustomed to personify Ireland by the shape and face of a beautiful woman.

What was the prognosis?

It will get worse and worse, she said, but very very slowly, and then I will die.

# Biographical Notes

John Banville  Born in Wexford in 1945, he was educated at St Peter's College. His first book, a short-story collection, *Long Lankin*, was published in 1970. Many novels followed – one of them, *The Book of Evidence*, was shortlisted for the 1989 Booker Award – and in 2005 his novel *The Sea* won the Man Booker Prize.

Vincent Banville  Born in 1940 in Wexford, he is a novelist, short-story writer and critic. In 1970 three of his stories were included by Faber in *Introduction 4* of their young prose writers anthologies. His first novel, *An End to Flight*, based on his experience as a teacher in Nigeria, was published by Faber in 1973. It won the Robert Pitman Prize for fiction, and in 2002 it was reissued by New Island. In recent years the author has written bestselling detective novels and stories for children.

Sebastian Barry  Born in Dublin in 1955, he read Latin and English at Trinity College, and received the Iowa International Writing Fellowship in 1984. A playwright and poet, he has also published four novels, the most recent being *A Long Long Way*, which was shortlisted for the Man Booker Prize in 2005.

Dermot Bolger  Born in Dublin in 1959, he studied at Beneavin College. His first poems were published in *New Irish Writing* in 1976, and since then he has written five books of poetry. He has also published four novels, *Night Shift*, *The Woman's Daughter*, *The Journey Home* and *The Family on Paradise Pier*.

Mary Byrne  Born in Ardee, Co. Louth, in 1948, she graduated from University College, Dublin, and worked in Ireland, England, the USA and many other countries. Her first story, 'The Listener', was published in *New Irish Writing* in 1986 and won her a Hennessy Literary Award. She was invited by Lawrence Durrell to collaborate on his final book of essays – published by Faber in 1990 – and she was awarded the *Bourse Lawrence Durrell de la ville d'Antibes* in 1995.

Harry Clifton  He was born in Dublin in 1952 and was educated at University College, Dublin, where he took a Master's Degree in Philosophy. His first poems and short stories were published in *New Irish Writing* and he won the Patrick Kavanagh Poetry Award in 1981. He taught for two years in

Nigeria, and he worked and travelled extensively in Europe, Africa and Asia. He has recently returned to live in Dublin.

EMMA DONOGHUE She was born in Dublin in 1969, and is a novelist, playwright and literary historian. She has published historical fiction as well as fairytales – *Kissing the Witch*, and contemporary fiction – *Stir-Fry*, *Hood* and *Touchy Subjects*. She lives in Canada with her partner and their son.

MARY DORCEY She was born in Co. Dublin in 1950 and has lived in England, France, USA and Japan. Her stories and poems have appeared in numerous journals and anthologies in Ireland, Britain and the USA and her short-story collection, *A Noise from the Woodshed*, won her the 1990 Rooney Award for Irish Literature.

ANNE ENRIGHT Born in Dublin in 1962, she went to school there and in Vancouver, Canada, and she then attended Trinity College, Dublin, and the University of East Anglia. Her first collection of short stories, *The Portable Virgin*, won the Rooney Prize in 1991. Uncollected stories have appeared in the *New Yorker*, *Granta* and the *Paris Review*. In 2004 her story 'Honey' won the Davy Byrne Award.

MICHAEL J. FARRELL He grew up in the Irish midlands and spent a quarter-century in journalism in the USA before retiring to East Galway in 2003 to do personal writing. His award-winning novel, *Papabile*, was published in the USA in 1998.

CARLO GÉBLER Born in Dublin in 1954, he was reared there and in London. He has written many stories and novels, one of the latter being an historical work, *How to Murder a Man*, published in 1998. He has also written a travel book about Cuba, and a work of non-fiction reportage, *The Glass Curtain: Inside an Ulster Community*.

ANTHONY GLAVIN Born in Boston, USA, where he taught for four years in a public high school, he and his wife came to live in Ireland in 1974 in Co. Donegal. He has published two story collections, *One for Sorrow* and *The Draughtsman and the Unicorn*. His highly praised novel, *Nighthawk Alley*, was published in 1997 by New Island.

DESMOND HOGAN Born in Ballinasloe, Co. Galway, in 1951. His first stories were published when he was seventeen. His first collection, *The Diamonds at the Bottom of the Sea*, won the John Llewellyn Rhys Memorial Prize in 1980 and was followed in 1981 by a second collection, *The Children of Lir*. He has also written four novels, and plays produced in Dublin and London. In 1971 he won a Hennessy Literary Award and in 1997 he received the Rooney Award for Irish Literature.

MARY LELAND Born in Cork, she worked as a journalist and feature writer with the *Cork Examiner*, the *Irish Times* and other newspapers. She has published two novels, *The Killeen* and *Approaching Priests*, and a short-story collection, *The Little Galloway Girls*.

# Biographical Notes

AIDAN MATHEWS Born in Dublin in 1956, he was educated at University College, Dublin; Trinity College, Dublin and Stanford University, California. He has published a number of poetry collections and has had plays produced in London, Dublin, Boston, Avignon and Paris. Winner of the *Irish Times* Award in 1974, the Patrick Kavanagh Award in 1976, the Macauley Fellowship in 1978/79 and an Academy of American Poets Award in 1982. He has published a novel, *Muesli at Midnight*, and two collections of short stories, *Adventures in a Bathyscope* and *Lipstick on the Host*.

PATRICK McCABE Born in Clones, Co. Monaghan, in 1955, his first story, 'The Call', was published in *New Irish Writing* in 1978 and won the Hennessy Literary Award. His novels include *The Butcher Boy*, which was shortlisted for the Booker Prize in 1992 and won the *Irish Times* Aer Lingus Award, *Breakfast on Pluto*, and, most recently, *Wintering*, published in 2006.

PHILIP MacCANN Born in England in 1966, he came to Ireland at an early age. A graduate of Trinity College, Dublin, his short-story collection *The Miracle Shed* was published by Faber in 1994.

FRANK McGUINNESS Born in Buncrana, Co. Donegal, in 1953, he studied English at University College, Dublin. From 1974 to 1978 he wrote only poems, almost all of them appearing in *New Irish Writing*. In 1979 he produced his first story, *Hearing English Spoken*. He has also produced versions of plays by Ibsen, Chekhov and Lorca, and has written a film script for Brian Friel's *Dancing at Lughnasa*.

EOIN McNAMEE Born in Kilkeel, Co. Down, in 1961, he was educated at Queen's University, Belfast, where he graduated in Law. A novella, *The Last of Deeds*, was published in 1989, and was followed by the novels *Resurrection Man*, *The Blue Tango* and *The Ultras*. He has also written screenplays and he received the Macauley Fellowship in 1990.

ÉILÍS NÍ DHUIBHNE She was born in Dublin in 1954, and studied both at the University of Denmark, Copenhagen; and at University College, Dublin, where she was conferred with an M. Phil degree. She has published three short-story collections, *Eating Women is Not Recommended*, *The Inland Ice* and *The Pale Gold of Alaska*; and two novels, *The Bray House* and *The Dancers Dancing*. She works as a keeper in the National Library of Ireland and also lectures in folklore.

JOSEPH O'CONNOR Born in 1963 in Glenageary, Co. Dublin, he studied at University College, Dublin, and graduated in 1986. He started to write full time in 1988 and in 1989 he won the *Sunday Tribune* Hennessy First Fiction and New Irish Writer of the Year Awards. His debut novel, *Cowboys and Indians*, was published to great acclaim in 1991, and his first short-story collection, *True Believers*, was also published in 1991. His most recent novel was the highly acclaimed *Star of the Sea*.

JOSEPH O'NEILL Born in Cork in 1964, he was educated in the Netherlands and at Cambridge University. His two novels published by Faber are *This is the Life*, in 1991, and *The Breezes*, in 1995. In 2001 *Granta* Books published his non-fiction account of the lives of his Irish and Turkish grandfathers. He practised as a barrister in London from 1990 to 2000, and he now lives in New York.

BRIDGET O'TOOLE She was born and brought up in the south-west of England, and came to Ireland in 1970 to teach at the University of Ulster. She now Lives in Donegal. Her stories have appeared in the *Honest Ulsterman*, the *Sunday Tribune* and *Phoenix 2000*.

BREDA WALL RYAN Born in Co. Waterford in 1951, she worked as a language instructor after graduating from University College, Cork. Her stories have appeared in literary magazines and anthologies. Having completed the M. Phil in Creative Writing at Trinity College, Dublin, she is now working on a short-story collection and a novel. She lives in Bray, Co. Wicklow.